St.Peter's Finger

GLADYS MITCHELL

St. Martin's Press
New York

Library of Congress Cataloging in Publication Data

Mitchell, Gladys, 1901–
    St. Peter's finger.

    I. Title.
PR6025.I832S7   1987   823'.912   86-24782
ISBN 0-312-00192-4

First published in Great Britain by Tom Stacey Reprints Ltd.

First U.S. Edition

10 9 8 7 6 5 4 3 2 1

"And can a man his own quietus make
with a bare bodkin?

"With daggers, bodkins, bullets, man can make
a bruise or break of exit for his life;
but is that a quietus, O tell me, is it quietus?

"Surely not so! for how could murder, even self-murder
Ever a quietus make?"

D. H. LAWRENCE : The Ship of Death.

CONTENTS

CHAPTER 1

CYCLIST

" Then did of th' elements' dust Man's body frame
A perfect microcosm, the same
He quickened with a sparkle of pneumatic flame."
EDWARD BENLOWES : Theophila.

GEORGE SAT ON A BIT OF BOARD LAID ACROSS THE TOP
of an upturned bucket, and read the Sunday paper.
He was in his shirt-sleeves and was without his leggings.
A slight breeze rustled the pages of the paper and stirred
his hair, for his peaked cap hung on a bush. Two dogs
lay near him in the sun; a faint smell of horse-manure
mingled (despite their appeal to different senses) with
the pleasant sound of a far-off mowing machine; and a
lilac tree by the wall was bold with buds. The stable
cat was watching birds near by, and the newly washed
car stood gleaming at the doors of the garage.

At the end of the lane which connected Mrs. Bradley's
house with the main road through the village, three elm
trees were in thick, dark-clustered flower. The elders
already had their leaves, and an almond tree at the gate
was in bright pink blossom. Emulating it, but not
happily, since the colour made her yellow skin look
dirty, was Mrs. Bradley in a pink spring suit. Her black
eyes were brilliant as she listened, with a faint and
sceptical grin, to the half-bullying persuasions of her son.

Ferdinand was earnest, and Mrs. Bradley, apparently
contemplating not his face but the yellow-starred

11

jasmine behind his black-clad shoulder, had given him close attention for more than twenty minutes, while they stood together at the gate, for, characteristically, he had given no hint of the object of his visit until he was ready to depart.

"So, you see, mother, it really is exceptionally interesting, and it would be a good thing for the convent if you would go and look into the matter. It may be nothing, but the Superior is a pretty shrewd old lady, and if she smells a rat there must be something that wants nailing to the mast. In any case, you need a rest after that long American tour, and the country is lovely there now."

"So it is here, dear child."

"Yes, but you need a change, and the air on the moors is like wine. (Yes, I know, but juries like clichés, so I practise when I get the opportunity.) Now, mother, please, do go. I half-promised Father Thomas that you would. Look here, let me drive you down."

"I would rather be driven by George. Where is Father Thomas now?"

"He has gone back to Bermondsey. He was living in the convent guest-house to recuperate after a break-down. That is how he came to know what had happened. I could arrange for you to meet him, but I'm sure I've told you everything he said."

"I have no doubt of it, child. Well, I will think it all over. Give my love to Juliet, and I hope you get the better of Mrs. O'Dowd."

"Not a hope, mother. If I do, I'll pay your consultation fee. It's quite certain that the convent won't be able to afford it. The guest-house and the boarding-school keep the orphanage going, and what other income the sisters have is microscopic, I believe, and in any case they've a mortgage round their necks like a millstone. Well, good-bye. I'll come down in Easter week-end and see how you're getting on. Hilary ends on the thirteenth, so, if you're still there, I'll come and compare impressions with you. Good-bye, good-bye."

Mrs. Bradley watched his car swirl out of sight, and then walked alongside the house, through the kitchen garden, past the rainwater butt, and into the yard. George stamped on his cigarette and rose when he saw his employer.

"What do you know about convents, George?" she asked.

"I had a sister who changed to Catholic, madam. There's nothing in it, really, I believe. It seems as sensible, in essence, as—pardon me, madam—your religion or mine."

"Yours being—what, George?"

"In the army I was a Seventh Day Adventist for the reason that they had no Church Parade. Nowadays I should think perhaps you might call me a sympathetic agnostic. Religion has altered, madam, since I was a boy. It's a far cry, now, from the time when the Creed and the Catechism carried one through. But the Catholics really do appear to have a point of view, madam, and support it very ably in argument."

"Excellent. Get your things, George, and have the car ready for half-past three. We are going away for a day or two, unless I change my mind by the end of lunch."

She turned to walk back to the house, but it occurred to her that here was an excellent opportunity of passing on the story as her son had told it her to a reasonably unprejudiced listener, so she went back to the chauffeur and said:

"There was once a child of ten who sneaked into the guest-house of a convent and had a bath. The hot water was supplied by a geyser, which must have given off fumes. The child became unconscious, fell back into the water, was submerged and consequently drowned. I can't smell the rat, George. Can you?"

"I remember my sister's little girl of ten, madam. The only water she would ever go into, without being actually ordered, was the water of the municipal swimming bath, and there she took impetigo. Not at all nice, madam, children at certain stages of development."

"Good heavens, George! But the incident I have just related to you happened several years ago. The other day—you may have seen an account of it in the paper—a girl of thirteen did exactly the same thing, only it seems that there was nothing wrong with the gas apparatus and that the child was not drowned, but actually succumbed to carbon monoxide poisoning, although her head was under water when they found her. The coroner gave a verdict of suicide, and the convent, naturally, doesn't like it much, and neither do the relatives, nor, on the face of it, does it appear to be a reasonable inference."

"I saw the account, madam. The paper I've been reading gives the details. It all happened actually last Monday, so this is the first cut the Sunday papers have had at it. This paper states that the young lady was in trouble with the convent authorities, and was expecting terrible punishment, the nature of which is hinted at, not described. It indicates that this fact was instrumental in assisting the coroner to arrive at his conclusions."

"Lend me the paper, George, if you've finished with it. Oh—*that* paper?"

"Yes, madam. I should say, myself, they're skating on the edge of libel in this particular instance, but I dare say they know the type of reader they cater for, and that the nuns won't take any action. Still, it's a bit thick in parts, and, I should say, highly-coloured and untruthful."

"Convents are always news, George."

She walked away briskly, taking the paper with her, and settled down in her sunny sitting-room to read. A double page had been devoted to the story.

"Suicide or——?" it was headed; and underneath, in slightly smaller type, "Four Nuns in Court. Strong Local Feeling Over Child Found Dead at Convent School. *We Want The Truth*, say villagers."

Mrs. Bradley read the two pages very carefully. It was not an ordinary report of the proceedings at the inquest, but claimed to be an eye-witness' account. Mrs. Bradley disentangled what the coroner actually had said from what the *Sunday Flag* would like its readers to believe that he had said, and then gave her particular attention to a paragraph in heavy type which emphasised the fact that the gas apparatus, a water heater of the ordinary domestic kind familiarly known as a geyser, had been found by the gas company's experts to be in perfect order.

"Untampered with by guilty hands," the paragraph ambiguously and actionably stated, "the water heater could have poisoned nobody. *What happened*," it went on to demand in italics and in the name of its readers, "*in that fatal bathroom, to that young and innocent girl?*"

Mrs. Bradley, almost with reverence, put the paper aside, and went to the telephone.

"Is Philip at home?" she enquired of an unseen listener.

"Yes, Beatrice. How are you? Do you want to speak to him?"

"Doesn't his department handle all the statistics about gas suicides?"

"Don't do it, dear. You go a horrible pink. It wouldn't suit you."

"It does suit me. I am completely clad in it. Ask Philip to come to the telephone, dear child."

"Good morning, Aunt Beatrice! Gas? Oh, Lord! Are you on to that convent case already? It's not in your line. You leave it alone. It's going to cause a fair amount of stink. We're still quite Gunpowder Plottish in England, you know."

"Was it really suicide, Philip?"

"According to the coroner and the Sunday papers there's no possible shadow of doubt. Plus the fact that the convent system of education is out of date nowadays. Did your paper give due prominence to the coroner's rider warning all those who have charge of the young not to be too 'arsh with the innocent children?"

"Never mind the coroner. What did the gas people say?"

"Geyser all present and correct. No escape of gas. No evidence that apparatus had been tampered with. Correctly fitted flue to carry off all dangerous waste products. In fact, exit the geyser without stain!"

"Does that mean that if the verdict is correct, the child turned off the gas before she lost consciousness? It doesn't make sense to me. And how do they know that the geyser was perfectly safe?"

"Look here, if you're really interested, you ought to go upstairs and test your own geyser, if you've got one. The only thing you can actually turn on is the pilot light."

"I'll go and see in a minute. But, Philip, tell me your opinion of the verdict."

"Punk."

"Yet the child did inhale gas, apparently enough to kill her."

"Must have done, I take it. No argument about it, and the medical evidence quite clear."

"So what, child?"

"Oh, Lord! I don't know. Of course, she may have turned on the pilot light and sucked in the escaping gas, but, if she did, your point holds good. She couldn't have turned it off again before she became unconscious. Seems to me it must have been an accident. Rather tough on the family, and also the convent, if that's a fact, although, I suppose, from their point of view, it would be a little better than having it brought in suicide. Either way the convent will be blamed."

Mrs. Bradley rang off, and went to inspect her geyser. It looked, she thought, a fairly harmless contraption. She lit it, watched the water falling into the bath, twisted the pilot-light round and blew it out. Then she shut the window and door, stood outside on the landing and waited for five or six minutes. Then she opened the door, walked over and turned off the gas. The smell was detectable, but there did not seem to be any dangerous quantity in the air. She shut the door again, quickly, locked it and went downstairs. She picked up a book, settled herself to read, and was still reading when her maid Celestine came in to report that a relative was on the telephone, "and invites you, madame, to a holiday in the south of France until Easter, while the young nephew and niece are still away at school."

"That settles it," said Mrs. Bradley firmly. She went to the telephone, refused her sister-in-law's invitation with the maximum amount of charm and urged, in her own defence, when her sister-in-law became reproachful, that she expected to be working very hard until after

Easter. Then she wished her a pleasant holiday, hung up and ascended the stairs to the bathroom.

The smell of gas hung faintly upon the air. The twelve per cent of carbon monoxide present with the gas seemed negligible, judging by her own reactions. She opened the window wide to clear it away, put the key back on the inside of the door and went downstairs again.

"I'll go down to-day and have a look at this convent and its startling geyser," she thought.

It was Célestine who expressed horror at the summary nature of the proceedings. She then packed a suitcase in record time, and offered her husband, Mrs. Bradley's cook, as escort on the journey.

"He has a veritable gun, and is also as good as a gangster. He is a ruffian, that one," she observed, in hearty recommendation of her spouse. "He knows not fear, and, if madame proposes to cross the moors—oh, the stories one hears!"

"Delicious," said Mrs. Bradley, tying a veil over her hat and underneath her chin. "Were you ever in a convent, Célestine?"

"But certainly," replied the Frenchwoman. "Was I not taught by the good nuns everything that I know? More, too, which, alas! I have forgotten. Madame should recuperate, after the long American tour, at a convent. It is incredible, the care that is given."

"On the contrary," said Mrs. Bradley, "it is more than likely that I shall be gassed in my bath. Put in my heaviest walking-shoes, and I shall require a shooting-stick, golf clubs, field-glasses and a camera."

"Madame disguises herself," said Célestine, with a sniff. "And the walking-shoes will go by themselves, apart from the rest of the trousseau. Georges has put ready the golf clubs, and Henri is preparing food for

madame to eat on the journey. There may not be good
wayside food at English hotels so early in the year.
In France, of course, it is different. There we are
civilised people. It is curious what brutes are the
English.''

Mrs. Bradley, accustomed to this criticism, did not
reply. In twenty minutes she was off, and, before
darkness fell, George had drawn up the car outside a
village inn not far from Ferdinand's convent. But for
the reek of petrol which came from a garage near by—
for the village was on a main road—they might have
fancied that they could smell the sea; it was less than a
mile away. The host was not surprised to hear them
enquire about the convent.

"Had a mort of people," he said, "come in their cars
since Tuesday to have a look at the place. Taken the
public fancy, this case has, as though it had been a
murder. 'Course, there's them as says it *is* a murder,
and holds to it, but what I says is, if Coroner don't know
what he be at, no business to be coroner, I says; and
after that holds my peace.''

"So the convent has a bad name?" said Mrs.
Bradley.

"*Didn't* have—no, not a murmur. More to the
contrary, like, in the village before. But a few folks
wagging their tongues can soon make mischief, and
there's them in the know that says charity may cover
a multitude of sins, but where there's children they
ought to be very careful, and not go exposing them
where there's been temptation.''

Behind the inn was a garden, and beyond the garden
the rolling common, deep woodland and misty pools
of what had been a royal forest from the time of the
Norman Conquest to the days of Henry III. The road
through the village ran beside it, mile after mile.

Opposite the inn a spread of moorland mounted a mile-long hill to great cliffs sheer to the sea.

Mrs. Bradley washed and dined, and after dinner walked across the moor in search of the convent. The white path, wide enough for small cars, but boulder-strewn here and there and deeply rutted by cart-wheels, led to its gates, she was told.

The evening was cool, and the climb up out of the village fairly steep, but she took the slope briskly and soon was warm. It was easy to find the way. A bright half-moon lit the path, and against its light the convent church stood bold and black and solid, a landmark to pedestrians on the moor. As she drew nearer she could see, between her and the church, a huddle of lower roofs. Some part of these, she surmised, must belong to the convent guest-house, and the rest to buildings abutting on to the cloister.

Whilst she was standing still at the top of the slope before exploring further, she was aware of the approach of an elderly man with a bicycle. She noticed him first when he was still some distance away because of the headlamp of the bicycle, which appeared to bob up and down owing to the uneven surface of the stony moorland track. She did not move, and in a minute or two he came up beside her, and both of them stood gazing at the buildings.

"Death-traps," said the man.

"I beg your pardon?"

"Yes, and death-traps is what I mean. Lures little children to their doom."

"What does?"

"Nuns."

"Interesting."

"I call it 'orrible. Soon as I 'eard, I said to my old girl, 'I'll be off and hold an inspection of that there lazar-'ouse,' I said. Come be road in seven hours and a quarter, less two hours' rest and refreshment. Always give yourself a chance when you're on your old jigger, and you'll still be cycling at ninety.''

"You follow up sinister happenings, Mr.——?''

"Gossage. Ah, I do. 'Obby of mine this twenty-four year and seven months, ever since me and the old girl found ourselves next-door neighbours to a man what cut seven throats in the one 'ouse between ten-thirty-seven, when the other next-door was speaking to one of the corpses, engaged in putting out the cat, and six-fifteen, when the early-round milkman see the blood on the front-door step, it having run that far in the interval between the 'orrid deaths and their dramatic discovery.''

"And you suspect that a horrid death——?''

"Took place with that little girl in that sinister bathroom? Ah, that I do. And I'll tell you for why. That inquest was in our paper. Perhaps you never see it—ah, you did, though, or else you wouldn't be 'ere. Kept very small, at first, to the bottom bit of the page, but even then what I call suggestive, and look how it's 'otted up now. The whole place was wrecked last night by 'furiated villagers. And the coroner's remarks, if you noticed, were what I calls—what's the word— muffled? No, that ain't quite it. Now, what do you call it——?''

"Vague?''

"Vague, that's the word. Ah, vague. And the coroner's name was 'Iggins.''

"Higgins?''

"That's right. The only other 'Iggins I ever knowed was a absconding slate-club treasurer. Now what do you make of that?''

"Coincidence.''

"Not a bit. It was like an 'and pointing. I swallowed me breakfast, pumped up me tyres, tested me brake-blocks, told the old girl to expect me when she see me —retired last year, I did, so free to indulge me fancies —and then, to prove 'ow right I was, I find you 'ere a-gazing your fill by moonlight. I meant to 'ave a read of the Sunday paper, but mother lit the fire with it by mistake."

"And what do you think really happened in that bathroom?"

"'Ad 'er 'ead 'eld under."

"Really?"

"Not a doubt of it. Easy enough to do, and leaves no trace. That little girl was a heiress, near enough. Only one life between 'er and 'er grandfather's money, and that was the grand-dad 'imself."

"Are you sure of your facts?"

"They says so, down at the pub."

"Who say so?"

"A couple of chaps I run into. Nobody round these parts is talking of anything else. Irish, that little girl was, and her grandfather went to America and made his pile in the Prohibition trade. Champagne was 'is lay, and whiskey. Done well, and cleared out. Never copped. Not even suspicioned, so far as he knew. And now collects art treasures, like any other millionaire. Very tidy placed, 'e is. It's common talk in the village. There's another girl at the convent, so far un'armed. Two other girls, I believe. But what will the 'arvest be?"

Mrs. Bradley could not tell him. He remained in earnest contemplation of the buildings for a minute or two and then looked at his watch, and asked her what she made the time.

"A quarter to ten," she said, as she held out her arm to throw the light of his head-lamp on to her watch.

"Crikey! They'll be shut," he remarked, as he turned the bicycle about and headed in the direction of the village. "So long! And you take the advice of one what knows, and keep well away from them gates. You never know who might be lurking."

He swung his leg over the bicycle with an ease remarkable in an elderly man, and wobbled unsteadily over the stony path. As he carried no rear lamp, but only a red reflector, she soon lost sight of him. With a little cackle, for the chance encounter had amused her, she approached the convent buildings more closely. They seemed to be surrounded on every side by a very high brick wall which rose behind the guest-house garden and the gardens of two private houses which adjoined the guest-house on the west, and completely enclosed the other buildings. The gatehouse was set some yards farther back than the gates to the houses, and was in the ancient form of a small room over an archway closed by a massive door. The window looked over the hill. A building to the left of the gatehouse, larger than any of the private houses, but again in a line with them, Mrs. Bradley later discovered to be the convent Orphanage. There were lights in several of the buildings—sure sign of untoward happenings, for the convent hour of lights-out was nine-thirty. Even the gatehouse window showed a glimmer, like that of a candle, to wayfarers coming from the village.

Doors to the convent were few. The Orphanage had its separate entrance, but evidence, supplied later on, proved what appeared, even at first glance, and at night, to be the case, that the entrance was barred up and never used. There was no entrance to the convent grounds, in fact, except by way of the gatehouse. Even the convalescents, if they wished to walk in the gardens of the convent, were obliged to come out by one of the guest-house doors and go in through the gatehouse entrance.

Seawards the breeze freshened. The church, with its high boundary wall running parallel, almost, with the coast, had its north side fronting a cliff along which ran a little path. The moon showed the path up clearly, and Mrs. Bradley followed it westwards for about a quarter of a mile, and discovered that it branched off from a coast-road which swung south of the convent and which had crossed the track by which she had mounted the hill.

The sea beneath the moon looked calm, as though the waters themselves, in meditation, induced the long thoughts which she found herself thinking as she watched them. The tide was in and came to the foot of the cliffs. Below, she supposed, there were caves. The landscape was a perfect setting for smugglers, and the hill-track by which she had come was their mule-road, she thought, across the moor.

She looked back at the convent buildings. High in the church tower burned a steady light. Saint Peter's Finger they called it in the village. It was the warning to ships which the convent still made it a duty to show every night, although a new lighthouse, half a mile farther along the coast, had released it, in effect, from its ancient obligation to mariners. But as Saint Peter's Finger its glow was still noted on charts, and the nuns kept watch, two by two, in the lamp-room at night. The light itself, Mrs. Bradley thought, looked friendly. The high walls and the gaunt, stark church threatened those without, yet gave an impression of guarding those within. But all dark deeds seemed possible—she had noticed it before—in tall buildings seen by moonlight. One view of the convent made it look as though it had been gutted by fire. There seemed no glass in the windows and the buildings had an empty, neglected look. She turned back and continued her tour.

Along the east wall she detected the presence of pigs, but, apart from the fact that all lights, except the beacon-lantern in the tower and the glimmer over the gate, were now put out, there was nothing else to be discovered, and she turned to walk back to the village.

She found herself thinking about her chance acquaintance, the elderly man with the bicycle. She wondered how long he was going to remain in the neighbourhood adding to his collection of horrors. She remembered that some of his information had been picked up in the bar of the pub at which she and George were staying. George, too, was adept at acquiring information in pubs. She resolved to compare the results of his researches with what the cyclist had told her. If the child were an heiress, no wonder the village was full of sinister rumours.

The way back seemed short, with the slope of the hill in her favour, but the path was rough, broken and rutted, and several times she stumbled on outcropped stones.

CHAPTER 2

INMATES

"Hopeless immortals, how they scream and shiver,
While devils push them to the pit wide-yawning
Hideous and gloomy, to receive them headlong
Down to the centre!"

ISAAC WATTS: The Day of Judgment.

THE CONVENT, BEHIND ITS DEFENCES, SLEPT UNEASILY, and some of the inmates, nuns and lay-sisters, orphans and private-school boarders, did not sleep at all. The disturbances to which they had been subjected (beginning with the dreadful fact of the death of Ursula Doyle on the Monday, and ending with the hooligan attack on the building which had made the following Saturday night a time of anxiety and fear) were all too recent to make peaceful sleep a possibility.

There were twenty boarders, among them two cousins of the dead girl. The dormitories, presided over by the nuns in turn, were divided into cubicles, and, each in her narrow bed, Ulrica Doyle and Mary Maslin lay still, and feared and brooded.

The course of events had been bewildering, strange and terrible. On the Monday evening had come the news, broken to them separately by the Mother Superior, of their cousin's dreadful death. They were not supposed to know—Reverend Mother had not told them, and neither did she tell them at any time subsequently—that Ursula was believed to have killed herself, but of course it had come out, for although newspapers were forbidden to the boarders, the nuns could hardly keep the day-girls from them, and the tidings were all round the school on the Wednesday morning.

The two girls had not seen their cousin before she was taken away. Ghoulish accounts of bodies eviscerated by doctors doing a post-mortem examination had been passed in thrilled whispers round the school, and although they had not come directly to Ulrica's ears her nights had been waking nightmares ever since she had gathered, from overhearing them, the purport of all the rumours. Mary suffered less in this particular way. For one thing she was younger, for another less imaginative. Then, too, she was accustomed, and her mind acclimatised, to horrors, for her form was entertained by Mother Bartholomew once a week to the more revolting stories of the martyrdom of saints. These ancient *contes et légendes* were given by the old ex-actress with a lack of reticence which amounted to the Rabelaisian, and had stiffened the hair of many generations of girls, who, with the sadistic tendency of extreme youth, on the whole enjoyed them very much, but were not always edified by them in exactly the way that their mentors and preceptors might have wished.

Still, even Mary, when night fell and the buildings were hushed and dark; when the restless sea on the grim shore broke in a far-off thunder, cuddled her knees to her chin, and lay and watched the curtains of her cubicle to see when horror entered; to be ready to fight for her life and, if necessary (so, in anti-climax, do the thoughts of children run), to scream and scream with fear.

It was all particularly upsetting; to young Mother Mary-Joseph, whose week on duty it was in the senior

dormitory, as much as to anybody except, perhaps, the
cousins. Four times since Wednesday she had guided Ulrica back to bed, for, like a sleep-walking Lady Macbeth,
Ulrica, nervous and clever, strode and muttered, waking
the lighter sleepers and causing Mother Mary-Joseph the
most acute uneasiness, for the dormitory was right at the
top of the stairs, and to the stairhead Ulrica's steps each
time had been directed, except once, when she went to
an open window instead.

In the junior dormitory Mother Patrick, blessed, in
spite of an apparently domineering personality, with the
kindly spirit of *laisser-faire* which is one of the glories of
the Irish, made silent rounds every night and paused beside Mary Maslin and did not rebuke her for her unor-
thodox, pre-natal, curled-up attitude in bed. Instead, she
bent over her, murmured a benediction, and tucked in
the warm, protective bedclothes to a reassuring tightness.

She knew nothing of Mother Mary-Joseph's anxious
vigils, for the young nun did not mention them except in
confession to the Reverend Mother Superior, for on the
Friday she had fallen asleep and had only just wakened in
time to get to the girl at the stair-head before she
pitched headlong down.

Mother Patrick herself did not sleep. There was evil
abroad, and all the Community, not only the Irish, knew
it. The horror of the child's death, the dismay at the
verdict of suicide, the realisation that things went on in
the convent of which, with all their perspicacity and
careful supervision of the children placed in their charge,
the nuns knew, it seemed, less than nothing, darkened
the solemn season, gave dreadful, intimate meaning to
the customary Lenten fast, and made voluntary penance
this time acutely personal.

In her lodging over the Sacristy the seventy-five-year-

old Reverend Mother Superior watched and prayed with
her daughters. The blow had fallen sharply in its suddenness, inevitability and weight, and it had brought with it
lesser shocks—newspaper comments, notoriety for the
convent, serious allegations brought against the Community by an hysterically overwrought woman, Mary Maslin's stepmother, the dead child's aunt by marriage. Then
there had been the local ill-will and rumours, and the
terrifying attack, on the previous night, by a gang of village hooligans.

Worse than all, to the Mother Superior's mind, was a
nagging feeling of doubt. She was an intelligent and
widely experienced woman; had lived a brilliant, worldly
life before her acceptance of the veil; and had prayed,
when Father Thomas first told her of Mrs. Bradley, for
Mrs. Bradley to come and solve their problem. But what
if Mrs. Bradley's researches could not alter the coroner's
verdict? Or what if things were made worse instead of
better? For, although she had mentioned it to no one,
and although she prayed daily that it might not be the
truth, the horrid thought of murder lay in her breast like
lead.

There was everything to suggest it, and the Mother
Superior, daughter of a royal house, was not the woman
to shirk an unpalatable situation. The character of the
dead child, the fact that she was heiress to a fortune,
some peculiar features of time, place, opportunity, all put
together, made a formidable array. She had thought and
she had prayed, and, in the end, she had decided that,
whatever the result of it, a further investigation must be
made. But it had been a difficult decision, and she had
made it heavily.

CHAPTER 3

RELATIVES

"For Dissections
For Sculptures in Brass,
For Draughts in Anatomy,
For the contemplation of the Sages."

THOMAS TRAHERNE: A Serious and Pathetical
Contemplation of the Mercies of God.

THE FUNERAL WAS OVER. HAD BEEN OVER, DONE WITH, and, from its ceremonial aspect, almost forgotten, and Mrs. Maslin, who had brought the child's body from the convent, and looked, a fox-faced, quick-eyed, wiry little woman, her very worst in black, sat behind the tray and handed tea to her husband.

"But I don't see why you want to go back there," he said. "You can send for Mary if you want her. Personally I can't see why she shouldn't stay."

"It must be morbid for her," his wife, Mary's stepmother, replied. "It makes an unhealthy atmosphere, a thing like that happening at a school. Mary was fond of Ursula."

"It won't make her any happier to bring her away from school, and so insist on what happened. Much better to let her stay there. The sisters are perfectly sensible women. The excitement will soon die down."

"I see no reason for referring to the sudden death of your own relation as something exciting, Percival."

"Isn't it exciting? Don't be a humbug, Nessa."

30

At this plain speaking Mrs. Maslin cast a sharp glance behind her, and, lowering her voice, hissed at her husband to silence him. Mr. Maslin, however, refused to be advised, and continued, in his ordinary tone of voice.

"Well, face the facts, Nessa. Isn't it?"

"*Will* you be quiet! It's—well, it's scarcely decent to take that attitude now."

"But, Nessa, face the facts. We've always said that with Ursula out of the way—she was never a very good life, poor child—delicate, and with the family tendency, as we know—and Ulrica (according to Mary) bent on taking her vows as soon as she's old enough —it would—it would be a very fine thing for us! Why try to pretend that you're thinking of anything else?"

"Because I *am* thinking of something else."

"Oh? What?"

Mrs. Maslin lowered her voice still further and replied, while her harsh-skinned, brown little hands picked restlessly at a fringe on the cushion beside her:

"I told you, didn't I, that the Reverend Mother Superior had been trying to get hold of some private investigator or other, to try to prove that the death was not suicide, but simply an accident?"

"Well? What's the matter with that?"

"Nothing . . . except that I don't want Mary mixed up in it all, and questioned. It isn't good for her. It's morbid."

"Well, I don't see what you can do."

"I want Mary home, that's all. I don't want her there, being got at."

"Got at?"

"You never know what these unprincipled people will say. They ask the most innocent children dreadful questions."

"A thing I've wondered," said Mr. Maslin, suddenly lowering the paper, and again enunciating with the clearness which his wife was finding so embarrassing, "is . . ."

"Don't," said Mrs. Maslin, snapping him off. "I shall go down again to St. Peter's as soon as I've had another talk with Grogan and Grogan. I want to know how we stand before I see the Mother Superior again."

"I suppose you've cabled your father-in-law?"

"No, not yet. It can make no difference to him."

"I thought he was fond of the child."

"The Mother Superior cabled him, of course."

"Oh, I see. He does *know*."

Mrs. Maslin made no reply. Then she said:

"Of course it means that, if Ulrica enters, the money comes straight to Mary."

"I don't see that at all."

"Timothy Doyle would never let all that money go to the Church!"

"We can't tell what he will do. Do you mean you think he'll disinherit Ulrica?"

"You must see to it that he does. In any case, I shall see that Grogan and Grogan fight the girl to a finish if she dares to claim the money on Timothy's death! You will have to stand up for your own child's rights in this! Her mother was Timothy's daughter. *I* can't do any more."

"We had better go over and see the old boy, I fancy. Word of mouth is the best way of communicating some ideas. I don't believe, any more than you do, that he'd like his money to go to the Church as the dowry of a nun. And go and take Mary away, Nessa, if you like. She can come to New York and we'll let her make her impression on the old chap. He hasn't seen her since she was quite a baby, and she's not a bad sort of kid."

"And, after all, her mother *was* his only daughter!" said Mrs. Maslin, emphasising the point.

"Yes," said Mr. Maslin, dealing with this observation as briefly as possible. He had liked his first wife better than he liked his second. "But let me remind you, Nessa, that's it's no good to force the old boy. I met him once, and I know what I'm talking about. I don't say there isn't a chance, because, after all, Ursula was the kid he was really fond of. Her father, Michael Doyle, was the apple of the old chap's eye, and he nearly pegged out when Mick was killed. He's never thought for an instant of the money coming to Ulrica, or, for the matter of that, to Mary. I should say there's an even chance to upset the will. But if once he gets the impression that you're trying to get him to alter it in Mary's favour, you might as well buy your ticket home and catch the next boat to Southampton, for he's as obstinate as a mule. Look how he stuck to that Ming vase, when the police were after it as stolen property."

"But *he* didn't steal it, Percival. He knew he was perfectly safe. And over in New York, too. After all, it was only in England that all the fuss was made."

"But the police knew jolly well that whoever had bought the thing had bought it cheap, and knew it to be stolen ! He'd have been in an awkward fix if they'd ever traced it to him."

"Well, they didn't, and there you are."

"That's what I say. You can't rattle him. If we do go across, and I think it's a pretty good plan, all things considered, you leave the talking to me. Even if he divided his money between them there'd be a nice lump for Mary. He's done pretty well, the old coper!"

CHAPTER 4

ATHLETE

"My unwashed Muse pollutes not things divine."
THOMAS CAREW: To my worthy friend, Master George
Sandys, on his translation of the Psalms.

MRS. BRADLEY SLEPT WELL, ON A BED NEITHER HARD
nor soft, in a room where the window would not open.
The sheets were rough and smelt of lavender, and the
floor was linoleum-covered except for a strip of what
seemed to be discarded stair-carpet which had been
placed by the side of the bedstead.

A little maid woke her in the morning and offered
her tea and toast.

"A nice morning," she remarked, as she set down
the tray on a table near the head of the bed. She
arranged Mrs. Bradley against pillows and carefully shut
the door, which all night long had been left wide
open.

"Did you leave the door gaping all night?" she
enquired, returning to the bedside. She cut the toast
into fingers, and brought the tray to the bed. "Can
you balance it? There! That's clever."

Mrs. Bradley cackled.

"Air, child," she said. "The window doesn't open."

"And why should it? Night air is no manner of good
to anyone. Would you not fear to be murdered in your
bed? I could never sleep with the door gaping, come
what would! I'd sooner be smothered, I know."

"Smothered?" said Mrs. Bradley. "Has anybody ever been murdered on these premises?"

"Lord, no, I hope not! Oh, what a dreadful idea!"

"It was yours," said Mrs. Bradley, sipping tea.

"Oh, no! I'm sure, then, it wasn't. But you can't help thinking things, with all you see and hear."

"You mean the convent?"

"Ah, that I do." She sat down, folded her hands in a sociable manner and leaned forward, prepared to gossip. "Such goings-on, I can't tell you. Some poor little maid poisoned in her bath, so they do say."

"When? Lately?"

"Come a week. Happened last Monday afternoon, the poor little dear."

"I suppose there had to be an inquest?"

"That's the scandal of it."

"What were the findings?"

"Soocide! A little dear of that age! As if she'd think of such a wicked thing! Of course, the coroner couldn't speak against the convent."

"Oh? I didn't understand. But how do they know she was poisoned?"

"It's common talk in the village. One of the school-children brought it home to her dad, and he's tooken her away and put her to the High School over to Kel-sorrow. And I reckon other parents 'ull do the same. I know I would if I had a little dear there."

"People nearly always exaggerate when they write or talk about convents. I don't think we have the right to assume what has not been proved," said Mrs. Bradley.

"Can't get over Gunpowder Plot, though, can 'ee?" This reference to a deplorable historic event, the second she had heard since first she had taken up the case, roused Mrs. Bradley to retort,

"But what about 1829?"

"I dunno," said the little maid cautiously, treating this date with respect. "But the name of the people is Waller, and they live in one of they little bungalows just this side of Hiversand Bay, and for why should they take their child away and send her to a school all that way off, if there wasn't sommat nasty going on? More tea? I'll pour it. Happen you might have an accident, awkward like, if you pours it out settin' up in bed." She poured out the tea with motherly good nature and then went to the window and looked out.

"Some of they lads over Brinchcommon way enjoyed theirself Saturday night when they had a couple of beers or so inside 'em," she volunteered, turning her head.

"You mean they made a demonstration?"

"Ah, I should just say they did. Oh, it *were* a mess up there at the convent, too; and rude words writ on the gate, and dirt put into the letter-boxes, and songs sung and all of them yowling like wolves. Would a-frit me into a fit if I'd been there. We could hear it, too, from this house, and that's a mile away, and see the sky rockets, nearly a hundred of 'em, all of 'em yowling like wolves," pursued the little maid, composing the hooligans and the sky-rockets into an Elizabethan medley of fire and terror. "But then, come yesterday early morning, all the mess was cleared up, and you wouldn't have known, bar a couple of windows broken, that anybody went there that night. Wonderful tidy the nuns are, and Tom Shillen asleep in his bed, and nobody able to wake him to put on his helmet and go and owst they lads. Be you going to eat that toast? Another cup? I'll take it all off of you, then, and you can have a nice half-hour before you needs to get up. Breakfast don't be before nine."

Hiversand Bay, Mrs. Bradley discovered, exploring by car a little later, was reached by a secondary road which

branched off north and a point by east across the moors
and avoided the convent which was left away to the
west.   The small seaside resort was still in process of
development, and most of the houses and bungalows not
directly facing the sea were not finished or else still for
sale.   The shops, small, single-fronted lock-ups, were
new, for the most part, too, and enquiry at the first of
them, a butcher's, produced the exact address of the
Wallers.

Mrs. Waller was at home, and the little maid who
opened the door left Mrs. Bradley on the front door-
step whilst she went in search of her mistress.   In a
minute both came to the door.

"Says she would be glad of a word," Mrs. Bradley
heard, as they came from the kitchen towards her.
Then the little maid retreated, and Mrs. Bradley was left
face to face with the lady of the house. Mrs. Waller
was a large, benevolent woman in horn-rimmed glasses
which, at the moment, were clouded by kitchen steam.
She removed them, revealing kindly, protruding eyes.

"I can't think who you are, but come in, do," she
said with brisk hospitality.   "Everybody comes to see
us now we live near the sea.   You'll have to excuse the
house.   You know what it is, Monday mornings."

"I ought to tell you," said Mrs. Bradley, "that I am
not proposing to claim acquaintance with you, Mrs.
Waller.   In fact I can make no possible claim at all,
either on your time or your hospitality."

"Oh, I don't want to *buy* anything," said Mrs.
Waller, looking disappointed.

"No, I have nothing to sell.   I had hoped to get some
information from you, that is all."

"Oh—you mean about taking Ellie away from the
convent?"

"It can't be as easy as this," thought Mrs. Bradley.

But it was. Mrs. Waller had had the reporters and she had loved them. Even when she knew that Mrs. Bradley did not write for the papers she was still interested in her visit, and took her into the drawing room and produced, with the little maid's help, various "elevenses," including a wine cocktail ready mixed and purchased in bottle, biscuits, chocolates, sherry, small home-made cakes and a bottle of ginger wine.

" Of course, I don't say I welcome it, poor child, but if I've said to Stanley once that a convent wasn't the place for Ellie, I've said so ninety-nine times. You see it isn't though we're Catholics, and she'll learn all the deportment, and all the French, too, that *she's* ever likely to need, at Kelsorrow High School. I said, too, that she needs her games, does Ellie, and although the convent grounds are very lovely, it's hardly like hockey and cricket."

"And so, when you heard of that poor child's death, you removed your daughter from the school?"

"Well, what do you think? She came home full of it. 'Oh, mother,' she said, 'whatever do you think? A girl called Doyle—not Ulrica Doyle, but her cousin, Ursula Doyle—has committed suicide at school, and Ulrica, who's quite old—in the Fourth Form—had hysterics and had to be taken to the sick-room by Mother Francis.' It was just like one of those horrid things in the papers. Well, of course, this has been in the papers. I gave five or six interviews myself. 'You ought to be on the films, mother,' Ellie said."

"Are you sure that Ellie mentioned suicide on the very day it happened?" asked Mrs. Bradley.

"That was the story that all the girls had got hold of. Strange it should turn out right. I always say to Stanley that children know more than we think. According to Ellie, this girl was never in trouble at school, and last week she had done something wrong—most unusual for her—and the nuns, or some of them, were angry. She was such a sensitive little thing, it seems—no parents, and her old grandfather in America with all that money to leave—it really does seem most sad. So Stanley withdrew all his arguments, and the High School had a place because a girl went back to India— a little Indian girl—always wore the native dress, so pretty, isn't it, and graceful?—so down went Ellie, on their books, and this morning off she goes on her bicycle to Kelsorrow, just as pleased as Punch. 'I'm sick of that old convent, mother,' she said. 'The nuns are ever so sweet, but we only have Miss Bonnet four half-days a week, and the Kelsorrow girls get her all the rest of the time; and another physical training mistress full time as well.' Miss Bonnet takes the physical training, you know. Stanley doesn't agree with so much of it for girls, but, as for me, I love it. I go to Kelsorrow every week myself, for the League of Health and Beauty. It keeps me cheerful, and Ellie and I do all our practice together. 'Oh, mother!' she said, the first time she saw me in shorts. But now she's got quite used to it."

"I'm interested to hear that the girls themselves concluded that Ursula Doyle committed suicide. Were the punishments at the convent very severe?" Mrs. Bradley said, as Mrs. Waller sat back and sipped her drink.

"Well, I shouldn't call them anything at all, and Ellie always said they made her hoot. Of course, she's very non-suggestible. I mean, it's the atmosphere does it. I mean, actually, I believe, they just lose a badge which all the good girls are entitled to wear, but it's the atmosphere. And not being allowed to be in the processions, I believe, that's another thing; and not being asked in to sing and recite to the nuns while they do their mending. 'Good Lord, I shouldn't want to,' said Ellie's little cousin when she came down here for Christmas, but Ellie, who, mind you, as I said, is simply most non-suggestible, said, 'Oh, yes, you *would* want to. They make you want to want to, whether you want to or not.' And, of course, they do creep about, and that always gets on children's nerves, I think. I've always said to Ellie, 'Make a noise. When you're making a noise I know what's happening. If you're quiet you're probably in mischief.' And I never found myself far wrong."

There seemed nothing more to glean, but Mrs. Bradley felt that to take too early a departure would be unkind. When she did get away the car crawled slowly along the coast road and discovered three-quarters of a mile of promenade, untidy at the ends, and a café or two, closed at that season, for Easter was some weeks off and there was scarcely a visitor in the town. Mrs. Bradley did not care for Hiversand Bay, and directed George to drive on. They inspected Kelsorrow, a respectable market-town about a dozen miles farther east, and then Mrs. Bradley announced her intention of turning about and presenting herself at the convent.

Six miles on the road George stopped the car in the middle of open moorland because Mrs. Bradley thought that they would be too early, and sat on a boulder and smoked whilst his employer strolled off to take the air and admire the rolling scenery. Whilst both were thus occupied, a small car, driven fast, shot by, two wheels on the road and two on the heather, and suddenly pulled up. The driver, a stocky young woman of medium height dressed in a tweed three-piece suit and a little suède hat, got out, slammed the door, and came briskly up to George, who rose and saluted.

"In trouble?" the young woman asked, in a deepish, self-confident voice.

"No, thank you, miss." He looked at her with respectful interest, and continued, "Just killing time, because my employer thought she might be a bit too early at the convent."

"The convent? Oh, they've finished lunch, if that's what you're thinking of. I've just had mine there, so I know. I believe they're full up, though, at the guest-house; or has your employer booked her room?"

"I couldn't say, miss. We're lodging, just at present, in the village."

Mrs. Bradley came up to them.

"I hope you've booked your room," said the young woman, extending a hand. "Friends of the nuns are friends of mine. I think they're simply splendid at that convent. Marvellous people! So simple and sweet, I think. Of course, I happen to get on rather well with them, working, as I do, for half-pay." She laughed loudly, stridently and unconvincingly.

"Interesting," said Mrs. Bradley. "A strange life, don't you think, though, that of a nun?"

"Shouldn't care for it myself. But there's no doubt some are called to it."

"I met a man yesterday who thought the life iniquitous."

"Men will think anything. Thank goodness I've no use for them."

"Still, a man," said Mrs. Bradley reasonably, "would have seen that a geyser was properly installed."

"Geyser? What do you mean? Of course it was properly installed! They had the Gas Company down to look at it the very same day, as soon as they had got the child out of the bath."

"No flue, then, I imagine."

"But there *was* a flue. Look here, are you a reporter?"

"No, no. The case was in the papers and I cannot accept the suicide theory, that's all. I suppose you were at the convent when it happened?"

"Well, I ought not to have been, but I was. Look here, I don't in the least know who you are, but I suppose, if you're not a reporter, it's all right, and you're bound to hear gossip if you're staying in the village. We—I mean the convent—have had a lot of trouble. There are some perfectly bloody people living round about here. After all, a child who intends to commit suicide will do it wherever she is. The fact that this little idiot, poor wretch, was at a convent, makes no earthly difference."

"So you were actually on the premises when it happened?"

"Kelsorrow School, where I do the P.T., had a day's holiday. I hadn't enough money to do anything decent, so I thought I might as well put in the time at the convent. That's how it was, and a jolly good thing it was so, too, in a way."

"What do you mean, I wonder?"

"Artificial respiration. No stone unturned. Worked over the child until the sweat streamed off me. Nobody could have done a better job. No go. Child quite finished. Been dead, the doctor said, at least three quarters of an hour—probably more—before we found her. That was accidental, too. I'd been playing netball with the orphans, and felt pretty sticky and grubby, so I asked Mother Jude for a bath. The kid was in it, of course, and a good old smell of gas. No window open. I flung open the window and we picked up the kid and took her into the nearest bedroom and there I got to work on her at once, but it wasn't a bit of good. Nice child, too, in her way—which wasn't mine."

"Not good at her lessons?"

"Lord knows. Probably. No good at games or swimming. Timid as a rabbit. Just the type for suicide, of course. These quiet, mousy kids are always the ones. You never know what they're thinking, then off they go and do it, and most people feel surprised. Not me, though. I've seen so much of it. Germany, now. Kids commit suicide there if they can't get through their exams. I knew two boys—most brilliant kids—hanged themselves when the results came out. Too terrible."

She produced a packet of cigarettes which looked as though it had been sat on, put Mrs. Bradley aside and got into Mrs. Bradley's car, where she spread herself over the seat—"too windy to smoke in the open," she explained—lit the cigarette by striking a match on her knee, waved the match carelessly to and fro and tossed it, still burning, on to the heather. George walked over and stamped on it. The young woman said, as an afterthought, speaking with the cigarette in her mouth:

"Hope you don't mind my getting into your car?"

"It is a pleasure to have you," Mrs. Bradley replied, getting in beside her and causing her to move up. "Tell me a little more exactly what you made of Ursula Doyle."

"Oh, I don't know. Do you know any Catholic kids? Always pick 'em out in any school. This one was Irish, though. The what-is-it kind of Irish, too. Not the devil type, but the——"

"But the—what, George?" enquired Mrs. Bradley, sticking out her head and addressing the chauffeur much as a witch might suddenly address her familiar.

"The Celtic twilight type, madam, perhaps?"

"That's it! Deirdre!" said the cigarette-smoker, dropping ash on the cushions. "Pale and interesting.

You know. Keen on poetry and afraid of a hard ball, rotten little ass. Although, of course," she added magnaminously, with a large, sporting gesture which just escaped burning a hole in the car's upholstery, "that sort can't help it. That's my experience. Calling them funks doesn't help. They only turn sulky on you. Teaching P.T. is no joke, you know, what with them and their sickening parents."

Mrs. Bradley sympathized.

"My name's Bonnet, by the way. Dulcie Theodora Bonnet. May have heard of me—I don't know. I row, you know."

"George," said Mrs. Bradley, again speaking out of the window, "Miss Bonnet rows."

"Oxford or Cambridge, madam?"

"Oh, club eight, club eight," said Miss Bonnet, answering the question herself a little testily. "Naiads."

"I place the young lady now, madam," said George. "She rowed at number five in the Naiad eight which took first place by four and a half lengths in the women's European championships, inter-club, last year. Later in the season Leander offered the ladies a six-lengths' start over three-quarters of a mile, but the ladies said they would start level or not at all."

"And did they start level?" Mrs. Bradley enquired.

"No," replied Miss Bonnet, annoyed. "I should have been Henleying this year," she added moodily. She got out of the car, tossing away her cigarette which George automatically stamped on. "Well, I'll look forward to seeing you again. That's an intelligent man of yours," she added, in a very much lower tone. "By the way, don't tell them up at the convent that I've said a word to you against poor little Ursula Doyle. They don't want to have the suicide theory elaborated, naturally. A thing like that hasn't done the place any good, as you can imagine." She got into her own car. "Still, it's straining at a gnat to pretend that she didn't when she did!"

Yelling the last words violently across the space between the cars, she drove off bumpily and at a tremendous rate.

"What did you make of Miss Bonnet, George?" asked Mrs. Bradley, motioning him to take his seat at the wheel.

"I think the convent must be broadminded, madam." He climbed into the drivers's seat, and gave an object lesson (unfortunately missed by Miss Bonnet, who had provoked it), in driving off along a bumpy moorland road. Before they had gone very far, however, a small car swept past on two wheels, screeched itself to a rocketing halt about thirty yards ahead, and then, as though as an afterthought, shot out a red warning arrow in lieu of the driver's hand.

George pulled up, with delicate preciseness, just a yard behind, got out and walked forward slowly. Miss Bonnet, for it was she, got out of her car and met him.

"Ah, there you are," she said. "I just came back to say don't take too much notice of Mother Francis, that's the headmistress, you know. She's just the slightest bit prejudiced. Quite a dear, of course—they all are, bless their hearts!—but, well, call it prejudice. That's the kindest way to think of it, I suppose."

"I will inform my employer, miss, of your observations."

Before he had a chance to do this, Mrs. Bradley herself came up to them.

"I was saying," said Miss Bonnet, "that you don't want to take too much notice of Mother Francis, the headmistress. Quite a darling, of course, but—well, better call it prejudice, as I said to your man."

"But am I likely to encounter Mother Francis?" Mrs. Bradley enquired.

"You *may* not, of course. Oh, well, perhaps you won't. But, remember, she doesn't approve of me, and if she mentions me at all—I mean, I'm not *touchy*——"

"I understand," said Mrs. Bradley. "You are not sensitive, but, all the same, you don't care to be misunderstood. Nobody does, of course. It is a common human desire to be praised above one's deserts."

"Not that I've ever met the person yet who understood me," Miss Bonnet interpolated swiftly, not pleased with Mrs. Bradley's observation. "Take some of the parents, now. Quite bloody. Oh, well, you don't want to hear."

"And do you like teaching, Miss Bonnet?" Mrs. Bradley enquired with naive, disconcerting directness.

"I—yes, of course. It's a bit of a strain at times, but it's necessary work, don't you think? And that gives one a feeling of—well, being necessary, and having a little niche," Miss Bonnet, somewhat incoherently, replied.

"Like a saint," Mrs. Bradley suggested.

"Oh, I don't know. I was quite a devil at school. When I think of the things we got up to, these present-day kids seem soft. Not, of course, that there was any harm in me. Just full of spirits, that's all."

"Interesting," said Mrs. Bradley, in a thoroughly damping tone. Miss Bonnet looked at her watch, which was barred all across its face to preserve the glass when she was playing games, and announced that she *must* simply *fly*.

Off she tore again. Mrs. Bradley, watching the disappearing dust, smiled grimly at George and observed:

"The plot thickens, George, don't you think?"

"Modern young ladies are usually up to snuff, madam."

"It struck you that way, did it? As a race, George, I don't think I like the athletic female young. I suppose she *is* quite as healthy and strong as she looks?"

"Not much doubt of it, madam, I should say."

"Um, well, I hope you're right. An oarswoman, too, you say."

"Quite a famous young lady, madam, in her way, but hampered rather unfairly by lack of funds. It takes a good bit to grease the wheels in amateur sport to-day, madam."

"Yes, I expect so. Back to Kelsorrow, George. I'm going to call on the Gas Company."

George turned the car by running it on to the heather, and they crossed the moor in the wake of Miss Bonnet. The Gas Company's showrooms in Kelsorrow were easy enough to find.

Mrs. Bradley inspected gas-cookers and then enquired for water-heaters.

"But I must have a *safe* one," she observed, as she followed a courteous young man up a short flight of stairs to a showroom on the first floor of the building.

"All our appliances are fully recommended to consumers as being thoroughly safe, madam."

"Yes, but—— Oh, well, I suppose, then, you are not the people who fixed the geyser at that convent near Blacklock Tor? I read the report in the newspapers, and almost decided upon an electric heater instead of something with gas, except that one hears extraordinary stories, just the same, about those."

"That was nothing to do with the water-heater, madam, that anything happened to the girl. I can answer for that. We fixed it ourselves, and the appliance was fully tested before it was ever used."

"Well, the child died, anyhow, didn't she? And I can't take risks. I may be having young nephews and nieces to stay."

"But, madam, there really is not the slightest danger, I can assure you. The case you are referring to was very unfortunate, but no fault of ours whatever."

"Something must have got out of order, though, mustn't it?"

"The little girl's brain was out of order. That's the truth, as, if you have read the case, you ought to know."

"Yes, but——"

"Look here," said the young man suddenly, "I tell you nothing was wrong at all with the apparatus. We sent our fitters the very same afternoon, as soon as we got the 'phone call from the convent, and I could show you their report. Everything was in order. We're going to publish the report. It's damaging when people get ideas that the apparatus must have been out of order. The only thing that could possibly have happened, unless the girl inhaled gas direct from the pilot burner, was this; supposing she'd loosened a joint, either in the gas-pipe or in the flue-pipe—anybody who could handle a pair of pliers or a fitter's pipe-grips or a footprint wrench could manage to do that, and they learn all about these things at girls' schools nowadays —my young sister learns it in domestic science lessons. Well, if a joint got loosened, she'd breathe enough carbon monoxide in a very short time to render her unconscious, and probably kill her. Then the inference is that somebody else got in and turned off the gas. I've thought a lot about this case—everybody talks about it round here—and so far as we are concerned there's been no negligence."

"How could anybody turn off the gas if it was not

known that the joint had been loosened? I don't follow your argument there."

"I know. That's just where it's funny."

"You can't explain that, then?"

"No. I can't. Well, I could. Do you know that word they use on the pictures——?"

"You mean——?" said Mrs. Bradley, looking startled.

"I'm not going to say what I mean. I thought it out for myself, and so can other people." He returned to his first manner rather abruptly, as though he had given away secrets. "Now, madam, if you like a nice, clean-looking model which will fit any scheme of decoration in your bathroom, I would advise this number, carried out in either cream or silver. The finish——"

He took her all round the showroom, talking without cessation, and gave her various leaflets. Mrs. Bradley finished up with a gas poker as a present for Mrs. Waller, who had said that she should like one, and with a very vague undertaking to think over the question of installing a geyser in her house. She had arrived at the young man's theory very easily, and had taxed him with it whilst she was buying the poker. He thought that the convent, hoping to get the doctor to sign a certificate so that an inquest could be avoided, had put right the joint that the child had tampered with before the gas-fitter and his mate had arrived.

"Do them a lot of harm, a girl committing suicide like that," he added, having admitted that Mrs. Bradley's guess was correct. "They'd sooner blame it on to us as accident. There doesn't always have to be an inquest when that's the case. We assume no responsibility, and they can't bring a court case, you see."

Mrs. Bradley gave Mrs. Waller's name and address,

so that the gas poker could be sent, and, having got back to the car, told George to hurry.

"Lunch, madam?" said George.

"Good heavens, George! I'd forgotten all about it. Are you hungry?"

"No, madam, but it is now past one o'clock. I find that the *Crown and Quest* is reputed a very good inn."

CHAPTER 5

ORPHANS

*"Sleep, my babe; thy food and raiment
House and home thy friends provide;
All without thy care or payment;
All thy wants are well supplied."*

ISAAC WATTS: A Cradle Hymn.

BY DAYLIGHT THE CONVENT LOOKED DIFFERENT—BIGGER, but not so grim; shut away from intruders, but not so starkly withdrawn.   The car drew up at the guest-house entrance at just after half-past three, and Mrs. Bradley was admitted by a very neatly-dressed girl in cap and apron.

The room into which she was shown was simply furnished, but the chairs were comfortable, there were daffodils in glass vases on the table and on the bookcase, and the floor was carpeted.   An open grate at one end of the room, and a portable gas-fire, attached to a snake-like flex, at the side of it, gave promise of comfort in cold weather.   A picture of Saint Ursula and her eleven thousand virgins, not all of whom were depicted, hung on the wall above the mantelpiece.   The room had gas lighting, and there were candles on a side table.

"If you please, madam, I am to ask you to do exactly as you like.   Reverend Mother Superior sends her compliments by Mother Saint Jude, and Mother Saint Francis is in school at the moment, but can be fetched if you would like to talk to her," said the girl, coming back and curtsying.

"And who are you, child?" Mrs. Bradley enquired.

"If you please, madam, I am Annie, the eldest orphan."

"And do you know, Annie, why I'm here?"

"Oh, yes, madam. Bessie and me have both been told, because we're to wait on you specially." She smiled, and added, "And, madam, we *are* so glad, because you're really somebody from outside."

"Outside?"

"Yes, madam. Not a priest, or a relation of one of the private school children, or anybody *connected*."

"I see. Well, Annie, the first person I ought to talk to is you yourself."

"Oh, madam!" She twisted her apron between her fingers, noticed quickly what she was doing, and smoothed it out again.

"Yes. Sit down and let's begin. Did you know the little girl who died?"

"No, madam, not to say know her. I believe I had seen her about, but we have very little to do with the private school children, even the boarders, and only meet them adventitious."

"I see. Who cleaned that particular bathroom, Annie?"

"Me and Kitty, and other times me and Maggie, or, it might be, Kitty and Bessie. It all depends."

"Which days?"

"Why, every day, madam. Every morning at half-past ten."

"Did you notice a smell of gas in the bathroom last Monday?"

This question, put to test Annie's degree of suggestibility, evoked no reply for a minute. Then the girl answered,

"It would be easy enough, madam, now I think it over,

to say that I did smell gas, but, honestly, madam, I
didn't, and Mother Saint Ambrose can't shake me on
that, for I know well enough that I didn't, and Mother
Saint Ambrose wouldn't want me to lie. I reckon all
that anybody smelt was the creosote."

"Did Mother Saint Ambrose say that she knew there
would be an inquest?"

"Not to me, madam. She wouldn't be likely to say
such a thing to me."

"How long have you lived here, Annie?"

"Since I was nine and a half. Father was killed on the
line—he was a platelayer, he was—and mother went on
the drink and took up with a horse-racing man."

"Do you like the convent life, Annie?"

"Oh, madam, yes, I do. But I can't stay on after
May unless I become a lay-sister, but Mother Saint Jude
and Mother Saint Ambrose don't seem to see me like
that."

"What will it be? What will you do, I mean?"

"Domestic service, madam. But I'm so afraid I'll
feel odd. It won't be like the convent, and I don't know
what mistresses are like. I shouldn't care to be awkward
and do the wrong things. Then—gentlemen. We have
so few gentlemen to wait on, and most of those are
priests who come here because they've been ill."

"I expect you've been very well trained. There is
nothing to dread. People have need of good servants.
I'm sure you'll like it very much if you get a good place."

"But I don't expect to *like* it, madam—not as I've
liked it here."

"So you do like it? I've often wondered what the
feeling was. Is anybody unhappy here, do you think?"

"You mean that poor little girl, madam? I couldn't
tell you. Us orphans aren't, except Bessie. I couldn't
answer for her. My belief she'd be a misfit anywhere.

But we all dread leaving, except Bessie, and now there's been this dreadful upset, and all this questioning, and nobody knowing anything, it's worse.''

"Are you girls trained for anything besides domestic service? Are there other prospects?''

"We can learn the typewriter and the shorthand, madam, if we wish. The clever ones do. But I want to be a real cook, madam. Still, I do dread to think about leaving here, especially now. Because what could have made her do such a dreadful thing? Not anything here, I do know. It must have been something *outside*, and that's what frightens me so.''

"But, Annie, there's nothing to dread. Your mistress, I'm sure, will take to you because you have pleasant manners and you know your work and like it. You are sensible and good, I am sure. How many young men have you met?''

"Oh, madam, that's the part that worries me most. I'm sure they'll think I'm odd, and I dread their ways.'' Her young, clear eyes sought comfort. Mrs. Bradley's brilliant gaze met hers, and both of them smiled.

"You mustn't dread them, Annie. That will never do. Don't you meet the butcher and the baker?''

"Nobody but the milkman, madam, and he's been changed since Mother Saint Ambrose found out he gave Maggie some cream with a rose stuck through a bit of string round the carton.''

Mrs. Bradley cackled.

"There you are, you see. He didn't think Maggie odd. He obviously thought her pretty and attractive.''

"Yes, madam, so she is. We don't have the baker and the butcher because we bake all our own bread, and kill our own meat, partly. The rest comes in from Kelsorrow twice a week, and the butcher's wife brings it by car.''

"I see. Now, Annie, how much of the day are you girls on duty here in this guest-house?"

"Every morning from nine-thirty until eleven, madam, and on Monday, Wednesday and Thursday afternoons from half-past two until seven."

"So some of you were actually on duty over here— or may have been—when that poor child entered the guest-house? You did not see her come?"

"I wasn't here myself. It was Bessie and Kitty. But nobody saw her. At least, so everybody says. We always work in pairs, madam, over here, though the pairs aren't always the same, in case we get too friendly."

"I must talk to Bessie and Kitty. Now, please, think carefully, Annie. Did anything out of the ordinary come to your notice that day?"

"No . . . Yes, madam. The gardener was putting creosote on the fence, and Miss Bonnet gave up her holiday from the other school she attends to stay here and give the younger orphans some netball."

"Is that all?"

"Yes, that's all, but, of course, she wanted a bath, like she always does after games when she's took part herself and got hot, and that was how we found out about the poor little girl."

"Did the orphans get dirty and hot?"

"Oh, yes, but there wasn't no baths for them then. They had theirs just before bedtime. They all had a wash, though, before they went back into school."

"I see. At what time did Miss Bonnet take this bath?"

"Well, actually, of course, she didn't, madam, though the time was about half-past three, because of getting her lunch down. It was all the same bathroom you see, so she never had a bath after all, it turned her up so, finding the poor little girl."

"Very awkward and not very pleasant. Did Miss Bonnet select the bathroom she was to use, or did somebody else arrange that she happened to try the one where the child lay dead?"

"She said, 'Ah, this'll do, Annie,' and walked herself in. She wasn't used to waiting to be asked. She's Physical Training, you see."

"And did she—how did she react to what she saw?"

"I don't hardly remember, madam. I think she just went white and stuck her head out and shouted, 'Annie, fetch somebody, quick!' So I hollered to Bessie to fetch Mother Saint Ambrose quick, because I could see that something must have upset Miss Bonnet proper, and she came out quick and shut the door."

"And Mother Saint Ambrose came?"

"Yes, ever so quick. Bessie went for her, and I reckon Bessie was frightened at me yelling out like I did."

"Was Mother Saint Ambrose frightened?"

"You can't tell that with the religious. She acted quiet and gave orders to fetch Mother Saint Jude, and they was the two that carried the little girl out, Miss Bonnet going as well to do the first aid."

"Where did they take the little girl?"

"To one of the bedrooms which didn't happen to be occupied. The little girl's auntie had had it, but said the springs of the bed was not too good. Miss Bonnet tried everything she knew, and Mother Saint Ambrose telephoned for the doctor, but nothing was any use."

"I had better see Mother Saint Ambrose and Mother Saint Jude. Where are they to be found?"

"I'll go and find them, madam. Would you want them both at once?"

Mrs. Bradley said that she would, and while the girl was gone she examined the dining-room closely. A silver vase, without flowers, attracted her attention, and so did two metal ash-trays, obviously and beautifully made by hand. She was still admiring these when Annie re-entered the room.

"If you please, madam, Reverend Mother Superior sends her compliments by Mother Mary-Joseph, and if you can spare the time, she would be very glad to meet you. That is, unless you are employed, in your opinion, more usefully."

Mrs. Bradley put down the ash-tray and went with Annie to the door.

"By the way, Annie," she said, "you said that you showed Miss Bonnet to the bathroom. But you also said that you weren't on duty that day."

"Yes, madam, that's right. I was over at the Orphanage, and got sent over with Miss Bonnet."

They left the guest-house by its entrance, went round to the gatehouse, were admitted by a smiling lay-sister portress, passed an asphalt netball court set among grass, and then went through a wicket-gate into an orchard. The orchard was bounded on its north side by another low hedge, similar in every way to the first in which the wicket-gate had been set. Both hedges were carefully kept, and were composed of box shrubs set close together. But this time there was no wicket, and they turned sharp left through a gloomy arch of green, a tunnel in the higher and thicker hedge which separated the nuns' garden from the orchard. A path through the herb garden and beside a rock garden brought them to a brick-roofed passage several yards in length, and this opened on to the cloister. At the far end of the passage was a flight of steps which reached a round-headed door-way infinitely ecclesiastical. At the base of the steps stood a young nun. She inclined her head to dismiss Annie, who curtsied and retired, and then held out her hand to Mrs. Bradley.

"I am Sister Mary-Joseph. Reverend Mother Superior is glad you have come," she said. Mrs. Bradley followed her up the outside staircase, walked past her, by invitation, when they came to the round-headed door-way, found the door ajar, and went in. The nun followed, and closed the door very quietly.

"I have prayed," said the Mother Superior gently. "This is the answer to my prayers."

Mrs. Bradley, unaccustomed to such a theory as applied to herself, bowed and grinned. The Mother Superior, a tall old lady with a voice as thin and sweet as the notes of a spinet, came towards her. "I am glad to see you," she said, a statement which Mrs. Bradley could more easily credit.

"I am glad to have come," she said.

"It is good of you to give up your time. You must tell us how much to pay."

"I am here on holiday. I shall be pleased to do anything I can."

"It is good of you. Our income is small. God will bless you." She accepted Mrs. Bradley's unpaid services with gentle matter-of-factness, and both of them sat down. "The others will tell you the details. We have been very unhappy."

"I know the story in outline. Will you tell me why you want to have it investigated?"

"Tell me, first, the story as you know it."

"My son met Father Thomas. Since then I have talked to Annie and to Miss Bonnet."

"That is a good child, that Miss Bonnet. She is not a Catholic, but she has a good heart. She comes here for half her usual fee, and stays often to help our poor orphans—that for nothing. There are so many good people. . . . We are thankful. But this death. . . . Tell me what you have heard."

Mrs. Bradley told her of the conversation with
Ferdinand, who had recounted Father Thomas' version
of the story, and described her own investigations,
including the questions she had put to Annie. As she
talked, she studied the austere room and its occupant,
and the young nun in the door-way. In contrast with
the comfort of the guest-house, the Superior's lodging
was noticeably, uncompromisingly bare. Except for the
two chairs there was no furniture except a writing-
table, a praying-desk and a religious picture. Through
an opening in the wall was a smaller room containing,
as far as Mrs. Bradley could determine, nothing except
a mattress on the floor, a washing-stand and a crucifix.
There might have been other furnishings, but from where
she sat she could not see them.

In the room in which she was, the walls were patched
with damp, and the one window was medieval in scope
and placing, little more than an embrasured slit high
up in the bare brick wall.

"And you want to know why we wish to have that
story investigated?" the Mother Superior said, with a
courteous use of Mrs. Bradley's own expression which
its originator was quick to appreciate. "I will explain."
She remained for a moment as though she were thinking,
and then said, "We know our children. This one, little
Ursula Doyle, came to us when she was six. We have had
her for seven years. She would not, under any circumstances, have taken her own life. It is unthinkable.
So grave a sin——"

"I understand that she was in trouble at school."

"Yes, I know. It was suggested by the coroner
that that was a reason. . . . It is impossible."

"Children exaggerate the importance of these things,
do they not? A reason which might appear inadequate,
or even ridiculous, to a grown-up person——?"

"No amount of exaggeration would account for such a terrible reaction. The child's death was an accident. It must have been. You will find out. . . . You will help us?"

"I will find out what I can, but I am not a Catholic. Scientific truth concerns me—nothing else—and you will understand that I shall remain entirely unbiased."

"Love concerns you," said the Mother Superior, with a gentle smile. "We give you a free hand. Go and talk to the others, those who teach in our school. They are among the children—they knew the child, poor mite!—very much better than I did." She broke off, her frail voice leaving no echo in the room. Then she added, as Mrs. Bradley rose, "God has laid on us a burden, and I, my dear friend, thankfully transfer it to you. I will pray for your good success." She patted Mrs. Bradley's shoulder, and signed to the motionless young nun to go with her back to the cloister.

"I take it," said Mrs. Bradley, as they walked through the nuns' garden towards the guest-house, "that I shall not be allowed to interview any of the Community alone? If, for instance, I were to begin to question you about the death of the child, you would refuse to answer except in the presence of another of the nuns?"

Mother Mary-Joseph smiled. She could not, Mrs. Bradley decided, be more than twenty-five years old.

"We are always permitted to talk to visitors," she said.

"Which day did the child die?"

"Last Monday, just a week ago to-day."

"When was the inquest?"

"On Tuesday."

"Were any relatives present?"

"An aunt from Wimbledon. Her husband is the nearest living relative except for the grandfather in

New York and the cousins, a girl of fifteen, and another of thirteen, who are at school here."

"Were you acquainted with Ursula Doyle?"

"Yes. I teach English to her form."

"What kind of girl was she?"

"She was very quiet and docile. Her nature was gentle, and, I would have said, good."

"Have you altered that opinion, then?"

"It cannot be good to contravene the will of God," the young nun answered sadly.

"I am here to try to establish that the child did not take her own life. I am interested to know that you at least concede the possibility of suicide. Were you present at the inquest?"

"No, I was not."

"Which nuns were present?"

"Sister Saint Ambrose, Sister Saint Jude, Sister Saint Francis and Reverend Mother Superior."

"Anyone else from the convent?"

"No one. That is, Miss Bonnet was there to witness to the finding of the—of the child."

"Nobody else? None of the lay-sisters?"

"Nobody else, so far as I know."

"How do you come to know what happened?"

"Sister Saint Francis, with the permission of Reverend Mother Superior, told us, before morning school on the day of the inquest, what had happened. Later we were told of the verdict given by the coroner."

"Do all the nuns teach?"

"Yes, except for Reverend Mother Superior. Sister Saint Francis is the headmistress, and so does not do as much teaching as the rest, but she is always in school. Sister Saint Ambrose, who is matron of the Orphanage, and Sister Saint Jude, who is kitchener and hospitaller, do no teaching, ordinarily, in the private school."

"And I suppose I am keeping you from your teaching now?"

"I have set the top form an essay. They will not be idle."

By this time they had reached the convent gatehouse. Here Annie was waiting to conduct Mrs. Bradley again to the guest-house parlour.

"Good-bye, then, Mother Mary-Joseph," said Mrs. Bradley. "Thank you for answering my questions." The young nun bowed and smiled. Mrs. Bradley passed through the gate, but paused beside the lay-sister who came out and pushed it open.

"Who are you?" she asked.

"I am lay-sister Magdalene."

"And do you always keep this gate shut?"

"Shut, yes, but not locked until sunset. But I come down now and open it for everybody who goes through, because we think *she* must have come through this way to get into the guest-house bathroom."

"Are you the only person who keeps this gate?"

"Why, yes." She seemed not in the least puzzled by this persistent questioning, but still smiled as she closed the convent gates behind Mrs. Bradley and Annie.

"Now, Annie," said Mrs. Bradley, when they were again in the parlour, "I want you to show me the bathroom in which the child was found."

The guest-house was nothing more than three detached houses, built originally for private purchase, but now made into one by means of covered ways which joined them together. Next to them were two more houses, and these were still occupied by private families unconnected with the convent. Annie led the way across the hall, up some stairs to a landing, and then pointed.

"That's the one, madam. That's the bathroom where she was found."

"Are you afraid to go in?"

"No, madam, not in the least."

"What did you do whilst Bessie had gone running along for Mother Saint Ambrose and Mother Saint Jude?"

"I stayed where I was with Miss Bonnet."

"Where was that? Will you stand in the same place again?"

Annie walked a couple of paces forward.

"It would have been here, madam."

"Now tell me where I should stand, supposing I had been Miss Bonnet."

"Forward of me, madam, not quite so near the door. She went bursting in, do you see, and came bursting out again."

"What, once again, did she say?"

"She began with an oath, madam. Do you order me to repeat it?"

"Just as you like."

"She said, 'Good God! Annie, run and get someone! I'm not going to touch her! I can't!'"

"Now, look here, Annie, I want you to think very carefully for a minute. I have in my notes"—she turned back the pages—"that when Miss Bonnet came out of the bathroom she did not scream out; she merely said, 'Annie, fetch somebody quick.' Which were her actual words? Those, or the words you told me just now?"

Annie looked distressed.

"I didn't think you'd want me to swear," she said.

"Very well, Annie. Then Miss Bonnet really said, 'My God! Go and get Mother Saint Ambrose!'"

"No, madam. 'Good God! Annie, run and get someone. I'm not going to touch her! I can't!' That's what she said, and I shouted to Bessie, and Bessie must have run fast."

"Then Mother Saint Ambrose arrived. Now what did she say?"

"She sent Bessie off for Mother Saint Jude, and told me to get some towels from the airing cupboard, although as a matter of fact there was one in the bathroom already, and I suppose she beckoned Miss Bonnet in to help her, because Miss Bonnet said, 'I can't! I can't!' Very upset she seemed."

"Now then," said Mrs. Bradley briskly, "I want to see Bessie. Please go and fetch her, and bring her up here to this landing."

"Very good, madam."

She went, and as soon as she was gone, Mrs. Bradley stepped inside the bathroom, and closed the door. The little room was as bare and clean as a cell. It was tiled to a height of four feet, and above the tiling the walls were covered with washable distemper. There was a window which opened casement fashion, and beneath it was a wash-bowl. Under the bowl was a cork-topped bathroom stool, and beside the bowl, over the outlet end of the bath, was the gas water-heater. This Mrs. Bradley examined minutely. She lit it, let water run, turned it off again, examined the gas-pipes, and noticed nothing amiss except that the room had no ventilator. The geyser, however, had a correctly-fitted flue.

She heard footsteps outside and went on to the landing again. A short, dark, sullen-looking girl was standing a yard behind Annie. Mrs. Bradley sent Annie away for Mother Ambrose and Mother Jude and then turned on the second eldest orphan, summed her up, and spoke sharply:

"Now, then, Bessie," she said. "The truth, and quickly."

"Don't know nothing, and don't want to," said Bessie with discouraging abruptness.

"I see," said Mrs. Bradley. "No use to ask you, then, whether the bathroom window was open or shut."

"I don't know. I heard Annie yelling, and I run."

"Annie, I suppose, is a very excitable girl."

"Nothing don't excite her. That's why I run."

"Did you hear quite clearly what she said?"

"No, but we always runs for Mother Saint Ambrose when anything over either house goes wrong."

"I see. So you took it for granted that you were to fetch Mother Saint Ambrose. Where, by the way, did you find her?"

"Same place as usual."

"And she came immediately?"

Bessie, slightly nonplussed by this calm acceptance of her uncouth behaviour, replied, still doggedly sulky but with a greater degree of animation than, so far, she had displayed:

"Most immediate she come, and when she gets there she sends me darting off for Mother Saint Jude."

"And was Mother Saint Jude also in the same place as usual?"

"She was in the kitchen, if that's where you mean."

"Supervising the baking?"

"How do you know?"

"Routine."

"She was telling off young Maggie."

"An unusual occurrence?"

"Eh?"

"Did she often tell Maggie off?"

"Every day. So did Mother Saint Ambrose. Young Maggie don't half muck about. Wish I had half her sauce."

"But she stopped as soon as you burst in."

"I never busted in. Trust me! *You* won't go busting in, neither, time you've been here for a bit. Busting's a thing of the past."

"How long have you been here, Bessie?"

"Best part of a year, since I left the Industrial School."

"Are you a Catholic?"

"Me mother was. That's why Father Thomas bunged me in here when she died. I don't care. They'll have to let me go when I'm eighteen, else I can have the law on them."

"Did you see them carry the little girl out of the bathroom to the bedroom?"

Bessie's sullen face softened.

"Ah, poor little nipper," she said. "Tell you what I reckon, but for God's sake don't go passing it on. I reckon the coroner was right, and she *did* go and do herself in, that's what I reckon. Always scared she was, I used to notice. I had the job of laying the tables, see, for the paying kids' lunch. Only a few are boarders, but plenty stops to lunch. And I used to see her, and my heart didn't half used to bleed. Some horrible things can happen in these here convents, take my word for it."

"Has anything happened to you?"

"Oh, I can take care of myself. I'm tough, I am. 'Tisn't everyone that's been sent incorrigible to an Industrial School for two years. You wait till I get out of here, and then you watch my smoke!"

Sorrowfully Mrs. Bradley agreed to do this.

"What happened after the child had been carried into the bedroom?" she enquired.

"I don't know. Mother Saint Ambrose put her head out and told me to go on downstairs, and *she* went down to the telephone."

"Did you go downstairs when you were told?"

"Course I went. What you think?"

"I think you did go. Where was Annie then?"

"She let the water out of the bath and cleaned up the bathroom, and shut the window up what Miss Bonnet had opened."

"How do you know what she did if you were downstairs?"

"I heard the water running out, then there wasn't nothing except the water running, then I heard the bang of Annie shutting the window. Here's Mother Saint Ambrose. Better look out what you're saying. She don't stand for much, I can tell you."

"Bessie," said Mrs. Bradley, stretching out a thin yellow claw and yanking Bessie with unceremonious adroitness into the bathroom and gently closing the door, "do you dislike Miss Bonnet?"

"I got no use for any of her sort. More like a police-woman, she is, and not of the best of them."

"You do dislike her, then?"

"I never said so."

"You're intelligent, though," said Mrs. Bradley. "You tumbled to the point about the window. Miss Bonnet didn't open it, Bessie, did she?"

"I thought as how she did. No, that's right! Annie said she did. I never see her."

"What class were you in at school—before you were sent to the Industrial School, I mean?"

"Class Two."

"Not the top class, was it?"

"Next to the top."

"Queer. I should say you had brains."

"Nothink to do with brains. If you're lousy they doesn't put you up to the top class, see?"

"And were you lousy?"

"Yes, I was. Think they can get me clean, sending me to that old bitch at that bloody clinic!"

"But you're clean here, Bessie, aren't you?"

"Ain't no louses, that's why."

"Have you ever taken an oath in a court of law?"

"Course I have. Didn't me step-father do a seven-year stretch?"

"And are you prepared to tell me the truth, the whole truth, and nothing but the truth about what happened here?"

"About the little nipper?"

"Yes."

"I dunno."

"Bessie, did Miss Bonnet *shut* the window?"

"No, that was Annie, I tell you."

"Miss Bonnet then, neither shut nor opened the window, as far as you yourself know? Don't answer for Annie, please."

"O.K. Suit yourself what she did. Don't matter to me."

"I will suit myself. Ask Annie to come in here."

"I suppose you know you're keeping Mother Saint Ambrose waiting," said Bessie, with a last impudent fling as she went outside. Annie came almost immediately.

"Annie, was the bathroom unlocked, then, so that Miss Bonnet could walk in?"

"Why, yes, madam, certainly it was."

"Was it usual, do you know, for the children to leave the bathroom door unlocked when they had a bath? I know it is sometimes done."

"I couldn't say about the boarders, madam. Us orphans never lock the door, but it's different in the Orphanage from here. It's all our own place. There's no strangers."

"Now, Annie, one more thing. You say that Miss Bonnet asked you to go for help. Why didn't you do as she told you, instead of shouting for Bessie?"

"Miss Bonnet clutched a-hold on me and said, 'Don't go! Don't leave me, Annie! There will have to be witnesses of this!' "

"What did she mean? Do you know?"

"I think she was just took a-back, madam, finding the little girl dead."

"Did you see the dead girl?"

"Well, yes. She looked kind of peaceful, in a way. But her head was right under the water, and I never see such a lovely colour on anybody."

"What colour was she, then?"

"Ever so pink. I only ever saw one other dead person, and they was as white as death. That's what you say, madam, ain't it?—as white as death."

"Quite right, Annie. Go on."

"Yes, well, she wasn't, see? And her little eyes shut, and her little mouth just a bit open, as though she might be asleep. I don't think she *suffered* much, madam, really I don't. She had gone to join the blessed saints, I'm sure."

"So you don't believe in the suicide theory, Annie?"

"What, kill herself? That little dear? Oh, madam, I'm certain she never. It must have been an accident. She could never have looked so peaceful, lying in mortal sin."

"Perhaps not. Thank you, Annie. And you heard Miss Bonnet close the window?"

"*Open* the window, madam. She *said* because of the gas, but I think as how she felt faint. I'm sure I couldn't smell gas, let Mother Saint Ambrose persuade me how she will, not until I went in to clean up. But they'd all had a fidget with the pilot light, I reckon, before then. I know the doctor did later. And then that stink of creosote off of the fence."

Mrs. Bradley stepped on to the landing and apologised to the nuns for keeping them waiting.

CHAPTER 6

NUNS

"These iiij figures, combyned into one,
Sette on thy mind for a memorial;
Erthe and iren, foure trees, and the stone
To make us fre, whereas we were thral."

JOHN LYDGATE: Let devoute peple kepe observance.

"I WANT TO KNOW ALL THE DETAILS," SAID MRS. Bradley. Mother Ambrose, buxom, black-browed and tall, her meek habit declining to look, upon her, anything but militant, gazed straight ahead without a glance for little, apple-cheeked, dimple-chinned Mother Jude, and then said in a deep voice resonant as an organ:

"Bessie came to me in the ironing-room and asked me to go over to the guest-house immediately. I rebuked her for her state of mind, which seemed to me an unnecessarily excited one, and then hastened to this landing with her. When I discovered what had happened I sent Bessie off again for Sister Saint Jude."

"You say 'when I discovered what had happened.' What did you think had happened?"

"I could see that the child was dead."

"You felt certain of that?"

"Yes. Illogically, however, I bent over the water and raised the child's head."

71

"Was the head completely submerged when you saw the child first?"

"Yes, indeed. The water was very deep—almost up to the top of the bath."

"What was the temperature of the water?"

"I could not say, except that it was quite cold."

"When you say that——?"

"I mean that it was a shock to me when I plunged my hands into the cold water. I suppose I had taken it for granted, subconsciously, that the water would be warm."

"Yes . . . thank you."

"Sister Saint Jude arrived very soon after I had sent for her," Mother Ambrose continued, "and came into the bathroom. She said: 'Oh, poor little Ursula!' Then we lifted the child out of the water and I had to call to the two girls, Bessie and Annie, to bring some towels from the airing cupboard, as I could not see any in the bathroom, although, later on, one was found beneath the bathroom stool. It was wet, as though it had fallen into the water by accident, and had been wrung out."

"At first, did you not think it very odd to find no towel?" asked Mrs. Bradley.

"I should have found it incredible," Mother Ambrose replied, in her deep voice, "if children were reasoning beings. I doubt whether they are. The apparent absence of towels did not surprise me. When we had rolled the child in the towels that were brought, we carried her into the nearest bedroom, and, leaving Miss Bonnet and Sister Saint Jude to attempt artificial respiration, I telephoned for the doctor."

"May I have his name and address?"

Mother Ambrose gave them, and continued:

"All efforts to resuscitate the child failed. Miss Bonnet then volunteered to acquaint Sister Saint Francis with what had happened, but Sister Saint Jude and I thought it better that the news should be delivered by one of us. In the meantime, Annie, acting on my instructions, had cleared up in the bathroom, and had found a saturated towel.''

She closed her lips and indicated by her bearing that nothing else presented itself to her mind as having any immediate bearing upon the subject under scrutiny. Mrs. Bradley finished writing and then turned to Mother Jude, who had stood by, silent as a Rubens' picture, as clear, as fair, as motionless, whilst the other nun had been speaking.

"I must ask you, Mother Saint Jude," she said, "to corroborate or contradict what Mother Saint Ambrose has said.''

The little nun beamed.

"I can corroborate every word," she said, "except with regard to the towels. As soon as Bessie came into the kitchen I knew that something was wrong. I thought it was the dining-room fireplace again, and I was vexed, because we had it done in the autumn and it was very, very expensive. We had to instal the portable gas-fire while the work was being carried on. I did not see how the guest-house was going to balance its books if the fireplace had to be done again so soon. All Bessie would say was 'Come!' So I gathered up my habit and I *flew!*''

Mrs. Bradley grinned sympathetically. It was easy and pleasant to imagine little, rotund Mother Jude, with her full skirts gathered in her hand, sprinting from the kitchen to the gatehouse, and through the archway round to the guest-house door.

"There's just one other thing," she said, "before we come to the towels. Was the window open, Mother Saint Ambrose, when you first went in?''

"Indeed it was. Wide open. I was startled. It seemed immodest."

"Ah, yes. And talking of that—is it true that you get the children to cover themselves with a sheet or shift, or such, when they take a bath?"

"It is the custom," replied Mother Ambrose. "There was no such covering on the child, or visible in the bathroom," she added immediately.

"The people who stay in the guest-house——"

"I cannot say. Coverings are provided, and are always served out by the maids. Whether they are always used I cannot tell. They are usually wetted to make it appear that they have been used."

"Tactful," said Mrs. Bradley. "People have very nice natures, more's the pity."

The nuns made no verbal reply to this remark, although Mother Jude's eyes twinkled. Mrs. Bradley wrote again, and then asked:

"Can either of you tell me anything about the dead child herself? I take it that such an exploit as stealing into the guest-house during school hours and taking a bath would be regarded by the girls as a highly daring proceeding?"

"It would be so regarded," Mother Ambrose agreed, after a moment's thought.

"It has been done once before, and once only, so far as we know," supplemented Mother Jude. "A girl called O'Donovan did it in 1925, when the guest-house was one-third its present size. She did it because she was dared, but she was found out because she was obliged to call for help. The key broke off in the lock, and the girl, having had the bath, could not get out of the bathroom again."

She broke off to laugh. Mrs. Bradley regarded her with affection.

"It has been a permanent 'dare' in the school since then," Mother Ambrose contributed after a pause. "It grieves me to have to tell you these things," she added, with a fleeting glance of immense disapproval directed towards Mother Jude, "but we are all under obedience to assist this enquiry in any way that presents itself. Your questions guide me to tell you that the girl in question was expelled."

"She is now," Mother Jude interpolated neatly, "a Franciscan nun, doing missionary and medical work in South India."

"What is the nature of the 'dare'?" enquired Mrs. Bradley. "Merely to take the bath?"

"There is a condition attached. The girl who dares another must first have performed the feat," replied Mother Jude.

"You throw new light, so far as I am concerned," said Mrs. Bradley, "upon the mentality of children educated in convent schools."

"Children vary very little," said Mother Jude, with her blissful, charitable smile.

"I suppose that the child's clothing was found in the bathroom," Mrs. Bradley observed.

"Oh, yes. And in such a state! Tops torn out of both her good black woollen stockings, one suspender broken, the neck of her vest torn and the tape knotted and broken. Sister Genevieve, who acts as matron to the boarders, was horrified when she saw the state the clothes were in. She said that she had never known Ursula Doyle to be so careless and destructive, and would not have believed she could tear and damage her clothes, and soil her good tunic."

"Interesting," said Mrs. Bradley.

"Of course, if the unfortunate child was breaking the rules by being in a guest-house bathroom, I suppose she would naturally tear off her clothes in a hurry," Mother Ambrose observed.

"I wonder whether it would be possible for me to examine the clothing at some time? I must see Sister Genevieve about it. And now, Mother Saint Jude, I must ask you to let me have, at your convenience, a list of all the guests who were here when the death occurred. I should like to be able to find out exactly where they were, and what they were doing during that afternoon."

"I will write you a list and I can tell you what they were doing," said Mother Jude promptly. "They took the youngest orphans to the cinema, and they and the children had lunch very early. The cinema at Hiversand Bay charges at a cheaper rate until three o'clock in the afternoon, and the guests, including the priest from Bermondsey, Father Thomas, had arranged to leave the convent at half-past twelve so as to arrive for the commencement of the performance, which was at half-past one. One of the contractors at Hiversand Bay had lent a lorry, in which the party travelled, and Sister Saint Ambrose and I, and the older orphans, saw them upon their way before we had our own meal."

"And every guest went with the children?"

"Every one. I will write you the list."

"It was the day before Shrove Tuesday, was it not?" said Mrs. Bradley. "I see. So that means that none of the guests would have been using the bathrooms, and nobody will be able to give any information about the movements and operations of the child."

"That is so. It was because I knew that the bathrooms would not be required that afternoon that I was able to tell Miss Bonnet that she might use one, after the game."

"That brings me to my next question. It was unusual,

I take it, for the guest-house to be completely denuded
of guests?"

"It was most unusual," said Mother Ambrose
vigorously, and almost as though Mother Jude was in
some way to blame. "I do not declare that it has never
happened before, but I do not recollect its having
happened."

"Nor I," said Mother Jude, with matter-of-fact
placidity.

"Now, then: to how many people, besides the guests
themselves, was it known that the guest-house would
be empty that afternoon? And for how many days
beforehand had it been known?"

"The younger orphans, those who were given the
treat, had the news on the previous Thursday, at the
end of morning school. The guests had made all the plans,
and then had sent the invitation half-way through
Thursday morning. I do not know which other people
had information that the guest-house would be empty,
although I see the purport of your question. You want to
know, I think, whether the children of the private
school could have known?"

"Yes, but I see that you cannot tell me. Perhaps
Mother Saint Francis would know that. It is indeed
kind of you to have been so patient in answering my
questions. I think I had better see Mother Saint
Francis next."

"There is one more thing," said Mother Ambrose,
determined, it seemed, to find Mother Jude somewhere
in fault. "Did lay-sister Bridget go to the cinema that
day?"

"No, she did not." Mother Jude turned to Mrs.
Bradley, who was writing hasty hieroglyphics in a note-
book. "This Sister Bridget is a poor, afflicted woman
who is staying in our guest-house. She was not told

about the outing because, for one thing, she does not go to the cinema, and, for another, because she is tiresome, poor thing. We take her out ourselves, but we do not let strangers go with her. It is embarrassing for them. You will understand when you see her."

"I wonder," said Mrs. Bradley, "whether we might go downstairs to the parlour?" When they were seated— the nuns bolt upright on the straightest-backed chairs they could find—she added, "That is extremely interesting. Did Sister Bridget remain in the guest-house, then, whilst the others were out with the children?"

"Not all the time. It would have been dull for her. She loves company. She went into the Orphanage," Mother Jude explained. "And washed currants," said Mother Ambrose, taking up the tale. "She is quite good, and does not eat the fruit."

"She says," observed Mother Jude, "that all dried fruit belongs to the good Saint Paul. She has heard, at some time, I think, that currants take their name from the city of Corinth."

"She came over at twenty-past twelve——"

"I did not want her to see the others go——"

"And she had her dinner with the older children, and then washed currants until a little before two o'clock."

"From two until half-past two she was with us at Vespers, and when we resumed our duties after Vespers she had her afternoon sleep in her bedroom here."

The nuns, concluding this triumphant duologue, closed their mouths and modestly dropped their eyes.

"In her bedroom here in the guest-house?" asked Mrs. Bradley.

"Yes," said Mother Jude, for the guest-house was her province.

"Did the noise made by Miss Bonnet, when she discovered the child's body, disturb Sister Bridget, do you know?"

"I do not know. Her room is on the same floor, but I saw nothing of her. I did not think of her. There was so much to be done, and the whole affair was so dreadful that my mind was filled completely."

"And you, Mother Saint Ambrose?"

"I saw nothing of Sister Bridget. I did think of her, though. I hoped that she would not come out upon us because we were so much occupied."

"Can you tell me anything more about her? I labour the point because it seems as though she must have been the only person in the guest-house, except for the girls in the kitchen, when the child entered the bathroom. Is she usually left by herself?"

"Oh, no!" said both the nuns immediately. Mrs. Bradley looked mildly surprised.

"We never leave Sister Bridget entirely alone anywhere, except in her bedroom," Mother Jude explained, "and even then there is a lay-sister or one of the other orphans within call, and often I am here, too, with Sister Saint Cyprian, who teaches needlework to both orphans and private-school children. On the afternoon in question Kitty and Bessie were on duty together here, Mother Saint Ambrose was supervising laundry work in the laundry (a separate building with its drying-ground just behind this guest-house). I was in the kitchen—the Community kitchen, that is, which adjoins the frater on the south side of the cloister—and Sister Saint Cyprian was taking a needlework class at the school. But you must not think of Sister Bridget as usually being alone and left to her own devices."

"That is quite clear. Is it likely or unlikely that Kitty and Bessie would have seen the child when she came to the guest-house for the bath?"

"It is quite likely they would be unaware that anybody had come in. Generally we use only one door, and that is in the front of the house, and the wall along the end of the guest-house garden is far too high to climb. If Kitty and Bessie were sitting in the kitchen doing some mending or getting on with their compulsory reading, they might not know that the house had been entered from the front. We do not lock the front door until sunset or after."

"Is the entrance to the convent grounds also kept open during the daytime, then? I mean, would the child have experienced any difficulty in getting past Sister Magdalene at the gate?"

"It depends upon the time. The gate is left unlocked from about eight o'clock in the morning until the late afternoon, and the portress is nominally in charge of it. But, of course, she has other duties, and it would not be difficult for a child to slip through the unlocked gate without being seen. If she went through while the portress was at Vespers, she certainly would not be seen."

"I see. Thank you." She made another note. "And now about Miss Bonnet. What was she doing, Mother Saint Ambrose, when first you saw her that day?"

"Taking off her trousers," was Mother Ambrose's startling reply.

"Taking——?" Mrs. Bradley looked nonplussed.

"Miss Bonnet described to me once how essential it is, if one wishes to succeed in sports or games, to keep the limbs *warm*," said Mother Jude.

"She was going to play netball with the orphans——"

"She always played games in shorts——"

"And over the shorts she wore trousers."

"These she took off at the moment that play commenced."

"She is quite a *modern* young woman."

"I understand, I think," said Mrs. Bradley, not knowing whether to admire most the quick comedy-patter of the duologue, or the self-control with which, having said their say, the nuns switched off, as it were, an electric current, and lapsed into immobile silence. "Pardon me for having put my question so ambiguously. I meant, what was she doing when you came into the bathroom that day?"

"She was on the landing, just outside the door."

"Doing nothing?"

"Nothing at all, so far as I remember. She looked very pale, as though she might be going to faint or turn bilious," said Mother Ambrose.

"What was she wearing then?"

"She was wearing her drill tunic and a jersey."

"Not her trousers?"

"She had her trousers with her, but for going about the school she always, at the special request of Reverend Mother Superior, put something over her shorts for modesty."

"Were the trousers actually in her hand when you saw her first?"

"No, on the bathroom floor, as though she had dropped them and forgotten them in the shock of seeing the dead child."

"And the window, you say, was wide open."

"Quite wide open."

"Miss Bonnet, Annie thinks, had opened it."

"And had dropped what she was carrying to do so?"

"That would be my inference."

"Very sensible of her, I should say. I suppose she wanted to let out the smell of gas."

"Did *you* smell gas, Mother Saint Ambrose?"

"Certainly. Not strongly, because, of course, the open window must have dispersed the fumes, but strongly enough to be noticeable, and to make obvious the cause of death."

"Yet Annie declares that she could smell no gas."

"Then her sense of smell must be defective."

"Did *you* smell gas, Mother Saint Jude?"

"Certainly. I looked to see whether the pilot light of the geyser had been turned off."

"Had it?"

"Yes, quite securely."

"But had not the guest-house fence been coated with creosote?"

"Oh!" said both nuns, as though this point had escaped them.

"Tell me, please," said Mrs. Bradley, as though she had decided not to labour it, "about the guest-house towels."

"The guest-house towels are distinctive," said Mother Jude, "and the wet towel seems to have come from one of the rooms. The towels are striped in blue and white, and carry the name of the convent, 'Sisters of St. Peter in Perpetuity,' embroidered in red across the corner."

"Was the wet towel mentioned at the inquest?"

"It seemed of no importance."

"No? Yet surely that towel might have changed the verdict from suicide to accident? Would a suicide take a towel?"

"I don't believe it would have helped to get the verdict altered," Mother Jude sadly interposed. "People do so many things from habit."

"Yet Mother Saint Ambrose said, a short while ago, that she was not astonished to find no towels in the bathroom. That, in her opinion and according to her experience, children were feckless beings whose common sense could never be relied on. Perhaps, however, you are right. The towel makes a small point only, although an interesting one. There is one thing more; what happened when you found that it was impossible to resuscitate the child?"

"Miss Bonnet and the doctor went to have another look at the bathroom, which Annie, by then, had tidied. Sister Saint Ambrose and I went together to Sister Saint Francis to let her know what had occurred. Annie and Bessie were told to remain in the kitchen until they received other instructions, and on no account to let anyone know what had happened."

"Did you speak to the doctor again before the inquest?"

"Yes, he returned with the police."

"That seems an extraordinary thing."

"He was frank with us. He said that, although he could smell gas when he went into the bathroom with Miss Bonnet—although, now you have mentioned the creosote, it might have been that—he could detect nothing wrong with the water-heater—he is quite a practical man—and that the circumstances needed explaining."

"He refused to sign the death certificate, then?"

The two nuns bowed their heads.

"And what view did the policeman take?" asked Mrs. Bradley. Mother Jude smiled.

"He did not confide in us. He took notes, and was exceedingly nervous, and addressed Reverend Mother Superior throughout the conversation as 'Your

Worship.' He wiped his boots, too, which we thought was nice of him.''

''And when did the demonstration take place?''

''On Saturday night,'' Mother Ambrose answered. ''We were disturbed after dark by a nu ^ber of wild young men from neighbouring villages.''

''Were the gates locked?''

''Fortunately they were. Bessie very bravely volunteered to go for help. She has good qualities although she lacks self-control.''

''You did not let her go?''

''We did,'' replied Mother Jude. ''I myself assisted in helping her over the west wall so that she could get past the attackers without being seen.''

''It was thought best,'' said Mother Ambrose, ''that she should go with our assistance and permission rather than that she should be led into the sin of disobedience.''

''When once the idea had occurred to her, she would have gone in any case,'' said Mother Jude, simplifying the other nun's statement.

''I see,'' said Mrs. Bradley. ''And did she obtain assistance?''

''No. No one would come to our help. It proved impossible to wake the village policeman.''

This was not news to Mrs. Bradley, who had heard as much from the chambermaid at the inn, and she remarked: ''So the policeman who wiped his boots was not the village policeman?''

''No. He was a man from Kelsorrow. The doctor lives in Kelsorrow, and telephoned from here to the police station. He knows the inspector there.''

''I see. Thank you, both of you. You have been most kind and patient.''

''You will doubtless, as you suggested, go next to see Sister Saint Francis,'' Mother Ambrose suggested.

"I think so. Are you going that way? Shall we all three walk together?"

The nuns were bound respectively for the Orphanage and for the convent kitchen, so, Mother Ambrose stately as a cassowary, Mother Jude like a cheerful, plump little robin, and Mrs. Bradley a hag-like pterodactyl, they proceeded, at the religious pace, to the gatehouse to enter the grounds.

CHAPTER 7

HEADMISTRESS

"He that hath found some fledged bird's nest may know
At first sight if the bird be flown;
But what fair dell or grove he sings in now
That is to him unknown."

HENRY VAUGHAN: They are all gone into the world
of light.

SISTER MAGDALENE SAW MRS. BRADLEY AND THE NUNS
before they arrived at the gate, and was there to open it.
The nuns passed through, but Mrs. Bradley halted.

"You don't, of course, remember seeing Ursula
Doyle go through to the guest-house?" she enquired,
with what she felt to be unnecessary persistence. It was
one of the major problems in need of solution, this fact
that nobody appeared to have seen the child's approach.

"I've been thinking things over," the portress
observed, as she shut the gate again and accompanied
Mrs. Bradley a short way into the grounds. "I believe
she must have come through the gate during Vespers."

"During Vespers? At what time is that?"

"From two o'clock until half-past two. I don't
know whether the children are bound to attend, but
I know that some, if not all, of those who stay to dinner,
go to church then. All the choir nuns go, and all of us
whose work can be so arranged, go also. It seems to
me that if she had slipped away then and gone to the
guest-house, no one would be the wiser."

86

"A very important suggestion," said Mrs. Bradley, too tactful to let the lay-sister know that it had already been made. "I am obliged to you, Sister Magdalene. That clears up a difficult problem. What about the orphans? Do they attend Vespers, too?"

"The youngest don't, but they had gone for their outing. The others, if they were not in church, would be in the Orphanage, or the guest-house, I should think, and in either case would not know who came through the gate."

"Yes, I understand. Thank you," said Mrs. Bradley. She walked on past the laundry, and bent her steps towards the orchard and the field. It was with considerable interest that she looked forward to her first interview with the headmistress of the convent private school. She had spent some time already of the short, early spring afternoon, and it was towards the time of the afternoon break, when, having crossed the orchard in a west to east slant, she passed the school gardens kept by the children themselves, and entered by a wooden door in the high board fence of the playground. There were two entrances into the modern, one-storey building, one in the south, the other in the west wall. She chose the first, went in, knocked at a classroom door and asked for Mother Saint Francis.

Mother Francis was a grey-eyed, gracious woman with a red, sensuous mouth, white hands, and an extraordinarily lovely complexion. She was between thirty-five and forty, Mrs. Bradley supposed, and had superimposed the dignity of bearing required of her by her vocation upon natural alertness and energy.

Although her speech did not betray the fact, it was obvious that she was not an Englishwoman. She received Mrs. Bradley with warmth and great charm of manner, and, when both of them were seated, she observed:

"I am particularly anxious to have this investigation made, because the child's stepmother is coming back in a short while to demand a further enquiry into the circumstances of the death. She has made it very hard for us."

"Indeed?" said Mrs. Bradley. "Is she not satisfied, then, with the verdict given at the inquest?"

"By no means." The nun, who gazed straight ahead of her as she talked—a habit in the religious which Mrs. Bradley was finding disconcerting—paused for a moment and then added: "No one is satisfied with it. I have prepared, if you would care to have it, an exact account of the circumstances, so far as I can discover them. I believe that you have already begun your investigation. Perhaps you can check these facts against any others which have been given you."

She opened a drawer in her desk and handed out from it a typed, foolscap document. Her eyes met Mrs. Bradley's, and rested on them for a short time as though she were trying to communicate something which was in her mind without having to use the medium of words. Apparently she was successful, for Mrs. Bradley said:

"I think you mean me to understand that you have already made up your own mind on this matter, and that you are inclined to think that I have made up mine."

The nun bowed her head, and spoke without looking up.

"In this school," she said, "apart from the quite little children, we have just over eighty girls. They are of all ages, from nine to nineteen. We get to know them very well indeed. In fact, I do not suppose there is anything about them that we do not know. As that is the case, as soon as anything out of the ordinary happens, it is possible for us to be able to fix, with absolute certainty, nearly every time, upon the child responsible for what has occurred. I had a very long conversation with Father Thomas before he went back to Bermondsey. He said that he knew your son, and would ask him to do his best to persuade you to take up our trouble."

"Why me?" asked Mrs. Bradley. It was a point to which she had given some little thought.

"Because all that we can offer in support of our strong belief that the child did not bring her own life to an end—and suicide is a shocking thought to all people, and especially so to Catholics—is evidence of character, disposition and training. Mrs. Bradley, you are a psychologist; you understand the workings of human minds. We knew this child, and I declare to you that she could not have done this thing! If ten million juries declared her guilty of this sin, I would not believe them. I could not believe them, knowing her as I did."

"Tell me about her. I am anxious to learn all I can."

"She came here when she was six. She was then, and has been, ever since, one of the sweetest children we have ever had in the school. She was not good at her lessons—not nearly so good as her cousin, Ulrica Doyle, who now becomes the grandfather's heiress, and not much better than her good, stupid cousin, Mary Maslin, whom we put in the form below. But her religion was part of her life, in the most genuine sense of those words, and under no circumstances whatever can I imagine her, of her own will and wickedness, putting an end to that life. People never do things out of character. You agree?"

Mrs. Bradley, with a mental reservation (for she

wondered whether her interpretation of the statement would coincide with that of Mother Francis if both defined their meaning), said that she agreed.

"Well, it was entirely out of character for Ursula Doyle to have ended her life by suicide. Her death was not of her own premeditation. She died by some terrible accident. Look! I will show you her picture."

She opened a drawer of her writing-table. A photograph lay on top of a large portfolio. She took up the photograph, glanced at it, and passed it to Mrs. Bradley. It showed a group of six children in fancy dress, apparently at a garden fête.

"Our last school concert. Ursula is the one on the extreme left," she said. "That comes slightly in profile. Here is another full-face. Both are extremely good likenesses."

Mrs. Bradley studied the photographs closely. They conveyed very little to her mind. Ursula Doyle, a slender, delicate-looking, apparently fair-haired child, might have been one of a hundred or so almost identically similar children whom Mrs. Bradley had looked at in school photographs. She handed the likenesses back with a very slight shrug.

"She looks a nice little girl, but so did Constance Kent," she observed with crude directness. Mother Francis, however, appeared not to know the name of Constance Kent, and put the photographs very carefully away without replying. Then she looked up and said:

"She *was* a nice little girl. Who is Constance Kent?"

Instead of replying to the question, Mrs. Bradley asked another.

"What are the possibilities of accident?" she enquired.

"Obviously, that something went wrong with the water-heater."

"Yes, that is so. Now, apart from the fact, which you know, and which formed the basic evidence in favour of the verdict of suicide, that there was nothing wrong with the water-heater, tell me this: was Ursula Doyle the kind of child you would envisage as having done a thing which, I hear, was strictly forbidden to the children, and for which one girl has been expelled?"

Mother Francis took up a pen and tapped restlessly upon the table. She was obviously greatly agitated, and when she spoke it was in a low voice and as though the words were being dragged from her.

"I know," she said. "She was no more the child to have acted so disobediently and wildly than she was the child to have killed herself deliberately. I don't know what to think. I can't *bear* to think. She was the heiress to a vast fortune. . . . I was saying to you just now that we know our girls, and I say to you also that I have been the headmistress of this school for nearly ten years and never once, in investigating the little charges of naughtiness, disobedience, wilfulness which can be laid at the doors of even the sweetest children, never once have I been at fault. I say it in all humility. Where, in my own mind, I have apportioned blame, I have discovered that the facts, when I had them, invariably bore me out. I have thought long and earnestly about this dreadful occurrence. I have prayed. The result is a terrible conviction for which I can give no reason except—that I knew the child. You understand me, I think?"

Mrs. Bradley said nothing for more than a minute. When she did speak, her question seemed irrelevant.

"Tell me," she said, "what you know about Miss Bonnet, please, Mother Saint Francis."

The nun looked up.

"You have a quick mind," she said. "I did not think you would ask that quite so soon. Miss Bonnet is not a Catholic. She is a fully qualified teacher of physical training, and had a very good post in the Midlands before she took up her duties at Kelsorrow High School. I do not know quite what happened, but she did not get on very well at her first school, and—well, it is only fair that you should have the facts, as you have undertaken this investigation—it appears that she stole some rather valuable pictures. She comes of quite a good family, and had a kleptomaniac aunt—a genuine case, by the way; this aunt, now dead, spent a considerable part of her later life in a private mental hospital. The school did not press the charge against Miss Bonnet, but they felt they had to dismiss her, and she was lucky, I understand, to be appointed at Kelsorrow—really a very good school. The full-time post there, however, is held by another physical training specialist and Miss Bonnet's post is a temporary one in which she is employed by the half-day. The school has expanded considerably during the past two years, partly owing to the development of the seaside resort of Hiversand Bay, so Miss Bonnet is now employed for seven half-days a week, but is not yet counted a member of the regular staff. That is to say, she still has the position of a visiting mistress only. The other three half-days of the ordinary school week, namely, Monday morning and all day Thursday, she comes to us here, and we also employ her on Saturday mornings, when Kelsorrow High School is closed."

"And what of the girl herself? Do you like her?"

"She is efficient."

"How did she manage to get another post?"

"Her father has some influence with the governors

of the school, I believe, or she might not have been taken on at Kelsorrow or anywhere else. But I know very little of what happened, and should not ask to be told more."

"But you do not think her an undesirable person to have here among your children?"

"She works well, and the girls are under good supervision—our own. One of us is always on duty when she takes the physical training lessons here."

"You do not trust her, then?"

"It is our custom to keep the girls under our own supervision when they are taught by visiting mistresses. As for Miss Bonnet, she has a good heart and is willing to give good service, but she lives in a drama, I think, of which she is not only the heroine, but in which she occupies, always, the centre of the stage. That is sometimes a little boring for the audience, and may lead the actor into trouble."

"Would you call her a truthful person?"

"Truth, in her, is subordinated to her conception of herself."

"You believe that she might tell lies?"

"Oh, yes," said Mother Francis. "In fact, she does tell lies. But she is really a very good teacher, and comes here for half her usual fee."

"So the Mother Superior told me. Now, these two cousins who also come to the school: I should like to talk to them at some time when it is convenient."

"Whenever you like." She glanced at the large school time-table. "Ulrica——"

"She is now the heiress?"

"Yes——is in the fourth form. She is rather an unusual kind of girl. It is a sad case. The father left the Church, and the poor child, until she came to us three years ago, had never been to church at all. Now, of course, she is anxious to do all in her power to combat the evil that has been done. We allow her more liberty than some of the children have. She is by nature solitary, loves long walks (which she is allowed to take quite often without supervision) and is an interesting child altogether. Mary Maslin, younger, of course, is in the second form. She is rather a backward girl in most school subjects, but does not lack intelligence, I believe. She will be doing elocution after break with Sister Saint Bartholomew."

"That isn't——?"

"Yes, Rosa Cardosa. She entered the religious life after the terrible catastrophe at the Duntrey Theatre in which she lost every penny. She wasn't insured, you know, and, as I expect you remember, the theatre was burnt right out."

"Poor Rosa! But I thought there was a fund?"

"Her friends agreed to support her. Hundreds of pounds were collected. She sent them all back, and said that she was going to take what she had—a little money her mother had left her, and which, for some superstitious or sentimental reason, she had never used for her theatrical enterprises—and give it to God. So she brought it along as her dowry, and has been with us now many years. She taught me when I was fifteen, at our other house."

"And she has never wished to go back, and begin again?"

Mother Francis smiled, raised her hands in a gesture so slight as to be almost unnoticeable, and answered:

"Who can tell?"

"Her father-confessor?"

"Yes, or Reverend Mother Superior, and they will not."

There was a pause; then Mother Francis, as though

she felt that she had rebuked her visitor and wished to make some amends, said: "Tell me, ought I to send those two children home? Both are suffering from shock, and Mary from grief. Ulrica seems afraid. She is highly strung; a rather peculiar girl, although very clever."

"As I do not know either of the girls, I cannot offer any advice," said Mrs. Bradley. "Have you any seculars besides Miss Bonnet on the staff of the school?"

"Yes. There is Mrs. Waterhouse. She teaches all the children under six, orphans and others. We pay her forty pounds a year and she has a cottage next door to the presbytery at Hiversand Bay, which was rather a pleasant little place before the speculative builders came."

"What are her qualifications?"

"She was an elementary schoolteacher employed by the London County Council before her marriage. She is a widow now, and lives in this district for her health. That is why we get her so cheaply. She lives rent free, and has her midday meal, and, if she wants it, her tea, with the orphans. She has no children, and lives alone."

"Is she a Catholic?"

"I have no reason to think so."

This, Mrs. Bradley thought, was an extraordinary reply, so she noted it. Then she asked:

"Are all the children Catholics?"

"All the orphans are Catholics. Of the private schoolchildren about nine-tenths are Catholics."

"The dead child——?"

"Yes."

"Mary Maslin?"

"Mary Maslin comes of a Catholic family, although her father's present wife, I believe, is not a Catholic. In the other case, the father lapsed from the Church, as

I told you just now—his father and mother were converts—and the child has been brought up without
religious knowledge. It is very sad. I have hopes,
however——''

Mrs. Bradley nodded.

"Do you find that the non-Catholic children tend to
become Catholics in their later life?" she asked.

"We do not use any influence," said Mother Francis
sharply.

"What proportion become Catholics later on?"

"A fair number." Her momentarily defensive
attitude melted. She smiled with great sweetness.
"Our Faith fights its battles," she observed.

"It has its attractions," said Mrs. Bradley, "in an
unstable, undisciplined world. Will you arrange to
have Ulrica Doyle escort me on a tour of the buildings
and grounds? I should like to meet her, as it were,
unofficially, as though I were an ordinary visitor to the
school."

"Certainly. The girls are accustomed to show our
visitors round the gardens. I will send for her now if
you would like me to do so. It is just as well that you
should get to know her."

"I should be very much obliged."

Mother Francis pressed a bell.

"Ulrica Doyle, from Mother Saint Gregory's music
class," she said to the girl who appeared. "That is
Ethel, one of the older orphans," she added, after the
girl had gone. "They take it in turns to sit in the
adjoining room doing needlework or practising shorthand, and act as messengers if I require it. I very
seldom do require it, but it is convenient to have
somebody there if visitors come, and quite good
practice for the girls to take courteous, correctly-
rendered messages."

Ethel was not long gone. She returned with a tall, blue-eyed girl, wearing the convent black pinafore and badge, whose face told of sleeplessness, strain and acute anxiety. She curtsied to Mother Francis, and waited with exaggerated meekness to hear what she was to do. She curtsied again when she had heard it, opened the door for Mrs. Bradley and then walked sedately beside her along the whole length of the corridor as silently as a ghost. She seemed to Mrs. Bradley as quiet as a nun. The disembodied manner in which the religious suddenly appeared and retreated without sound was startling, but not uncanny. In Ulrica Doyle this silence was disquieting.

The girl took charge of her, however, without awkwardness or shyness, and showed her the grounds and the buildings. It was not until they were walking in the nuns' garden that she mentioned her dead cousin. The fact that she did so at all surprised Mrs. Bradley and gave her occasion for thought.

"I suppose you have heard about Ursula?" Ulrica said.

"Yes, child." Neither looked at the other. Ulrica stared at the gravel, Mrs. Bradley at the wall of the frater.

"What do you think about it? Tell me, please, what you think. I want to know."

"I have no idea what I think about it, except that it was a very terrible thing."

"But you've come to find out about it, haven't you?"

"Yes, child. How did you know?"

"Father Thomas promised me that he would try to get you to come here. Ursula must have been killed. She would never have killed herself. I wish you would let me help you."

"You come first on my list of suspects,"

Mrs. Bradley observed, with a strangely mirthless grin.

"Because of the money, you mean? Yes, it's a motive, I suppose. It couldn't benefit me personally, though, because I am going to enter as soon as I am old enough."

"Enter?"

"Join the Community. Become a nun."

"I see. So you would get no benefit from the money?"

"All my property will come to the convent when I enter. Poverty is part of the Rule."

"Why do you suspect that your cousin's death was not suicide?"

"I knew Ursula very well indeed. She was a sweet child. She would never have done such a thing."

"Have you any idea why anybody should desire her death?"

"No—I don't think I have. At least, it isn't definite, and I would rather be torn to pieces than put suspicion on anybody unjustly. That would be awful, wouldn't it?"

"Do you speak literally, I wonder?"

"About what I would suffer? Saints have been torn to pieces, and what they endured, I can."

"I see. Does your cousin, Mary, share your theories?"

"Oh, Mary's a silly little thing. I should never dream of talking to her about Ursula. She didn't like Ursula; I loved her."

"That, of course, would make a good deal of difference."

"The part I can't understand is how anybody ever persuaded Ursula to do a naughty thing like going to a guest-house bathroom. It's dead against the school rules, and she was such a gentle, timid little thing that I can't imagine her letting anybody lead her astray. It must have been a grown-up person. Nobody -in the school would ever have persuaded Ursula to break the rules like that."

"Whom do you suggest?"

"I am not prepared to name anybody. And, besides, by the time you've taken out the nuns and Miss Bonnet and Mrs. Waterhouse, none of whom, I suppose, can very well be suspected, there isn't anyone else except the guests, who all have an alibi; and old Jack, the hedge-trimmer and gardener, and he wouldn't hurt a fly."

"There are the orphans."

"I know. Some of the older ones are awful."

"Motive?"

"I know. But—well, take Bessie. I can imagine her doing no end of wicked things."

"What makes you think it was murder? Why can't the death have been accident?"

"Because somebody *must* have taken her into the guest-house. She never would have gone there alone."

"I see."

They walked on in silence. Then, down one of the paths, they encountered a nun. Ulrica curtsied and smiled. The nun and Mrs. Bradley exchanged dignified, grave little bows.

"That's Mother Mary-Joseph. She's quite young and a perfect dear," said Ulrica, when the nun had passed out of earshot.

"Yes. I have met her. She teaches English, doesn't she?"

"Ever so well. We're all thrilled. We're doing *Macbeth* this term. It was set for Schools last year, and Mother Mary-Joseph thinks that by the time our form takes Schools it will be time for *Macbeth* again."

"*Macbeth?*" said Mrs. Bradley. Ulrica looked at her expectantly, but Mrs. Bradley had no more to say. They turned out of the nuns' garden and were going back towards the school when they came to a small wooden hut. Mrs. Bradley asked what it was.

"It's the handicraft centre," Ulrica Doyle replied. "Do you want to go inside? It isn't particularly thrilling, but visitors usually go over it. Mother Saint Simon-Zelotes doesn't like it if they don't. She spends all her spare time in there, copying the chalice and the paten. We are all excited about it. They're very old, you know."

"Is that where they make those charming silver vases and metal ash-trays which I saw in the guest-house, I wonder?"

"Yes, but it's very noisy, with hammering and all the other work going on. Still, they do make some nice things. But it's Mother Saint Simon-Zelotes' own work that you really want to see. The nuns here haven't many treasures, and can't afford beautiful things, and so they make them. My grandfather wanted to buy the chalice and paten—they're thirteenth and fourteenth century—but Reverend Mother Superior wouldn't part with them. She said that some day the convent might *have* to let them go, but that that day had not yet come. We're longing to see Mother's work. She was an artist in metal-work—ever so famous, I believe—before she joined the Community. Do you really want to go in?"

"I particularly want to go in," said Mrs. Bradley. "I greatly admired the art room and the laboratory." The handicraft centre was far enough from the main building to ensure that the sound of hammering did not reach the classrooms, Ulrica went on to explain as they went inside. There were three benches, each under a window with a rack of tools above it and drawers and boxes by the side. The nun in charge was a briskly cheerful middle-aged woman with a face which looked as though it had been newly scrubbed. She had good teeth, a short, aggressive nose, and large, very fine, strong hands. Mrs. Bradley recognised her at once, and, to her pleasure, addressed her by the name she had borne in the world.

"We do not forget our artists," she said, with a startling cackle of laughter. She paused where two girls were working.

"It should be three to a bench, but that poor child, Ursula Doyle, it is her place that is vacant," Mother Simon-Zelotes explained. "The eight girls in this room are half the form. I have half of them, and the other half take theory of music with Sister Saint Gregory and Latin with Sister Saint Benedict. Then we change over to-morrow. Last week I did not take them. I did my own work instead."

The girls began to put away their tools. It was the end of the first period of afternoon school. Ulrica took Mrs. Bradley back to Mother Francis.

"I wish you would give me a copy of the school time-table, and a list of the teachers' duties and free time," said Mrs. Bradley, when Ulrica, having curtsied to both of them separately, had gone.

"I have them ready. I anticipated that you would require them," Mother Francis observed, as she handed them over.

Armed with these, Mrs. Bradley was escorted back to the guest-house by Ethel and handed over to Annie.

"I want you to ask Mother Saint Jude to let me have that list of the guests who were staying here last week, Annie," Mrs. Bradley said, "and I want their home addresses. Perhaps she has put those down beside the names, but just in case she hasn't——"

"Very good, madam. We got you a room ready, madam, as we weren't sure whether you were going to stay here or not."

"Is there a room to spare?"

"We've put Sister Bridget in the Orphanage. She won't mind."

"I don't like to turn out Sister Bridget."

"She really won't notice, madam. She's very biddable and harmless. She never notices nothing, except the matches, which we generally keep out of sight, and her little mouse."

Annie went off to get the list of guests and their home addresses, and Mrs. Bradley was making notes when Bessie entered abruptly and rather rudely, and announced that she had been sent by Mother Saint Ambrose to show Mrs. Bradley her room.

"I'm glad I don't sleep here meself," she observed sincerely, as they passed the door of the bathroom in which the dead child had been found. "Frightened of ghosts, I am, and I bet she walks of a night."

"I thought that Catholics didn't believe in ghosts?"

"You got another think coming. 'Course they believe in 'em. What's done can't be undone. It's only common-sense, after all."

With this majestic retort, Bessie led the way along a landing to a door marked with a black number seven.

"You got a lucky number, anyway," she said. "Old Sister Bridget *would* have this room with a seven. Young Maggie's been give the job of painting it on the door of her cubicle over the Orphanage now, to let her think she's at home. Seems more than a week ago that that there happened, don't it?"

"I cannot say, Bessie," Mrs. Bradley replied. "Is there any means of sending to Blacklock Tor for my things?"

"Father Clare would give the word at the pub, if you asked him. He's over here now with Reverend Mother Superior. Daresay he'll stay to supper. He often do of a Monday. Nothing much at the Presbytery, I suppose."

"Does that mean that he was here last Monday, then?"

"Course he was. What you think? Didn't he go with our little 'uns to the pictures? No more pictures for us till after Easter, Mother Saint Ambrose's orders. Who do you like the best? Somebody 'ighbrow, I suppose?"

"Katherine Hepburn," said Mrs. Bradley, after a suitable pause for thought.

"Ginger Rogers for me. Oh, boy! She's lovely! Her and Fred Astaire! See her and Hepburn act in that one about the chorus girls and that? That bit where Ginger gets lit! Oh, glory, didn't I laugh! On the Q.T. I see that. Supposed to be hout on an 'ike. Only Annie knowed, and she wouldn't tell. Not bad, old Annie isn't."

"Oh, Bessie," said Mrs. Bradley, suddenly interrupting, "how long after Annie did you go into that bathroom?"

"Me? I never went in. You can't pin nothing on me!"

"Why do you use that expression? The little girl committed suicide, didn't she?"

"Did she? Let them as think so fry in their fat, I says."

"But it was you who suggested to me how cruelly treated the children were, and how natural it was that they should be driven to dreadful deeds."

Bessie seemed taken aback, and for once had no answer ready.

"So you didn't go into the bathroom at all," said Mrs. Bradley, in gentle, musing tones. Bessie glowered suspiciously.

"Suppose I said I did?"

"I should not suppose anything so improbable," said Mrs. Bradley briefly. "Were you going to show me my room? Later on, I think. I have to go back to the private school for a bit."

CHAPTER 8

RETROSPECT

"And from these springs strange inundations flow
To drown the sea-marks of humanity."

FULKE GREVILLE, LORD BROOKE: The Nature of a
True Religion.

IT WAS THE TIME OF THE AFTERNOON BREAK. MRS.
Bradley stood in the school grounds and watched the
girls come out. With them came two nuns to supervise
the recreation period. The girls came out with decorous
quietness, but soon conversation became animated,
groups formed, the see-saw and the netball posts were
requisitioned, and girls linked arms to walk about.
Some went up to talk to the nuns, but Mrs. Bradley
decided that this was too good an opportunity to be
wasted, so she, too, joined the group. The girls made
way for her politely, and drifted off. The nuns bowed
and smiled.

"I believe," said Mrs. Bradley, "that when visiting
mistresses take lessons, it is the custom for some of you
to be in attendance."

The nuns bowed again. Mrs. Bradley, remembering
the curious silences and clipped-off conversation of
Mother Ambrose and Mother Jude, proceeded:

"May I have your names, please, for my note-book?"

"I am Sister Saint Timothy," said the elder of the
two.

"I am Sister Saint Dominic," said the slightly younger
one. Mrs. Bradley wrote down the names, putting

Mother, instead of Sister, as the title, a complimentary manœuvre which the nuns received with smiles, and then said briskly:

"On the afternoon that Ursula Doyle was found dead, the orphans had extra netball.   Which of you supervised that game?"

The sisters lowered their eyes, and concentrated deeply on the question.   Mother Timothy spoke first.

"I do not think anybody did."

"There was no arrangement," said Mother Dominic. "It was something quite out of the ordinary, you see, for Miss Bonnet to take the game then."

"Do you know how long the game lasted?"

Neither of them knew that.

"Miss Bonnet will be here again on Thursday," volunteered Mother Timothy.   "She took the game. She will know."

As soon as the break was over, the nuns, with further bows and smiles, went in, and Mrs. Bradley, watching them go, decided that the time had come to ask a few questions of the orphans with whom Miss Bonnet had taken the extra netball.

She went first to Mother Ambrose whom she discovered in the dayroom counting sheets.   She asked permission to talk to the orphans.   Mother Ambrose gave it readily, and offered to send for the children so that Mrs. Bradley could interview them apart from their classmates.

So the fourteen orphans who had had the extra netball practice were paraded in the Orphanage dayroom, and stood in a deferential semi-circle to be questioned.   Mother Ambrose remained in the room with the lay-sister who was helping to check the laundry count, but she removed herself to a courteous distance from the questioner.

"Now, children," said Mrs. Bradley, "sit down and answer me carefully."

They sat on the floor in silence, and fixed their eyes upon the middle button of her blouse.

"You remember last Monday dinner time when Miss Bonnet kindly took you for extra netball? At what time was that game over?"

"Two o'clock, madam," they replied, more or less in chorus.

"And what did you all do then?"

"If you please, madam, we all went and washed," volunteered a child of thirteen.

"And what did Miss Bonnet do while you had all gone to wash?"

"She came with us to see there's no noise," said a twelve-year-old.

"How long did it take you to wash?"

They could not answer that with any certainty.

"What did you do when you had washed?"

"We went in school and learnt our spellings ready for half-past two," said the girl who had spoken first.

"Who was with you, then, until half-past two?" It turned out that no one was ever with them at that time. From one o'clock until two they had recreation, and then from about ten past two until half past, whilst the Community went to Vespers, the children were set to learn some piece of work or other in the classroom, and lessons proper began at half-past two, when the nuns came back from church.

"Who generally supervises the games on Monday dinner times?" was Mrs. Bradley's next question.

"If you please, madam, nobody don't. We plays by ourselves of a dinner time. Reverend Mother Superior put it to us to be good, and let Mother Saint Ambrose have a rest."

"Oh, I see. That's a very good idea. So you always look after yourselves from one o'clock until two, and then in the classroom from two until half-past two?"

When they had all been dismissed to go back to their lessons, Mother Ambrose volunteered the information that one of the orphans had been fairly badly hurt during the early part of the game.

"The child who was playing in the centre position fell and hurt herself, and was brought to me here in the Orphanage where I spent about twenty minutes in attending to her injuries," she said.

Mrs. Bradley took out her note-book.

"How did she come to hurt herself so badly?" she enquired.

"She jumped for the ball at the same time as Miss Bonnet jumped for it. Miss Bonnet, being considerably heavier than the child, got the better of the encounter. The child was knocked down and sustained a fair number of abrasions, which I bathed, anointed and bound up. By the time I had finished, the game, I think, was over. Sister Saint Jude came over from the guest-house and gave me some assistance, I remember."

"Miss Bonnet played centre, then, did she?"

"Oh, no. She always said that no one could direct the game from the centre position. When she took part in the games, she always played against the shooter."

"Inside the goal circle?"

"Yes, with her whistle between her teeth, which always seemed to me dangerous."

"The child was not badly hurt, then?"

"No, but the asphalt is rough. If the players fall they always cut their hands and knees. Then they must darn their stockings. It is all good training for life."

Mrs. Bradley digested what was to her a novel view, and then asked:

"You came out into the playground, perhaps, before Vespers?"

"Certainly. Five minutes, I should think, before time, to make sure that the game was over and the children had gone off to wash."

"Thank you, Mother Saint Ambrose. What happened to Miss Bonnet between the end of the game at about five minutes to two, then, and the time when she went for her bath, so very much later?"

"She had asked permission, I understand, of Sister Saint Francis, as the afternoon was at her own disposal— she would ordinarily, but for the holiday, have been at Kelsorrow School—to give some extra gymnastic coaching to some of the girls at the private school."

"That would have been between two o'clock and two-thirty?"

"Yes. While the Community were in church."

"I suppose she did give them the coaching?"

"I assume that she did. It is no concern of mine, and I know very little about it, and nothing directly—that is to say, from Miss Bonnet or Sister Saint Francis."

Mrs. Bradley thanked her again, and then went to find Mother Francis, in order to get permission to speak to one of the girls. She wanted a girl who was friendly with either of the cousins of the dead girl, but not with the dead girl herself. She disliked the necessity for questioning the children at all, and was resolved to cause as little distress as she could.

"Oh, child," she said, when a girl of twelve was sent out to her, "did you know Ursula Doyle?"

"Yes, a little. Not as well as I know her cousin, though."

"On the day Ursula died Miss Bonnet gave extra teaching to some of the girls in the gymnasium, didn't she?"

"Yes. I was one, and Ursula was supposed to have been another. Then there were two of the sixth form, and a girl who is terribly good. The rest of us had the extra coaching because we're fairly bad at gym, and Miss Bonnet wanted to improve us before the drill inspection."

"Drill inspection?"

"All this Keep Fit—*you* know. They send people round to the schools. Miss Bonnet was very anxious to have us make a good impression."

"She seems a hard-working young woman."

"Oh, she's ever so keen. I wish I could do P.T. better. It's lovely for the girls who can. She took us individually. I was the last one she came to."

"How do you mean—individually?"

"She gave us all an exercise to get on with, and then she went the rounds and put each one right in what she was doing."

"You were all in the gymnasium at once?"

"Oh, yes. One had rope-climbing, another the parallel bars, two others had to practise the box work, with two more acting as supports, somebody else had ribstalls, and I had the balancing form because my balance is so frightful."

"And Miss Bonnet was with you all the time up to half-past two?"

"Well, twenty-five past. She was quite disappointed she couldn't have us for longer."

"I see. Yes, thank you, child." The girl went back to her class, and Mrs. Bradley went back to Mother Francis.

"I would like to question all the girls who took extra physical training with Miss Bonnet last Monday afternoon between two o'clock and two-thirty," she said.

Mother Francis looked at her in perplexity.

"But no one took extra physical training then."

"I have just been told that Miss Bonnet took a few girls—half a dozen or so—for extra gymnastic work on that day at that time."

"Oh, well, she may have done so, then. There is no reason why she should not, if she had the time to spare. Only—I knew nothing about it."

"Mother Saint Francis, are you certain?"

"Perfectly certain. Does it matter?"

"I don't know. The child who told me about it certainly thought that your permission had been given."

"My permission was hardly necessary in the circumstances, except that it would have been more courteous to ask for it. That would not occur to Miss Bonnet, I daresay."

"Except also that I thought the girls were always supervised when they were in the charge of visiting mistresses," Mrs. Bradley remarked.

"Yes—the whole form. But an extra piece of recreational work is not, perhaps, quite the same thing. Nevertheless, I am glad you have found out about it. On Thursday, when she comes again, I will have a word with Miss Bonnet. She is very zealous. I suppose she did not think."

"One could almost imagine she thought very hard," said Mrs. Bradley. Mother Francis looked at her, but if she felt any curiosity it went ungratified, for Mrs. Bradley remarked:

"May I ask you *not* to mention the matter to Miss Bonnet just at present?"

Mother Francis gave the promise, and also gave permission for the girls who had participated in the extra physical training to be questioned.

The girls—there were nine of them—were unanimous in the assertion that Miss Bonnet had been with them until two-thirty or just before.

"And Ursula Doyle?" said Mrs. Bradley. They agreed that she had not been there.

"What happened when the practice was over?"

"We dashed to wash."

"Was Ursula Doyle with you then?"

They looked at one another, and one by one replied that they could not remember. At last one child burst out:

"I'm sure she wasn't! There are only six basins, and Kathleen and I shared one, and so did the two third form girls, and the rest had one basin each, so Ursula couldn't have been there, and, anyway, she hadn't been at the practice. Miss Bonnet didn't seem to notice her absence, though. But, really, she was such a little quiet thing we hardly ever noticed whether she was with us or not, so I don't suppose Miss Bonnet noticed, either."

"And what did Miss Bonnet do after she had left you?" Mrs. Bradley enquired.

"She went to the Orphanage, I think. At least, she said she was going there. She said that one of the children had been hurt playing netball. She said, too, that she felt very dirty, but that it was much too soon after lunch to have a bath, although Mother Saint Jude had promised her one in the guest-house as soon as she was ready," said one of the girls.

Mrs. Bradley went back to Mother Francis.

"Where would Mother Saint Ambrose have got the impression that you had given permission for the girls to have that extra gymnastic instruction?" she demanded.

"No doubt from the girls themselves. Sister Saint Ambrose is a great favourite in the private school. She does not teach the girls there, and that gives her a certain distinction in their eyes." She paused, and then added, with the disquieting *naïveté* of the religious: "To her I am indebted for all sorts of information which I should not otherwise obtain."

Mrs. Bradley, English enough to feel uncomfortable at the thought that Mother Ambrose could be guilty of breach of confidence, did not reply to this. Instead she said:

"Did. Miss Bonnet spend time at the Orphanage between two-thirty and the time she went across to the guest-house for her bath, Mother Saint Francis, do you know?"

"I have no idea. It seems possible, as she had been taking the netball game with the orphans."

"She did not go to the guest-house until half-past three or so, did she?"

"I believe not. It was after four o'clock when I received the news that the child was dead."

"That allows for the interval during which they were trying artificial respiration, telephoning the doctor, and so on."

"Yes, I suppose so," Mother Francis agreed. "But to obtain a full report of her movements I am afraid you will have to go to see her at Kelsorrow School or wait until she comes here again on Thursday. She lives in Kelsorrow. I do not know her private address or I would give it you."

"There is no particular hurry," said Mrs. Bradley. School finished for all the children at twenty past four. Tea at the guest-house was at half-past four, so Mrs. Bradley missed it in order to question the child who had been injured in the game of netball.

She proved to be a big, strongly-made girl of fourteen. The scars of her injuries were still visible, and she showed them with obvious pride.

"Dear me!" said Mrs. Bradley, examining with very great interest the marks of battle. "You must have had a very bad fall."

"I did, madam. Didn't half hurt."

"Yes, I should say it did. Do all you children come from London?"

"Mostly, except for the Irish. And lots of them are London born. Father Thomas sends us, mostly, and helps to pay for some of us, too and all."

"He must be a very wealthy man."

"He's rich in good works, madam," the child quaintly responded, "and his place is prepared in heaven."

As this proposition was unarguable, Mrs. Bradley accepted it with a nod. She had heard much from her son about Father Thomas and his London-Irish flock.

"Now, how long were you out of school on the afternoon that this happened?" she asked, pressing a kneecap delicately with her long, thin, yellow fingers. "That hurt? Yes, and you limp a bit still, don't you? You ought to rest that leg. I'll see Mother Saint Ambrose about it."

"I never went in school that afternoon. I couldn't walk, and the classrooms are up the stairs," the girl responded.

"I see. Who was with you all that time?"

"At first, when Miss Bonnet carried me in, Mother Saint Ambrose came. Then Mother Saint Jude, she came. Then they had to go, and Miss Bonnet came, but she didn't stop very long."

"How long?"

"Not hardly five minutes. Then she said: 'Oh, lor! I'd forgotten those private school kids. You'll be all right here, won't you?' So I said I would, and she give me a comic, what I shoved away under the cushion if I

heard any steps, because we're never allowed to have
comics because Mother Saint Ambrose says they're low
and wicked, although the lay-sister winks the other
eye——"

"So Miss Bonnet left you and went to the private
school. Did she come back later on?"

"Just poked her head in at half-past two, and asked
me how I was, but my belief she meant to bunk straight
off again, only we heard Mother Saint Ambrose coming
back, so Miss Bonnet took a seat and never moved off it
until Mother Saint Ambrose had gone off to check all
the laundry."

"Does she check the laundry every Monday afternoon?"

"Yes, to see what we've tore, and whether we've
kept ourself clean. She tells by the pillow-cases
mostly."

"I understand. What does she do, then, on Monday
mornings?"

"She learns us in school."

"I see."

"The private school washing gets done of a Monday,
you see, and ourn gets done of a Tuesday."

"Ah, yes. I understand. Did Miss Bonnet come
back any more?"

"Yes, popped her head in about playtime, and asked
how I was, and said she was going to ask for a bath and
go home. She said she was ever so sorry she knocked
me down, and give me a tanner, and then she hopped it.
She never came in any more."

"Thank you very much, my dear. What's your
name?"

"Minnie Botolph."

"I see." Mrs. Bradley wrote it down and added a
note. "Now mind you rest that leg. There's slight

fluid, and we must disperse it. Have you had the doctor?''

"No."

"Why not?"

"I said it never hurt."

"Silly to say that when it does."

"Don't want no doctor messing me about."

"Probably not. You sit where you are for a little while, anyway, Minnie, and I'll go and talk to Mother Saint Ambrose."

"Want me tea," said Minnie, *sotto voce*, to Mrs. Bradley's back. Her tea and Mother Saint Ambrose came in seven minutes later. Mrs. Bradley walked into Hiversand Bay and had tea and buttered toast at the hotel.

CHAPTER 9

DOCUMENTS

"Which they have written in their inward eye;
On which they feed, and in their fastened mind
All happy joy and full contentment find."

EDMUND SPENSER: Hymn of Heavenly Beauty.

MRS. BRADLEY'S BEDROOM IN THE GUEST-HOUSE WAS large, airy and clean. It smelt of lavender, yellow soap and, most unaccountably, mice. The gas lighting was adequate, and a small table having been especially imported about an hour earlier by a willing and almost mild-mannered Bessie, Mrs. Bradley seated herself at it after the evening meal, and studied the papers with which she had been provided. The school time-table and the list of guests she put aside at first in favour of the detailed account of the circumstances of the child's death.

Mother Saint Francis had done her work with all the neat and loving thoroughness of a nun, and the document gave Mrs. Bradley some valuable information. Her own thoughts at this point in the investigation were mixed. The Community, in desiring her presence at the convent, had had in mind, she knew well, the possibility that her investigations might change the theory of suicide into one of accident. If, as she began to perceive most clearly it must, the case resolved itself into one of murder (person or persons unknown at that point in her enquiry) she wondered in what light her services would continue to be appreciated. She realised, too, that, apart from any shock that might be in store for the nuns, her own intelligence shied from the thought of murder in such a connection for much the same reason as a horse, accustomed to motors, will shy at a piece of white paper fluttering down a country lane. The effect was too startling to be in tune with the surroundings.   Murder and the conventual life were mutually contradictory.   The theory of accident she had been inclined to discard as soon as she had heard the report of the man in the Gas Company's showrooms. She knew that there had been cases of gas poisoning in which no escape of gas was traceable, and it was possible that this was one of them, but such cases were rare, and the law of averages was not in favour of too frequent a repetition of such coincidence.

Another strange feature, even as far as she had gone, was the mutual contradiction of possibly unimportant points of evidence.   The most striking, she felt, was Annie's confident assertion that there had been no smell of gas when she first went into the room.   Yet Miss Bonnet had opened the window wide, and both the nuns had smelt gas in spite of the fact that the window, by the time they arrived, was open.   Of course, there was the creosote, she reflected; a substance with a most pungent, gas-like odour, yet none of the witnesses appeared to have taken it much into account.   The smell, in any case, would have been greater downstairs in the rooms at the front of the house than in the bath-room right round to the side.

A curious feature, too, was that the child's head should have been completely submerged.   If murder had been committed by the administration of carbon monoxide gas, and as there was no way of hiding the method of killing, it seemed redundant to add apparent drowning to the affair . . . unless, of course—and at this

Mrs. Bradley frowned in an attempt to reject an idea which was becoming increasingly persistent—unless the death had been accomplished not by an adult, but by another child, who had plotted it carefully, but did not feel sure that the method would be efficacious. On the other hand, there was Miss Bonnet. Mrs. Bradley desired to be perfectly just with regard to Miss Bonnet, and her first act of grace was to acknowledge to herself, fairly and squarely, that she disliked Miss Bonnet very much indeed, and that so far as she herself was concerned, if the thing turned out to be murder, she would sooner suspect Miss Bonnet than anybody else in the place. Then she dismissed all prejudice from her mind, and settled herself to examine the fact that Miss Bonnet —sinister sign very often in a case of murder!—had been the very first person, so far as anyone knew, to come upon the body.

She studied the report again. It was certain that the child had been present at the midday meal. What, to Mrs. Bradley's mind, was very much less certain, was that, according to Mother Francis, the child had also been present at the beginning of afternoon school. Mother Francis based this statement upon the fact that she had not been noticed to be absent, but recollections of the exploits of her own nephews and nieces at school caused Mrs. Bradley to reflect that it is by no means unheard-of for a child to answer a name or sign a sheet for an absentee member of the form, and never confess to the fact.

Obviously, if this had been done, no later confession had been made, or Mother Francis would have said as much. Mrs. Bradley went back to the school time-table, and noted again the lessons for Monday, but this did not help her. According to the readings, Mother Gregory should have been taking Ursula's form for

music at the beginning of the afternoon, and had made
no report of her absence. Mrs. Bradley made another
note, and then put down the names of all of the Community who were engaged in teaching on Monday
afternoons. These, she found, were Mother Cyprian,
who taught needlework all the afternoon; Mother
Simon-Zelotes, who taught in the Orphanage first, and
then took metal-work; Mother Mary-Joseph, who taught
English and History at the private school until twenty
minutes past four; Mother Gregory, who took music
until the same hour; and old Mother Bartholomew,
whose time was occupied in teaching dancing and
elocution.

Mrs. Bradley put a tick against all these names,
because if the child had gone into class at half-past two,
none of the people employed in teaching from half-past
two until after four o'clock could have been directly
occupied in making away with her. If it could be
shown that she had not gone into class at all on that
Monday afternoon, the field was considerably wider,
because the Community had an hour of recreation
between one and two o'clock (except for those who had
duties during that time, and whose activities would have
to be taken note of), and the child might have been
dead before the end of that recreation period. There
had been nothing in the medical evidence to render
such a possibility void. It was significant that she had
not turned up for that physical training practice at two
o'clock.

But still—and Mrs. Bradley found herself continually
referred back to this extraordinarily difficult problem—
by far the most important point at issue was to ascertain
the means by which the child had been forced or
induced to breathe the carbon monoxide which had
killed her. One whiff of the deadly gas would have been

sufficient to make the little girl unconscious, but with a gas water-heater in perfect order, and no clue to the way in which sufficient gas had been administered to the victim to kill her, Mrs. Bradley felt that her theory of murder would scarcely carry conviction.

Still, the Community's theory of accident was even less capable of proof; in fact, in the face of the evidence, it was nonsense. And yet—Mrs. Bradley nodded very slowly—why the turned-off gas, the turned-off taps, and the water to the rim of the bath? It almost seemed as though it might have been suicide, after all, and that the dead body had been discovered earlier than the time at which Miss Bonnet invaded the bathroom. In this case, it might be that an innocent but panic-stricken person—one of the older orphans, very likely—had turned off the gas and the running water, but had failed to report the death in case she found herself involved in its awkward consequences.

But, if this were so—and it was quite a likely hypothesis—why the singular manœuvres of Miss Bonnet? Why, in particular, the obviously staged attack on the unfortunate Minnie Botolph? It was unusual, to say the least, for the centre player to be knocked out, in netball, by the goal defence.

She left the point for the moment, and came back to her newest theory. The more she examined this idea, the more improbable it seemed, however, for in such case—accidental discovery of the body of a gas-suicide— the gas would probably have rendered the invader unconscious. Apart from that, Mrs. Bradley could not believe that Annie, in particular, had guilty knowledge, or that Bessie would have lacked courage to report to Mother Ambrose the accident if she had discovered it. Of course, there was Kitty, who had been on duty that day. Kitty might have to be interviewed.

There was also to be considered the slightly mysterious Mrs. Waterhouse, but she, presumably, had been
fully employed, and had had no opportunity for murder.
All the infant orphans, it was true, had been taken off
her hands for the afternoon, but there were a number of
private school children of kindergarten age who had to
be taught. She looked up Mrs. Waterhouse in Mother
Francis' report. Mrs. Waterhouse, Mother Francis
deposed, had been engaged in teaching five little children
from the private school until a quarter to four—that is
to say, until after the body had been found. Moreover,
at a quarter to four she had taken them, by invitation,
and as a special treat, to see the Mother Superior, who
gave them sweets, and whom they were accustomed to
address as Grandma. Unless Mrs. Waterhouse had
managed to sneak away from her charges during the early
part of afternoon school, therefore, or had committed
the murder between the end of the morning session and
the beginning of the afternoon one, she seemed to be
fully covered.

But Mrs. Bradley paused. Waterhouse? Waterhouse? Memory flooded back. A woman of that name
had been tried, five years before, for the murder of her
husband in a London tramway depôt. It had been an
extraordinary case. Ferdinand had defended the
woman, and she had been acquitted, amid considerable
female hysteria, of a crime which it seemed quite
certain she had committed. Ferdinand affected a
complete belief in her innocence, Mrs. Bradley remembered. Brave of her not to have changed her name, she
thought.

She folded the document from which she had made
her notes, compared what she had written with the
information supplied by the school time-table, and then
studied Mother Jude's clearly-written list of guests. It

suggested nothing until she came to the last name on the paper. "Mrs. A. P. Maslin," she read; there followed the woman's address, and a note, written neatly in the margin, to state that the wet towel found in the bathroom had come from her room. A sufficiently startling entry, this, Mrs. Bradley thought. She had not understood, from conversation with Mother Ambrose and Mother Jude, that an aunt of the dead girl had been staying at the guest-house at the time when the death occurred. It was this aunt, then, who had taken the body home for burial. It was she who was coming back later to hear the result of Mrs. Bradley's enquiry. In view of the provisions of the grandfather's will, there was something extraordinarily sinister in the fact that this aunt had been living at the guest-house at the time when the death occurred. There was a large fortune for Mary Maslin, Mrs. Bradley remembered, if two people between her and the money could be removed; one had gone already; there remained the pale, self-possessed girl who had taken her on a tour of the convent grounds at the end of afternoon school. On the other hand, why had the woman made such a fuss about the verdict? That did not look like guilt.

She picked up the list and went through it carefully again. Father Thomas' name came first and was followed by those of Miss Philippa Carey, Mrs. George Trust, Kathleen O'Hara, professed nun, Monica Temple, the same, Dom Pius Edmonds, Mademoiselle Yvonne Darnier, Mademoiselle Jacqueline Darnier, Señorita Mercedes Rio, and then, as though placed there for special attention and notice, Mrs. A. P. Maslin.

Of these, the two nuns had arrived on the Wednesday following the death of the child, and from no point of view could be involved. The foreigners, too, Mrs. Bradley was inclined to leave out of serious consideration.   The Benedictine monk was probably, she thought, not a murderer, and she entertained no suspicions of Father Thomas.   Of Miss Philippa Carey and Mrs. George Trust she knew nothing except their names, and was inclined to the opinion that that was all she would need to know.   But Mrs. Maslin, with only one life now between her step-daughter and the fortune of Timothy Doyle, was in a different category, in spite of the fact that she had not accepted the verdict, and Mrs. Bradley added her name to a short neat list which read thus:

> Ulrica Doyle.
> Mary Maslin.
> Miss D. T. Bonnet.
> Person or persons unknown.
> The Community of Saint Peter.
> Mrs. Waterhouse (?).
> Mrs. A. P. Maslin.

Then she glanced at her watch.   Her room was at the back of the house and overlooked the grounds of the convent.   There was not a light to be seen.   Bed-time seemed depressingly early in that house of the religious, but she knew that the lay-sisters were up before half-past five and the choir-nuns before six every morning.   She turned her back to the window and looked at the narrow bed which had been assigned to her, and speculated, not without sympathy, upon its last occupant, the half-witted lay-sister Bridget, asleep by now, she supposed, in the grim-looking Orphanage opposite.

Suddenly she went to the door, opened it, and peered out into the passage.   She could not have said that she had heard anything, yet some sort of signal had been transmitted to her conscious mind through one of her senses, and that, almost certainly, the aural one.

A night-light was burning inside a small glass lantern, and Mrs. Bradley, though dimly, could see to the end of the passage. She waited, but a considerable interval elapsed before she made out a body, clothed in dark, bundled garments, flattened against the wall.

"How are you, Sister Bridget, dear child?" she said. "Come along into your room and let's have some cocoa and biscuits."

The motionless heap did not stir. Mrs. Bradley went inside the room again, but left the door ajar. She seated herself at the table and watched and waited. A quarter of an hour went by, and the room began to get chilly from the draught through the open doorway. Mrs. Bradley was beginning to think that she had been mistaken, and that it was not Sister Bridget outside, when the door opened very, very slowly, and the half-witted lay-sister, with her dead-white, puffy face, upon which was a calculating, slightly leering expression, and her shuffling, lop-sided walk, came inch by inch into the room. She seemed extremely nervous, and retained her hold upon the door. Still facing Mrs. Bradley, she shut the door behind her, and stood with her back to it, waiting.

At this, Mrs. Bradley smiled—not her usual rather frightening grimace, but with a gentle kindliness which softened the brilliance of her eyes—and patted the arm-chair near her to encourage her visitor to be seated. Sister Bridget, leaving what she evidently felt was the friendly locality of the doorway, at last came sagging across the room with the heavy, ungainly movements of the mentally enfeebled, and seated herself in the chair. The cheerful little fire had been replenished by Annie before she went to bed, and Sister Bridget, leering with satisfaction, stretched out her hands to the warmth.

Mrs. Bradley got up, without haste, and went over to

a small hanging cupboard. From it she took biscuits and some sweets. Quiet and unhurried although she was in all she was doing, the lethargic lump in the fireside chair watched her closely, following every movement with anxious, suspicious eyes.

"There now," Mrs. Bradley said, when she had arranged the sweets and the biscuits on plates. "We will settle down together and be comfortable."

So they ate the biscuits and sweets, and Mrs. Bradley boiled milk on the fire and made cocoa for her visitor. Then they began to talk. It did not take long to discover that, whoever might have knowledge of the events leading up to the death of Ursula Doyle, the poor half-wit knew nothing about it. Word associations, skilfully introduced into a rather one-sided conversation—for Sister Bridget ate too voraciously to have very much time for talking—produced nothing but negative results. Even a test which was given under light hypnosis (attempted and successfully concluded in about a quarter of an hour, the subject having previously become a little drowsy), failed to prove the slightest degree of guilty knowledge on Sister Bridget's part concerning the tragedy.

Mrs. Bradley had not thought that the lay-sister would be connected with the affair, but it was with a sense of thankfulness that she concluded her tests.

Sister Bridget remained drowsy for a while, then slept for a bit. She woke with a little squeal of fear, apparently out of a bad dream, and was alarmed, for a minute or two, to find Mrs. Bradley in the room. Her lips slobbered, and she made passes as though to ward off attack. Mrs. Bradley talked to her quietly, and reassured her, and the lay-sister, leering pleasedly, suddenly gave a peculiar little call, and out of the corner of the room came a large, fat mouse. Its intelligent eyes took in everything, and at Sister Bridget's command it swarmed from her dress to her shoulder, then sat on the corner of the mantelpiece. The half-wit gave it some biscuit which it nibbled with delicate grace; then it sat brushing its nose with a tiny paw.

"What is its name?" Mrs. Bradley asked. When she had repeated the question twice, Sister Bridget replied that he was her brother. She was silent for a time after that, but Mrs. Bradley could see that she wrestled with words, and wanted to give voice to something which was almost beyond her capacity to express. Mrs. Bradley waited patiently, her bright black eyes on the bright black eyes of the mouse. She placed a bit of biscuit near it, but Sister Bridget snatched it up and ate it herself before the mouse could have it. Mrs. Bradley handed the next bit of biscuit to the lay-sister, and, with sly chuckles, Sister Bridget fed her pet.

Suddenly, in her outlandish jargon, she began to talk. Her excitement was fearful to watch, and so were the contortions of her face and body. Mrs. Bradley found it impossible at first to grasp the essence of the outburst, but concentration plus a little imagination brought its reward. The mouse had nearly died. Something had nearly killed the mouse. The mouse had lain for dead. His little paws had been bent; he had lain on his back, his little eyes had been glazed and his tail had not moved even when Sister Bridget had slightly tweaked it. He had been dead. He had been dead. And then, like Lazarus, he had been alive. Both miracles, Sister Bridget apparently understood and firmly believed, had been worked by divine agency.

Mrs. Bradley was almost as excited as the lay-sister, although not as obviously so, and not for the same reason. She began, very carefully, to lead the feeble mind back to the occasion on which the near-death of

the mouse had come about.   She did not want to suggest
time, but thought it could do no harm to lead towards
locality.   Not immediately, but in a minute or two, she
induced Sister Bridget to name the place in which she
had found the mouse lying unconscious on the floor.
The lay-sister, full of her subject, which had affected her
deeply—so deeply that she had not (extraordinarily,
considering her mental condition) forgotten the occurrence—took Mrs. Bradley's hand and shambled, mopping
and mowing, towards the door.   Mrs. Bradley produced
a small electric torch with her free hand from the deep
pocket of her skirt, and switched it on as they reached
the dimly lit corridor.

Sister Bridget led the way to the bathroom immediately above that in which the dead child had been found
—a curious mental aberration, Mrs. Bradley thought—
and showed the exact spot on the floor where the mouse
had lain unconscious.   Mrs. Bradley focused the light of
her torch upon the spot and took a very small box of
drawing-pins from her pocket.   She instructed Sister
Bridget to press one into the floor on the spot where
the mouse had lain.   Then they went back to the bedroom and again fed the mouse, who had supplied the
first direct evidence, apart from that produced by the
medical examination of the body, that the gas supply in
the bathrooms might be faulty or had been tampered
with.

Mrs. Bradley remarked, as together they watched the
mouse:

"What a pretty colour he is."

Sister Bridget agreed, took Mrs. Bradley's hand and
fondled it, mumbling affectionately.   The suggestion
as to colour aroused no reaction, and the evidence
remained unconfirmed.   Either Sister Bridget had not
noticed, or the mouse had not produced, the usual

symptoms of carbon monoxide poisoning. Nevertheless, the clue, as a clue, remained.

It was shortly after this that Sister Bridget decided to
go to bed. She omitted every formality attendant upon
this inclination except for removing her shoes, which
were very muddy. Mrs. Bradley sat still until she was
sure that the lay-sister was asleep. She slept as nuns do
—stretched flat upon her back in the bed, her old arms
crossed on her breast, her loose-hanging mouth closed
firmly. So she slept every night, and so she would
sleep in death, Mrs. Bradley reflected. She turned out
the gas, lighted a candle, placed it on the table and took
up the documents again. A tap at the door made her
turn her head. The door-handle twisted, and Mother
Ambrose, still fully habited, although it was long past
midnight, came noiselessly into the room.

Mrs. Bradley got up and went towards her, carrying
the candle so that it lighted her face. She thought that
the nun was startled, but Mother Ambrose's voice was
calm and low-pitched as she said:

"Sister Bridget is not in the Orphanage bedroom
where we put her. I thought perhaps she might have
wandered back here. She is greatly attached to this
room."

"She is here asleep," Mrs. Bradley observed, as she
raised the candle to let its yellow glow illumine the
lower part of Sister Bridget's face. "What is more,
she has been of material help to me."

"She told you about the mouse, I suppose," Mother
Ambrose surprisingly remarked.

"You knew about the mouse, then?"

"Certainly I did. Sister Bridget talked of nothing
else for two days."

"Was the mouse—who discovered the mouse in the
bathroom?"

"You were going to suggest that the mouse was rendered unconscious by breathing carbon monoxide gas," said Mother Ambrose. "How can I tell? It seems likely. As to who discovered it—Sister Bridget discovered it herself. It was fond of the bathroom. Sister Saint Jude spoke to Sister Bridget, because it would nibble soap, a habit which disgusted the guests and was expensive for the convent."

She folded her hands—a tall, Amazonian woman, military, faithful, and, to Mrs. Bradley, enigmatic—and waited, with the unique patience of her sisterhood. Mrs. Bradley chuckled, and then looked guiltily towards the bed. But Sister Bridget's rest remained undisturbed.

"And at what time in the day—I am assuming that it was on the day of the child's death—did Sister Bridget find the mouse?"

"The mouse was not found on the day of the child's death, but on the previous Thursday, after Compline."

"If the mouse had been found on the Monday, I suppose you would have mentioned it to me?"

"I think I might have done so. I cannot tell. It proves, of course, that the Gas Company were wrong, and that there must be an escape of gas in at least one of the bathrooms."

"I don't think it proves that unquestionably, but we shall see. Did people continue to use the bathroom after the mouse had been found there?"

"When we had heard Sister Bridget's story, we made every effort to discover whether there was an escape of gas in the room, but we could not find one. We tried every joint in the pipes, for instance, with a lighted taper, and Annie and Kitty sniffed their hardest to detect the smell. There was nothing. Kitty, who is inclined to be nervous, declared several times that she could smell gas, but neither Annie nor I, when we tried, could agree with her. We thought it safe, therefore, to allow the guests to use the bathroom, but we put up a warning placard, advising them to keep the window open at the top."

"I am surprised that you did not mention all this to me," said Mrs. Bradley. The nun bowed her head politely at the tone of rebuke, but said nothing in explanation of her omission. "Do your guests attend all the religious services?" Mrs. Bradley went on, after a very slight pause.

"Neither the guests nor the children," Mother Ambrose replied, in tones of imperturbable courtesy. "They may do so if they wish, of course, but we do not suggest nor particularly desire it. Of our spiritual exercises, only Compline is sung. Everybody here attends Mass. Mass is served by Father Clare, except during the visits of ordained priests of our own order. Father Clare, of course, is of the Order of the Society of Jesus."

Apparently deciding once again that she had sufficiently answered the question, Mother Ambrose retired into immobility again. Mrs. Bradley sighed inaudibly, and then remarked that she supposed that Mother Ambrose would be glad to go to bed.

"What would *you* like to do?" Mother Ambrose asked. "I could wake Sister Bridget and take her back with me, and put clean sheets on the bed——"

"By no means. Let me sleep in the Orphanage. I shall enjoy it," Mrs. Bradley replied. So they went down the stairs and out at the front door together.

The night was very dark and still. There was no sound to be heard except the distant wash of the sea at the foot of the cliffs, and the fall of their own footsteps as they walked to the gatehouse and pushed the iron gate open.

"Compline is an evening service, I believe?" Mrs. Bradley observed.

"We sing it at five o'clock," the nun replied, "and, except at Pascal time, the Angelus bell is rung at six."

"At what time did Miss Bonnet leave the school on that Thursday?" Mrs. Bradley enquired.

"She is free to leave at four-twenty," Mother Ambrose replied; but beyond this bare and uninformative statement she volunteered no further answer to the question, and Mrs. Bradley did not press the point. She waited whilst the nun both closed and locked the gates. She could not see the key, because the night was so dark, but she was interested to notice that Mother Ambrose seemed to have no difficulty in finding the lock.

"I wonder what brought Sister Bridget to this pass," she said, as Mother Ambrose fumblingly put back the key on a chain at her waist. "I suppose that she must have been of normal mentality when she was accepted as a lay-sister?"

"Certainly. She suffered a considerable shock once when the part of the building in which she was working with two others caught fire, and the other two were suffocated. Sister Bridget was badly burned in trying to save them, and was very ill for months afterwards. When she recovered she seemed normal, but gradually lapsed until she was as you see her now. The curious feature is that she loves to play with matches."

Mrs. Bradley nodded. Shock had strange effects, and in the case of Sister Bridget must have upset the work of the thyroid gland. She had not had a similar case, and was interested.

"I would like to undertake her case," she said. "I am pretty sure she could be cured. How old is she?"

"Sixty-seven." The nun hesitated and then added: "She has been like this, afflicted, for twenty years."

They talked no more, for the Orphanage was in darkness and its occupants presumably asleep. Mrs. Bradley was shown into Sister Bridget's room to find that the bed had been occupied and that the lay-sister, moreover, must have gone to bed in her muddy outdoor shoes.

"Oh, dear!" Mother Ambrose exclaimed, and, despite Mrs. Bradley's protests, she insisted upon entirely remaking the bed. Then, giving the counterpane a last twitch and the eiderdown a friendly and comradely pat, she bade Mrs. Bradley good-night, commended her to God, and disappeared with the same complete and ghostly celerity as that with which it appeared she had arrived at the guest-house bedroom.

Mrs. Bradley went to bed and was glad to get there. The day had been extraordinarily fatiguing. Bessie came in in the morning with tea and toast.

"Ah, Mother Saint Ambrose *said* you was here," she pronounced, with extreme satisfaction. "That slobbering old—that Sister Bridget went and pinched your bed."

Mrs. Bradley cackled. There was something refreshingly unregenerate about Bessie. Excellent although she believed the training of the orphans to be in some respects, she hoped that it would not have the effect of altering Bessie's high spirits and racy language. She considered her with a bright and birdlike eye over the rim of a cup of tea, and thought of her own youth, which had been spent in a village and had been guided, so far as religious matters were concerned, by the Church of England. She could hear the vicar, with his delicate emphasis on the personal aspect of Christianity . . . "Wherein I was made a member of Christ, *the* child of God, and an inheritor of the Kingdom of Heaven!"

"By the way, Bessie," she said, as she lowered the cup. "I suppose Miss Bonnet *was* the first person to find the dead child in the guest-house?"

Bessie's uncomprehending stare was answer enough, she felt, without the characteristic reply.

"Dunno what you're getting at. Sounds as if you might be coming round to my point of view, after all. They done 'er in; I'll always hold to it, poor little innocent kid."

CHAPTER 10

QUESTIONS

"Either his slippery knots at once untie
And disentangle all his winding snare
Or shatter too with him my curious frame."

ANDREW MARVELL: The Coronet.

ANNIE WAS CLEANING TAPS. SHE SMEARED ON THE polish very evenly, thinly and carefully, and then rubbed with such energy and goodwill that the metal seemed to burst into sunshine underneath her hand. Mrs. Bradley watched her, and the girl, unconscious of her presence, worked on, her breathing a little laboured, her cheeks brightly flushed, and a stray quiff of hair hanging loose from her neat mob cap.

"Good work, Annie," said Mrs. Bradley pleasantly, as the girl gave up and began to screw the cap on the tin of polish. Annie, accustomed to the unheralded comings and silent going of nuns, looked round and smiled.

"Good morning, madam. Did you sleep well at the guest-house?"

"Not at the guest-house; here, in the Orphanage," Mrs. Bradley replied, surprised that Bessie had not passed on the fact of her presence.

"Really, madam?"

"Yes. Sister Bridget decided to come home to roost. Annie, did you know she had a tame mouse?"

"Certainly, madam. Last Thursday week it nearly died, or something. She was that excited we could

135

hardly get anything out of her. Not as it's easy, any time, to quite make out all she says."

"I can't think why nobody told me about this mouse. I want to go across and have a look at the bathroom. Will you ask Kitty to come with me? And can you come as well?"

"I'll just speak to Mother Saint Ambrose a minute, then, madam."

She put away her cleaning things, washed her hands, and went off in search of the nun. Mrs. Bradley, who had wandered into the kitchen from the dining-room, wandered back again. The Orphanage was rather sternly be-texted, and religious pictures simpered from most of its walls, but the walls were also cheerful with yellow paint, and there were branches of hazel in vases. Mother Ambrose came in less than three minutes, and readily gave permission for Annie and Kitty to go with Mrs. Bradley to the guest-house.

The drawing-pin was still in position, and, watched by the two girls, Mrs. Bradley knelt down and scrutinised it. Kitty involuntarily giggled, but was nudged into silence by Annie. Near the drawing-pin, which marked the spot on which, according to Sister Bridget, the unconscious mouse had been found, the gas pipe connected to the geyser came up through a hole in the floor. Mrs. Bradley poked an inquisitive, long, yellow finger into the hole in the boards, but could touch nothing.

She sat back on her heels, turned her head and spoke to the girls over her shoulder.

"If I become unconscious, drag me away and open the window and door, children," she said, with a ghastly cackle. "Shut both, and then I shall begin."

Annie closed the window, Kitty the door. Mrs. Bradley lay full length, her face above the hole. After a full three minutes she got up.

"Do you feel all right, madam?" asked Annie. Mrs. Bradley blew her nose and nodded.

"Unfortunately, quite all right," she said. "Kitty, why didn't you tell anybody that you had found someone lying unconscious in the bath?"

"When, madam?" Kitty's prominent eyes opened wide. "Sure, you wouldn't be meaning that poor little girl?"

"Why wouldn't I?"

"Well, madam, I thought it was in the bathroom underneath this one she was found. Anyways, Miss Bonnet found her, not me. I never was after finding her. Indeed, I know nothing about it, beyond what I'm hearing from Annie."

"But surely you should have been on duty here?"

"Sure and indeed I should have been, only, do you see, I was doing a Little Penance for coughing in Silence Time. 'Tis by way of being a privilege to work in the guest-house. We lose it if we are offensive."

"I see," said Mrs. Bradley. "What were you doing instead?"

"Cleaning pigs."

"Is that a penance?"

"Not to me; I like it. But to most here it is."

"Kitty pulled it out of the bag, madam, and Mother Saint Ambrose couldn't change it, you see," Annie politely explained. "Cleaning pigs, cleaning water closets, weeding gravel, killing slugs, making bread-crumbs, gutting fish, is all Little Penances, and you fish for one out of the bag if you've done something wrong, whether Mother Saint Ambrose knows or not; we're on our honour, us older ones, we are."

"What happens to all those jobs when nobody has qualified for a Little Penance?" Mrs. Bradley enquired. The two girls looked at one another.

"Sometimes some of us do one to gain merit, but that don't happen very often," said Annie, pensively. "There's Bessie, for one. Always in trouble, she is. And swapped her Little Penance, once, for a Grand Penance Maggie got given her, because she liked it better."

"What was the Grand Penance, then?"

"Not to see Reverend Mother Superior for a fort-night."

"What did she change it for?"

"Killing slugs. You see, you can't be found out in that, because Reverend Mother Superior don't know who's allowed to see her and who isn't, and as long as you can show a fair number of slugs, nobody watches while you find them. So Bessie pulled it off, only Maggie let it out by mistake."

"What happened then?" asked Mrs. Bradley, hoping to get more light on the character of Mother Ambrose.

"Nothing *happened*," said Annie, inconclusively. "Not as we know of, anyway. But Maggie said she would never do it again."

"I think I'd like to see Maggie. I wonder, Kitty, whether you could go back now and send her over?"

Maggie proved to be fat and fair, and, looking at her, Mrs. Bradley felt that it was incredible that she should have achieved a Grand Penance. So intrigued was she that she asked, point-blank, for an explanation.

"Oh, madam——" said Maggie. She twisted up her apron, drew in her breath with a sudden, sharp hiss, and then laughed until Mrs. Bradley was afraid she would suffocate.

"Oh, madam——" said Maggie again, with another hysterical burst. Mrs. Bradley was beginning to regret that she had embarked upon the subject when Maggie, gathering herself together, said, with a rush, so that laughter should not eclipse speech: "I told a lie, madam! I really had to. It was all through the milkman, madam. He left a rose in a carton of cream—for Kitty, we thought, only it was really for me, only neither of us didn't like to tell Mother Saint Ambrose, it made us feel so awkward—so I told Mother Saint Ambrose we didn't know who it was meant for, and there was poetry on it and everything, only we hadn't seen it. It was tied round the carton under the rose, and I suppose Mother Saint Ambrose must have read it and found my name on it, and she gave me a Grand Penance for lying—only, you see, it wasn't really a lie —and made me do my hair back tighter."

"Well, that's very interesting, Maggie. By the way, why didn't you call somebody to help you when you went into the other bathroom and found the little girl dead?"

"I never went in there, madam. I never do." Maggie looked puzzled, not scared.

"Do you mean that you never do the work in that bathroom?"

"No, madam, not in that bathroom. It's Kitty's and Annie's work. All of us have our own work, though we don't always have our own partners."

"Have you never been inside it before?"

"Yes, madam, but only when fetched. I came into *this* bathroom, madam, when Sister Bridget's mouse was found. I picked it up, madam, as nobody else fancied touching it."

"Didn't Sister Bridget touch it?"

"No. She spoke very blaspheemious, although nobody thought she could help it. It was just the devil taking advantage of her, being as she's simple, madam."

"But she didn't pick up the mouse?"

"No, madam. Mother Saint Ambrose ordered Bessie to, but Bessie said she couldn't, not for nobody, so Mother Saint Ambrose said: 'Fetch Kitty.' So Bessie said (only she muttered it, so she told me) to the effect that 'Maggie's the one for your money! She's our little old slug-catcher!' So she fetched me along, against order, but acting innocent, like she do."

"You didn't mind picking up the mouse?"

"What's the use of minding? My father was a mole catcher. Help him put 'em out in rows, I have, many's the time, and wish I could help him again."

She began to whimper and, at a nod from Mrs. Bradley, who added: "The other two," Annie led Maggie away. Maria, aged fifteen, and Ethel, aged fourteen and three-quarters (whom Mrs. Bradley had already seen as Mother Francis' monitor), were as innocent as the others, it appeared, of having opened the bathroom door and found the body. This left Mrs. Bradley where she had started, except that to have eliminated the orphans led one step further from suicide or accident, and one step nearer murder, she decided, since an innocent adult person would surely have summoned assistance and made the death known.

Shaking her head, she went over to the school for Mother Gregory. She knew that the Sacristan did no teaching on Tuesday mornings, so, after a glance in at the doorway of the staff-room where the nuns, if they wished, could sit and correct exercise books without having to carry these off the school premises, she wandered across to the cloister, and heard the sound of the organ. Quietly she went into church, and knelt for a moment, as she would have covered her shoes with over-slippers if she had been entering a mosque. Then she got up and moved quietly towards the organ.

The church was almost all new, although it stood on

the site and was built on the foundations of the monastic church which had commanded that high headland before the Dissolution. The Community had purchased the site very cheaply from a local Catholic landowner, and much of the labour of putting up and restoring the conventual buildings had been done by the nuns themselves. It had been an heroic task, and, later, Mrs. Bradley had the story of it from the Mother Superior, who, except for Mother Simon-Zelotes, Mother Gregory and a very old lay-sister named Catherine, was the only person who remembered those days of toil and of glory.

Mrs. Bradley walked on, found the steps leading up from the chancel to the organ, mounted them and stood at the organist's side. Mother Gregory, spectacles on nose, dim eyes, even so, strained closely towards the copy of the music, played on, regardless of, or else indifferent to, the proximity of the listener. Then she finished; turned on the stool, faced Mrs. Bradley, smiled kindly and vaguely, as old people, well-disposed, do, and extended a fine, large hand. Mrs. Bradley helped her from her seat, made way for her, and followed her out of the church.

"Who wants me now?" Mother Gregory hoarsely enquired.

"I do." They walked through the archway which led from an angle of the cloister into the nuns' garden. "Can you cast your mind back to yesterday week?"

"A Monday. Yes, I can. That was the day I had a double class for music, because Sister Saint Dominic took those poor children to the dentist."

"Is that all? Does nothing else come to your mind about that day?"

"Wait. Yes, it does. That was the day when that poor little child was found drowned."

"Now that is what I want to talk to you about. Do

you remember her going out of class? According to
the school time-table, you take the third form—her
class—for music at the beginning of the afternoon."

"Nobody went out of class. Why should she?"

"I cannot say. Are you certain that nobody went
out?"

"The last time that anybody went out of class in one
of my lessons was when a girl called Farley—Clarice
Farley—was sick after eating trout. Nonsensical," said
Mother Gregory, hoarsely. "As if trout could make
anyone sick!"

"And when was that, do you remember?"

"Certainly. That was in the last week of last term—
just before Christmas. I remember perfectly well
saying to the poor child: 'If you can do this with trout,
what do you suppose you will do with your Christmas
dinner?' "

"And what did she suppose she would do with
her Christmas dinner?" Mrs. Bradley could not help
but enquire. Mother Gregory snorted, and then
observed aptly:

"*La varieté des viandes, si elles sont en grande quantité,
charge toujours l'estomach; mais s'il est faible, elle le ruine.*"

Mrs. Bradley chuckled, and the nun cocked a witty
eye and added: "And that is not the best use to make of
the letters of Saint François de Sales, unless——" she
resumed her normal expression, "you know how to take
a hint."

Mrs. Bradley was silent for a minute or two, and they
strolled on, the nun majestic in the dignity of her
habit, Mrs. Bradley insignificant as a sparrow, for, in
deference to her surroundings, she was dressed in drab
brown with no more than a touch of yellow to enliven a
withered, autumnal uniformity of colour.

"How many children are there in the **third form**?"

she enquired, to end the pause, during which she had thought furiously hard.

"About twenty, I believe,"Mother Gregory answered. Her face was benign in repose, and had the curiously self-satisfied expression which spectacles can bestow upon some countenances.

"I suppose you would have noticed if anybody had been absent from your class? Had not shown up at all, I mean, to the lesson?"

"I might have done in the ordinary way, but as I was taking the two forms together and am, as no doubt you have observed, particularly short-sighted, it is highly probable that I should not have noticed whether any particular child was there or not. Choral singing is not quite like most other lessons. One has no direct dealing with individuals. I have already discussed all this with Sister Saint Francis."

Mrs. Bradley, no longer surprised to learn that there were a good many facts which she was *not* told by the religious, merely nodded.

"And now," she said, "forgive me for pressing the point, but it may be extraordinarily important— do you think you would have noticed if *two* children had been absent from that double class?"

"I don't know that I should have noticed," Mother Gregory admitted.

"It is possible that two children might have been absent then," Mrs. Bradley observed. She made a note. "Do you call a register, by the way?"

"I do not. There is no need. The children like music."

Mrs. Bradley was aware of a cocked eye again. She frowned. The nun was still hinting. She accompanied her to the further end of the garden, from which there was a short cut back to the church, saw her enter by the west door, and herself went over to the private school again. She did not seek Mother Francis immediately, but seated herself in a small, light-panelled vestibule and wrote out Mother Gregory's quotation from *La Vie Parfaite*. Then she knocked at Mother Francis' door.

"For how long beforehand," she asked, "had it been known that Mother Saint Gregory was to have a double class on that particular day?"

"For a week," Mother Francis replied. "Sister Saint Gregory gave out the notice herself to both forms on the previous Monday, because she wanted the words of two or three songs learned in readiness for choral singing."

"I see," said Mrs. Bradley slowly. "I believe you told me that Ulrica Doyle is in the fourth form, and Mary Maslin in the second?"

"Yes. Mary is six months older than poor little Ursula was, but is rather a dull child, as I think I said before."

"Then Ulrica will be able to tell me whether Ursula was in class for the music lesson, I dare say," Mrs. Bradley observed, "since forms three and four were taken together that Monday afternoon. Have you any objection to my questioning her about it?"

"None whatever. Please do whatever you think best. Would you like me to send for her?"

"I will talk to her during the dinner hour. It will be less formal then. This news of the double lesson is important. I wish I had known it before."

Mother Francis lowered her eyes. It seemed to Mrs. Bradley as though she were fated always to be finding fault with one or other of the Community, and their docility in accepting rebuke unnerved her. She said, when the nun looked up again:

"Mother Saint Francis, I am going to ask a direct

question, and I would like the frankest answer which you can give me."

The nun's grey eyes were fixed on hers. Mother Francis was summing her up. She smiled.

"What is your question?" she asked.

"What is your own belief about the circumstances of the child's death?"

"I regret to say that I cannot give you any answer at all to that question."

"You believe that she was murdered?"

The nun did not reply. Her eyes, which remained meeting Mrs. Bradley's, lost focus, as though she were looking through the back of Mrs. Bradley's head to the window behind her, and out of it across the school garden. Her lips moved, but no sound came from them. Mrs. Bradley read the lip-signs and followed the Latin words. She grinned. Slightly startled, and, exceptionally, betraying the fact, Mother Francis apologised. Mrs. Bradley said briskly:

"As doctor to prospective patient, I would remind you that it is early in Lent to be feeling the effects of fastings. Remember the ears of corn which the disciples plucked on the Sabbath. Your work is trying, and you are under continuous strain. There has been, and is, among all of you here who knew her, acute and painful anxiety over the death of this child. Take my advice, and do not over-estimate the powers of bodily endurance."

"Thank you," said Mother Francis with great composure. "I am accustomed to fast." Snubbed, Mrs. Bradley left her and went to find Mother Benedict. The teacher of Latin, beautiful as an angel, was in the nuns' common room, copying a page from an illuminated manuscript of the thirteenth century. She showed Mrs. Bradley her work, and they talked about it. Then

Mrs. Bradley asked her about the Monday afternoon on which the child had died.

"I understand that you were not teaching until half-past three," she said. "Where were you during the first hour of afternoon school?"

"In here, getting on with my work. This." She touched her copy of the picture. "I do it in here, and nowhere else at all, because the psalter is one of our treasures, and I have special permission to make a copy of this page for Reverend Mother Superior on condition that I never remove the original from its case. I sit here, looking at it through the glass, and I must never touch it."

"I see," said Mrs. Bradley. "Did anybody come in whilst you were here?"

"Yes. Sister Saint Dominic came in at about a quarter to three to tell me that she was going into Kelsorrow with some children who had to see the dentist. She asked me whether I wanted any more colours for my work, and I gave her a list."

"How long did that take?"

"Less than five minutes—I cannot tell exactly."

"Did anyone else come in whilst you were here?"

"Yes. Old Sister Catherine came in to sit by the fire. She is over ninety, and does whatever she likes. She is near to God now."

She smiled, very sweetly and tenderly.

"And how old are *you*?" Mrs. Bradley asked abruptly.

"I am thirty, a blessed age."

Mrs. Bradley did not contradict the statement. Any age, she thought, as she looked with pleasure upon the lovely face, would be blessed in Mother Benedict. "Did you know the dead child?" she asked aloud.

"Yes, certainly. I take all the forms for Latin, and I had had her form, the third, that very morning. I remember the lesson vividly, I suppose because of the dreadful accident later."

"Oh, you think it was accident, do you?"

"Why, of course," said the beautiful nun. "It could not be that so sweet a child would kill herself. It is unthinkable. She was so excited, so pleased with life that morning, one could not help but notice her. She had learnt her work better than anyone else in the form, and shone in translation as I have never known her to do in all the time that we have had her. Sister Saint Simon-Zelotes said the same thing about her Science."

"Was she usually bright in class?"

"Well, no. She was shy and quiet. But on that particular morning—I wanted to give evidence at the inquest, but could not get permission—she was—it was as though she was on fire with the resolve to work hard and do well. And at the end of the hour, when I pulled her back to give her a little badge—a merit badge— we give them for very good work, but never in front of the rest of the form—she caught my hand and whispered: 'Oh, Mother Saint Benedict, it's good to get a merit badge at last! I am so very happy!' I kissed her when I pinned on the little badge, and pushed her out, because I knew she had to catch up the rest of the form to go into Sister Mary-Joseph's lesson at the other end of the building, so I shall never know what it was that had happened to change her so much."

"I shall be able to tell you, later on," said Mrs. Bradley. Mother Benedict stood looking after her in great surprise, her painting forgotten for the moment, in her eyes the picture of the happy child, in her ears Mrs. Bradley's grim promise.

CHAPTER 11

SUSPECTS

"The lamb thy riot dooms to bleed to-day,
Had he thy reason would he skip and play?"
ALEXANDER POPE: An Essay on Man, Epistle 1.

(1)

Tuesday

ULRICA DOYLE SAT IN CLASS SEWING HER HOPES AND FEARS
into a calico nightdress. The material was harsh with
'dress,' her needle—the second one that morning, for
she had broken the first and, in consequence, had been
presented with a Little Penance by Mother Cyprian for
carelessness—was too fine for the type of work, and she
was in morbid dread of breaking it as she had broken the
first one. Since the death of her cousin Ursula, she had
been nervous and clumsy over everything. Her ordinarily pale face was paper-white, and her eyes were
blue-shadowed. She looked completely exhausted, as
though she had not slept since the occurrence.

The fourth form began the morning on Tuesdays
with needlework, and as a rule Ulrica was glad. The
subject, in Lent, when the choice of the garments was
guided, the children thought, by the penitential nature
of the season, was not as attractive, to most of the form,
as at other times of the year, when they learned
embroidery, knitting and the drafting of patterns for
clothes to fit themselves. But to Ulrica, who had the

148

outlook of a mystic, there was something satisfying, in a harsh season, in the harsh material, the roughening of her fingers, even in a Little Penance for breaking needles. She needed to suffer, she felt, and wished that the suffering could be greater so that she could identify herself more closely with the solemnity and preparation of the time.

Her hopes, as she sewed, were high, and trembled on the brink of fulfilment. Already she had felt the call to the religious life, and her grandfather, her guardian now that her father was dead, had not attempted to dissuade her, in his letters, from pursuing the vision to the end, from entering one of the enclosed religious orders as soon as she was old enough to do so.

Her fears were as genuine as her hopes. She had had an interview, difficult for them both, with her aunt by marriage, after Ursula's death. Mrs. Maslin had told her that she approved of her desire to enter upon her novitiate as soon as she was old enough, and had drawn a convincing picture of the dead child as another candidate for entry.

Ulrica, however, was not a fool. She disliked Mrs. Maslin intensely, and was always very polite to her in consequence. She saw through the attitude of approval, and reached back to the cause of it without difficulty.

"She doesn't believe that grandfather will let his money go to the Church," she said to herself. The thought troubled her, because Mrs. Maslin's doubts were equally her own. She did not know how her grandfather's fortune had been made, and she did not remember ever having seen the old man, for, although he had been her guardian for several of her fifteen years, he had had her brought up in England, and, except when they were invited to spend the holidays at Wimbledon with Mary, she and Ursula had remained at the convent, spoilt by the lay-sisters and mothered by the nuns.

"If Mary were out of the way . . . if Mary died," she thought, her needle pushing carefully into the stiffness of the calico, her finger, where she had pushed the needle with it instead of with the covering thimble, springing red, "grandfather would not be tempted . . . he would have to leave me the money . . . there isn't anybody else. . . ."

After needlework came French with Mother Dominic, and, following French, in which she always shone—but why was the verb "tuer" that morning, and why did Mother Dominic ask her to give a sentence in the past tense, and why did she begin "*J'ai tu*——" and then stop and suddenly burst into tears?—there came history with Mother Lazarus.

Mother Lazarus was small, white-faced and uncannily energetic. She reported upon King Henry VIII as though he were a personal enemy, and upon Martin Luther as upon a man who had cheated her at cards. She was a Frenchwoman, and had all the logic and sentimentality of an extraordinarily gifted race, so that usually Ulrica came away from a history lesson in tears, much as some Irishmen will cry at the mention of Ireland—or would, before the days of Home Rule—for history caught at all that was romantic in her nature, and with historical persons, especially the martyrs to religion, she completely identified herself. But on this particular morning she heard scarcely a word of the lesson, was all abroad when pounced on suddenly by Mother Lazarus for an answer, and achieved another Little Penance, which this time she took to her bosom with a smile as being simple, easy and near. It was to translate back into Latin and learn in the recreation hour to recite at supper that evening, a Lenten hymn. It was to Ulrica's taste to do

this, and she remained in the room to tell Mother
Lazarus so. But the aged nun, with a chuckle, declined
to alter the gift, and gave her a comfit out of a small tin
box. It was extraordinary, Ulrica thought, as she
walked sedately after her classmates to put away her
books in her own form-room, that people should be so
kind.

Having put away her history books, she tidied the
desk meticulously against Mother Dominic's daily
inspection of lockers, put her hymnbook into the pocket
of her overall so that she need lose no time after dinner
in commencing her task for Mother Lazarus, and went
along to the refectory. Seated next to Mother Francis,
who presided, was the little old woman whom Ulrica
had conducted round the grounds on the previous
afternoon.

(2)

Tuesday

Mary Maslin ate slowly, and talked, in the low-
voiced convent tones, to her neighbours. She was
hungry; she was always hungry, and the discipline of
eating slowly was for her a real one. At home she
gobbled her food and talked very fast, about school. At
school she conformed to the rules, because that was the
easiest plan and led to the fewest complications.

After the meal was over, grace was said, and the girls
went out for games. Mary played defending centre in
netball, played well, and enjoyed herself. A sixth-form
girl umpired the game, and two nuns, Mother Simon-
Zelotes and Mother Cyprian, watched, with austere
detachment, from the side-lines. That the religious
took it in turns and always in pairs to supervise games
and physical training lessons was a thorn in the flesh of

Miss Bonnet, who regarded it as approximating to a vote of No Confidence in her, but, although she had made, at the beginning, a vigorous protest to Mother Francis upon the subject, the system of supervision was continued.

"We think it best," Mother Francis had replied to every spirited argument. Against the rock of the head-mistress' invincible faculty of never engaging in controversy, Miss Bonnet's protestations hammered in vain. Whatever the weather, so long as the children could be out in it at play, the two nuns on duty, stout in their habits like black birds with feathers ruffled against the cold, stood on the touch-line and watched, or appeared to watch, everything that went on.

When the netball practice was over, the girls went off to wash, and then followed half an hour's reading in the classroom, or the time could be given to a hobby or to sewing, whilst the choir nuns were at Vespers. Mary was no reader; she took out of her locker a pillow-case which she was hemstitching for her stepmother, sat down and got on with the work. As she sewed she thought, for most of the form were reading and the room was comparatively quiet, although there was no rule of silence. She thought about Mrs. Bradley, and wondered why she had come to lunch in the refectory when she might have had more interesting food at the guest-house. She also thought about tea, which would not be served for another two hours and a half. There would be, of course, currant buns. She always looked forward to tea-time. She licked the end of her cotton and re-threaded her needle; the action recalled to her her cousin Ursula. Ursula had been hemstitching pillow-cases, too. Each was to finish a pair for Mrs. Maslin's birthday. Ursula, Mary remembered, had kept her work cleaner than she had, and had done it a

good deal more quickly. She thought, with a shiver, of
the night that was to come. For four or five nights now
she had dreaded to be left alone in the dark. It was a
chance remark overheard on the Wednesday evening
succeeding Ursula's death which had opened, as it were,
a chasm in her imagination up which crawled dreadful
things, shapeless, black and evil. One of the sixth-
form girls had made it to another during the time,
which the children spent as they pleased, between tea
and preparation.

"She wouldn't have gone there unless she'd been
enticed. . . ."

Enticed . . . it was the most sinister, horrid word that
Mary had ever encountered. There was an unmistakable
smack of the devil about it. It was serpentine, sinuous,
plausible, coaxing, sensuously soft-handed and impure.
Gilded vice was in it, and something terrifying, like a
nightmare begun as a pleasant dream and suddenly
slipping into horror.

Who had enticed the mild Ursula? Mary remembered
trying to tempt her to eat a sweet in Mother Mary-
Joseph's English hour, whilst the serious young nun
read them stories and a surreptitious sucking, so long as
it remained inaudible, was indulged in fairly generally by
the class. The sweets had come from Mrs. Maslin and
were confiscated promptly, as soon as the postman
delivered them. Then they were given out to Mary
once a week on Saturday afternoons. Mary hoarded
them sometimes. They helped a little to stay the pangs
on days when prunes and custard were on the menu.
But Ursula was firm, and did not appear to fight with
temptation at all. *Enticed* . . . Mary's mental reactions
to the idea, especially after nightfall, were compounded
of horror and fear.

(3)

Wednesday

Miss Bonnet cast an approving eye on the Lower Fourth at Kelsorrow High School for Girls. She was proud of the Lower Fourth. Bequeathed to her slack and disorderly, with a tendency to stand, graceful but insolent, with one knee bent, whilst requesting to be allowed to sit out of the physical training lesson because they were not very well, they were now, she felt, a credit to themselves, to her, to the school and to one another. She had worked very hard for this. Once she had boxed a girl's ears.

Her superior, the full-time instructor in the subject, always handed to her the rottenest classes—got them in a mess and then got rid of them, was Miss Bonnet's private judgment on this behaviour—and the present Lower Fourth was a case in point. Now, to see them, under their leaders, at practice in the four corners of the big hall, doing group work of an advanced and difficult kind, was to see the fruits of last term's terrible grind and lengthy warfare.

"Pity somebody from the governing body can't see them," she thought, as she kept a watchful eye on running somersaults over a two-foot rope. "But, there! You'd have to see what they were like this time last term to get any idea of what's happened."

She blew a whistle, and the four teams formed file and stood still. Briefly and clearly she explained a new game they were to play. The girls ran to their places. The game began, and picked up speed. The girls were laughing and happy; their play was accurate and bold. They took risks, and the risks came off. There was a first-class exhibition of swift, clean, neat-handed passing.

She blew her whistle; breathed the form; dismissed it; sat on the edge of the platform to wait for the next class to come. Her thoughts, as at all times now when she was not completely occupied, turned again to that bathroom in which she had seen the dead child. She flicked her head nervously, as though to flick away the vision. She supposed that in time she would get over the shock, and forget it. She forced her thoughts, as she had been doing for a week, away from the subject and on to something more pleasant. She wished she could afford to give up her job at the convent; ten shillings a day was all they paid her; five shillings for the half-day; charwoman's wages. She knew they would double the pay if she said the word. They had to have a qualified person to take the physical training. Amateurs at the job were inefficient and dangerous. The Community could not, however tiny their income, afford to lose Miss Bonnet for the sake of a little more pay. But she would not say the word. She liked to think that she could not. It was a fancy of hers, a vanity, she pretended to the Kelsorrow staff, to go to them for half-pay. Besides, she had hoped to get a testimonial out of them later on; one from Kelsorrow, too. That other unlucky business—she flicked that away as well. It seemed as though there was no clear, happy course for her wandering thoughts to take; death, ignominious dismissal—the one had been a shock, the other still rankled. It was not as though they could prove that she had done wrong. The evidence of children ought not to be accepted against adults, she felt, especially in a case of lost property. Their answers had been suggested to them, and by the headmaster, too! Mixed schools were the devil, anyway. She hated giving P.T. lessons to girls who were taught their academic subjects by men. Dismissal or a court case! What a choice!

Naturally, she had chosen to go. They could not have
proved her guilt—she knew that perfectly well—but
other things might have come up. That was the worst
of having no testimonials to show except her college
one. Lucky to have got to Kelsorrow, she supposed, even
in a temporary capacity. Her appointment had never
been confirmed. They could dismiss her without notice,
she supposed. She wished she were independent of a
job, and could please herself what she did. She supposed
she would take up golf. There was good publicity in
golf. She had a pretty good handicap, as it was, when
she played only during week-ends and at holiday times.
With practice and regular coaching, and money to
spend, she believed she could be very good. It was a
game one could play for years; not like these team
games—hockey, lacrosse—not like swimming or rowing
—in which, speaking generally, one was not much good
after twenty-four or so. . . .

She jumped down to take the next form who were
trickling into the gymnasium, dancing up and down to
warm up, as she had taught them; long-legged girls in
shorts and thin white blouses; nothing on their feet
but socks and rubber shoes; nothing in their heads,
when first she took them over, but cinemas, boys and
dodging compulsory games. . . . She looked them over
complacently. Good stuff now. She cracked out an
order. Nice to give up the military style of command,
out of date, really, nowadays, but until one was certain
of these girls. . . . Thank goodness none of them
looked in the least like the dead, pink-faced child in
the bath. It had been like a tinted waxwork, that still,
dead face; like the Little Mermaid, asleep, or the
angel, that troubled the waters, drowned in them
after all.

(4)

Wednesday

Mrs. Maslin sat straight and looked at Mr. Grogan. "I *couldn't* contest it?" she said. Mr. Grogan shook his head. He was a good-looking man whom a judge's wig would have suited. He screwed the top on his fountain-pen and slightly pulled in his lips as though the task were a ticklish one, and he not sure of success. Then he laid the pen down between the open pages of a book and opened a box of cigarettes.

"You smoke?" he said. Mrs. Maslin took a cigarette and tapped it exasperatedly upon the enamelled lid of the flap-jack from which she had powdered her nose some three minutes previously.

"I can't understand it," she said. Mr. Grogan, who had always regarded Mrs. Bennett's remarks about the entail as giving a very fair view of women's general incapability of grasping even the less abstruse points of testamentary law, shook his fine head sympathetically.

"Well, there it is," he said. He smiled, and made a joke. "You would have to prove that the young lady murdered her cousin before you could justly claim the estate for your stepdaughter, my dear lady."

Mrs. Maslin went home very thoughtful. As soon as dinner was over, and the servants had cleared, and coffee was on the table, she said to her husband:

"I've been thinking about the death of poor little Ursula."

"Seen Grogan this afternoon?"

"Well, yes, I *did* see him. He wasn't particularly helpful."

"Well, face the facts, my dear. How could he be?"

"Percival," said Mrs. Maslin, laying down her coffee spoon and speaking with great distinctness, "do you think there's anything at all in Grogan's suspicion that *Ulrica killed her little cousin?*"

"Good Lord, no! Why, Nessa, what a terrible idea! Damn' silly, too. Surely Grogan couldn't have said such a thing?"

"Didn't he, though? And, you know, there might be something in it! A most extraordinary girl!"

"What nonsense, my dear! Face the facts! The girl's got religion. You told me so yourself."

"I know, and that's just what I mean."

"Look here, Nessa," said Mr. Maslin, for once asserting himself, "I don't believe it, and I won't have you suggest it. Grogan must be mad. I'd as soon believe you killed the child yourself!"

(5)

Thursday

To say that Mrs. Waterhouse loved her work would be not so much to contradict facts as to avoid them. Her work was a refuge, and she buried herself in it much as an ostrich will bury its head in sand. But it had always been understood, except by the victims themselves, that primary school teachers loved their work, and Mrs. Waterhouse, far from being irritated by the assertion (which had been made in her hearing by her former headmistress and by various committee members, as they were called), fostered it. It gave her, in the eyes of those who supervised and employed her, a palpable *raison d'être* which she felt she was the safer for possessing.

The truth was that she neither loved nor hated her

work; she merely did it. To her it was a job, like other jobs; a good deal more tiresome, perhaps, and a little better paid (not at the convent, certainly, but in the old days, before her marriage) than other jobs she might have got, but a job, nevertheless; not a vocation, a hobby, a life-work or a missionary enterprise; merely a job, and one that she did very well.

When Mrs. Bradley discovered Mrs. Waterhouse— on the Thursday, the day following that upon which she had dined with the school—it was turned ten minutes past twelve, and Mrs. Waterhouse was in the middle of a weltering democracy of four- and five-year- old children, some of them orphans, some of them of noble and one of royal blood. She was taking (like and unlike Miss Bonnet) a physical training lesson. Little mats were laid upon the netball court, but the children had abandoned these, and, when Mrs. Bradley first saw them, were fiendishly scrumming for a small light football, of the kind known as a handball. All were shrieking their heads off.

Mrs. Waterhouse clapped her hands, picked up the only naughty child to prevent her from grabbing the ball when everyone else had obediently let it alone, and turned to Mrs. Bradley.

"Good morning," she said, and as she said it she suffered a sudden, unceremonious return of a peculiar feeling she had always experienced in the old days when she knew that His Majesty's Inspectors of Schools had arrived on the premises and were seeking whom they might devour.

"My name is Bradley. I am the mother of Ferdinand Lestrange," said Mrs. Bradley equably. Mrs. Water- house went white. Mrs. Bradley could see a vein throbbing in her temple. She said, in the voice of one speaking from a parched, constricted throat:

"Oh—yes? I'm—I'm glad to meet you. Would you like me to take you over to Mother Saint Francis?"

"No. I've seen her. I've been here since Monday afternoon. I heard you were here, and I thought my son would be interested to know that I had seen you," Mrs. Bradley went on, in a false, district-visitor voice.

"It's very kind of you," said Mrs. Waterhouse. "It's—I owe your son a great deal—in fact, my life."

"I know. He always believed you innocent, of course."

"Yes, but I wasn't," said Mrs. Waterhouse suddenly. "He couldn't have thought so really." She put down the only naughty child, and it immediately ran to another little girl and pulled her hair.

"That's what she'd have loved to have done to me while I had her close enough," Mrs. Waterhouse remarked more naturally.

"Is she an orphan?"

"Oh, lor', no. She's the Grand Duchess Natalie —well, over here we call her Smith, because nobody's supposed to know her name. There's a rumour that her family know all about the disappearance of that wonderful pearl, the—what's-it-called?—the—I don't know—began with P—a French name, somebody told me. It was worth about forty thousand pounds before the war, and got lost from a Russian museum."

She looked at Mrs. Bradley with the expression of one who seeks feverishly to postpone an evil moment, and then flew to separate the two children, who were now screaming and fighting.

"I suppose," said Mrs. Bradley, when Mrs. Waterhouse came back again with Natalie whilst the others played nicely together with the ball and two or three hoops which they dumbly gave up to one another on demand (as they had been taught, Mrs. Bradley supposed), "that you never let these children out of your sight?"

"That I do not," Mrs. Waterhouse replied. "Why, that Natalie would tear the hair off little Pamela, if I left them, and the orphans would teach the others naughty words."

"I should have thought it would be the other way about," said Mrs. Bradley. So saying, she shed her benevolent smile, as the moon its light and the rain its mixed blessings, alike on the just and on the unjust, and slowly walked away. She looked back after a moment, for a howl of anguish had arisen. The Grand Duchess had tumbled over, but Mrs. Waterhouse, in a scolding, motherly voice, immediately reduced the howls in volume, and shortly silenced them.

Mrs. Bradley went back to Mother Francis. "In which room does Mrs. Waterhouse teach the little children?" she enquired.

"In the room opposite mine," said Mother Francis. "I like to have the little ones near me."

"And were you in your room, do you remember, at the beginning of last Monday week afternoon?"

Mother Francis glanced up at the framed time-table which hung opposite.

"I was, without doubt," she replied. Mrs. Bradley thanked her, apologised for disturbing her so often, and went outside again. Mrs. Waterhouse was letting the babies collect up the mats and the other apparatus of the lesson. Screams from the Grand Duchess Natalie announced to the world her determination not to give up her mat without a struggle.

Mrs. Bradley grinned, and then sighed. It was impossible to suspect that Mrs. Waterhouse had left her class on that Monday afternoon. The Grand Duchess would certainly have brought Mother Francis into the room if Mrs. Waterhouse had been away long enough to get to the guest-house bathroom, unless— Mrs. Bradley stopped short in her walking and looked back. Holding her teacher's hand in a pudgy fist, and looking proud, animated and happy, the Grand Duchess was leading the line across the netball court back into school.

"If she'd taken her with her," Mrs. Bradley decided, walking on again, "that would have been a solution."

She amused herself by walking over to look at the pigs who were housed along by the north-east angle of the grounds. There were other pigs opposite the little square laundry building, but these were managed, Mrs. Bradley understood, by the gardener. The pigs she was aiming for were the charge of the lay-sisters, who were proud of them. She halted at the sties and then looked over, but, lacking her nephew's guidance, she failed to appreciate to the full the special points of their occupants, and turned away after a minute or two to stroll past the school and the children's own small gardens, across the orchard where the pear-trees were already promising blossom, and through the low archway in the hedge towards the gatehouse. There was still Miss Bonnet to be interviewed, but that could be done after lunch.

CHAPTER 12

GUESTS

"What a blessed change I find
Since I entertained this Guest!
Now methinks, another mind
Moves, and rules, within my breast."

CHRISTOPHER HARVEY: The Enlarging of
the Heart.

SISTER MAGDALENE, SMILING, AS USUAL, OPENED THE
gate for her, and stood beside it, waiting to shut it
again.

Mrs. Bradley stopped in the entrance and said:

"Who else has a key to the gate?"

"A key hangs in the Common Room, Reverend
Mother Superior has another, and a third is in the
possession of Sister Saint Ambrose for letting the
orphan children in and out to the guest-house after
sunset."

So that was that, Mrs. Bradley thought. She thanked
the lay-sister, passed through the gate and walked into
the guest-house just as the gong was being sounded for
the midday meal.

The dining-room was twice as long as its width, and
a table ran almost the whole length of it with a place
set at the head and another at the foot. These places,
she found, were allotted to herself and to the Dominican,
a merry-looking man of forty or so, with a jowl which
no amount of shaving could make any colour but blue,
black eyes as sharp and bold as sloes, and a very beautiful

voice. He was, Mrs. Bradley learned, convalescent after long illness, and was hoping to return to his monastery in the near future. He had read all her works, and discussed them with her during most of the meal. He was a learned, entertaining companion, and the fact that the length of the table lay between them did nothing to abate his enthusiasm. Mrs. Bradley attempted, now and again, to talk to her neighbours, but the Spanish lady, another refugee, Señorita Mercedes Rio, and one of the two young French girls, who were going to Rome later on for their novitiate in the mother house of the Order, had scarcely a word to say.

"My father, my brothers, my lover, all are killed," the Spaniard said, and lapsed into a silence which Mrs. Bradley hesitated to disturb. When the meal was over and Dom Pius had, for the second time, said grace, Mrs. Bradley met him, of set purpose, in the doorway, and laid a claw on his sleeve.

"You have something you wish to ask me?" enquired the monk, inoffensively but definitely drawing away from her touch.

"I want to talk to you about something of considerable importance. Will you walk with me in the garden?"

They passed through the convent gate again, the Dominican, who was in orders, automatically blessing Sister Magdalene as he passed, and began to stroll together towards the orchard.

"Last Monday week, father," said Mrs. Bradley slowly, "the day on which the guests took the little orphan children to the pictures . . ."

"I remember. I did not go. Oh—we are allowed to go—that is to say, there is nothing forbidden about it—the theatre, yes, the cinema, no, not at present —but actually I did not accompany the others."

"That is exceedingly interesting. Did anyone else not go?"

"You have good reason, doubtless, for asking me this, and I know, of course, why you are here. I cannot remember that anyone else did not go. But, then, I should hardly have troubled myself, I think, to find out who went and who did not."

"Father Thomas?"

"Yes, he went in. It is not forbidden, you see, and the little children loved him. They would not have been so happy, had he not gone, therefore he went to please them. It is good to be loved by children."

"What did you do, then, whilst the others were at the cinema?"

"I went into the local museum and studied the exhibits in the cases. I have seen better, but these were quite interesting. Palæolithic, Neolithic, Bronze Age —some Roman things, of course—Saxon, a mediæval pot or two—it was not rubbish—nearly so, not quite. I was there for three hours, and then we all had tea."

"Where?"

"In the guest-house, here, and the little children had theirs here, too, and then we played with them at bears, and then the good sisters came and took them to put them to bed. We did not know then of the dreadful thing that had happened, of course, in the guest-house."

"I suppose you did not talk to the doctor, father, after he had examined the child?"

"I did not see him, no. I knew that the child was not dead by half-past twelve, but that you also know. I went up to that bathroom at the last, before we left, to bring down a watch which one of the ladies had left. This death is strange and terrible. Such things happen; I have known of them; but not where it is peace, as it is here." He hesitated, and then said charmingly, "But

I am keeping you, and you will wish to be away pursuing your enquiries. It is quite dreadful, and a great family, yes."

"Not, I believe, a great family. Certainly a wealthy one," Mrs. Bradley replied. "And the little girl was the heiress."

"Where there is much wealth there is sometimes much wickedness. It is like that, money." They were back at the great gates. He bowed, and Mrs. Bradley smiled, and let him go. There was a service at two o'clock each day, she remembered. Probably he wanted to attend it. She wondered whether all the other guests would go, too. Since the monk could not provide an alibi for anybody else, and since his own was (only technically) suspect—she could not imagine the Dominican killing a child—it would be just as well to establish that the rest of the party had actually spent their time at the cinema, and that none of them had sneaked back to the guest-house to meet Ursula Doyle.

She was fortunate, for, even as she stood thinking, a girl she had noticed at table, a frail, black-eyed creature who looked extremely ill, came past the gates and smiled at her as she passed. Mrs. Bradley arrested her progress.

"It is a little warmer," she said. "Are you going to Vespers, possibly?"

"No, I am sorry. I am to take the air for an hour every afternoon that it is fine. Did you wish for a companion to go with you?" Her foreign accent was almost undetectable.

"No. Please walk about the garden with me for a little while. I, too, have to take the air," Mrs. Bradley, partly mendaciously, explained.

"Ah, yes, that will be pleasant. I am not good alone. There is much to think about. Do you think much?"

"I think a good deal," Mrs. Bradley admitted. "I think I should like to have been with you when you took the little children to the cinema."

"Yes, I, too, would like to have gone, but, alas!———"

"Oh, you did not go with the children?"

"No, I did not go. I have trouble of the chest. I went out walking when they had all gone inside."

"Did you go part of the way with Father Pius?"

"No, no. I went to the door of the cinema with the others. He left us at the turning to go to a little museum, so he said."

"So he said? You think that perhaps he did not go to the museum after all?"

"I did not mean that. I mean that I heard him say that was where he would go. Why, please, should he not go, if he said he was going?"

"I have no idea. We must assume that that is where he went."

"Perfectly."

"Have you stayed here before?"

"Never. It is beautiful. I love the wildness. How do you call it—this wild country?"

"The moors."

"Ah, yes. The moors. On them I walked whilst the others were inside the cinema, and above the sea, on the top of the cliffs."

"How far did you go?"

"Not so far. It is not allowed to become too tired yet. I walked out, and I walked back, just enough to be interesting, and then I sat in a small little house———"

"A shelter?"

"A shelter—on the top of the cliff that is of the town. There was an old lady there, and a nursemaid who had a baby in a baby-carriage, and we talked. I liked it very much."

"Did you not become cold?"

"No. I was well in clothes, and I wore the little stockings over the long stockings, and large gloves, and the sun shone, not so warm as we have it, but it was very pleasant."

"Then you came back when the others came out from the cinema?"

"But very much sooner. The man, who had driven us over, took me back, and then returned for the others."

"At what time, then, did you get back here to the guest-house?"

"To the guest-house, no, I do not come there. I was in the church ten minutes, perhaps, and then I was in the cloister in a long chair, and Sister Lucia— she is of my country and very kind—I am only English of my husband—Trust, his name is—she brought me some hot soup and put over me blankets and left me to rest as it is ordered. I fell asleep, it was so warm and comfortable."

"And at what time, then, did you go into the church?"

"It would have been—let me see—I am to answer you as well as ever I can, because you are asking all these questions for a purpose—so much I can tell— well, now, Vespers are over, and the church is silent when I go in. How much over—that is what you wish to know. My friend, I cannot tell you. It is not long, I think—perhaps it was about a quarter to three. Sister Lucia will know. She came to me in the cloister— she will know at what time she came. Oh, and I think perhaps I was not alone in the church. Someone was praying, too. That person, perhaps, would know."

It was all perfectly convincing, Mrs. Bradley thought, and nobody with lungs in the condition of this poor girl's could have risked either a struggle or the carbon monoxide gas. Not that there was the slightest reason for suspecting her. The interesting thing was that, once again, the facts she had been given were proving not to be facts. *All* the guests had *not* gone to the cinema with the children. Counting poor old Sister Bridget, three, at least, of the convent's visitors had been elsewhere at the time of the death.

She walked with the consumptive girl to the sunny side of the cloister, saw her tucked up by Sister Lucia, and then obtained the approximate time at which this had all been done on the afternoon on which the child had died. Not that it helped. Mrs. Bradley felt in her bones that it could not make any difference. How interesting it would have been, though, if somebody had gone to the bathroom before the arrival of Miss Bonnet at half-past three or just after.

She went back to the guest-house parlour in search of another victim, and found one in the person of the English girl, Philippa Carey, who was residing at the convent for a week or two before she went across to France to take up her novitiate. She was quiet, intelligent and, to Mrs. Bradley's mind, irrationally enthusiastic at the thought of becoming a nun. This girl remembered that Dom Pius had left the party to go to the museum, and she remembered that the poor young married woman with the troublesome cough had left them at the door of the cinema. She agreed that she herself had gone in with the children, and stated that all the other guests had also gone in to see the show.

"It was Mickey Mouse," she said, "and some cowboys. A very good programme for children."

"Then the aunt of the poor little girl who was drowned was at the cinema that afternoon with the rest of you?" Mrs. Bradley exclaimed.

"Yes, certainly she was. She went in just in front of me, and, although, of course, it was dark whilst the films were being shown, I do not think that anybody went out.''

"Did she sit in front of you?''

"Why no.   I do not know where she sat.   We sat with children on either side of us, and attended to them and not to one another.''

"Did she come home with the rest of the party?''

"I do not remember noticing.   But what a dreadful thing for her to come home to!''

"Do you remember how she was dressed?''

"I think so."   The girl looked at her curiously, but Mrs. Bradley offered no explanation of the abrupt and pointed question.   "She had on a greenish tweed costume, and over it a big musquash coat, and had a little plume of deer's hair—you know the ones they sell in Scotland to visitors?—at the side of her hat.''

"I hear she is coming back here after a bit?''

"I have not heard that.   Poor woman, she was terribly distressed.''

"Naturally.   I wonder whether she tried to get the coroner to bring it in as accidental death?''

The girl shook her head.

"I do not know.   I did not attend the inquest.   But here in the guest-house she said to me that she could not conceive that a child like little Ursula would dream of doing such a terrible thing.''

"The child was in trouble in school, though, wasn't she? I heard a rumour that she was exceedingly unhappy.''

A curtain seemed to be drawn over the girl's eyes. She replied very stiffly.

"I have no knowledge that she was unhappy or in trouble, but no happy child would commit mortal sin, I am certain.''

"I was sent for to prove that the child's death was accidental,'' Mrs. Bradley meekly explained.

"And can you prove it? How wonderful that would be!" Her face lit up as she said it. Mrs. Bradley slowly shook her head.

"Whether I can prove it remains to be seen," she said. "I think the chances are exceedingly remote. There seems so little to go on."

"But the evidence of character?"

"Yes, the evidence of character. The last kind of child to be involved in a fatal accident due to disobedience, wouldn't you say? Quite the last child to break into the guest-house against the very strictest rule of the school. No, no." She shook her head.

CHAPTER 13

PICADOR

"Fluttering, piercing as a needle's point,
No armour may it stay, nor no high walls."
WILLIAM LANGLAND: The Vision of Holy Church.

MISS BONNET TOOK A NETBALL PRACTICE WITH THE private-school girls from half-past one until two, and then went off to wash. Mrs. Bradley waited in the school hall and waylaid her as she came back. Miss Bonnet, in the trousers which she had worn to referee the game—for the March wind was fresh and blew cold from seawards—looked subtly different from the stocky young woman in tweeds who had spoken to Mrs. Bradley on the moors.

"Half a second; must climb into a skirt," she observed, rather nervously. Mrs. Bradley vetoed the suggestion with some promptness, and led her firmly towards the staff room.

"Here we shall not be disturbed," she said. "Sit down. I have a number of questions to ask you."

"Oh, but look here," said Miss Bonnet, "I can't help you, you know. You see, I've got to be pretty careful what I say."

"How do you mean?"

"Well, rightly or wrongly, *I* was the person responsible for the blinking kid committing suicide, you know. I mean, it was no fault of mine. All in the day's work, and that kind of thing, of course, but there's no doubt whatever that the poor wretched kid had got me up her nose a bit.''

"Because you take the physical training lessons?''

"You've got it in one. What's more, I had arranged particularly to give her extra coaching. I figure that she funked it, and bunked to that beastly bathroom and finished things off. I've been in the devil of a stew ever since, as you can imagine.''

"So that,'' said Mrs. Bradley, regarding her shrewdly, "is why you, almost alone of all the people I have questioned, are convinced that the child committed suicide.''

"That's about the size of it,'' Miss Bonnet readily agreed. "You see, my methods aren't all that gentle and tactful, I'm afraid. I admit it, but I can't alter them. It goes down all right with the majority of kids, and then you get some poor little misfit like this one—and off she goes and shoots up the whole outfit. I feel pretty much like a murderer, I can tell you.''

"Yes,'' said Mrs. Bradley, "yes, you must do.'' She made a few notes, and then rose. "I suppose,'' she said suddenly, as Miss Bonnet also got up, "that you can account for all the children who were supposed to have that extra physical training practice with you during the Monday dinner hour?''

"Account for them? Yes, I think so.''

"And you yourself. What were you doing between the time that practice ended, and the time you went for your bath?''

"Doing? Oh—I remember. That wretched kid I knocked over at netball—I went to see how she was getting on, and stayed a bit, and then went over to Kelsorrow in the car—and then I came back, and—well, that's when we found her.''

"Ah, yes. You saw nothing of Ulrica Doyle, I suppose?''

"Ulrica Doyle? I shouldn't expect to see her."

"Is she good or bad at her physical work?"

"Average. She could be very good indeed, but she isn't keen. Pretty rotten family, the whole lot of them, really, I think."

"Most likely. Well, thank you, Miss Bonnet."

"Of course," said Miss Bonnet, as she was going off, "you can't prove or disprove a single thing I've said, but take my tip: suicide don't suit the nuns' book. Accident is what they're after. But it wasn't accident. Couldn't have been! Look at the facts!"

"I have," replied Mrs. Bradley. "Ad nauseam," she added to herself, as Miss Bonnet cantered away to change her trousers. Mrs. Bradley walked back to the guest-house, but suddenly changed her mind about going in, and hurried off across the moors to meet George at the village inn.

George was finishing his lunch—roast beef, Yorkshire pudding, potatoes, cauliflower and beer, followed by boiled suet pudding with butter and sugar.

"Good heavens, George!" said Mrs. Bradley. She ordered the first course herself, regardless of the fact that she had already lunched at the guest-house, ordered half a pint of beer, and finished up with biscuits and cheese.

Fortified, she got into the car, and George drove her to Hiversand Bay.

It was easy enough to check Dom Pius' alibi. The assistant curator at the small museum, who happened also to be assistant librarian—for the exhibits were housed in the vestibule of the library and on its first-floor landing—testified, without having to stop to think, that a gentleman in the dress of a monk had visited the collection and seemed interested

"Quite an Oxford man, by his speech," said the

assistant librarian and curator, "and interested in the local history. I put him on to some books, and he seemed very pleased. Stayed until nearly four o'clock. The nuns come occasionally, of course, to look up stuff for their school work, but we've never had a gentleman before. Very cultured, he seemed, and spoke very nicely of the collection and the way we'd got it set out."

For Mrs. Trust the evidence was not as easy to collect, and Mrs. Bradley took no particular trouble to collect it. She haunted the two shelters which were all that had been erected on what, later on, she supposed, would be a made-up promenade, and questioned a nursemaid with a perambulator. A foreign lady, looking very ill, had sat and talked a bit one afternoon; she could not remember which. Oh, wait a bit, though. Yes, perhaps—no—yes, it would be a Monday. They had had the cold lamb and nothing but mashed potatoes and, of all things, boiled rice to follow. No, well, you could not hardly expect to have the oven on, not with no roast joint, but—boiled rice! Well, she asked you!

Mrs. Bradley expressed comprehension, sympathy and amazement. The evidence made no difference to the enquiry. No time could be established, the nursemaid saying definitely that she had not the very foggiest, only Brian was being a bit awkward, and she took him in earlier than usual, fancying he felt a bit cold and it made him pulish.

Mrs. Bradley, treasuring the Shakespearian derivative, got up and walked west towards the convent. The coast road, high and lonely, led away from the raw little town until from its eminence nothing could be descried but rough grass, cloud and sky. Even the sea was hidden, for the road did not follow the cliff, but kept, for safety, inland. Gorse was in bud, and at one place she came upon a goat tethered to a thick, tough stem. It ran at her with its head down until its chain brought it up short. Further on she met a man with a dog. There was no other sign of life, apart from the promise of heather, bramble and bracken, except for the gulls.

She reached the convent at four, having sent George back with the car some hour or so earlier, had tea in the guest-house, and then walked into the village of Blacklock Tor. Three minutes after her arrival at the inn she was in the car again, being driven to Kelsorrow High School. Although school hours were over by the time she arrived, she had planned her visit well. Several of the mistresses were still on the building, and the headmistress was still in her room. The caretaker, an ex-soldier, who gave her the information, recognised George. Mrs. Bradley left them in delighted conversation whilst the caretaker's wife conducted her to the secretary's office, and the secretary took her in to the headmistress.

"If you had come an hour earlier, you might have given a travel talk to the school," was the headmistress' characteristic lament upon recognising her visitor. Mrs. Bradley grinned, and stated her errand.

"I want to know all you can tell me about Miss Bonnet," she said.

"But you don't suspect Miss Bonnet of murdering a child of thirteen?"

"I should if I could find that she had a motive," Mrs. Bradley replied. The headmistress rang for the secretary and asked her to make some tea. She was a young headmistress, and had held the post for three years.

"I don't know much about her, you know," she said. "She's efficient, and I don't make the private lives of the staff my concern as long as their work is satisfactory."

"I understand that she was lucky to get a post here, even a temporary one."

"I don't know what you mean by a temporary one. She's been here longer than I have, and I shouldn't dream of trying to get rid of her. I believe she was dismissed from her last post for theft, but—*you* ought to know—aren't these cases so often pathological? It turned out that she'd had a row with her young man, and the thefts followed hard upon that."

"She didn't go to prison, I believe?"

"No, but the school governors dismissed her without a testimonial. Then it turned out that she had a friend —her father's friend, actually—on the governing body here, and he persuaded the rest of them to give her a trial. That was four years ago, or very nearly. She's been here ever since."

"And you've no fault to find with her at all?"

"Her discipline is military, but I don't know that I object to that, within reason. She is not too popular with the girls, but neither is she disliked. The girls respect efficiency, and like to be bossed—more's the pity."

"What did she steal?"

"Pictures."

"Valuable ones?"

"Yes, very."

"Did she sell them?"

"She didn't, no. But whether she was caught too soon, or whether she never intended to part with them, I don't think anybody knew. Personally, I feel sorry for the girl. Of course, if the case had gone to the police, as some people, I expect, thought it ought, no doubt they would have found out whether she was in touch with a receiver and so on. But my view, and I've known her for three years now, is that the girl passed through an

abnormal phase consequent on this quarrel with her
lover. There was an abnormal aunt, or something, too,
so heredity may be against her.''

"What happened to the lover, do you know?''

"Oh, yes. He married, and went to East Africa to
live. I suppose he has leave at times, but I don't think
she's ever seen him since they parted.''

"What made her confide in you?''

"She had been taking a hockey practice, and one of
the half-backs rolled the ball in from the side-line after
it had been hit out of play, and it slipped from her hand
and struck Miss Bonnet on the head. They had to carry
her here, and I looked after her a bit. She got a pretty
good crack on the temple—rather nasty—and spent the
afternoon in here on my settee. We talked a bit, and
she told me about herself.''

Mrs. Bradley was not surprised. There are people
who seem to be the natural confidantes of those with
whom they come in contact, and Mrs. Bradley could
readily understand that the head mistress of Kelsorrow
would give an impression of sympathetic understanding.

"How was it discovered that she was the thief?''
she asked.

"Rather oddly. Of course, Miss Bonnet said nothing
to me about the thefts, only about her young man, and
I should not dream of mentioning them to her. That sort
of thing is far better over and forgotten. But I was told
of her record when I received the appointment here.
The governors thought it fair to me to tell me. It
seems that she got rather drunk one night at a dinner.
The rowing club she belonged to had won an important
race at Henley, and were celebrating. During the
evening she happened to describe one of the pictures to
a man who knew that, unless she had stolen the picture,
the probability was that she couldn't even have seen it.''

"How extraordinary!"

"Indeed it was. Of course, she had no idea that he was an expert. She knew him only as the chairman of her rowing club, not as an expert in pictures. Actually he happens to be a dealer."

"Whose were the pictures, then?"

"They were the property of the school at which she taught, and were kept in the Governors' Room, as it was called, on the second floor. This room was sometimes used, apart from meetings of the Governors, but when it was, two of the pictures whose subject-matter was thought unsuitable for children—rather peculiar and horrid martyrdoms, I believe—were carefully covered up. The others were left on view, and were familiar, probably to the staff of the school. But the hidden pictures, one of which she described, were not. When the room was not in use it was always kept locked because the pictures were valuable. Of course, it was recognised that she *might* have seen the pictures at some time, but the chairman, who was anxious, naturally, to get them back, had enquiries made, and very soon they were recovered."

"What excuse did she offer?"

"None."

"What reason, then, for having stolen them?"

"She said she must have been mad."

"It is possible that she was right, and that it was a temporary mental aberration. How valuable were the pictures?"

"Christie's valued them at sixty thousand pounds. They would have been worth a great deal more than that if two of them had not been suspected of being contemporary copies."

"Contemporary copies?"

"That isn't as unusual a happening as one might

think. These pictures were painted for churches, and an interesting rendering of—you must remember—a traditional happening, might well be copied half a dozen times."

"To Miss Bonnet, I suppose, sixty thousand pounds would be a great deal of money."

"She wouldn't have got a quarter of that from a receiver."

"Not if the receiver had a market? There are plenty of wealthy people, especially in America, with collectors' mania, I believe."

"Oh, I see . . . a ready market. Anyhow, it all came out, and the pictures were returned undamaged. She had cut them out of their frames with a very sharp penknife, and had hidden them under the carpet in her room."

"Ah, yes. Where does she live?"

"In lodgings. The address is Nineteen, Hiversand Bay Road, Kelsorrow—quite near this school."

"Was she in lodgings when she taught at her last school?"

"Yes, she was. Her landlady turned her out as soon as the pictures were found. Gave her an hour to pack and take herself off. People are terribly heartless."

"Yes, aren't they?" said Mrs. Bradley; but she spoke absentmindedly, her eyes on the clock on the desk.

"How do you know her landlady turned her out?" she asked, comparing her watch with the clock.

"She told me, but not the reason. That I guessed. That clock is ten minutes fast. I must put it right."

"And I," said Mrs. Bradley, "must be off. You did not, of course, see Miss Bonnet at any time on that Monday, the day that the child was found dead? She

was engaged to teach at the convent that morning,
I believe?''

"Oh, yes, I saw her. She turned up here at about
a quarter to one, to ask whether, as there was a holiday,
I wanted her to do extra coaching.''

"She came here, then, immediately she had finished
her morning's work at St. Peter's School?''

"Yes, she must have done. She drives most
recklessly.''

"How long did she stay?''

"I cannot tell you. She was in here less than five
minutes. I thought it rather nice of her to come. There
was no reason why she should.''

"She went back to St. Peter's and gave the orphans
some netball.''

"Yes, she would do a thing like that. She's a very
good-natured sort of girl, in a coarse, hearty sort of
way, and tremendously keen on games.''

"But didn't she come again in the afternoon?''

"Not to my knowledge. Besides, there was nobody
here except the caretaker and his wife. It was a
holiday, you see.'' So Mrs. Bradley applied to the
school caretaker for information as soon as she had
left the headmistress.

"Miss Bonnet, mam? Turned up at a quarter to one,
when all the girls had gone home, and might have
stopped the time it would take her to smoke a cigarette,
I should think. I couldn't say exactly to the minute,
but she certainly wasn't here long. Left again before
one o'clock, I reckon, because I was out there doing
a bit of repairs to the bicycle shed when she came,
and hadn't, I'm sure, done fifteen minutes at the job
before she went. Her little car stood in the drive where
I could see it, and she drove off very fast, like she always
do—have a smash-up one of these days, I shouldn't

wonder—and I got on doing the job till four o'clock. Chucked her cigarette-end down, I remember, on to a heap of shavings.''

"And nobody else came here?"

"Nobody else that I know of, and that's as good as saying that nobody came.''

"The plot thickens, George,'' said Mrs. Bradley, as she got into her own car again to drive back to St. Peter's. "Can you think of any reason why Miss Bonnet should kill Ursula Doyle?''

"No, madam, but time will show. Not altogether a sympathetic character, the young lady.''

"I believe, however, that you and I are unique in that opinion. On all sides I am told how unselfish and good-hearted Miss Bonnet is.''

"At the pub, madam, in Blacklock Tor, there's a feeling that the nuns know all about it.''

"That wouldn't surprise me, George. They are a very reticent body, and, I'm sure, know more that they say.''

"They withhold information, madam?''

"I don't suppose they would like that way of putting it. They don't want a murder, George, naturally.''

"Artful, madam, some of them. Wrong-headed, too, in a way. Did you ever study the history of the Jesuits?''

"That reminds me, George,'' said Mrs. Bradley. "Stop at the cinema at Hiversand Bay. I want to bounce the box-office clerk into giving me information.''

This proved a simple matter. At that time of day business in the cinema was slack. Mrs. Bradley asked the clerk whether the gloves had been picked up.

"What gloves?'' the girl enquired.

"A pair of doeskin gloves, dark brown. My friend believes she must have dropped them off her lap when

she rose from her seat in the cinema last Monday week.
I understood she had enquired about them herself—
a woman in a musquash coat over a greenish tweed
costume, with a green hat to match.''

"Oh—her as walked out early? One of them as
brought the little children?"

"I didn't realise she walked out early. Ah, that
accounts for it, then. She wasn't feeling well, and came
out in rather a hurry."

"I should say, too and all, she did. Didn't look ill,
neither. Fair raced to the bottom of the road, and took
Bill Gander the taxi. Does for us and the station.
Walked out of here to see her go, I did. Well, no gloves
haven't been found, so far as *I* know."

"Thank you so much. She must have dropped them
on her way, then. They were rather expensive gloves
—she'd like to find them. I wonder—I'd better ask
at the police station, perhaps. Do you know when
she left the cinema? I should have to tell them that,
I expect, should I not?"

"Two o'clock, as near as I can remember. She hadn't
been in long, I can swear to that."

"Oh, thank you so much. That's helpful." Armed
with this unexpected bit of evidence that Mrs. Maslin
had, as matters stood, no alibi for the time of the
child's death, she got back to the guest-house to discover that Mrs. Maslin herself had arrived the day
before she was expected, and was at that moment
walking histrionically up and down the guest-house
dining-room, to which she had laid claim for the purpose
of a private interview, waiting to see Mrs. Bradley.

Mrs. Bradley found a small, ferrety-looking woman,
sharp-featured and pale, with hard grey eyes, foxy-red
hair and a thickish coat of inartistic make-up, and
Mrs. Maslin saw a small, black-eyed, elderly woman

with a fiendish smile and an air of being able to see
through to the back of Mrs. Maslin's head.

"I hear that nothing has been done to clear up the
mystery of my niece's death," Mrs. Maslin announced
belligerently, instinct warning her that with an adversary
of this calibre it would be as well to get her word
in first.

"Let us sit down," said Mrs. Bradley, taking the
most comfortable chair she could see, and fishing out
a mangled length of knitting from an untidy, brightly
coloured bag.

Mrs. Maslin complied with this suggestion, and, as
she had had no reply to her question and did not propose
to repeat it, sat in what was intended for haughty
silence whilst the newcomer knitted a couple of rows
and carefully counted her stitches.

"And purl two," said Mrs. Bradley, nodding slowly
and agreeably. She looked up suddenly and said:

"Why didn't you stay in the cinema all the
time?" The question took Mrs. Maslin entirely by
surprise.

"What cinema?" she said, hedging rather too
obviously. Mrs. Bradley took up her knitting again,
bent her gaze upon its intricacies, and said:

"On the afternoon when your niece was found dead,
you went to the cinema with the other guests here and
the younger children from the orphanage."

"Yes, I did. And—oh, yes, I remember now. But
who told you that I left early?"

"How early?" asked Mrs. Bradley, again not
answering the question.

"I don't know. It was hot. I was bored. I wanted
some air. I expect, now I look back, that some instinct
warned me."

"Warned you of what?"

"Why, naturally, that something had happened to Ursula."

"Why should it do such a thing?"

"Well, I am, I suppose, the relative—I mean, I *was*—most nearly in touch with her, poor child."

"Only by marriage, though, aren't you?"

"What I want to know is—what has been done about the death? The sisters promised me that the death should be fully investigated," said Mrs. Maslin, leaping away from the question with very suspicious celerity.

"Why do you want it investigated?"

"Well, surely, my own niece—and such a terrible verdict!"

"You mean you think the child's death was accidental?"

"I do not believe it was suicide."

"No," said Mrs. Bradley, "neither do I."

"M-murder?" said Mrs. Maslin, a gleam—was it of hope?—in her calculating grey eyes.

"There is no evidence that one could give to the police."

"Oh, *isn't* there?" said Mrs. Maslin, becoming volcanic. "You tell me what you've found out, and I'll soon get something for the police, with that and what I know!"

"I have discovered," said Mrs. Bradley, "that with Ursula Doyle and her cousin Ulrica dead, your step-daughter Mary would inherit the grandfather's fortune."

"Yes, but that's no good," said Mrs. Maslin vigorously, refusing to admit the implication. "It's Ulrica we must look at. Have you examined her movements? She's a most peculiar child. Her father was a most dreadful man—an atheist—believed in nothing."

"And Ulrica proposes to enter a convent."

"Yes, don't you see?—— It's abnormal."

"What is? To enter a convent?"

"Well, in my opinion, it is. But that's neither here nor there, and I'm sure you know what I mean."

"Yes, yes," replied Mrs. Bradley, taking up her knitting again and doing some rapid decreasing which she felt she would regret later on. "You want me to trump up a case against your niece Ulrica to show that she murdered her cousin. As the law stands, no murderer may stand to gain by the results of his murder—in this case the family fortune—so the money, you hope, would automatically come to Mary."

"I don't think you're being serious! You are *not* being serious!" said Mrs. Maslin, flushing in sudden fury. "It's intolerable! It's just making fun! No one would think that a dreadful tragedy had occurred— or that you were being paid to investigate it," she added spitefully.

"On the second count he would be quite right," said Mrs. Bradley, unperturbed, and counting stitches again. Mrs. Maslin bristled. Had she had hackles on her neck they would certainly have stood upright. Mrs. Bradley let her simmer, and then said:

"So you refuse to account for your movements on the afternoon of the crime?"

"Of course I don't! It's ridiculous! I walked back here to have a look at the school?"

"You *walked*? How long did it take you?"

"I don't know, but all this is silly."

"Did you speak to anybody here when you arrived?"

"No. I walked round the grounds."

"Who opened the gate?"

"It was open."

Mrs. Bradley reflected sadly that this was true. The gate was always left open during the day.

"Didn't *anybody* see you?" she said. Mrs. Maslin suddenly looked frightened.

"It can't possibly make any difference whether anybody did or not!" she blustered feebly, her foxy little face quite sharp with anxiety and fear. Mrs. Bradley wagged her head.

"A difficult position, most," she observed without compunction.

CHAPTER 14

HOBBIES

"The ever-flourishing and fruitful soil
Unpurchased food produced: all creatures were
His subjects, serving more for love than fear."

GEORGE SANDYS: Deo Opt. Max.

MOTHER PATRICK WAS GRAFTING FRUIT-TREES. IT WAS the Saturday half-holiday for the private-school children, and the day, although dull, was calm and not cold. She descended the ladder when she saw Mrs. Bradley, and waved her grafting knife.

"Go and find me two sensible children, dear," she said. Feeling rather like a sensible child herself, Mrs. Bradley grinned amiably and walked towards the school. But no children, sensible or otherwise (and, in any case, how she was to pick out the one kind from the other, since she could neither see with Mother Patrick's eyes nor think with her mind, she did not know), were anywhere to be seen. At last, in a corner of the vestibule, she found a child, who, challenged, said that her name was Mary Maslin. Mary Maslin was crying.

"I beg your pardon," said Mrs. Bradley formally, "but I have been asked by Mother Patrick to find her two sensible children. Can it be that you are a sensible child? For, if so, half my task is accomplished."

"But I don't want to help Mother Patrick. I don't want to help anybody," said Mary Maslin, through sobs. Mrs. Bradley sat down beside her on a bench which covered school boot-holes, and observed that it was not a very nice day for anybody to be out of doors.

"It isn't that," said Mary, obviously in need of a confidante. "It's because my mother's come back here to take me away."

"To take you away from school?"

"Yes. She's going to let me have a private governess, and perhaps I'm to go to New York. But I don't want a private governess. I want to stay here with the girls."

"It certainly seems rather trying," Mrs. Bradley agreed, "to be obliged to leave school in the middle of term like this."

"All because of what happened to Ursula," Mary observed without reticence. "It's so stupid. As if I should do a dreadful thing like that! They know quite well I shouldn't!"

"Of course not. But I can understand your mother's feelings."

"She wants Ulrica to come away, too. She wants to have her stay with me, and for us to share the governess. And I don't want that! I don't like Ulrica much. She's clever and I'm not, and I'm glad I'm not. I'd hate to be clever and horrible, and I don't want her anywhere near me! I suppose I can't say so to mother, but Ulrica scares me. I don't feel comfortable with her."

"But you don't feel comfortable at all," Mrs. Bradley pointed out. "Look here, Mary, I think I can make you a promise. I will speak to your mother, and although I shall not be able to prevent her from taking you away from the school—in fact, it's just as well that you should go—a change will do you good— I certainly will see to it that Ulrica doesn't go with you."

"Will you?" said Mary Maslin, cheering up a little.

"Well, that'll be something, anyway. Thanks a lot. Well, all right, then, I'll go and hold bits of stick for Mother Patrick. Doesn't she look lovely on a ladder?"

Off she went, and Mrs. Bradley, left with a new idea, walked out of the building in quest of one more child. Failing to find one, she went back herself, and meekly assisted in the work. Some of the orchard trees were large and old, and had been cut back by the gardener some weeks earlier in preparation for Mother Patrick's talents. She first cut them back a little more, and then made a slit between the bark and the wood. Mrs. Bradley and Mary Maslin held delicately-prepared grafts and handed them up on demand, to be inserted in the slit like rather spiky trimming on a hat.

Mother Patrick on a ladder certainly was a fearful and wonderful sight. She had a man's trick of balance whilst using both her hands, and yet it seemed all the time that her large, ungainly body, its bulk apparently added to by her habit, must at any moment descend, among splintered wreckage, on to the snowdrop-sprinkled orchard ground below.

When the grafts were properly inserted, Mrs. Bradley and Mary handed clay which Mother Patrick clapped upon and moulded round the tree to keep the air, Mrs. Bradley supposed, or curious insects, or, possibly, prying eyes, from the delicate grafts. There was need for something to speculate on, for, as is the way with those who merely stand at the foot of a ladder and hand things up to the master-builder above, the assistants grew tired a long time before Mother Patrick was ready to give up.

"That's all," she said at last. "You are a good child, Mary. You must try to do as well in my subjects as your cousin Ulrica can do. Still, to-day you have done well. I shall pray for our work to be blessed. I

cannot give you a merit now, because it is holiday time,
but remind me to give you one in the next mathematics
lesson—*however* badly you behave!''

''She always calls it 'behaving.' She really means
'answering' or 'working,' '' Mary explained, as she and
Mrs. Bradley went to wash. ''She *really believes* that
everybody can do her sickening old algebra and geometry
if they like. Just like Mother Saint Simon and her
science. And they're for ever throwing Ulrica up at
me. Did *you* have a clever cousin when you were at
school?''

''Never. There were no clever members of our
family,'' Mrs. Bradley replied. ''Now I remember,
though, I did not go to school.''

''Did *you* have a governess, then?''

''Alas, no. My father taught us. We merely learned
to read, and not to lose our tempers when we argued.''

''What did you read?''

''Oh, Lewis Carroll, and the Bible, and the *Swiss
Family Robinson*,'' Mrs. Bradley replied.

''I have never read any of those. Perhaps that is
why we are different.''

''It is quite likely. And now, is it time for tea?''

''You don't fast, do you, during Lent?''

''No. But I never eat much, except when I come upon
my chauffeur eating roast beef and Yorkshire pudding.''

''Ulrica is trying to fast, but Mother Saint Francis
won't let her. She says we are growing children, and
need our food.''

''Most sensible.''

''Yes, it is, really. That's what I think.''

''Mary,'' said Mrs. Bradley, with some suddenness,
''was Ulrica in class, do you know, on the afternoon that
Ursula died?''

Mary stared at her.

"I really don't know," she said.   "We're not in the same form, you see."

"The third and the fourth forms did have a lesson together that afternoon, though, didn't they?"

"Yes, but I'm only in the second form," Mary replied, "and Ulrica thinks I'm much too stupid to be helped with my work the way she'd begun to help Ursula."

Mrs. Bradley nodded, and asked, again with some suddenness, whether Mary would like to go to tea with her in the guest-house.

"I'd love to," the child replied with considerable eagerness.   "Mother asks us once a week, while she's staying here, one of us at a time because we're not supposed to go to the guest-house in pairs.   But mother's gone to Kelsorrow.   If you asked permission, I could come.   They'd let me.   They always let us if anyone asks.   Oh—but——"   She paused, and looked slightly embarrassed.   "You'll have to write me down on the slate, you know."

Mrs. Bradley nodded.

"You mean that the cost of your tea will be added to my bill.   Of course.   Come along.   Do we have cake in Lent?"

They walked over to the school refectory and Mrs. Bradley obtained the required permission.   Tea in the guest-house was over by half-past five, and as Mary had to get back in her classroom by six to do her preparation, they parted immediately, and Mrs. Bradley strolled over to the nuns' Common Room, to which she had been bidden, earlier in the day, by Mother Simon-Zelotes, who wanted to discuss Mendel's theory of heredity.

Mrs. Bradley had not forgotten that from five o'clock until half-past six the nuns sang Compline and went on to Matins and Lauds, and the Common Room, she thought at first, was deserted. In the corner by the fire, however, was the old lay-sister Catherine, her gnarled hands, brown as the fruit trees which Mother Patrick had re-vitalised that afternoon, lying folded together in her lap, her lips moving easily in prayer, the facile, comforting prayers of habit, her rheumed eyes focused vacantly on heaven—or purgatory, perhaps—Mrs, Bradley could not guess. Her broad feet—not essentially nun-like, just the broad and easy-shod feet of any very old woman—were planted upon the fender for warmth, and to help support in an upright position the soldierly, hard, old body.

Mrs. Bradley seated herself without a word, and watched how the rosary passed through the brown old hands. So they sat for a long time, until the old woman looked up from her beads, nodded and mumbled a bit, and then said, in the abrupt manner of the aged, who always speak the middle and not the beginning of their thoughts, "I told them it would not do. I always said so."

"The hot water system?" Mrs. Bradley intelligently enquired. The lay-sister nodded.

"When I was a girl, we boiled every drop in the copper, and carried it up in pails. There was none of the danger then."

"I suppose not, sister. Didn't the people scald themselves sometimes, though?"

"I never heard of it. Things ought to be done in God's way, and if water is going to be heated it ought to be boiled on a fire. Brother Fire. Good Brother Fire." Her voice mumbled on. She had forgotten Mrs. Bradley, and her thoughts were lost in the wide and echoing halls of dim-lit memory. Content to be left to her own thoughts, Mrs. Bradley sat motionless. The darkness gathered. Soon the old lay-sister slept.

The first of the Community to join them was Mother Cyprian, who, under special dispensation, was to get on with some embroidered bookbindings. She lit the lamp —there was no gas laid on in the buildings which abutted on the cloister—exchanged smiles and bows with Mrs. Bradley, seated herself beneath the light and began to mount the embroidery she had done on a square of fine, strong linen. Mrs. Bradley asked permission to look at the work. It was exquisitely done on satin, and Mother Cyprian explained that after the backing had been put on she would be able to do the heavier work in braid, which the satin, without its backing, could not support.

"Then, too," she said, delighted to show her work, "the paste which I shall use to connect the embroidery with the book which I wish to bind would damage the delicate satin if I applied it directly. The backing is useful. It comes between. It is like——" She paused for a simile which should be at once intelligible to her hearer and satisfying to herself—"it is like——" Invention failed her, but old Sister Catherine, awakened by the light and the sound of talking, piped out, in a voice like a badly-played viola:

"It is like the blessed saints who intercede for us. Holy Saint Joseph, protector of the Blessed Virgin Mary . . ." Her mumbling voice droned on.

"She is Irish," Mother Cyprian observed, as though this was both an explanation and an excuse, but of what oddity the explanation, and for what impropriety the excuse, Mrs. Bradley did not understand. Sister Catherine went to sleep again, and made small moaning noises in the corner. Mrs. Bradley woke her very gently, and led her to the door and down the steps. Docile, the old woman said good night to her and went away to her bed. When Mrs. Bradley came back to the

Common Room, Mother Cyprian had finished her work, and was pressing it out to lie smooth.

"Did you teach Ursula Doyle?" Mrs. Bradley enquired.

"Yes. I teach needlework," the nun replied, looking up. "All the children come to me at some time during the week, both the private-school children and the orphans."

"And what did you make of Ursula?"

"She was a good child, very quiet. Very happy at the end—I mean, the last time I saw her."

"That would have been——" Mrs. Bradley now knew the school time-table off by heart—"on the Thursday morning, Mother Saint Cyprian, I think?"

She had not known the nun's name until Mother Cyprian mentioned the subject she taught, although she had guessed it from seeing her with her embroidery.

"On the Thursday, yes, madame," said the nun. She leaned forward, and, contrary to the habit of the religious, who either looked directly in front of them or else kept their eyes cast down, she looked Mrs. Bradley in the eye. "We cannot believe that that poor child took her own life. She was so happy at the end. She was quite beautiful with happiness. Her cousins will tell you the same."

Her cousins, Mrs. Bradley reflected, ought to be able to tell her a very great deal, but she shrank from questioning either of them too closely regarding the death of the child. It would do no harm, though, she felt, to interview Ulrica again. She enquired of Mother Cyprian how long the children spent over preparation.

"Until seven o'clock when they are aged ten to twelve; from twelve to fourteen until half-past seven, and the others until eight o'clock," Mother Cyprian answered. "But if you wish to speak to Ulrica, or to any of the children, during the Preparation time, no doubt it could be arranged."

"I should like to speak, not to Ulrica, but to somebody else in her form," Mrs. Bradley said. Mother Cyprian nodded.

"An excellent idea," she agreed. "I think it is time that Ulrica was cleared of all suspicion of knowing anything about her cousin's death."

At this Mrs. Bradley, who had supposed her secret thoughts to be hers alone, positively started with surprise. Mother Cyprian smiled very slightly.

"But, of course, we have all thought what *you* think," she remarked. "Was she not the heiress, if her cousin should die? And, behold, her cousin did die."

To say that Mrs. Bradley was taken aback by this candid statement would be to speak less than the truth. So the Community *had* considered murder! They had even put a name to the murderer, which was more than she herself so far had done.

Mother Cyprian smiled with seeming guilelessness. Mrs. Bradley had the helpless feeling that, even if she stayed in the convent for the rest of her life—and her parents had averaged eighty-seven point nine four years, and her grandparents, counting all four of them, just over fifty—she would never understand the workings of the minds of the religious, either individually or as a community.

She sat, and pondered, and scribbled, and Mother Cyprian took up needle and silks, and commenced another piece of embroidery, already backed, this time, because it was on velvet.

Until eight o'clock they sat there, and then Mother Cyprian put her work away, turned out the lamp and lighted the candles. Then she stood still beside the door as the Mother Superior, followed by most of the

Community, entered the room. It was the hour of recreation before the De Profundis bell at nine.

Mrs. Bradley was interested to find out how the recreation hour would be spent by the nuns, but thought it incumbent upon her to leave them to their devices. They welcomed her presence, however, and asked her to stay, so she seated herself in a corner, took out her note-book and busied herself—or appeared to busy herself—while they took their places at the great, semi-circular, deeply polished table and took out darning, mending and patching. This they had brought in calico bags tied with tape.

The fire glowed strongly and brightly red, the yellow candlelight doubly-lined the faces of the older nuns, and gave more than their due of beauty to the smooth soft cheeks of the younger. It pleased Mrs. Bradley to do nothing but sit there and watch them. They were a fine and comforting picture, for the older nuns had the largeness of aunts in her childhood; the beautiful nuns were like Virgins stepped out of their frames. They sat so still, except for their busy fingers, and their calm, fresh faces were so smooth, benign and comely, that they made a group for a painter, and Mrs. Bradley's one regret was that her nephew Carey Lestrange could not be there. With keen pleasure, seated in the shadows, she watched them, aware of a faint nostalgia, aware of sadness and a most curious feeling of envy.

Then they talked with her—Mother Simon-Zelotes discussing Mendel's theories, and the others (heads nodding, Mother Amrose's long nose twitching with militant zeal, Mother Timothy's false teeth gleaming more bone-like than whited bones under the moon), making good use, as they were expected to do, of the hour of recreation. Mrs. Bradley, discussing Mendel, the Spanish war, a bye-election in the Midlands, plainsong, electric fires, watched the age-sharpened, delicate profile of the gentle-voiced Mother Superior and Mother Francis' sharp eyes; mused on the loveliness of Mother Benedict, the youthfulness of Mother Mary-Joseph, the cherubity of Mother Jude and the charitable brow and large, fine, craftsman's hands of Mother Simon-Zelotes as she sketched swift diagrams of pea seeds, and talked about blue eyes in rabbits, and negroid characteristics as a Mendelian dominant.

There came a tap at the door, and, in response to a quiet reply from the Mother Superior, a little girl, about eight years old, came in and stood, with her hands behind her back, opposite the centre of the table.

"Well, Kathleen?" said Mother Francis, from the Mother Superior's left. Kathleen, it appeared, was prepared to recite to the nuns, and, encouraged by the Mother Superior, began in a big, bold voice, got stuck half-way, was prompted by the young nun Mother Mary-Joseph, and finished gamely, rather fast, but remembering the rest of the words.

"Thank you, Kathleen," said the Mother Superior, nodding. The child came round the table to her side, and the old woman kissed her gently, blessed her, and commended her for the night to the keeping of God.

This ritual was repeated six or seven times with different children, and apparently was a feature of school life to which the boarders were accustomed. When the children had all gone to bed, Mother Benedict read aloud, in a clear, grave voice, a chapter from the life of the founder of the Order.

Then the Mother Superior turned to Mrs. Bradley, who had long since put away her note-book.

"My friend . . .?" she said; and left the whole of the sentence a question. Mrs. Bradley rose, under the eyes of all the Community, and came to the centre of the table. Mother Mary-Joseph from the right-hand end of the semi-circular arc, brought up a straight-backed chair. Mrs. Bradley thanked her, and sat down. There was the kind of expectant hush to which she had grown accustomed, and scarcely noticed, but to a sensitive stranger it would have seemed as though the nuns were all holding breath, and that in the air was a tension as keenly stretched as the string of a violin; but Mrs. Bradley spoke briskly, and without hesitation or preamble.

"I have found out nothing of importance, but I think that both Mary Maslin and Ulrica Doyle should be sent to their homes," she said.

"To their respective homes?" asked Mother Francis. "But Ulrica has no home, except with her aunt, Mrs. Maslin. She usually spends her holidays here, at the school. Otherwise there is the grandfather in New York."

"They ought not to go together," said Mrs. Bradley.

There was no movement among the nuns. They sat as still as carved wooden figures in their high-backed, uncushioned chairs, while the surface of the deeply polished table reflected the candle-light and the flashing of Mother Cyprian's steel needles, for Mother Cyprian, alone of the Community, had continued her work after Mrs. Bradley had spoken. The atmosphere had changed, although not a sister had moved. It was as though she had shouted loudly, and they were all listening to the fading away of the echoes. Peace was gone, and she felt like a bird of ill-omen, and looked the part, too, with her yellow skin and brilliant eyes, and her mocking, crocodile grin. It was almost as though the devil had got into the Common Room. The candlelight accentuated her ugliness as it did the beauty of Mother Benedict and the white hands, made smaller by contrast

with the wide heavy sleeves of their habits, of young
Mother Mary-Joseph and red-lipped Mother Francis.
The only one of the Community whom Nature permitted
to keep Mrs. Bradley in countenance, was the old nun
Mother Bartholomew, the ex-actress Rosa Cardosa, who
retained, in the religious life, the marked features, the
mobile, expressive mouth, the raddled complexion and
the endearing, extravagant gestures of the profession
she had outgrown. Discipline, however, had imposed
its iron gag even upon Mother Bartholomew, and,
although her eyes spoke clearly, her tongue made no
remark. In fact, the dead silence, by its very con-
tinuation, soon became slightly uncanny, until, at a
sign from the Superior, the black-habited, white-coifed
religious took up their patching and darning and again
bent their eyes upon their work. The Mother Superior
leaned forward across the table, her needle between
finger and thumb.

"You mean that there was no accident, but that the
child was killed intentionally?" she said.

"That is what I mean," replied Mrs. Bradley.

"Will you tell us—" the old voice was so gentle
that Mrs. Bradley, conscious of the blow which her
news must be to many of those who heard her, wished
heartily, not for the first time, that she could have
found something different to report "—why you have
come to this conclusion?"

Mrs. Bradley read all her notes aloud. She offered
no comments, and, when she had finished, she felt,
rather than heard, the long sigh which went up from
those who accepted her findings.

There were some who did not. Mother Benedict
said, when the Superior had invited the nuns to speak:

"I cannot see that you have proved your contention.
Pardon me if I am stupid."

"I will re-examine the theory of suicide, if that is the general wish," said Mrs. Bradley, "but the theory of accident seems to me untenable."

"I agree that it could not have been accident," said Mother Benedict slowly, but she spoke without conviction, and as though her common sense and her intellectual acceptance of the facts were not in agreement.

"The police would not be prepared to act on this amount of evidence," said Mrs. Bradley soothingly. "But I do suggest, for your own sakes, that you get rid of those children at once—and separately. Ulrica Doyle, as I said, must not go home with Mary and Mrs. Maslin."

"But you are not accusing Mrs. Maslin of having killed her niece!" exclaimed Mother Simon-Zelotes. Mrs. Bradley shook her head.

"I have scarcely a shred of evidence at present against Mrs. Maslin, but, all the same, I think that Mary Maslin and Ulrica Doyle should not both go to the same house. I mention this because I believe that Mrs. Maslin has proposed it."

"Yes, Mrs. Maslin did wish that," said Mother Mary-Joseph, gazing, bright-eyed, at Mrs. Bradley.

"It is nearly the end of recreation time," said the Mother Superior, almost in tones of rebuke. "We thank you for your advice, my friend," she added. "We must think it over carefully. We will pray."

She rose, and the nuns rose with her, and they filed out, taking their work, and left Mrs. Bradley alone. In less than a quarter of an hour, she knew, they would enter the church for night prayers. She had half an inclination to follow them, but, instead, she put out all but one candle, and by its flickering, solitary light —there was a ghostly draught somewhere that would not allow the candle flame to grow upright—she took out a little book of pictures—a British Museum copy of some of the pages of a late medieval Book of Hours.

" 'The Flight into Egypt,' " she read, " 'and the Massacre of the Innocents.' "

The draught blew more strongly. The door the nuns had carefully closed was opening. Mrs. Bradley ducked, saved by the never-sleeping instinct of self-preservation which still plays sentry even for the highly civilised. There was a loud crash. The door slammed to; the missile, whatever it was, had landed squarely and then had fallen to the floor. Mrs. Bradley stayed where she was and counted fifty. Then she got up, walked over to the door and locked it, lighted a second candle and searched for what had been thrown. It was a hammer. She had seen several like it in the metal-work hut, and had no doubt that it had come from one of the racks. It had smashed a religious picture. The glass was all over the floor.

CHAPTER 15

ATTACK

" . . . the night
Is dark and long;
The road foul, and where one goes right
Six may go wrong."

HENRY VAUGHAN: "Stars are of mighty use."

HOLDING THE HAMMER IN HER RIGHT HAND, MRS. Bradley unlocked the door with her left and descended the steps to the cloister. They were not many, but were cloaked in utter darkness. She had heard no sound of footsteps either coming or going, but she felt quite certain that whoever had thrown the hammer was far enough away by the time she herself left the Common Room. As she came out into the dimness of the cloister she could see the nuns in front of her ready to enter the church. She drew a large, thick motor-veil out of her pocket, tied it over her head (catching the hammer between her knees) and followed them into the building. She seated herself as near the entrance doorway as she could, placed the hammer noiselessly beside her, and sat back, almost hidden, in the pew.

The church was vast and high. The sound of the nuns' chanting came as though from a very great distance, and to the fastness of God penetrated the sullen, booming crash of breakers on rocks—sure sign, they had told her, of tempest—a sound she had not heard at the convent before.

The unusual size and grandeur of the church was

due to the fact that before the Dissolution, when St. Peter's had been a house of monks, the church had been used by the villagers as well as by the Community. Lighted only by candles at its eastern end, it was a vastness of shadows, and, sitting there, she could imagine that the place was peopled by ghosts. She could hear—or was it all imagination?—the slight, fidgety rustlings of a rustic congregation, the sighs of children compelled to a pretence of devotion, even a muffled cough from somewhere away to her left on the north side of the church. She strained her ears, but a rush of wind round the north-west angle of the building, shrieking at gale force, eighty miles an hour, filled the church with its fury. When it died away the sound of the nuns' voices was all that could be heard.

The prayers were not long. When they were over the sisters remained for a quarter of an hour's meditation, and then filed out, and Mrs. Bradley followed closely behind. She fell in with Mother Ambrose and Mother Jude, and walked as far as the Orphanage door with them. They entered by the door which opened on to the convent grounds, and she was left to make her way through the gate and round the front of the guest-house alone.

She did not fear molestation, but naturally intended to avoid it if she could, so she got indoors quickly and found supper set and Annie on duty in the dining-room. She still held the hammer and noticed that Annie eyed it. She laid it beside her plate, and as everyone seated at table was too well-bred to remark upon it, she herself was able to hold her peace. She ate sparingly, drank some water, and, when the meal was over, went to bed. Another room in the guest-house had been made ready for her, so that she and Sister Bridget were now lodged under one roof, neither inconveniencing the other. Mrs. Maslin had also been accommodated, for two of the guests had voluntarily taken beds in the Orphanage.

Mrs. Bradley locked her door as a precautionary measure, and very soon fell asleep. She had not been asleep for more than half an hour before she was awakened by a sound of shrill squealing which appeared to be directed into the keyhole of her door. At the same time she was aware that a high wind was still shrieking round the house, and she could hear the sullen booming of the sea like gunfire a long way off. She woke completely, put on a dressing-gown enriched with peacock designs and colourings, and shouted through the keyhole:

"Who's there? What do you want?"

"Fire! Fire!" squealed the unknown. There was a nerve-trying noise of crackling somewhere at hand, but Mrs. Bradley, sniffing, could not smell any smoke. She gripped the hammer, which she had placed underneath her bolster, and flung open the door, prepared for trouble. Nobody but poor Sister Bridget stood outside. She clutched at Mrs. Bradley, gibbering anguishedly. Mrs. Bradley gathered, fairly soon, that she thought her pet mouse was in danger. Mrs. Bradley went with her to her room. The crackling here was now a triumphant roaring. The bed was on fire, and part of the window curtains, as Mrs. Bradley entered, fell in a mass of flame. Mrs. Bradley picked up the bolster which the smouldering fire on the bed had not yet reached, and used it to put out the flames, beating away with the heavy, unwieldy thing as men beat out a prairie fire with branches.

Suddenly there was a squeal of triumph, and in the midst of what looked like hell, with Mrs. Bradley chief devil, danced Sister Bridget. She had the mouse on her arm. She ran to the door, pulled it open and then shut it behind her with a crash, leaving Mrs. Bradley inside. Fortunately the lock did not jam, as Mrs. Bradley half thought it might with this treatment. She picked up the ewer, which was empty, dashed for the bathroom, filled the ewer and, returning, emptied it freely all over the bed. After the third jugful the flames gave up the fight, and she went out to find Sister Bridget. She called her name quietly in case she was in hiding but there was no response, so at last she went back to bed, but lay awake with something nagging at her consciousness. She turned over several times, fretted, racked her brains, but could not account for her own disturbed state of mind. She was too much accustomed to dealing with homicidal patients to allow her nerves to be upset by the hammer-throwing incident, and Sister Bridget, she was certain, had not been hurt in the fire. It was of no use to try to reassure herself, however, so she got up again, lighted the gas, took out her notebook and studied it. Any last doubts which she might have had respecting one aspect, at least, of the affair, had been dispersed by the hammer-throwing incident. She had no doubt that the hammer had been slung directly and deliberately at her head, which must have made a good target, dead black against the light of the solitary candle before which she had been seated to read her little book and look at its pictures. Somebody obviously held the opinion that she was becoming a nuisance, and this fact gave Mrs. Bradley the considerable satisfaction which some American editors experience when people begin to plug at them through the window. She wondered whether, when she told her tale in the morning, Mother Benedict would still refuse to consider the possibility that the child had been murdered. She began to dissect her mind to

discover the true cause of her uneasiness, and decided
that she was thinking of Sister Bridget.

"Nonsense," she said, denying the truth of her own
diagnosis of her symptoms. "There's nothing to fear
from that source." She even felt under the bolster for
the hammer as soon as she got back to bed.

So her nagging mind let her alone, and she slept at
last, but not deeply. When she woke, she discovered
that her hand, almost paralysed with cramp, was under
the pillow, and that she still had the hammer in her
grasp.

(2)

The hour of Prime was ordinarily at six-thirty, and
the choir-sisters, upon rising, always went straight to
the church. The lay-sisters rose about half an hour
earlier than the choir-sisters, and did more than an
hour's work before their half-hour of meditation.

Mrs. Bradley was not the only person in the guest-
house who had slept badly. Sister Margaret, whose
week on duty it was, had been disturbed, as had everyone
else, to some extent, by the storm which had swept
on its way south-westward until two o'clock in the
morning, but even when it died down she had not
settled to sleep. Why this should be she had not the
least idea. Her conscience was clear, except for a few
uncharitable thoughts about Sister Genevieve, the
boarders' matron, with whom she had never found
herself in complete accord since that time last summer
when they had had a difference of opinion over some
towels torn on the gooseberry bushes where Sister
Margaret had spread them out to dry. These uncharitable
thoughts she proposed to confess, as usual, to Father
Clare, together with one or two other specific but
undetailed sins of a venial nature which she customarily

added as makeweight in case Father Clare should think her confession lacking in Christian humility, but, beyond all this, which was pure routine, there was nothing, and yet she could not sleep. So she got up and said a few prayers, but even these did not bring her repose, although she found them as comforting as usual. At four o'clock in the morning she was still awake, so she got up, dressed, and very quietly got through most of her Sunday morning's work. Then she went noiselessly out of the guest-house with the pious intention of cleaning the windows of the metal-work room—a job, as she had noted on the previous afternoon, that badly needed doing, and was usually given to the orphans as a penance.

She did not get far, however, for there was work to do nearer at hand. She picked up the key of the gate-house from the table in her room, and, holding it in her hand—it was a large, impressive key about five inches long—she walked briskly round the angle of the wall from the guest-house to the convent entry. It was Mother Ambrose's key, and Mother Ambrose had been vexed at having to lend it, for the key which Sister Margaret should have been able to borrow was the spare one which hung in the Common Room. That key, unaccountably, had not been there when she went to look for it on the Friday. It was seldom that anyone wanted it, and enquiry had failed to elicit the exact last time when it was known to have been hanging on its hook on the chimney-breast, underneath a little metal plaque of St. Anthony.

So, key in hand, and shivering in the raw cold of the early March morning, she came to the convent gate.

But the gate was already open, and not far along the gravelled path lay the sprawling obscenity of a body clad in a thick, long-sleeved nightdress over most of its underclothing. It was the thick black woollen stockings which, for some reason, struck the most disgraceful note, in Sister Margaret's opinion. Perhaps it was because there was so much of them, for death— if this were death, and it looked exactly like it—is no respecter of persons, and had contrived to make poor Sister Bridget—for she it was, as Sister Margaret could see at half a glance—look not so much dead as completely and shockingly inebriated, and this effect was enhanced by her iron-grey, short, sprouty hair which was matted with dried and clotted blood. The weapon with which her injury had been inflicted was lying on the gravel path beside her, where her assailant had dropped it after striking her on the head. It was a hammer, and there was no doubt of its complicity in the affair, for the end was bloody, and a few grey hairs adhered.

Sister Margaret, innocent of all knowledge of police procedure, picked it up and rubbed the blood-stained end upon the grass. Then she laid it aside very carefully, because it was convent property and the convent was very short of money, and turned her attention to the body.

She found herself reluctant to touch poor Sister Bridget, but she straightened and tidied her clothing as well as she could, and then, taken suddenly with panic, a feeling for which she could not afterwards account, ran screaming like a maniac towards the cloister.

(3)

By nine o'clock the whole household, including the boarders and the orphans, were in receipt of the exciting news, although how it had been passed round was not, in the opinion of Mother Francis, at all easy to conceive. She stood before the twenty private-school boarders at nine-thirty, dead white except for two red spots on her cheeks (frightened, said some of the children, furious, said the others), and her mouth in a dead straight line, but to the general disappointment she did not refer to the cause of all the excitement except indirectly.

"You will not, my dear children," she said, firmly, "go beyond the limits of the school garden to-day on any pretext whatever. You will remain in church" —it was Sunday—"until you are sent for to go across to the refectory."

And that was very nearly all the share that the boarders had in what happened during the rest of what they felt, with envy, and a certain amount of reason, must be a very exciting day. Even so, they told one another, they had scored over the day girls, who, so far, knew nothing about it.

Sister Bridget, by some miracle, was not dead, and Mrs. Bradley and the doctor who usually attended the convent worked with goodwill to keep in her the little flicker of life which still remained.

She was, as the doctor remarked, a tough old party, and Mrs. Bradley was tough, and the doctor himself was a man who took pleasure, as he informed them, in keeping the religious out of heaven as long as ever he could in order to spite them. His view was that unmarried women were unnatural anyway, but that women who remained unmarried from choice and took vows of chastity were anti-social, and should be persecuted for this reason.

"Whole lot of you ought to be in gaol," was his expression of this opinion to Mother Jude, who liked him. She beamed upon him when he was present, and prayed for him when he had gone. So did Mother Ambrose pray for him, but this chiefly because he charged the convent only half a crown a visit instead of his customary fee.

It became a battle for Sister Bridget's life, and Mrs. Bradley and the doctor laboured, and the nuns watched and prayed. They also fetched and carried, obeyed every instruction as though upon it depended their salvation, and reaped some part of their reward when it became increasingly evident that Sister Bridget would live. Upon receipt of this news, Mother Mary-Joseph, Infirmarian to the Community, occupied a brief and popular period of notoriety by pitching down the Common Room steps into the cloister and breaking her left arm. She had borne the brunt of the night-nursing in addition to heavy teaching duties during the day. She was also keeping the Lenten fast, and in various ways was mortifying the flesh. Therefore, said the doctor (who, in addition to a general disapproval of the religious life, held strong views on the subject of fasting, putting it on a par, loudly and violently, with the twin crazes of slimming and Physical Fitness), she deserved to faint and fall down steps, and smash herself up, and have to take time off from school.

"But I am not going to take time off from school," said Mother Mary-Joseph in the deceptively gentle tone of the iron-willed; neither did she remain away from her classes for so much as half an hour. Mrs. Bradley protested to the Superior, but the old woman answered:

"Be easy, my dear, and let her be. She is young and very ardent. If the life is not a soldier's life, what is it?"

As Mrs. Bradley had no idea, she could not make an adequate reply.

"If her health were likely to be seriously endangered, she would take the doctor's advice and follow his orders," the Superior went on. "She is under obedience, you understand."

Meanwhile Mother Ambrose and Mother Jude had been far from idle. They had examined carefully Sister Bridget's room to see whether they could find any cause for the outbreak of fire, and had discovered an over-turned candle thick with grease, and also a quantity of cotton-wool, purloined, it turned out, from the medicine chest in the staff room cupboard at the school. The quantity of cotton-wool found by the nuns coincided, so far as they could tell, with the amount that was missing from store. It had not been burnt in the out-break because it had not been placed near the candle which appeared to have caused the fire. Sister Bridget herself had purloined it, they were almost certain, to make a soft bed for the mouse.

All this they reported, but Mrs. Bradley, who had her own reasons for wanting to know a good deal more about the matter than this meagre information implied, asked that the room should be kept permanently locked and that she herself should be the only person in possession of a key. Three more keys to the room were sur-rendered, thereupon, by Mother Jude, who merely smiled beatifically at Mrs. Bradley's expression of surprise. This was on the Thursday following the attack on Sister Bridget. Mrs. Bradley sent George with the keys to her bank in London. George returned next day with Ferdinand Lestrange, who remarked that he could stay until Tuesday.

"Not here, dear child," his mother observed immediately. She banished him to the village, chided George for bringing him anywhere near her, and went to find Mother Francis. As it was Friday afternoon Mother Francis was teaching. Her subject was drawing, and, although she was not the equal of Mother Benedict she was a very fair artist of the photographic-likeness school. That this was again coming into its own, Mother

Francis was not aware, Mrs. Bradley concluded; this for the simple reason that she did not realise that it had ever given place to the impressionistic school, cubism, post-impressionism, or the erotic iniquity of surrealism.

"Ah, so you have come to look at the children's work!" Mother Francis exclaimed, the teacher in her come uppermost, Mrs. Bradley was interested to remark. Shuddering slightly—a gesture of dissent which was noted and appreciated by the eighteen girls in the fourth form, who received it with leering triumph— their opinion (taken collectively) of their work being on a par with the visitor's own—Mrs. Bradley was drawn to the supererogatory work of inspection.

That over, and comments suitable to Mother Francis' rather hen-like attitude having been passed, Mrs. Bradley, whose eyes had been alert for Ulrica Doyle, remarked, as Mother Francis accompanied her to the door,

"I see that those children are still here."

"We are still waiting for Mrs. Maslin to leave the guest-house and take Mary with her," Mother Francis' replied, as she followed Mrs. Bradley into the corridor and closed the class-room door behind them both. "I spoke to her on the subject yesterday, but she replied that she was glad of the rest and change because she had been so much worried by family business matters arising out of Ursula's death. I know that you expected us to send the girls off last week, but we have had so much anxiety in connection with the attack on Sister Bridget, that, short of sending Ulrica to New York, I have not been able to think of what to do with her."

"Have the police found anything to go on?" Mrs. Bradley asked, more for the sake of prolonging the conversation than for the gaining of knowledge.

"No. They suspect, as we do, that the attack was

the work of those uncontrolled young men from the village of Brinchcommon who came here after the death of Ursula Doyle and did so much damage then, but it seems very difficult to prove it.''

"There have been no more of those demonstrations, have there?''

"You would have known as soon as we should, if there had been. They made, last time, the most dreadful howling noises for more than an hour. The orphans, poor children, were terrified, and so were some of the guests. The Spaniards said to Mother Jude that they had supposed this country to be free from terrorism. It was very dreadful for them. Their nerves are very bad. Some who were ill were set back in their convalescence.''

Mrs. Bradley said sympathetically that she supposed so, and reverted to the question of the cousins.

"I fear I did not urge you sufficiently strongly to get rid of them from the school,'' she said. "I meant it most sincerely. They are a danger to themselves and to one another. I have no doubt that the grandfather's great fortune is somehow at the root of the business, and I think you ought to act immediately. It is only because of the excitement and terror consequent upon the accident to Sister Bridget that nothing more has happened in the Doyle affair, I believe.''

"You speak of the *accident* to Sister Bridget,'' said Mother Francis. "Are you convinced this time, then, that what happened was accidental?''

"I most certainly am,'' said Mrs. Bradley with emphasis. The nun looked as though she were prepared to argue the point, and Mrs. Bradley was ready with an explanation of the presence of the hammer with which the aged sister had been struck. But all that Mother Francis asked her was:

"Then why did you insist upon our calling in the police?"

Mrs. Bradley replied:

"I thought it would do no harm in the village if the youths there learned that there was a point at which the police were prepared to act, and the convent to ask for protection."

"I see," said Mother Francis. She said no more, but Mrs. Bradley felt, not for the first time, considerable respect for the self-control of the religious. Anybody but a nun would have asked questions, she was certain. She glanced at Mother Francis, and then remarked:

"The blow was not intended for Sister Bridget. I am sure it was intended for me. Whoever set fire to the room did so with the intention of driving out its occupant, thinking that I still slept there. This person, whoever it was, did not know that Sister Bridget had been given her old room back again."

She told Mother Francis then about the hammer-throwing incident in the nuns' Common Room.

"I see," said Mother Francis again. "I ought to remind you, however, that Sister Bridget loves playing with matches, and probably set her bed alight by accident."

"Thank you," Mrs. Bradley replied. "But you will agree, I think, that she did not hit herself on the head with the hammer. Further to that, although, as I said before, it does no harm to let those youths feel that we are under the protection of the police, I think it unlikely that they had anything whatever to do with the attack. But the real culprit may as well be misled into imagining that we blame the youths, I think. By the way, did Mrs. Maslin arrive by car?"

"Yes, I believe she did. In fact, of course she did. She was angry, Sister Saint Jude told me, that we have no garage at the guest-house, and grumbled at the inconvenience and expense of garaging the car in the village.''

"I see. In church, on the evening when I had sat with you all in the Common Room—you remember?—and begged you to send those children home, there was a sound like a cough. You wouldn't have noticed it, perhaps?''

Mother Francis' eyes narrowed a little.

"Somebody started the engine of a car. I remember perfectly well,'' she said. "It was just as the storm was rising. The wind was very loud. Our singing sounded weak and thin against it, and I thought of the might of God. I was born in the West Indies. We have great winds there.''

"You are a Frenchwoman, then?''

"Creole, yes.''

"Your colouring, surely, is unusual?''

"Oh, the English!'' said Mother Francis. She laughed gaily. "You are so tolerant! Always you see the black blood! Creole! It does not always mean that, you know!''

CHAPTER 16

CHESSBOARD

"The milky way chalked out with suns; a clue
That guides through erring hours."

HENRY VAUGHAN : Sunday.

MRS. BRADLEY WALKED OVER TO THE GUEST-HOUSE FOR
Friday tea and brooded as she walked. Her suspicions
had now become certainties, and yet there seemed
nothing to prove that her theories were facts. The
police clues ought, she knew, to be the two hammers,
but the confused nature of the prints on tools which had
been handled by dozens of people, and on which, in any
case, her own prints were superimposed, since, except
for the police, she had been the last person to handle the
hammers, made the task of using finger-prints as part
of the work of detection extremely difficult. It was
rendered more difficult because, short of resorting to
the somewhat crude expedient of getting all the people
she had ever, even remotely, suspected of the murder to
grasp a postcard between finger and thumb and then
comparing the prints with all those found on the
hammers, it was not easy to decide whether or not the
weapons had been handled by the person she suspected.
Even then, if this person (as was probable) could show
reason for having had legitimate possession of the
hammers at some time, that piece of evidence would
automatically disappear. That was the worst of com-
munal property, she reflected, and was an objection

which would apply to almost everything on or in the convent buildings.

Tea, at the guest-house, was a formal meal, and the guests sat down at table, but Mrs. Bradley had a working arrangement with Annie, Bessie, Kitty and Maggie for having hers served in the kitchen. The girls liked the arrangement and enjoyed her company, and even Mother Ambrose, concealing her real feelings, allowed the two orphans who were not on duty in the guest-house to sneak off on slight excuse from their other tasks to make a cheerful party of five in the guest-house kitchen. Mother Jude did not have any feelings to conceal, but, if she could fit it in with her other duties, she joined the party, eating nothing, but enjoying the conversation. A firm friendship, in fact, was growing and flourishing between Mrs. Bradley and the saintly, tubby little Hospitaller.

"I don't reckon," said Bessie, speaking first, for Mother Jude was not present, on this occasion, to be deferred to in the matter of beginning a conversation, "as you'll ever find out who done it."

"Why not, young Bessie?" enquired Maggie.

"Less of the young," said Bessie. "You ain't the the only one got a boy friend. She won't, and she knows she won't, because there isn't anything whatever to go on, without the sisters tells her a damn sight more than they have."

"What makes you say that?" asked Mrs. Bradley, startled. Bessie turned up her eyes and folded her hands in scandalous imitation of Mother Ambrose.

"What makes me? Ah, well, I'll tell you. Look here, stands to reason. Young Maggie, turn down the gas under that there kettle and shove in a couple more spoonfuls. Seems to me they got everything to gain and nothing to lose by that kid being done in."

"But she wasn't done in! It was accident!" interpolated Maggie, going off to do as she was bid, for they
all took orders from Bessie, Mrs. Bradley had noticed.

"Oh, was it? Well, then, what's Mrs. Bradley still
here for? Can't you put two and two together? She
wouldn't still be here if it was accident! And who 'it
that poor old kite on the 'ead with an 'ammer? And
what's that ferret-faced Maslin bitch still hanging about
for round 'ere? You mark my words, and you, too,
Annie, for all I suppose you'll split on me later on to
Mother Saint Ambrose, there's more in this 'ere dope
than meets the eye."

"Go on, Bessie," said Mrs. Bradley, calmly, watching
her very closely.

"Garn!" said Bessie, suddenly on the defensive.
"Like me to give meself away?"

"Why not, in the interests of justice?"

"Justice nothing! What's justice! Seven years 'ard
for taking what ought to be yours! Don't talk to *me!*
I've 'ad some! Wait till I gets out of here, and watch
my smoke. Queen of the gangsters, that's me." She
made a loud whooping noise, and cocked a snook,
presumably at the innocence of her past.

"Bessie," said Mrs. Bradley, "don't be idiotic.
You've said too much to begin to sidetrack now. Out
with it, there's a good girl."

"You won't tell Mother Saint Ambrose?"

"Why not?"

"Oh, have it your own way. What I says is this:
this kid got a fortune, hadn't she?"

"If she had survived her grandfather she would have
had one, yes."

"Same thing, for all I see. She conks. Who gets
the dough?"

"Well, who?"

"The other gal Doyle, the cousin."

"How do you know, young Bessie?" demanded
Maggie, whose last Little Penance had been for smuggling
forbidden twopenny printed matter of the Cinderella
type into Religious Instruction, where it almost
immediately caught the eye of Mother Timothy, who
sometimes taught the orphans, and was confiscated.

"Talked to the Maslin nipper when she come over
here to tea."

"Oh, dear!" said Mrs. Bradley. "And I brought
her!"

"Well, shan't give her fleas or nothing, shall I?"
Bessie enquired, wilfully misunderstanding the purport
of the interjection.

"I am not in a position to determine," Mrs. Bradley
gravely replied. As it was by remarks of this character
that she had won Bessie's good opinion, Bessie greeted
the reply as a sally of the ripest wit, grinned amiably,
and continued:

"Garn! You win! Anyway, had a little chat, and
gets quite an earful of the dope. Seems this other Doyle
goes batty on being a nun. That being that, the dough
all goes to the convent. Well, got two ears and a nose
each, 'aven't us? Or 'aven't us?" she demanded
triumphantly of the others.

Annie looked shocked, and Maggie mystified but
impressed. Kitty looked disapproving, and remarked:

"And you to be after thinking the holy Reverend
Mother Superior no better than a thief and a murderer?
Bad cess to you, Bessie Lampeter, and the back of my
hand to you now!"

"Course not," said Bessie, uneasily. "Who brought
Reverend Mother Superior into it? Never said nothing,
did I?"

At this point Mother Jude arrived, and room was

made for her at the table between Kitty and Annie,
Bessie moving up closer to Mrs. Bradley, and the good-
natured, rather vulgarly pretty Maggie taking, as usual,
the path of least resistance, and moving in the direction
in which she was pushed.

"There is rain in the air," said Mother Jude.

"We have been discussing the Maslin money," said
Mrs. Bradley.

"The Doyle money, surely? Mrs. Maslin is in very
great distress. Have you heard the news? Old Mr.
Doyle is thinking of leaving all the money to endow a
hospital."

"Really?"

"Spike somebody's guns," said Bessie, with fierce
satisfaction.

"I thought you didn't believe in hospitals," Mrs.
Bradley remarked.

"No more I don't! Taking poor little kids away
from their mum and dad just because they got a few
spots, and shutting 'em up till they gets the diphtheria
and dies! Cruel, I call it. Ought to be put in prison!"

"Bessie happens to know of a very sad case," said
Mother Jude. " But I came to tell you some joyful
and interesting news. Sister Saint Simon-Zelotes has
at last finished the copies of our famous paten and chalice,
and the work is to be on view."

"That *is* very interesting," said Mrs. Bradley cordially.
"Shall we all be allowed to see it?"

"Surely we shall! Sister is proud of her work, and
so are we all. We hope to have many visitors. An
expert is being sent from the Victoria and Albert
Museum, and a man is coming from Christie's. Sister
Saint Simon did not expect to finish her work until
Easter, but is very happy to have completed it so soon.
At Easter it will be shown to all the old pupils of the

private school, and we shall put a notice in the paper to let the old orphans know that they are welcome to come and see it, too. It is a better time for noise and rejoicing than now, but as the work is finished, Reverend Mother Superior is willing to have the experts come down to see it. The originals, too, will be on view, so that people can compare them.''

''I suppose you will have the originals carefully guarded?'' said Mrs. Bradley.

''Oh, yes, we shall have the police.''

''That will be rather expensive. How many do you think you will have?''

''Half a dozen, so Reverend Mother thinks. We shall not have to pay. The Chief Constable is going to send them. He does not want a big robbery in his district, so he says!''

She laughed gently and happily, and added:

''Sister Saint Benedict's work will be on view too —those beautiful illuminated pages. And Sister Saint Cyprian's bookbindings. We are fortunate to have so many gifted people.''

''What about Mother Saint Patrick's fruit trees?'' Mrs. Bradley enquired with great solemnity, ''I regard them as no less a work of art, and one in which I had some share.''

''Dear Sister Saint Patrick! She is very proud of the orchard. She told me that you had helped her with the grafting.''

''So did Mary Maslin. We spent Saturday afternoon in handing up twigs for crown-grafting—the older trees, you know. The whip-and-tongue grafting she did by herself, I believe.''

''Like transferring of your blood,'' said Maggie, with horrid relish.

''Bessie offered her blood for transfusion to Sister

Bridget," said Mother Jude, smiling at the remembrance of this kindness. Bessie scowled, and Mrs. Bradley remarked:

"You will never qualify, Bessie, as queen of the gangsters, I fear. Your instincts are purely humanitarian and Christian."

Bessie muttered:

"Garn! You watch my smoke!"

"There is a great deal of good in Bessie," Mother Jude remarked, when all the orphans had gone. Two went on duty to wait at tea on the guests, the others went back to the Orphanage.

"She is all good," Mrs. Bradley replied very firmly. "And a girl of character, withal. If you felt inclined to set her free—so to speak," she added hastily, "—I think I could get her a very good post, and one which she would like."

"It would be a weight off Sister Saint Ambrose's heart," said Mother Jude simply and truthfully. "What is the situation you have in mind?"

"I have a friend who has opened, at her own expense, a small seaside home for poor children. She needs a nursemaid to take the children out and put some of them to bed and wash them, and so forth. It is not exactly domestic service, and I think it would suit Bessie well. She manages people beautifully, and is very sympathetic and kind-hearted."

"I will ask the permission of Reverend Mother Superior. It is kind of you. Bessie is not a good influence here. Our system is not the best for one of her nature."

"And experiences," said Mrs. Bradley, nodding. "I should like to do something for her. She interests me and I admire her."

They parted at the door of the guest-house, Mother

Jude to go to the church, and Mrs. Bradley to write to her friend about Bessie. She read in her room for an hour and a half after that, then bathed and changed for dinner. They called it supper at the convent, but it was always a hot meal, usually soup, fish, meat and a pudding. The oldest orphans cooked it, supervised by Mother Jude and one of the lay-sisters. Two of the orphans also waited at table.

Mrs. Bradley deliberately chose a seat next to Mrs. Maslin.

"I hear you are leaving us," she said. Mrs. Maslin looked annoyed.

"I most certainly am not leaving yet," she said. "There is far too much to do."

Mrs. Bradley could scarcely ask what she meant, and so she filled what might have been a pause in the conversation by remarking:

"I hear that the copies of the chalice and paten are finished."

"Yes, so I heard. I suppose we shall all be expected to go along and admire them," said Mrs. Maslin. "Personally, I don't suppose I shall know the originals from the copies unless they are labelled. Will the new ones look shinier or something? One hates to appear too ignorant, don't you think?"

Mrs. Bradley replied that she scarcely thought there would be any difference in shine, and turned to her other neighbour, a newcomer to the guest-house. Dom Pius had gone back to his monastery, and this man was a diffident, thin-faced Carthusian lay-brother who, from the age of sixteen, had never been out of his monastery until he had been sent to St. Peter's to recuperate after influenza followed by double pneumonia.

"I talked with a man to-day who said he had seen the devil," he said gently. Mrs. Bradley was interested,

and they spent a quarter of an hour discussing such
phenomena, Mrs. Bradley being tenderly corrected
from time to time in her theology by a white-haired
priest on the opposite side of the table.

Mrs. Maslin then drew her attention by saying:

"I hear that you have arranged to send Ulrica to
New York. I happen to know that her grandfather hates
the sight of her. I think, too, that I might have been
consulted before such a step was taken."

"It is a good plan to send her to New York," said
Mrs. Bradley, unperturbed by the waspish tones.
"I had not thought of it."

Mrs. Maslin, rendered more than usually irritable
by this blandness, observed that nothing was going to
be done in a hurry, and that, for her part, she should
be glad to know how the enquiry into Ulrica's death
was going."

"It isn't going. The enquiry is finished," said Mrs.
Bradley. "There is no doubt at all but that *Ursula*
was murdered." She watched the slow red spread over
Mrs. Maslin's face and neck.

"Of course I meant Ursula," she said. Mrs. Bradley
nodded.

"Of course," she said pleasantly. "The names are
somewhat like, and one is apt to become confused in
moments of panic." That the wish is father to the
thought had seldom achieved a more apt exposition,
she thought.

Mrs. Maslin achieved a kind of snort, which she
hoped the company would interpret as a spasm of
grief for her niece, Mrs. Bradley supposed.

"I am taking Mary home at the end of the week,"
said Mrs. Maslin, later on in the meal.

"And you really think the New York idea is a good
one? For Ulrica, I mean."

"I think it's ridiculous!" said Mrs. Maslin, shrilly. "Her grandfather hated her father, and has never seen Ulrica in her life! In any case, my husband must be consulted."

"I feel that Ulrica is a nervous, temperamental girl who is being influenced to her harm by the associations of this place," Mrs. Bradley concluded, "but by all means let your husband know what I propose." She left the table and went in the darkness out of the guest-house, across the grounds and through the orchard to the cloister and the Mother Superior's lodging. She climbed the steps, found the door open and went in. The Mother Superior was at Recreation in the nuns' Common Room and would remain there until she went to night prayers at nine. The little room was pitch-dark. Mrs. Bradley, who always carried a small electric torch, flashed it about to find a chair. It was peaceful in the dark little room, except for the sea, which boomed and thundered restlessly on the other side of the church, and Mrs. Bradley spent a quiet hour, or a little longer, meditating—not, perhaps, precisely after the fashion of the religious—and discovering that, with her work there nearly over, she would be very sorry to leave the convent and more than sorry to give up the society of the nuns. In spite of the nature of her task, the investigation had proved, because of its surroundings, a rest cure, as Célestine had foreseen.

It was nearly ten o'clock when the Mother Superior returned. Mother Mary-Joseph came first, stepped inside and lighted a candle. Mrs. Bradley saw her shadow blocking the doorway, and said:

"I am here, dear child. Is the Reverend Mother Superior coming with you?" For she knew, by the height, that this was not the Reverend Mother. Mother Mary-Joseph lighted the candle and put a small globe round the flame to keep it steady. Then she turned her head, and answered:

"Reverend Mother Superior is just behind me." She went out again to help the old woman up the steps.

"It is Mrs. Bradley, Reverend Mother," she said. Mrs. Bradley did not speak until the aged Superior was seated. Then she said:

"I want to know whether you will allow me to send the girl Ulrica Doyle to my own home for a time. I think she might be better there than here."

"I know. You told us, nearly a week ago, that we ought to send those children away. But Mrs. Maslin still stays, and her stepdaughter with her, and what to do with the other child we have not been able to decide. She has almost always stayed here during vacations. She has no home, and her grandfather in America is her guardian."

"So I understand. Mrs. Maslin must be allowed, I suppose, to do as she pleases with Mary, but I do think that Ulrica must leave, and at my house she would be safe and well looked after. My maid, a Frenchwoman, is a Catholic."

"It is good of you. It seems the best plan, if you are willing to have her. Send her away when you like. We are in your hands. I have been very greatly distressed, and very much mystified. The attack on poor Sister Bridget . . ."

"Unintentional. It was meant for me," said Mrs. Bradley, grinning. She grew serious in the face of the Mother Superior's expression of deep concern.

"My work here is coming to an end, but not in the way the guilty person intends," she said. "I have no proof yet, but soon I shall be able to make clear to whomever it may concern that it is only a question of time before that proof is obtained."

"It is horrible," said the nun. Mrs. Bradley inclined her head.

"I wish I could have come to another conclusion. I wish I could have proved that the death was an accident."

"I do hope we did the best thing in having an enquiry made."

"Do not have any doubts upon that score. At the least it has saved a life—possibly two lives—if that is any comfort to you now."

"I shall not ask you to name the guilty person."

"I will tell you immediately who it is, if you prefer to know, but I am not anxious to do so. One thing I do tell you. We shall manage without the police. So much I am prepared to promise for the sake of everyone here."

"I don't understand." She shook her head. "But you will know best. I shall leave it to you. God will guide you."

A comfortable belief, thought Mrs. Bradley, but one which did not necessarily involve a lightening of personal responsibility. "Pray as though all depended on God; work as though all depended on you," was the way the old priest at table had expressed it. She rose to take her leave, but before she went the Mother Superior said:

"We had hoped that you were going to join us in the Common Room to-night, but I expect you were far too busy. We shall have an immense debt to pay. You are very good to us."

"I should like to come and sit with you all again. By the way, Mother Saint Simon-Zelotes has kindly undertaken to effect the repairs to the picture which was smashed the other evening."

"She is clever. Her copies of our chalice and paten are to be on view—you have heard?"

"Yes; I am immensely interested. How long has it taken her to do them?"

"She has spent about six months on them altogether, and has given all the time she could spare, which, here, with the children to teach, is not very much. She has worked behind double-locked doors and fast-barred windows because of the value of the originals. The Insurance Company insisted upon that."

"Do you ordinarily keep the originals at the bank?"

"Oh, no. We keep them here, very safely locked away. But one of the children, with the best of intentions, I am sure, told her father that the copies were to be made, and so we had several journalists, and some less reputable people, all very anxious to interview Sister Saint Simon. She gave no interviews, but the project had become public property. The Insurance Company were not well pleased when they knew that, but they did not increase our premium. Sister Saint Jude saw the manager."

"You did not fear theft, though, did you? The chalice and paten are too well known, I should have thought, for thieves to take the risk of stealing them, and to sell the melted-down metal would not be worth while."

"Every private collector knows them, and so do all the museums. Nevertheless, there are some private collectors who are really, one supposes, a little mad, and will run any risk to obtain possession of something which they covet."

Mrs. Bradley agreed.

"I like, too, Mother Saint Cyprian's embroidered bookbindings, and Mother Saint Benedict's paintings," she said, to change the direction which the conversation was taking.

"Yes. They are beautiful, both. It is good to use great talents entirely to the glory of God."

"Are not all great talents so used? It seems to me that, whether consciously or not, all good work is done to the glory of God. But, Reverend Mother, I wish you would indulge a whim of mine."

"I will if I can. What is it?"

"When are your experts coming down?"

"On Monday or Tuesday."

"Not to-morrow?"

"No one is coming to-morrow. I thought, as it is a half-holiday, the school-children could see the work then."

"Could they not wait until Wednesday? That also is a half-holiday."

"Yes, they could."

"Will you let me have my own way?"

"Willingly. It cannot make very much difference. I will speak to Sister Saint Simon-Zelotes about it."

"Thank you very much. I have good reason for asking."

"I am sure you have," said the Superior, and blessed her before she let her go.

CHAPTER 17

DISAPPEARANCE

"I then arithmetic suspect
And on the past again reflect.
To number not by days but sins
My soul begins."

THOMAS KEN: Days Numbered.

SATURDAY WAS A FINE BRIGHT MORNING WHICH LATER
turned to rain. Mrs. Bradley interviewed Ulrica Doyle
before morning school, and arranged that she should
be driven to Wandles by George. Ulrica protested,
and demanded to be sent to Mother Francis. Mother
Francis in effect shrugged her shoulders, and Ulrica
went to her first lesson, Geography with Mother
Timothy, in tears.

By half-past eleven it was pouring with rain, and Mrs.
Bradley was loth to allow a message to be taken to
George. He drove over to the convent, however, a
few minutes after twelve, to ask for instructions, and,
while he was waiting, helped Miss Bonnet to change a
wheel, she having punctured the right hand back tyre
on a sharp flint somewhere on the coast road between
Hiversand Bay and the convent. Both got extremely
wet, for the work was done in the open. George was
soaked to the skin by the time he had done. Miss
Bonnet was no better off. Her last class should not
have finished until half-past twelve, but Mother Patrick
and Mother Gregory, who did not happen to teach on

Saturday mornings, and who, therefore, were free to supervise the Physical Training lesson, took charge whilst the wheel of the car was being changed. Owing to the rain, the lesson was in the gymnasium—actually the school hall—and the girls played some games and practised high jumping.

Both Miss Bonnet and George were asked into the guest-house and offered hot baths whilst their clothes were being dried. Miss Bonnet, obviously reminded of the last time she had been offered a bath at the convent, pointed out that she "only had to change"—she was wearing shorts and a blouse, both of which were clinging to her sturdy, well-developed frame whilst runnels of water chased each other down her large, muscular, ugly legs and on to the polished wooden flooring—but George remarked that he would be much obliged. So Mrs. Bradley herself conducted him, under a large umbrella (loaned for the occasion by Mother Francis, who used it on wet days in getting from the school to the refectory), over to the guest-house, and ushered him into a bathroom with orders to cast his clothes outside the door as he took them off so that they could be dried.

George, who was an only child and who was accustomed to be mothered, obeyed with alacrity and cheerfulness, and afterwards was provided with the dressing-gown allotted to penurious infirmary patients, and a spare pair of pants, much darned, provided by the old priest, Father Garnier.

"I suppose you know, madam," he remarked, as, the dressing-gown draped modestly and his wet hair plastered neatly to his head, he presented himself to Mrs. Bradley in the parlour, "that somebody's been and used pipe-grips in that bathroom?"

"But that's not *the* bathroom, George."

"No, madam. There might be such a thing as practice making perfect."

"I looked for indications in both bathrooms that pipe-grips had been used to open a joint, but could find no special indication, beyond the marks that any gas-fitter might leave."

"No gas-fitter left these marks, madam, that I do know. They look inexperienced to me."

"Thank you very much, George. That accounts for the unconscious mouse, at any rate. Are you quite warm? Don't take cold. Ought you to plaster your hair so close to the head?"

George rumpled his hair obediently with a dry towel which Kitty, giggling shyly, came forward and presented.

"He'll be having his clothes back soon, ma'am," she remarked to Mrs. Bradley, avoiding any direct communication by word of mouth with George.

"When they are dry, George, I want you to take a girl from the school back to Wandles," said his employer. "I suppose I had better come with you. The nuns won't care for her to travel alone. It's a nuisance, but cannot be helped. You must bring me back here to-morrow."

"Very good, madam."

The midday meal was served, and George sat down beside Mrs. Bradley. Bessie and Annie waited at table, the former with demure exemplariness, the latter with her usual good sense.

By half-past two George's clothes were dry; by three they were pressed and ready. He was grateful and tried to say so, but Mother Jude cut him short.

"You did good service to poor Miss Bonnet," she said. "She has a special engagement at Kelsorrow School this afternoon. They are having a Parents' Day, and she has to be there to conduct a display of physical training. Sister Saint Francis let her have her last lesson to make the repairs to the car, and she said she would not have been able to get away in time, even then, had she lacked your kind assistance.''

''The young lady hadn't any petrol, either, madam, so I gave her enough to get her twenty-five miles. We found, when we changed the wheel, she'd got a gash like you might expect she'd get if she'd run over an up-ended scythe or something. I've never seen such a gash, bar once, when I was in the States, and a tough slashed a tyre on a hold-up.'' He smiled reminiscently. ''Did I plug that baby!''

''George,'' said Mrs. Bradley, ''you're a marvel.'' She had no time to say more, for the front-door bell rang, and Kitty came in to announce that Sir Ferdinand Lestrange was at the door and would like to speak to his mother. ''Although who in the name of the holy angels *she* is,'' said Kitty, ''unless it would be yourself?''

''It *is* myself,'' said Mrs. Bradley. ''If he's not wet, show him in here.''

''He is only after having walked from his car, and it a large one, up to the door of the house,'' said Kitty, who had the Irish talent for sociability with its resultant liking for conversation at all times.

''Bring him in, then. George, this is luck! Sir Ferdinand can go with you to accompany the girl. That leaves me free to stay here. By the way, I do hope Miss Bonnet got to the school in time. I suppose, George, you *could* pick her up and get her there, even now, if by chance she has broken down again?''

Ferdinand, all smiles, looking even taller than usual by the side of little Mother Jude, came in on the heels of Kitty.

''Come for the week-end, mother,'' he announced.

"Staying at Hiversand Bay to get some golf.   Going back on Tuesday."

"Going back on Saturday afternoon," said Mrs. Bradley austerely.   "And it's no use to grumble, and protest," she added, with a good deal more urbanity. "You dragged me into this affair, and you'll have to help me out."

Nothing would please Mother Jude, made acquainted with all the circumstances, but that Ferdinand should have a meal in the guest-house before he went back to Hiversand Bay to let his friends know about the change in his immediate plans, and off she went to see about it. Mrs. Bradley waited until the door was shut and then drew nearer to her son.

"I want these Doyle and Maslin children got rid of," she said.

"But, mother, where are they to go?"

"You will have to take Ulrica back with you and put her in charge of Célestine at my house in Wandles Parva, dear child, that's all."   She grinned ingratiatingly—a horrible grimace which made him laugh— but she added immediately: "I am serious, Ferdinand. The other child was murdered, and I cannot take any more risks.   It's bad enough that they've been left here so long, and now that Sister Bridget is on the road to recovery—a fact which cannot very well be kept secret since the nuns see no reason for secrecy—I am really and horribly anxious."

"Very well, mother.   I suppose I may come back here to-morrow, when I've unloaded the girl on to Célestine?   And I suppose you can depend upon her to guard the young woman from enemies?"

"I shall write to Célestine and Henri.   I have it on unimpeachable authority that Henri has a veritable gun, and is as good s a gangster."

"Very well. I'll be ready to start as soon as George gets back." George, in obedience to a mysterious summons from Mother Jude, had left them. "There's a telegraph office in the village. I'd better wire Célestine to expect us. I might as well have the solace of eating one of Henri's dinners, since my week-end is to be ruined."

"You are very kind, dear child," his mother fondly replied. She liked him not so much on his own account as because she had liked his father, her first husband. Her son by her second marriage was really the apple of her eye, but he was, most of the time, in India, and she did not see very much of him. He was an authority on tropical diseases, and she had paid for his training, during her second brief widowhood, by writing her famous popular book on hereditary tendencies towards crime. Ferdinand, an unbiassed, entirely self-sufficient man, admired his mother's taste in sons, and fostered what he called "the romantic attachment," playing off the Freudian Oedipus complex against her with a delicate and admirable wit.

A little later Mother Jude appeared, followed by Annie and Kitty, and compelled Ferdinand to sit at table. She gave him two poached eggs for his tea, raspberry jam and some wine, which she insisted was strengthening and perfectly safe, as George, not Ferdinand, would be driving. She delighted Ferdinand, who kept her in conversation whilst Mrs. Bradley went across in the rain to obtain permission to place Ulrica Doyle in his charge on the journey to Wandles.

The Mother Superior listened sympathetically, and gave the required permission more readily than Mrs. Bradley had expected.

"I myself will speak to Sister Saint Francis," she said. "Do you get the child to ask Sister Genevieve to pack such things as are required. What of the other little one, I wonder? Do you suppose she is safe?"

"She is in the care of her stepmother," Mrs. Bradley replied.

"By the mercy of God, lay-sister Bridget is going to get well, the doctor tells me," the Mother Superior continued. "By the way, I have been wondering why you were perfectly sure that she was attacked in mistake for you. Now I should have thought that she could only have been mistaken for one of the religious."

"Not one of the religious."

"But the habit—and in the darkness——"

"Sister Bridget was not in her habit when she was attacked."

"But—of course, poor soul, she is not responsible. I had not understood, though, that she was not fully habited."

"Had you not? She had put on her nightdress over all her underclothes. The fire in her room was started to get the occupant running out into the open. Of that I am fairly certain."

"How truly dreadful this is! You do not think, then, that Sister Bridget herself set light accidentally to her bed?"

"No, I don't think she did. When we have the children safe I shall investigate. The room remains locked for the present, so that if any evidence is there I shall expect to find it—probably on Monday."

She went to the boarders' playroom to find Ulrica Doyle, and discovered her playing chess with an oval-faced child of eleven whose father, a Spaniard, was a master of the game.

"I give up and retire," Ulrica was saying as Mrs. Bradley came in. Both girls got up and curtsied at her entrance, and Ulrica gravely introduced her companion.

"This is Maria Gartez, Mrs. Bradley. She always beats me at chess, as you can see."

"Ulrica is good at chess," the Spanish child answered, "but I play like my father—very well."

"You are to find Sister Genevieve, Ulrica," said Mrs. Bradley, "and ask her to pack a suitcase for you. Your school holidays have begun a little earlier than usual. I have permission for you to go and stay at my house."

The girl looked at her with a mixture of amusement and defiance in her eyes, and said immediately: "I want some money to cable to my grandfather in New York. Will you lend it to me, please?"

"Yes, on Monday," Mrs. Bradley promised.

"And am I really to be taken away from here?"

"I am afraid so, yes. It may not be for very long."

"May I go and say good-bye to Mary? I suppose my aunt will take her away on Monday? I suppose we are both to go?"

"I suppose so, yes."

"Will you let me come back as soon as they find out who did it?"

"Did what?"

"Hit Sister Bridget on the head, and killed poor little Ursula."

"But it may not be the same person who did both."

"Oh, I should think it must be." She turned, in her grave and courteous way, to the other child. "Good-bye, dear Maria," she said. "God bless you and all your family. I shall see you again very soon."

She sauntered out, but turned at the door and came back to Mrs. Bradley.

"Where would you like me to meet you with my suitcase?" she asked, with another sketchy little curtsy.

"At the entrance gate, I should think. I will send my

chauffeur to receive the case from Sister Genevieve.
Where, I wonder, should he wait?"

"At the entrance to the nuns' garden. That will not
be very far for us to carry the suitcase. It need not be
heavy. I shall soon be coming back here, I expect. I
do not wish to go away, and shall cable my grandfather
so, and request his permission to return. I am not at
all convinced that he would approve of my staying with
strangers, but I know that it is being done for what you
all imagine must be the best."

So saying, she left them. The Spanish child raised her
eyebrows, gave Mrs. Bradley a pensive little smile, and
remarked, as though to herself: "*Ella tiene dolor de
cabeza.*"[1]

"I am not surprised," Mrs. Bradley said. "She
carries it off very bravely, but she must be having a
very worrying time."

"She is troubled since the death of the little
cousin."

"Yes. She looks strained and ill."

"She is ill. She is never like this, so not polite.
You must please to forgive her this time."

"I do not regard her as not polite. I do not think of
it that way. She has protested, as she has the right to do,
against being taken away."

Before they could say any more, Ulrica herself came
back.

"I cannot find Mary to say good-bye," she said. "If
she should come in here whilst I am packing, dear
Maria, ask her to wait, or come up to my cell, if you
please."

"Cell?" said Mrs. Bradley, when Ulrica had disappeared again.

"She has hopes of entering the religious life," Maria

---

[1] She has a headache.

reminded her. "*Más valdría no decir nada más,*"[1] she added, glancing towards the door.

"Possibly you are right," Mrs. Bradley agreed, so they said no more, and Mrs. Bradley, sitting on the floor where Ulrica had sat, and brooding over the chessboard like a crumpled bird of prey, waved a skinny claw to invite the black-haired child to continue the game which Ulrica had abandoned.

Nearly an hour later, Ulrica came down, not expecting, it was obvious, to discover Mrs. Bradley still there. She watched in absolute silence, while Mrs. Bradley moved on slowly to victory. Then she gave a little sigh, and the victor and the vanquished both looked up.

"This lady could beat my father," said the Spanish child, picking up a castle in slender, olive-brown fingers. Ulrica nodded, and asked:

"Did she continue the game from the point at which I left it?"

"Yes, she did, and you left it at very bad," Mrs. Bradley's opponent observed with considerable candour.

"Sister Genevieve has taken my suitcase to the top of the stairs, and Bessie is coming to carry it out to your chauffeur," said Ulrica, smiling to show that she felt no resentment of Maria's frank opinion.

In less than a quarter of an hour, she and Ferdinand had been driven away by George from the convent guest-house. George had just returned with a report of having seen Miss Bonnet's car in the grounds of Kelsorrow School.

Mrs. Bradley and Bessie watched Ferdinand, George and Ulrica out of sight, then turned to one another with the mutual congratulation of those who are left behind while others take themselves off. Bessie even wiped her hands on her apron. Her opinion of Ulrica Doyle was soon made clear.

[1] It would be better not to say anything more.

"Snitchy little tripe-hound," she observed. "Don't half fancy herself, I reckon. Ask *me*, she knowed what she was doing when t'other poor nipper conked out."

"I fear that your remark is highly actionable, dear child," said Mrs. Bradley, in gently remonstrative tones. Bessie grinned and spat. Then she said good night, and watched, bright-eyed, whilst Mrs. Bradley re-entered the guest-house doorway. She herself returned to the Orphanage for supper, which consisted of thick bread and butter, milk pudding and cocoa. It was greatly relished by the orphans, and got finished to the very last crumb; this to the perennial mystification of Mother Ambrose, who could not understand how children could be so hungry when, not many hours before, they had made a generous tea.

Mrs. Bradley, with the comfortable feeling of a job well done, went across to soothe Mother Francis, who so far had not been notified of Ulrica Doyle's departure. Mother Francis, looked greatly concerned, almost ran to meet her, and told her a long involved story, the gist of which was that Mary Maslin could not be found on the building, and had not been seen since just after a quarter past three.

"And if only I had listened to you," said Mother Francis, with all the disarming humility of her profession, "I should not have caused myself all this terrible new anxiety. I ought to have insisted that both the children were sent away when you said."

Mrs. Bradley took out a notebook, and asked for all the information which Mother Francis could give.

"Thank God we have got the other child away!" Mother Francis exclaimed more than once in the course of her detailed narration. Mrs. Bradley, longing to dispense with some of the conversation and get to work, had a sudden uneasy recollection of an hour she had

spent playing chess whilst Ulrica Doyle was supposed to
be packing a suitcase.

Mary, it appeared, had been well on the previous day,
when Mother Cyprian went in to take the needlework at
half-past two.   She had answered her name and, later
(perhaps at ten to three, Mother Cyprian thought), she
had had her work criticised and was shown how to do a
false hem.

And no false hem would have been necessary, Mother
Cyprian had reiterated, if only Mary were not such a
stupid girl.   Even over needlework she was stupid, than
which there could not be a pleasanter, easier subject, or
one which was in every way more suited to a young girl's
mentality.

This cry from the heart Mrs. Bradley was obliged to
receive in full from Mother Francis, who, weighed down,
apparently equally, by worry and humility, had lost the
faculty for selection, and let Mrs. Bradley have all the
material at her disposal in one great tangled muddle of
fact, opinion and emotion.

"And you, my dear friend," she finished up, almost in
tears, "you warned me, and still I would not listen!"

"But what makes you refer the matter back to yesterday afternoon, when the child did not disappear until
to-day?" Mrs. Bradley enquired.   Mother Francis threw
up her hands in a frankly Gallic gesture of despair.

"She was sick!   She was sick!   I fear the poor
innocent young girl has been poisoned!" she said, and
went on to make good her words in a mixture of French
and English which was not very easy to follow.

CHAPTER 18

SEARCH

*"That weary deserts we may tread
A dreary labyrinth may thread
Through dark way underground be led."*

RICHARD CHENEVIX TRENCH: The Kingdom
of God.

MRS. BRADLEY, ARMED WITH ALL THE FACTS THAT WERE known, quickly organised a search. The child had been taken ill on the previous afternoon at just after a quarter past three, because as soon as the form had had their afternoon break at the end of Mother Cyprian's lesson, Mary, according to the evidence of certain members of the class, had complained of feeling sick, and had gone off alone, refusing the comradely help and companionship usually given to one another by schoolgirls under these circumstances, and they had not seen her again that afternoon.

Two of them had made a tour of the water closets towards the end of break, but those within had all announced their identity, and Mary, it seemed, had concluded her attempts at being sick—'she *wasn't* sick,' they announced unanimously (this was the sort of information which, in a form of twelve-year-olds, could be relied on, Mrs. Bradley knew, for accuracy, and is always common property), 'but she'd certainly come out before we called to her, because everyone else inside answered.'

Mother Francis was sufficiently overcome by the shock

243

of Mary's disappearance to be incapable of delivering even
the mildest homily upon the indelicacy of these proceedings, and received all the tidings with a curt nod and an
order to 'go to your places and get *straight on* with your
extra preparation, and do not let me hear *another word.*'

This display of Old Adam had had the effect of crushing
an incipient outbreak of general conversation, and,
prompted by Mrs. Bradley, Mother Francis continued
the exposition, but would not be hurried into missing
out the smallest fact or most unimportant opinion.

After break, Mary's form had gone to Mother Mary-
Joseph for an English lesson, and here Mary Maslin
had not appeared at all. An excuse had been brought by
a girl named Ryan—Nancy Ryan—aged twelve. All she
had said was that Mary felt sick, and would come into
class as soon as she possibly could. Nobody added that
Mary's whereabouts at the time that the lesson began
were unknown to the rest of the form, and Mother
Mary-Joseph—very pale when Mrs. Bradley interviewed
her—admitted that she had forgotten the child and had
not sent out during the lesson to find out how she was.

"The children should have said something—little
donkeys!" said Mother Francis, in a pardonable burst of
asperity.

Mary, moreover, had not turned up at tea, had notified
nobody of what she had been doing in the meantime,
but had been sick twice during the night. She had gone
into Saturday school—French with Mother Dominic,
English with Mother Mary-Joseph (who asked her
whether she felt better), and Geography with Mother
Timothy. She had appeared at lunch, but had eaten
without much appetite, and then had gone off with
Nancy Ryan and some others of the day-girls, to play in
the junior dayroom. She had not been seen since.

Unfortunately Nancy Ryan was a day-girl, but five

of the boarders were girls in Mary's form, and the first thing Mrs. Bradley did, after having set in motion a search of the buildings and grounds—nobody to lose touch with the rest of her search party, and no search party to number fewer than four people—was to interview separately all these girls. They could tell her no more than Mother Francis had already found out. They had heard Nancy Ryan give Friday's message to Mother Mary-Joseph, and they had not been surprised when Mary Maslin did not appear at Friday tea. They assumed that she had gone to bed because she did not feel well, and had said so to Mother Cyprian, whose duty it was that day to supervise the boarders at table.

Mother Cyprian had paid very little attention, as she readily admitted. She was not the Infirmarian, and she had supposed that the child was being properly cared for. She had gone off to church at the usual time, and the boarders had enjoyed recreation. One girl, named Cynthia Parks, had broken rules, however, by sneaking up to the dormitory and peeping into Mary Maslin's cubicle. She came down and told the others that Mary was not there. When preparation time came, and Mother Timothy, on duty that evening, saw and commented on Mary's empty place, they told her that Mary had not been well, and Mother Timothy had taken it for granted that the child had been ordered to bed. She actually *was* in bed when the others all went upstairs, and then had been sick, but not violently so, twice during the night, and had been attended to by Mother Patrick, whose turn it was on duty in that dorter.

Mrs. Bradley could understand Mother Francis' panic-stricken insistence upon the events of the previous day, but they seemed to her to have very little bearing upon the fact of the disappearance. She tried to get further information from the children, but it was not long before it became obvious that they all knew no more than they had said. She abandoned the interrogation, divided the boarders into five groups, and ordered a further extensive search of the house and grounds.

She herself tiptoed up the stairs to the children's sleeping quarters. These had been a couple of very large rooms, but extra windows had been made, and these, together with thin wooden partitions and curtains, had made it possible to convert them into a dozen separate cubicles, each with half of a window for light and ventilation.

"Which is Mary's?" Mrs. Bradley enquired. The Spanish girl, Maria Gartez, who, unbidden but overlooked, had attached herself to Mrs. Bradley, stepped forward and pointed to one of the curtained archways. Mrs. Bradley went in, but the narrow bed was empty.

About a hundred and fifty different thoughts had been passing through Mrs. Bradley's mind. Two were paramount, and demanded most of her attention. One was common to all the searchers, both nuns and children: the highly dangerous nature of the purlieus of the convent: the high, steep cliffs; the rocks below; the sea; the wild moor; the wilder forest which encroached on it; the bogs, the pits, the paths that ended nowhere, the labyrinthine tracks through gorse and down steep gullies. The second thought, which was possibly hers alone, was that in all probability Ulrica Doyle had known, before she left, of her cousin's disappearance. True, she had been to look for her, so that she could bid her good-bye, but it seemed incredible that, missing her in her usual haunts, she had not enquired of the members of her form to know where she might be found; and if she had done this, she must have learned of her disappearance from the recreation room during the second part of the afternoon. She probably knew, too, of her cousin's illness of the previous afternoon and night, and ought to have made some attempt to find out how she was, and whether she had gone to bed again.

She turned to Maria Gartez.

"Did Ulrica know that Mary was lost?" she demanded.

"She said that somebody told her her cousin had been ill," said Maria. "She went to find her directly after tea."

"*Did* she find her?"

"I did not ask. We played chess."

"Yes, I know you did. What did she say when she came back?"

"I think she said: 'You have the board ready. I will have black. Black will win.' I do not remember anything else that she said."

"So you settled down to play, and were still playing when I found you?"

"Yes. It was almost time to go to preparation when you came. I was very glad you came. I do not like preparation."

"I see. You ought to have been at preparation whilst you were playing with me?"

"Yes. Ulrica had an excuse. She was to get ready to depart. I made it an excuse to play with you. Thank you very much for a very enjoyable game." She curtsied. Her dark eyes were grave. She seemed perfectly serious.

"And she didn't say a word about her cousin?"

"No. But about the board."

"I see. Thank you, Maria. That is all."

The Spanish child curtsied and, this time, went away. Meanwhile the Mother Superior had sent Sister Genevieve, the boarders' matron, and Sister Lucia, the assistant Infirmarian, for the police. They were to walk

across the moor to the village and to telephone to Kelsorrow from there.   They were not to use the guest-
house telephone for fear of alarming the stepmother of
the child.

Pending the arrival of the police, other search parties
were   formed.   Reverend   Mother   Superior   herself
went into the boarders' dormitory to do night-duty, and
the older nuns and lay-sisters Catherine and Magdalene
were left behind.   Old Sister Catherine, they thought,
could not help in any way; Sister Magdalene was to open
the convent gate to the police and explain to them, more
fully than could be done in a telephone call, exactly
what had happened.

Then   one   party   headed   by   Mother   Benedict and
including   Mrs.   Bradley,   and   the   other   headed   by
Mother Simon-Zelotes and including Mother Francis,
set out to search the neighbourhood.   Mrs. Bradley's
party carried the convent handbells, five in all, and the
other party had whistles used in games periods.   It was
expected that enough noise would be made to keep the
searchers in touch with one another and to warn the
missing child of the approach of friends if she had
wandered away and got lost.   Mrs. Bradley had her
electric torch and two spare batteries, and Mother
Benedict carried a hurricane lamp.   The others in their
party, following two by two as long as the nature of the
country allowed of this conventual method of progress,
were absolutely silent.   They were to explore the cliff-
top and the sea-shore, and Mrs. Bradley wondered, as
she led the way with Mother Benedict, whether theirs
or that of the other party, who were to comb the
heights and hollows of the moorland, was the more
unpleasant and dangerous task.

Soon it became impracticable to continue in the close
and unproductive formation of the crocodile, and so,

obeying orders, the searchers spread, half of them circling round Mrs. Bradley and her torch, the rest with Mother Benedict and her lamp.

Apart from almost frightening a tramp to death, their search of the cliff-top in the direction of Hiversand Bay had no result whatever. They went back along the path until they came to a place where steps had been cut to make a descent to the beach. Here the two groups separated completely, Mrs. Bradley and her followers to go down to the shore, the others to continue the search along the cliffs and to try the opposite direction.

All were tired but unflagging, and Mrs. Bradley, not for the first time, admired without stint the soldierly courage and cheerfulness of the religious, as, impeded, one would suppose, by their habits, stumbling often in the unevenness of the way, they carried out the thorough, patient search. The thought in her own mind was that all her theories had been false; that the mysteries bore another character from that with which she had been crediting them, and that Mary Maslin was dead, and through her negligence.

She could hear Mother Benedict praying as they went down the dangerous path, not for her own safety— although, in that wild search, and in the darkness, all of them risked their lives—but for the health, life and safety of the child.

The path kept turning on itself in sharp-angled bends. The steps were unevenly cut and were slippery with rain. Twice Mrs. Bradley saved Mother Benedict from falling, and twice Mother Benedict saved her. The sound of the sea grew louder. A table of tides had indicated that they would reach the shore on an outgoing tide, and soon they were walking on shingle and stumbling on great heaps of seaweed, wet, salt and sticky, and of hideous, fishy fleshiness, left high by the out-going sea.

The sea boomed on the rocks which it was gradually uncovering. They could see them as they approached— great black shapes like leviathans sleeping in the waters, up to the buttocks in the brine which leapt at their heads and fell back, foaming and streaming. Even by night the sky was pale above the water, but the towering cliffs shut out the heavens to the south, for the convent faced north to the sea, owing to the shape of the bay on which it was built.

Clanging their bells like lepers warning the unspotted, or like those in charge of the "dead cart" in time of plague, the untidy little procession, weary, wet-footed, wet-skirted, muddy and hoarse—for they called the child's name in addition to ringing the bells—walked for four miles up the coast, until they were two miles beyond the convent. Here the cliff was lower, and farther on it disappeared in sand-dunes covered with rough, spiked grass. Their shoes were full of sand, and they sat down as soon as they came to firm ground, and shook out the sand before they continued their journey. About a mile farther on, they heard the sound of a bicycle bell. Its continuous ringing attracted their attention. It was to bring them news that the child was found. The young policeman who was riding the bicycle got off and walked back with them to the convent. They were almost too tired to rejoice. Nothing more could be done that night. Those who had been left in charge at the convent had food and hot drinks ready for the searchers, and the Reverend Mother Superior put everyone under obedience to eat and drink.

The child had been put to bed. The police had arrived in time to round up the searchers. The story,

said Reverend Mother, must wait for the telling until
morning.

Mrs. Bradley, whose constitution was of iron,
nevertheless felt glad at the thought of bed. She
protested against being escorted by Mother Ambrose
and Mother Jude to the guest-house, but, tired as they
were, they would not leave her until she reached the
front door. In she went, and was asleep as soon as she
lay down.

In the morning she heard from Mother Francis the
story of the finding of the child. The second search
party had set off across the mile and a half of moorland
which led to the village. It had been rough, uneasy
going in the darkness, and they had no idea whether the
child, supposing she had crossed the moor, had travelled
east, west or south. Willing to obtain any help which
might be forthcoming, the nuns had asked for assistance
from the villagers, and a number of men had joined in
the search, for the village of Blacklock Tor was not the
home of the youths who had attacked the convent after
the death of Ursula Doyle. Some had made their way
to the big pond known as Larn Bottom, on the south
side of the village about two miles away from the inn,
in case the child had got drowned.

Whilst the search was thus progressing, the police
had arrived at the convent and had asked a good many
questions. Old Sister Catherine, however, had been
thinking matters over in the ruminating manner of the
aged, and, just before they arrived, had asked Reverend
Mother's permission to call upon the people who lived
in the two private houses adjoining the convent grounds.
So she, accompanied by old Mother Bartholomew,
called upon the builder who lived next door to the
guest-house (which he himself had put up in the form,
at first, of three private houses, making a row of five)

and straightway proved herself to be the most sagacious of all the people who desired the child's safety and well-being. She said to the man:

"Have you seen our little girl who ran away?"

"Sure," replied the man. "She had a nasty fall, and mother put her to bed and we telephoned the doctor. We dropped you a note in the door, and been expecting somebody over ever since tea. Didn't know how you was placed, but made sure she'd be missed before this."

Mrs. Bradley, in the morning, in conversation with Mother Francis, said:

"But what happened to the note that they sent?"

"It was found in the guest-house letter-box by Annie, and as it was not addressed to anyone, but bore the superscription, 'Urgent,' she put it on Sister Saint Jude's desk for her to see directly she came over from the convent kitchen. But the postman, later, called with a pile of accounts, and these were placed on top. Sister Saint Jude's habit is to deal with all her business correspondence in the morning immediately after church, so, of course, we did not find the man's note because it was hidden."

"And where is Mary Maslin now? In bed still, I suppose?"

"In the infirmary, yes. The doctor had said she could be moved if someone was there to carry her. She is not very badly hurt, but is suffering, the doctor thinks, from shock. Apparently she fell off the roof."

"I wish you would let me have a short talk with Sister Catherine."

Sister Catherine talked to Mrs. Bradley in the nuns' parlour, a small, bare chamber more like a dentist's waiting-room than anything else that Mrs. Bradley could think of, except that there were no magazines, and that a crucifix, very large, and carved with Spanish care for sadistic detail, hung on the high east wall.

"What I said to myself was: 'They're all alike,' " old Sister Catherine began. "They *will* do it. What one will do, another will do, just like sheep, as Our Lord knew, too."

She nodded and mumbled, and looked at Mrs. Bradley with a kind of good-humoured craftiness. "I've seen them! I've seen them! I know!"

"On the roof?"

"On the roof. And I've said to myself: 'She'll fall!' But the tricks these children get up to nowadays remind me of the time when I was a very young girl, and *he* climbed the balcony railings. Nearly seventy years ago, that was; and he was killed in battle, and so I came to the convent." She appeared to have fallen into a dream, and after a minute or two Mrs. Bradley roused her again with a gentle question.

"When did you last see somebody on the roof?"

"Not very long ago; no, not *very* long ago." She could not wrinkle her brow, for all her earthy old face was a network of wrinkles already, but her rheumy eyes became vacant in concentrated thought. She shook her head slowly, and smiled, a toothless, happy smile of great serenity. "No, I'm a stupid old creature. I can't remember. I know that when I heard of the other poor little one I said to myself: 'And lucky not to have broken her neck.' That's what I said to myself."

"That child would have been about the size of this one?"

"No, no, bigger. One of the older girls, surely."

"Was she dressed for climbing on roofs?"

"She was dressed as they dress for their drill, in a short tunic of grey serge and the scarlet girdle. When I was a girl we should have been whipped for appearing

in public like that. But times change, and perhaps it's
all for the best.''

This time Mrs. Bradley did not interrupt the old lay-
sister's thoughts, and they sat in companionable silence
until Sister Lucia, the assistant Infirmarian, came in to
tell Mrs. Bradley that the child was awake, had break-
fasted, seemed much better, and, in short, with the
doctor's permission, could be interviewed.

Mrs. Bradley walked from the parlour to the infirmary,
which was on the top floor of the Orphanage. The
spring morning was windy, with bright sunshine except
when, at intervals, the fast-moving clouds obscured for
a moment the sun. The nuns' garden was sheltered by
its hedges and high wall, and in it the early daffodils
were already in flower, and there were the last of the
crocuses at the base of trees, among the grass, and the
trim borders were brilliant with anemones of all
imaginable colours.

The fruit trees in the orchard showed traces of
Mother Patrick's labours. Bulges of clay on the crown-
grafted ancient trees, and neat criss-cross of bast on the
younger ones, which had been tongue-grafted with
delicate, precise insertions in T-shaped incisions,
proved that her leisure had been employed as pleased
her best. Mrs. Bradley nodded, reviewing her own
assistance in these labours.

CHAPTER 19

CULPRIT

"I leave the plain, I climb the height;
No branchy thicket shelter yields;
But blessed forms in whistling storms
Fly o'er waste fens and windy fields."

ALFRED, LORD TENNYSON: Ode on the Death
of the Duke of Wellington.

THE INFIRMARY, A LARGE, CHEERFUL ROOM WITH A view seawards which was partly blocked by the church, was, when Mrs. Bradley arrived, in the charge of Mother Mary-Joseph, who sat in a corner and, as it was Sunday, sedulously read from a book of religious character; what it was Mrs. Bradley did not know. She was seated out of earshot of any conversation which might be held between Mrs. Bradley and the child, and she kept this distance away all the time that Mrs. Bradley was there.

Mary looked pale, more from fear of getting into trouble than from the consequences of the fall, Mrs. Bradley thought. She greeted her cheerfully, whereupon the child burst into tears. This reaction, in one so obviously phlegmatic, provoked Mrs. Bradley's interest.

"Come, now," she said, with brisk kindness. "That's enough of that. You and I must not waste each other's time. What were you up to yesterday?"

"I thought I had a clue."

"What about?"

"About Ursula."

"Tell me."

"Ulrica always thought that Ursula was murdered. It frightened me at first, but then I saw that Ulrica was also horribly frightened, and I asked her why, and she said that she supposed she would be the next one, and she didn't want to die with her sins upon her. She isn't a Catholic yet, you know. She was sure she was going to be murdered."

"Rubbish. Accidents will happen," said Mrs. Bradley.

"Yes, I know. But this was no accident. I found that out last night. Any more than poor Sister Bridget was an accident."

"Sister Bridget," said Mrs. Bradley, who knew that the children had heard nothing definite beyond what the first spate of gossip had washed down to the schoolgirls at the very beginning of the affair, "had a nasty experience, and is lucky to be on the way to recovering from it. She is not quite responsible for her actions, as I think we all know, and things may happen to her which would not happen to others who are better able to take care of themselves."

"But they said she was hit on the head," said Mary, rightly disregarding this conventional and insincere explanation.

"Of course she was," Mrs. Bradley vigorously answered. "If people rush about the place at night as though they are burglars, naturally they get hit on the head if the people in charge have anything to hit them with."

"No one confessed to hitting her, though," said Mary, with irritating logic.

"Naturally not, since she nearly died of the blow," said Mrs. Bradley tartly.

"But——"

Mrs. Bradley, who had had considerable experience of adolescents who said: "But," decided to change the subject.

"You haven't told me your clue yet," she remarked.

"Oh, that! Well, I soon realised that things were more dangerous for Ulrica than for me, and, when I thought that, I cheered up quite a lot, because, you see, if it *was* the money, I can't get any until Ulrica is dead— I don't mean that to sound horrid; it's just common sense. So I decided to do a bit of snooping."

"Do a ——" said Mrs. Bradley, the accusing spectacle of Mother Mary-Joseph, teacher of English, there in the corner of the infirmary and immediately before her eyes.

"Oh, you know—snooping. Like detectives do. I thought perhaps the others had missed something that I might discover, and I thought how lovely that would be."

"Yes?"

"Oh, yes. Well, we're never allowed in the guest-house unless one of the guests invites us, so I made up my mind—I say, you won't have to tell Mother Francis this?—to get into the guest-house somehow and have a look at that bathroom—*only*—I didn't know, you see, which bathroom it was. That had to be found out first."

"And what were your plans for getting into the guest-house?"

"Well, Ursula managed it, didn't she? And she never broke any rules, as far as anyone knew. I thought there must be an easy way in, and it only needed finding."

"Now this," said Mrs. Bradley, "is what I've felt all

along was the very nub of the matter. She never broke
any rules, yet she broke one of the strictest rules of all.
I understand from the nuns that it is only the most
hardened offenders who ever dream of breaking into the
guest-house.''

"The last girl who did it was expelled."

"Were you willing to risk expulsion?"

"Oh, I shouldn't have minded in a way, as soon as the
row was over. Of course, I wouldn't in the ordinary
way want to leave the convent, but mother has been
such a beast about taking me away in any case, that it
didn't seem to matter in quite the same way. And
whether I am expelled or not, I am going to be taken
straight out to my grandfather in New York."

"Why is that?"

"Mother thinks he would like me better than Ursula
or Ulrica, if he saw me, because Ursula was a bit
mousy, and Ulrica really is rather fascinating, and, of
course, most awfully clever, but *I'm* decidedly stupid,
and as grandfather seems a bit stupid, too, mother—she
isn't my mother really, of course, she's only my step,
and I'm *not*, as a matter of fact, too terribly keen——''

"And as grandfather also seems a bit stupid," said
Mrs. Bradley, gently.

"Oh, yes. Mother thought he might like me a good
deal better than either of them, and give me the money
after all. It seems beastly to talk like this, but you do
want to know it all, don't you?"

"One moment," said Mrs. Bradley. She wrote in
her little notebook, the pencil that described her
hieroglyphic shorthand flicking over the pages like a
whip of silver fire.

"When did you know that your parents proposed to
take you to New York to visit your grandfather!" she
enquired.

"Oh, days! It was one of the first things mother mentioned when she got here."

"And how many people have you told?"

"Oh, dozens. Simply everybody, by now."

"And what made you sick on Friday?"

"I don't really know."

"Did you eat anything out of the ordinary?"

"No, but I don't like fat, and I had an awful lot on my plate at dinner, and, of course, we have to eat everything on the plate. I rather expect it was that."

"Why can't you see your grandfather during the summer vacation?"

"He goes away himself. Anyway, he wouldn't want us then. He says it's too hot in the summer to be pestered with friends and relations."

Mrs. Bradley could not regard this as a personal idiosyncrasy.

"I daresay he does. A good many people think the same. What does your father think about the trip to New York?"

"Daddy says while he pays school fees I'm to take advantage of them. It's mother who's always croaking about New York. All the same, I believe he's just as keen as she is. He'd love me to have the money, naturally."

"And it is your stepmother who is so much concerned about Ursula's death?"

"Yes, of course she is. She doesn't want anything to go wrong about the will. I don't understand what she means by that. You could ask her about it if you liked."

"I intend to do so. Well, did you manage to get yourself into the guest-house?"

"No."

"No?"

"I funked it. Oh, I did! I know it sounds awful, but you don't know *what* Mother Saint Francis and Mother Saint Patrick can be like. Mother Saint Patrick is my form-mistress, and I really believe she's worse than Mother Saint Francis, and Mother Saint Francis once made a girl cry two whole days on end. I couldn't explain how she does it, but she does."

Mrs. Bradley could believe this, and came back to the previous evening's exploit.

"Well, what about the guest-house?"

"I got an anonymous letter."

"What?"

"You know—those letters people write and don't put their name at the bottom. We had a poem like it, and Mother Mary-Joseph asked us why there wasn't a name at the bottom, and Rosalie Waters—always very cheeky—she's had three Major Penances from different people already this term—said, straight away, 'I suppose he must be ashamed of it.' Well, that might be true about some anonymous letters, I should think."

"What did the letter say? Have you kept it, by any chance?"

"No. It said to destroy it, so I did. I pulled the chain on it."

"A pity. It might, in itself, have been a clue."

"Oh, dear. I didn't think. It said: 'To-night keep your eye on Bessie at the Orphanage' and 'Orphanage' was spelt wrongly, I think, but I'm not too sure, because my own spelling's rather shaky."

"And is that what you were doing—keeping your eye on Bessie?"

"Oh, no! Do you read detective stories? We are not allowed them here, but at home I read a great many. I thought the letter was probably a blind. So I pretended to be keeping an eye on Bessie, but all the time I was

trying to make out whether anybody had an eye on
me."

"But was not that a frightening idea?"

"No. I thought of Ulrica. She'd got to have an
accident first, you see."

"I admire your ghoulish intelligence, but listen to
me: I want you not to take it upon yourself to do any
more of this snooping. It isn't really very safe."

"No, it isn't really. I got on to the roof of the guest-
house, and I *could* have got into the bathroom, but
didn't dare. And then I couldn't get down."

"Lost your nerve, I suppose, in the dark?"

"Yes, I did. I believe anybody would have. And I
thought I saw somebody lurking."

"Bessie's young man, I daresay."

"The orphans don't have young men! It isn't
allowed."

"Sometimes they have them," said Mrs. Bradley, with
a pleasant recollection of the carton of cream and the
rose. "Promise me, please, that you won't do any more
snooping by yourself."

"Very well, then. I'm glad you've made me,
because now I can't break the promise, and really I
didn't want to do any more hunting for clues. If I
hadn't fallen off the roof of the first private house,
though, and been helped by a gentleman who lives there,
I think I should have found out quite a lot. But I came
over sick again, and lost my hold, and crashed."

"Oh, yes. The private houses," said Mrs. Bradley.
She did not want to bring them any further into the
affairs of the convent if she could help it, but she
reflected that they might have information on various
points which the convent did not possess. There were
only two of them, and in time, she supposed, the
convent would absorb them into its guest-house just

as it had absorbed the other three which the friendly speculative builder had put up.

"So the gentleman helped you up?"

"Well, really, you know, I'd hurt myself. He picked me up, and then I got a sort of a clue, after all."

"No!"

"Oh, yes. He said: 'And how many more of you wretched kids am I going to spot on the roof?'

"I said: 'I'm terribly sorry. I slipped, and then I rolled. But I didn't know that anybody else had ever been on the roof.' I didn't like to ask him when it was, but it sounds like Ursula, doesn't it? You *can* get into that bathroom from the roof, because that's the way the girl who was expelled from school got in, only *she* was caught by Mother Saint Jude, and Mother Saint Jude was *terribly* upset at having to take her over to Mother Saint Francis, but she felt she had to, because the rule is so strict."

"You said that you received an anonymous letter. Have you no idea at all who might have sent it?"

"You know how the nuns write? Well, it was just like that. But all the girls can do it. It's very easy."

"What about your clothes?"

"A fearful mess. I daren't think what Sister Genevieve's going to say. Do you think that she'll report me?"

"I really have no idea. Did your stockings get torn?"

"Oh, yes. I took the skin off all down the side of my leg, and, of course, the stocking tore away too. And the roof is so terribly *dirty*. I got simply smothered in soot. Luckily I had my black overall on, and not my grey school tunic!"

"By the way, how did you manage to get on to the roof?"

"Oh, the man in the end house had a ladder already

up. He was doing some painting of the guttering. It was just light enough for me to carry, so, as soon as it was dark, I dragged it along and got up it. But I hadn't got to the guest-house after all, but only to the second of the private houses. Oh, dear! I *have* got bruises!''

"But, look here," said Mrs. Bradley, speaking sternly, "there's more in this than you've told me. Let's go over it again."

"No, please, I'd rather not. I shall only get into trouble as it is! I've told you all I can. I can't get other people into a mess."

"Do you mean Nancy Ryan?"

"Well, not only Nancy."

"Mary," said Mrs. Bradley, "don't be silly. What did you do on Friday between a quarter past three and bed-time?"

"I felt ill, and went up to bed."

"You were not in bed when Cynthia Parks went to look."

"I expect I was being sick again just then."

"Did you go into Preparation on Friday evening?"

"No. I went back to bed. I was sick twice in the night, you know."

"Why?"

"Well——"

"Why?"

"I ate soap."

"We're coming to it at last," said Mrs. Bradley. "All right, Mary. Don't begin to cry. You thought you were poisoned, didn't you? And now, what made you think that?"

"Ulrica gave me some sweets."

"Ulrica? Where did she get them?"

"She said that Mother Saint Gregory had given them to her. They were a kind of dark, awful yellow—very sinister. They tasted perfectly horrid, and I was nervous—because of Ursula, you know."

"Have you any of them left?"

"Yes, one."

"Good girl. Where is it?"

"In my needlework bag. It's collected up in Mother Saint Cyprian's cupboard. I'll get it for you next needlework lesson if you want it."

"How many did you eat?"

"Well, I ate three. I thought at first that the taste was simply peculiar, and that I might like it better if I persevered."

"Had Ulrica given you any directions about eating the sweets, I wonder?"

"Yes. She said not to guzzle them all at once. I thought she was just being nasty. I know I'm greedy. I always confess to the sin of greed, but I don't seem to get any better. I'm always hungry, that's all. I don't really *mean* to be greedy."

"Neither does a cormorant," said Mrs. Bradley, laughing. "Well, what happened next?"

"Well, my inside went funny," said Mary, delicately, "so I told the girls I was sick, which doesn't sound quite so awful. And then I *suddenly thought*——"

"What?"

"How easy it would be for Ulrica if I was out of the way. There'd be nobody then to go to New York and get grandfather's money instead of her having it all."

"So you suspect that your cousin tried to murder you?"

"Well, I didn't exactly *suspect* it, but it all seemed rather queer, so I thought the best thing I could do was to make myself sick with the soap and get rid of the poison, if any."

"Very sensible and commendable," said Mrs. Bradley,

nodding. Mary looked very uncomfortable. "I don't want to get Ulrica into trouble," she said.

"You won't," Mrs. Bradley promised her. "I will be the soul of discretion. I think we shall find that the sweets were merely brimstone and treacle tablets. Mother Saint Gregory provided them, you say?"

She was more immediately concerned with clothing than with sweets, and, upon leaving Mary, went to find Sister Genevieve. The lay-sister matron brought out the garments which had been found in the bathroom and brought the tape-measure which Mrs. Bradley also demanded. The clothes were as Mother Jude had described—torn and damaged. The rather long grey drill-tunic was black with soot from the roof. All the garments were marked with the owner's name-tab, U. DOYLE, sewn on with tiny stitches.

CHAPTER 20

GEORGE

*"What behaved well in the past or behaves well
to-day is not such a wonder. . . ."*

WALT WHITMAN: Stray Thoughts.

GEORGE CAME BACK AT HALF-PAST TEN WITH THE CAR, and Mrs. Bradley was notified of his arrival whilst she was still examining the clothing. George had brought a note from Ferdinand. Mrs. Bradley, standing at the door of the guest-house in the thin spring sunshine, read it, then read it again.

"Arrived safely in Wandles. Célestine all ready to receive us. Ulrica asks whether there is any objection to her going to New York to visit her grandfather, since she has been taken away from school. Says she thinks her relatives would give permission, if you think she would be safe. Let me know what you feel."

"So you arrived safely, George?" said Mrs. Bradley, looking at him with grandmotherly affection.

"Yes, madam."

It sounded noncommittal, and Mrs. Bradley was intrigued. She pressed the point.

"Quite safely, and in good time?"

"We were delayed a half-hour or so, madam, on account of the young lady's injury."

"Good heavens, George! My son has not mentioned her injury. What was its nature and location?"

"I am at a loss how to answer you, madam."

266

"Very well. Tell the whole tale. Come inside. There's nobody here. We can talk in guilty secrecy."

She led the way into the dining-room where the cloth was spread but the table not set, and motioned him into a chair. George waited until she was seated, and then, with his peaked cap held between his knees, and his feet set as though they were clamped in iron boots to the floor, he began his tale.

"We had proceeded through the village of Blacklock Tor and were about twenty-three miles upon our way when the young lady said she felt faint and would like some water. There being no water apparent, except what was in the radiator, madam, I drove on a couple of miles to the nearest village. There, while Sir Ferdinand ministered to the young lady, I purchased a packet of cigarettes for myself and a couple of cigars to give to Henri, me owing him these on account of a small wager which I had had with him some time previous, and conversed with the woman behind the counter. It was she who had supplied the young lady with a glass of water, and she mentioned to me that she thought the young lady had a sweet face, but looked exceedingly poorly. I concurred in this expression of opinion——"

"You don't really think the girl has a sweet face, George?"

"I had taken very little account of the young lady up to then, madam, for the reason of her being a passenger and hardly my business, but since you ask me, I thought she looked somewhat ethereal."

"Do you mean it, George?"

"Well, madam, I thought I did, but since you question the term, perhaps I don't."

"Now, be independent, George, and out with it like a man. What made you use the word ethereal?"

"She seemed to me not of this world, madam. She

reminds me of what I used to think nuns were like before we knew those here.''

''You don't call the nuns here ethereal?''

''They seem to me too practical, madam, to be warrantably called ethereal.''

''Wasn't the girl practical, then?''

''I don't know how to answer, madam, for here's what happened. After we got on our way again, Sir Ferdinand, I fancy, had fallen into a doze, and all of a sudden the left side back window cracked as though someone had struck it smartly with a halfpenny, and at the same minute I heard the young lady cry out. I stopped the car at once, got down and opened the door. She was whimpering and holding her arm—her left arm, madam—and was moaning out.

'' 'They've got me! Oh! They've got me!'

''Sir Ferdinand had awakened, and was staring at her and saying:

'' 'Pull yourself together, my dear child! Whatever is the matter!'

''He seemed a little testy, because, I think, he was startled, but I'd seen the blood running down, for our inside lights were on, and I said: 'Hold hard, sir, a minute, I believe the young lady's hurt!'

''We staunched the blood—a rather nasty cut, madam, that had slashed the sleeve of her coat and dress, and penetrated fairly deeply into the upper arm, about three inches, I should judge, above the elbow—and I drove on pretty fast to find a doctor. He dressed the arm—he thought she had cut it on broken glass from a car-smash, I believe, and none of us, not the young lady, either, said anything different to him.''

''She did it herself, I presume?''

''Very hysterical subject, I should fancy, madam. Rather like some of Herr Hekel's young ladies, I imagine.

Full of imagination, and out for sympathy and notice."

"And you still looked upon her as ethereal?"

"With all the colour gone from her face, madam, and her eyes all dark underneath, and a general limpness of demeanour consequent upon loss of blood, I must persist, madam, in the description. She wanted to tell us some long rigmarole about having seen a man on the running board of the car. Sir Ferdinand, who has not exactly taken a fancy to the young lady, madam, told her, somewhat abruptly, that this was nonsense, and she made matters not exactly better by referring him to the fact that he had been asleep at the time.

" 'Yes, but *I* wasn't,' I said. She told me I couldn't see behind me. I didn't argue, madam, but I know no man was there."

"But did you find the weapon that she used?"

"It was difficult without searching the young lady, madam. Sir Ferdinand remonstrated with her a bit, and told her she must calm down, and then Célestine gave her some milk when we got her home—she wouldn't have anything to eat, so Célestine told me later—and put her to bed. Then Sir Ferdinand had his dinner, and I sat down to supper with Henri and Célestine."

"I half-expected that my son would come back in the car."

"He thought he had better be there to keep an eye on the young lady, madam, I fancy. He specifically referred to her as the apple of your eye, and said he must watch his step, as you would expect an account of his stewardship."

"Quite right. I shall. Go and send off a wire, George, to tell my son that Miss Doyle can go to New York as soon as she likes, and that the next boat sails on Wednesday."

"Very good, madam." He hesitated. "I was to be

sure and ask after the other young lady, madam, so the young lady we took with us got me to promise."

"She's lucky to be alive, from what I can make out. She fell off a roof before you left."

"We heard nothing of it, madam."

"No. By the way, I suppose Miss Doyle said nothing about returning here when you found she had been cut on the arm, George?"

"She mentioned it frequently, madam, but Sir Ferdinand said he had his orders, and would proceed, as planned, to Wandles."

"Interesting. You knew she wanted to say good-bye to her cousin, and couldn't find her, did you?"

"I was not so informed, madam, no."

"Curious, George."

"She's a curious kind of young lady, if you ask *me*, madam."

"Yes, fanatical, very. I don't somehow think she will make a very good nun. She'd make a fine missionary, though. She's quite unscrupulous."

"Is it the young lady's intention to take the veil, madam?"

"It is her ambition, I understand. You go to Blacklock Tor, George, with the car, and get them to book me a room. I shall want it to-morrow night for certain, and very likely for to-night. So book it for to-night, in any case, and call for me at half-past nine or so. I feel I ought to go to Church this evening, as it's Sunday, and I'm not sure at what time to go."

"Very good, madam."

"Don't forget the telegram. If you can't send it from Blacklock Tor—and ten to one you can't—telephone it from Kelsorrow."

"Yes, madam, very good. If I may venture to make a suggestion, you'll keep an eye skinned for trouble, madam, with Mrs. Maslin still about the place?"

"I'll bear the warning in mind, George, thank you kindly."

He saluted, climbed into the car and drove away. Mrs. Bradley went back to the infirmary, this time to visit Sister Bridget. After that, she thought, it would be a good time to interview the inhabitants of the two private houses. The clue she had been waiting for—that she had known must manifest itself sooner or later—was now in her possession. There was little else to wait for.

She walked quietly up the Orphanage staircase and entered Sister Bridget's darkened room. She smiled at the nun on duty, and then bent over the patient. Sister Bridget's chief need was for rest and quiet. She lay like a corpse in the silent, darkened room, and either a nun or a lay-sister remained with her all the time. Their devoted nursing amazed Mrs. Bradley, used, as she was, to the selflessness of nurses.

She went down the stairs and out to the orchard where the trees were showing buds and the pear and the plum were nearly out. Nobody was about. She walked briskly to the gate and past the front of the guest-house.

The first man, in his shirt-sleeves, a hammer in his right hand, was not helpful and sounded surly. Yes, he had heard about the death of the little girl, and had complained to the police about the damage done by the hooligans who had demonstrated against the convent. Beyond that he knew nothing, cared less, and would not answer any questions.

"It ain't my business," he said, "and what ain't my business, I keep out of."

Outfaced by this admirable sentiment, Mrs. Bradley took her leave. She had learned from Sister Genevieve, the boarders' matron, a good soul not at all averse to gossip so long as it was not malicious, that the man had lost his wife and was very unhappy. He shut himself off from everybody, except when he went on wild jaunts (Sister Genevieve's words) to London, returning in a couple of days or a couple of months, just as the fancy took him. He was a superstitious man, and had told the builder next door to be sure to let the convent have the guest-house (three houses, actually) cheap.

The builder was a different kind of man from his neighbour. He and his wife invited Mrs. Bradley in, and were anxious and willing to discuss the roof-climbing feat of Mary Maslin. He described the episode fully. It appeared to have caused him some amusement. He was vague, however, about the date on which he had seen the other girl on the roof. Mrs. Bradley attempted to get a description of the girl whom old Sister Catherine had referred to, but this, she found, was impossible. The man appeared to have very little visual memory, and, in any case, the girl had been dressed like all the girls. There was nothing distinctive about her. She was a biggish sort of girl, he would say. Mrs. Bradley then asked him what time of day it was when he saw the first girl. He thought it was early afternoon. It was quite light, he remembered, yet he did not think it was in the morning, although it might have been. He remembered thinking it was a funny kind of convent to allow such goings-on, and suggested that if one of the children broke her neck the coroner's next set of remarks might be a little sharper.

"Did you go to the inquest, then?" asked Mrs. Bradley. Well, yes, he had; living in the neighbourhood, and so forth, he and his wife had been interested, especially as they had seen the girl on the roof.

Oh, he had thought of the child he had seen on the roof that afternoon, then?

Yes, it had crossed his mind.

Had he mentioned having seen the child?

Not until he mentioned it to the other kid who had tumbled off the roof into his front garden, and lucky for her he'd dug down a couple of spits that afternoon!

Did not he think it important?

He did not know whether it was important or not, but it wasn't on his roof she was climbing, and he wasn't going to get himself mixed up in anything if he knew it. Everybody knew that the girl had climbed somehow into that bathroom, didn't they? And if the nuns were not capable of looking after their pupils and seeing that they didn't turn on gas taps, and drown themselves in the bath, that was their look out, not his. No, he wasn't a Catholic. Had no time for religion. Frills, he called it; just frills—and got you nowhere. Cissy, he called it. No, it had been no trouble to answer the questions. He had liked the child he had rescued; nice little kid. No nonsense about her, either. Might have been bellowing her head off after a tumble like that, and must have been hurt, but if so, had not shown it. Wouldn't mind one of his own like her. No girls. A couple of boys; apprenticed, both of them. Not that there was anything doing anywhere, was there, nowadays? That's what they always said. Things were bad. Trade was bad. Nobody wanted skilled labour. All the professions were full. He believed neither in Fascism nor Communism. Thought they came to the same thing exactly in the end. Took away your liberty, and what did they give you in exchange? Look at Germany and—— No, been no trouble. Yes, there would be some good weather now, he thought. Yes, that was the ladder. He kept it in the front garden. Wasn't afraid of being burgled. Nothing worth nabbing in their house. Yes, quite a light ladder, considering its length.

He'd got plenty more round the back. Discount allowed to the trade, like in everything else.

Mrs. Bradley perceived that there was nothing more to be gained from the friendly man. George came at half-past nine, according to orders, and drove her to Blacklock Tor.

"Did you telephone, George?" she enquired.

"Yes, madam. Pardon me, madam, but don't you think it rather a risky proceeding to let Miss Doyle go to New York?"

"I do not anticipate that Miss Doyle will murder her grandfather, George."

"Very good, madam. May I enquire how the injured party is getting on now, madam?"

"Her head is quite hard, George. I don't know whether mine would have been as hard."

"So it *was* directed at you, madam?"

"It seems likely. Nobody would set out to murder poor Sister Bridget."

"That's if we're on the right tack, madam."

"Proceed, George. Are you sure you know the right tack?"

"I suppose the money *was* the motive, madam?"

"It often is, George, unfortunately."

"There's such things as guilty secrets, and people getting to know them."

"Perfectly true. So what?"

"I beg your pardon, madam?"

"So what, George. Neolithic American query capable of being couched in bellicose, disgusted or pseudo-pathetic style. The last was what I intended."

"Thank you, madam. It occurred to me that the young lady might have been in possession of somebody's guilty secret, and have been croaked for knowing it, madam."

"Whose guilty secret, George? Your perspicacity stuns me—and that is not meant sarcastically."

"One of the nuns. It stands to reason, madam, that a bevy of ladies of this type must house a considerable number of secrets, one way and another."

"Not necessarily guilty, though, George, do you think?"

"No, madam."

But he seemed to have something on his mind. She waited, but he said no more. He stared out over the moors—they had not yet left the vicinity of the convent —and towards the lights of the village.

"You know, George," said Mrs. Bradley, "the most mysterious thing about the whole business is that the dead child went into the bathroom at all. If I hadn't been entirely mystified by that, I would have turned Ursula Doyle's form inside out, schoolgirl code or not, and have found out what she was supposed to be up to that afternoon, for she certainly did not go into after-noon school. But from the beginning I was always brought up short by the problem of what on earth—or who!—persuaded a child who never broke school rules, and was sweet, gentle and timid, to do a thing which is immediately visited with expulsion."

"It certainly is a problem, madam."

"Think it over, George. She wasn't forced to go there. There were no marks of violence on the body, and, what is more, she didn't care whether she was seen to go or not. And she wasn't the girl on the roof. So much is clear from the description given by the builder, although he's not got a very reliable memory, and by old lay-sister Catherine. But what do you make of it all?"

"Sounds as if she was taken in there unconscious, madam. Had you considered that possibility at all?"

Mrs. Bradley looked at him with a mixture of admiration and affection. George modestly scratched his head.

"The cigar or coconut, George," said his employer, "is yours. You have only to choose. Let us get along to the inn. Is there a room for me, I wonder?"

"They were quite delighted, madam, at the idea of seeing you again."

"Drive on, then. I wonder whether it's the room I had last time? The window wouldn't open, I remember, and I had to leave the door ajar all night."

(2)

The same little chambermaid and same room, Mrs. Bradley found, were to serve her. She had supper—cold beef and pickles, slices of the last of the hostess' Christmas puddings fried up in the pan (slightly salt), cheese, biscuits and beer. George supped with her, and the two of them sat matily in the parlour behind red curtains, and with a baize-covered parrot between them on the table, when the meal was over, George smoking, and Mrs. Bradley knitting a shapeless garment slowly and very badly. Their conversation was about Charles Dickens, upon whom they held strong and diametrically opposite opinions, George maintaining his worth as a writer, Mrs. Bradley willing to concede him a sociological significance and proclaiming him to be a humanitarian of advanced views, great public spirit and considerable courage, but consigning him, as a writer, to a peculiar limbo of her own where existed also Mrs. Felicia Hemans, Henry Wadsworth Longfellow, Dean Farrer, Alfred, Lord Tennyson, and other eminent Victorians not mentionable because not yet removed from our midst.

At half-past ten George had some more beer and Mrs.

Bradley went to bed. At eleven o'clock the landlord locked the side door, and at half-past eleven George carried a small hard flock mattress, blankets and pillows stealthily on to the landing, and laid the lot down outside his employer's bedroom.

At half-past twelve the stairs creaked, and George sat up. Nothing else happened, and so he lay down again. At twenty minutes to one he sat up again. A beam of light was coming up the stairs, a round spotlight, the gleam of an electric torch. The hair on George's neck began to prick a bit. He remembered Sister Bridget and the hammer. He got up quietly and stepped in his stockinged feet to the opposite side of the passage. The light played on the walls and on the banisters. Then it lighted on the mattress and the pillows. It was switched off. There was darkness and silence. George waited where he was, knowing nothing better to do. Half an hour went by. There had been no sound, but he felt certain that the unknown prowler must have gone. He waited another ten minutes, then, feeling cold, went over to his bed again and crawled beneath the blankets.

He was wide awake, and realised that he was still straining his ears for sounds. Suddenly a horrid idea came into his head. It was possible that the intruder had found a way to climb up to the bedroom window. The next moment he reassured himself, for the window, he remembered, would not open. Anybody entering that way would have to break the glass and make a noise. Then he remembered how easy a thing it was to cut glass and make a way in. Training and common sense wrestled in George, but not for more than a moment. The door was half open. He stepped across his mattress and walked into Mrs. Bradley's room.

"Stand still!" she said, but not loudly.

"It's only me, madam. The night has had its suspicious

element, madam, and I wondered whether you were safe."

"Yes, thank you, George. Did somebody come upstairs?"

"You couldn't have heard them, madam."

"Second sight, then, George. I certainly thought I did."

"Well, I saw the beam of their torch, but I certainly didn't *hear* anything, and I'm not hard of hearing."

"It must have been instinct, then. What happened, and how did you know?"

"I happened to be about, madam."

"Sleeping outside my door? I call that very touching and noble, George!"

George, in the darkness, grinned.

"I didn't like the things that have happened with hammers, madam."

"No, George, neither did I. But I slept very peacefully, knowing that you were on guard, for I heard you come. Were you trained as a Scout in your youth?"

"I was a Scout, and then a Rover until I joined the army, madam, yes."

"Well, you'd better go back to bed. You must be tired. I shan't bother to sleep any more, so have no fears. Do you know, by the way, that there's a gas fire in this room?"

"Nothing doing, madam, I shouldn't think. The young lady wouldn't have been persuaded to come out here. Besides, the gas! The room 'ud be full of it, without a window open. The murderer would never have got out conscious, and the body was found at the convent, don't forget."

"No, I'm not forgetting," said Mrs. Bradley.

George retired, but no farther than his pallet on the landing. The rest of the hours of darkness passed without incident, and as soon as he heard the servants' alarum clock ring, he took up his bed and belongings and went back to the room assigned to him.

At breakfast, which he had in the kitchen along with the maids and the barman, one of the girls observed:

"Can't think how Miss Ada can come to leave the pantry window unfastened nohow. Seems to me that was shut all day long yesterday, on account of the wind being that way."

"Was the pantry door locked?" asked George.

"Lor', no. Why should it be?"

"I wondered. People sometimes lock the downstair rooms at night, just in case."

"In case of burglars, do you mean?"

George agreed that he did, but added carelessly: "Nothing to burgle here particular, I take it."

"Nothing to signify. All the big takings goes to the bank each day. Of course, there's the evening custom, but master sleeps on it all, as everyone round about know."

George went along after breakfast to have a look at the window. There was nothing to show it had been forced, and yet to suppose that the murderer—he assumed that the unknown prowler had been after Mrs. Bradley—had had the luck to find a downstair window open on the only night that it was necessary to get into the inn, seemed far too great a coincidence to be likely. He went outside and carefully examined the ground, but it was crazy paving, and told him nothing. It had retained no marks, and there was no scrape of shoes on stonework, wood or paint round the window or in the pantry.

He went to the landlord.

"Have any unusual customers yesterday, barring us?"

The landlord thought for a minute, then shook his head.

"Not as I recollect. Why, what's the trouble?"

"The pantry window was left open."

"That? Oh, that's my darter, I reckon. Does her Keep Fit in there each night, her do, and deep breathing opposite the window. Told her once to shut it after her and mind we didn't get cats, I've told her a dozen times."

"Does her exercises in the pantry, does she?"

"Ah, her do, on account of the window opening on to the garden. Mother won't have her gallivanting overhead, on account of the plaster from the ceilings; there isn't no room in the kitchen, and the other rooms downstairs is all public rooms, do you see."

George said that he did see, and went to Mrs. Bradley with the news.

"So it isn't a mystery, madam, and may have been the ordinary sort of burglar."

"Most likely," Mrs. Bradley agreed.

"Odd, though, madam, to pick the very night. And, after all, a good many people at the convent knew you were staying here, didn't they?"

"Quite true, George; so they did."

"Do you suppose it might be useful to prosecute an enquiry at the convent, madam?"

"No, George, I don't think so. The children don't seem to give one another away, and I can't believe, somehow, that the nuns have designs upon my life."

"Religion goes very odd at times, madam."

"Don't I know it, George! By the way, I had an interesting thought last night. There's one nun that I don't know at all. I've seen her but never spoken to her—the history teacher, Mother Lazarus."

"Would that be the lady like a wax candle, madam?"

"An apt description. How do you know her, George?"

"Well, madam, it was taking a good bit of liberty on my part, and I meant to let you know, but it slipped my mind."

"George, this is most intriguing! Don't tell me you've been taking the nuns for joy-rides in my car!"

"Well, it almost amounted to that, madam, really, I must confess. They wanted to catch up an expedition to a castle, madam, several miles away, and a museum. This Mother Saint Lazarus was supposed to be in charge of the party—a historical outing, madam, for some of the children—and one of the young ladies was always sick when she travelled by train. Well, it seems she's the star history pupil, and had to see this castle and museum if it killed her. So they wondered if they could hire a car off the landlord. Well, he couldn't oblige, his two being in commission moving young pigs, so, before I thought, I had offered, and off we went."

"So Mother Lazarus came here! And who was the child?"

"Well, madam, as it happens, it was the very same young lady I drove to Wandles with Sir Ferdinand."

"Ulrica Doyle? That's interesting. And which day, George, was this?"

"It would have been last Thursday morning, madam."

"But the fourth form don't have history on a Thursday."

"I couldn't speak as to that, madam, but Thursday is the cheap day's outing from the halt here."

"Oh, that explains it, then. Naturally they would want to do the outing at the cheapest possible rate. What was Mother Lazarus going to do if she could not hire a car?"

"I could not say, I'm sure, madam. She seemed

greatly relieved at my offer, and said that the rest of the party had gone on with Mother Saint Gregory and Mother Saint Francis, madam.''

''Oh, Mother Saint Francis was there! That explains, then, why Mother Saint Lazarus could leave her major charge to accompany a solitary girl. I suppose there was another nun with her?''

''Yes; an elderly lady by the name of Mother Saint Bartholomew, whom I recollect having seen in Restoration Comedy, madam, before she took the veil.''

''Good heavens, George! I shouldn't have thought you were old enough to have been taking an interest in Restoration Comedy when Mother Bartholomew was still on the stage. At any rate, thank you very much for your information. Again you have assisted materially in the enquiry.''

''May I be privileged to know in what way, madam?''

''I expected another attempt on my life on Thursday, George, that's all. By driving those three, the two nuns and the girl, to their castle and museum, you've probably—I should say certainly—saved me from attack. Somebody saw the car go out, I expect, and probably thought I was in it.''

CHAPTER 21

GIRLS

"What brighter throne can brightness find
To reign on than an infant's mind,
Ere sin destroy, or error dim
The glory of the Seraphim?"

JOHN WILSON: To a Sleeping Child.

"BUT THE LAST THING WE WANT," SAID MOTHER Saint Francis, "is a lot of gossip going on among the girls."

Mrs. Bradley agreed, but added that she supposed there was bound to be a certain amount of gossip, and that she thought her plan would lead to less of it, possibly, than might more secret measures. So the school, first thing on Monday morning, was surprised to have a little old woman with snapping black eyes and a terrifying, beautiful voice, step on to the platform beside Mother Francis, immediately prayers were over, and demand the writer of anonymous letters.

"Come here to me at once," she said. There was a movement of the ranks, and out stepped Nancy Ryan.

"Come along," said Mrs. Bradley, motioning her on to the platform. The child was so terrified that she added: "You have nobody but me to account to for your actions. I am Mother Saint Francis' delegate."

This did little to reassure Nancy, who stood, white-faced, and saw her surroundings through a mist, whilst her heart thumped horribly and she felt sure that if she were asked to say a single word she would be sick.

"How many letters did you write?" enquired Mrs. Bradley. There was no reply whilst Nancy struggled for control of her lips, which were dry with fright.

"One," she replied at last.

"To whom did you send it?"

"To Mary Maslin. If you please, it was only in fun."

"I believe that," said Mrs. Bradley. "But it might have led to serious trouble, you know. As it is, it has been of considerable assistance to me, and so this is the last you will hear of it. Go away, child, and don't write any more of the nasty, silly things. Get along with you."

Nancy retired, and Mrs. Bradley addressed the assembled school.

"I want next all the girls who knew that Ursula Doyle was not in class on that Monday afternoon."

There was barely a second's hesitation; then the whole of the third form, seventeen of them, came forward, single file, and made a straight line in front of the platform. ·Most of them looked scared and guilty, as though they felt they were going to be blamed for what had happened.

"Where was she, then?" Mrs. Bradley enquired, whilst the school stood silent but excited. A girl wearing a badge stepped out of the line and said:

"We didn't notice until we were ready for our lesson, and then we didn't say anything, as her cousin wasn't there either, and we thought they had both had special permission to be absent."

"Ulrica Doyle, do you mean, was not in class either?"

"Yes. The two forms, ours and the fourth form, had music together that afternoon, and we thought— and we thought——"

"I see. Very well, girls, thank you. Now, the fourth form—where was Ulrica Doyle that afternoon?"

Thereupon ensued one of those dramatic interruptions which schoolgirls dream about, and of which schoolgirl literature is full. Ulrica Doyle herself, who had been driven to Mrs. Bradley's home at Wandles Parva, came forward from the back of the hall, and looking even more pallid (from her self-inflicted injury, Mrs. Bradley supposed) than usual, said very calmly and distinctly:

"I spent that Monday afternoon in Church."

"In Church?" Mrs. Bradley betrayed no surprise at her sudden appearance. It was almost as though she had expected it. Ulrica came up to the platform. Still very pale, she was, as usual, entirely self-possessed.

"Did anybody else know this?" Mrs. Bradley enquired.

"No," the girl replied, and a faint smile, such, Mrs. Bradley thought, in a moment of irritation, as martyrs probably wore, appeared at the corners of her mouth. "Oh, wait, though. One of the guest-house people came in. She saw me, I believe, and may remember."

"But what made you go into Church?" Mrs. Bradley demanded, recollecting Mrs. Trust's evidence.

"Saint Jeanne d'Arc," the girl calmly replied.

"Voices?" said Mrs. Bradley sceptically, and with a considerable amount of distaste.

"You must believe what you choose," said Ulrica, quietly and firmly, her pale face lifted and her nostrils quivering slightly. "I was under compulsion to spend the time in Church, and school rules no longer had meaning. I shall explain this to Mother Saint Francis as soon as the Voices give me leave."

"Odd," said Mrs. Bradley; but she was not referring to the girl's last sentence, a fact which was patent to Ulrica but lost to the rest of her hearers, including Mother Francis. The nun, having promised to maintain a policy of rigid non-interference, was keeping silence, but her expression, to those who knew her—and even to Mrs. Bradley, who did not—boded no good to Ulrica, the embryo saint and martyr. Mother Francis was, in fact, as the girls remarked later on, positively seething with fury. At a nod from Mrs. Bradley she dismissed the school to their classrooms, but herself remained in the hall.

Mrs. Bradley fixed her black eyes on Ulrica.

"You will never make a nun if you disobey orders," she said, "and your orders surely must be to attend lessons, and fit yourself, through education, for life. I have a certain amount of sympathy, always, with rebellion, but I shall be interested to know why you did not remain at my house until my son sent you over to your grandfather."

"Saint Jeanne's orders," said the girl, speaking with a defiance none the less real because her voice remained quiet and her tone courteous, "were to disregard the orders of those who considered themselves her mental and spiritual superiors, and carry out orders from God. What would have happened to France if she had faltered?"

"How long did you stay in Church?" asked Mrs. Bradley. The abrupt question, cutting through an heroic daydream, apparently flustered the girl. She went very pale, turned suddenly crimson, and replied:

"I don't know, exactly. The girls were not still in school when I came out, so I went to find Mother Saint Benedict to apologise to her for having missed her Latin lesson."

"What about Mother Saint Gregory? Hadn't you missed her music lesson as well?"

"I knew she wouldn't have noticed I wasn't there," replied Ulrica, fixing a calm and fearless eye on Mother Francis. "Mother Saint Gregory is an artist. She is not conscious of other people, except in the mass and dimly. She also is very short-sighted."

"What had Mother Saint Benedict to say?" asked Mrs. Bradley, amused to think that artistry and short-sightedness should appear to be the same thing.

"I discovered, before I could confess to my absence from her lesson, that *she* had not missed me, either. She had taken the double class, while Mother Saint Dominic was at the dentist's, and had set some translation, and had gone round the class to help the slow ones."

"You were never a slow one?"

"No. I was always top."

"So she would not have come to you, probably, even if you *had* been in class?"

"I don't think she would, unless I had come upon a doubtful reading, and had actually asked her advice."

"What did she say when you went to her?"

" 'Not now, Ulrica. Go along and have your tea.' The nuns were always kind to me about food."

"She thought you had come for advice about your work?"

"She must have done. It was obvious that she did not know that I had come to make apology for absence."

"I see. And you didn't go again?"

"I saw no need. No harm was done by my non-attendance. The actual piece of translation which had been set I got from another girl and wrote out in my own time later. It would perhaps have grieved Mother to know that I had deliberately missed her lesson. It seemed kinder to let the whole thing drop."

These sentiments seemed to Mrs. Bradley admirably sensible, although she found the manner of their expression supremely irritating. She was aware, however, that her opinion was not shared by Mother

Francis, so she sent Ulrica to her formroom, and
grinned at the headmistress, prepared to argue the point
on behalf of the girl. Mother Francis forestalled her,
however, by remarking:

"The enquiry seems doomed to end in a cul-de-sac.
Nothing seems to lead anywhere."

"I wonder why Ulrica left my house and came back
here?" said Mrs. Bradley, determined not to be side-
tracked.

"I can answer that. She came to me before school
this morning, and said that there was no Catholic
church within twelve miles of your house, and that
your son had commandeered the car to go and play
golf."

"He is plus two," said Mrs. Bradley, in explanation,
Mother Francis gathered, of this selfishness. "That
would be the old car," she added. "I wonder he
could get it to go. Even for George its response is not
enthusiastic."

Mother Francis made no reply to this statement,
although she could think of several remarks which, to
her mind, would have been in keeping.

"Ulrica is not a Catholic, though," Mrs. Bradley
went on pensively.

"It is only a question of time, and of receiving formal
instruction," Mother Francis said quickly. "Still,
she should not have returned without permission, as I
explained when I saw her this morning."

"The temptation, probably, was strong. Where,
by the way, are the originals from which Mother Saint
Simon-Zelotes made her copies of the paten and
chalice?"

Mother Francis betrayed no surprise at the sudden
change of subject, but replied:

"Reverend Mother Superior was so much impressed

by your evident fear for their safety, that she had them
taken on Saturday morning to the Kelsorrow branch of
the Exe and Wye bank. It is in the High Street, almost
opposite the fire-station."

"And the distinguished visitors?"

"They have all been put off, except the Bishop. He
is to have a private view of the work on Wednesday
morning."

"But not with the originals for comparison?"

"That I cannot tell you. Reverend Mother seems
greatly impressed, as I say, by your anxiety not to have
the originals on show, but, on the other hand, Sister
Saint Simon's work loses interest if no comparison is
made with what she copied."

"Even so," said Mrs. Bradley, "they should not, on
any account, be shown publicly, even to the Bishop,
until Thursday." She glanced at the nun, and, yielding
to an impulse similar to the one which once before had
caused her to gratify what she felt must be the intense,
but unexpressed curiosity of hot-blooded, energetic,
repressed and self-controlled Mother Francis, she added,
nodding: "Ulrica Doyle is to sail for New York on
Wednesday. When she is gone, all will be well. Don't,
please, tell anybody that."

"I will say nothing. You regard Ulrica, then, as the
root of the troubles?" She did not sound at all surprised,
Mrs. Bradley noticed.

"She will be much better out of the way," Mrs.
Bradley answered.

Nobody knew better than Mother Francis, who had
given a good many similar answers in her time, how far
from the point of the question this reply was. She
folded her hands in her sleeves, bowed slightly, smiled
with a warm red mouth which no training could make
anything but sensuous and sadistic, and said nothing else

at all, but walked beside Mrs. Bradley out of the hall
and along the dim, cold corridor to her room.

"You will have Ulrica watched, will you not?" said
Mrs. Bradley, before they parted, the one to deal with
school stock required for the coming term, the other to
telegraph her son that his charge was safe at the convent.
"She ought to be under the supervision of at least two
people all the time."

George drove her to the Kelsorrow post-office.

"Letter follows," she telegraphed to her son, after
indicating that Ulrica was safe. Having sent off the
telegram she obtained a letter-card, and wrote immediately, remaining in the post office to do so:

"Dear Ferdinand,

"This in a great hurry, as I do not want to be
absent from the convent for a minute longer than I can
help between now and Thursday. Ulrica came back on a
milk train like Mr. Wodehouse's heroes, and arrived
here before the opening of morning school. Do not
worry about her. I had overlooked the point that we
have no Catholic church in the neighbourhood at home.
I wish, if you can manage it, you would put Ulrica on to
the boat at Southampton on Wednesday. I will send her
in charge of two of the sisters, who will make certain
that there is no hitch. It is absolutely essential that she
should leave this country on Wednesday. A train gets
into Southampton Docks at three, and the ship, the
Swan of Avon, sails at a quarter to five. Do be
there to meet the train. If you can't do it, please
wire me."

She sealed the letter-card and dropped it in the post-
box, then sent a second telegram to cover the information
in it.

"Meet Ulrica 3 p.m. Wednesday Southampton
Docks for s.s. *Swan of Avon*. Bradley."

She prepaid a reply to this, and then went back to the
car and told George to drive as fast as he could to the
convent. They arrived at the gate-house at just after
eleven o'clock. This suited Mrs. Bradley's purpose
admirably. She was admitted by the lay-sister portress,
and Kitty, who loved excitement and did not mind
running about, was sent to Mother Francis with notice
of her arrival. This was a new arrangement, and everybody entering the convent grounds was to be subject to it.

It was a clear, bright day, fairly windy but not at all
cold, and Mrs. Bradley strolled round the school gardens.
Then, attracted by the sound of a voice giving crisp
commands, she entered the school field and walked
over to watch Miss Bonnet giving a physical training
lesson to the sixth form. Miss Bonnet saw her, and
waved. Mrs. Bradley waved back, but remained away
from the class so as not to disturb the lesson. At a little
distance stood the two nuns on supervisory duty. So it
must all have looked, Mrs. Bradley reflected, on the
Monday that the child was found dead. The setting,
the time-table, the silent, black-robed observers—all
would have been the same. She wondered at what
point, and through what agency, the child could have
received the urge to go to the guest-house. The nuns
would have been out of the way—even the lay-sister
portress had been at Vespers—the guests from the guest-
house had gone out, except for poor Sister Bridget, the
orphans on duty in the guest-house had been shut away
in the kitchen, even the old gardener, who might
otherwise have been working in the grounds and so
have seen the child sneak by, had been round at the
front of the guest-house putting creosote on the fence.

It had been an ideal opportunity, and somebody had taken every advantage of the fact. Still brooding on this, Mrs. Bradley walked across to the metal-work shed. No one was there. Mother Simon-Zelotes was in the school laboratory teaching science, and all the girls who made a hobby of metal-work and woodwork were at lessons. The key was in the door, and Mrs. Bradley turned it and went in. The place was in workmanlike order, the floor clear of filings and shavings, the tools all put away or placed to hand on the racks above the benches. In a small, glass-fronted wall-cupboard stood the copies of the paten and chalice. Mrs. Bradley went up to them. The cupboard hung in a good light, and without opening the doors she could inspect the side of the chalice which presented itself, and the whole of the upper face of the paten. The work had been beautifully done. She could not have told, from looking at them, that they were not the original vessels. Mother Simon-Zelotes must be one of the cleverest craftsmen in England, she thought. She took a small lens from her pocket, opened the cupboard doors, and, without touching the objects, examined them through her little magnifying glass without revising her opinion. Mother Simon-Zelotes had done a first-class job, and Mrs. Bradley's heart warmed fully towards her because of it.

The nun herself came in at the conclusion of morning school, her science overall voluminous over her habit, and found Mrs. Bradley still there.

"You like them?" she said.

"They are good beyond praise."

"I thank you. It is kind of you to say so."

"Tell me—would it be possible for you to confuse the pairs?"

"The new with the old? Me, no. Others——"

she smiled, and waved a large, finely-made hand—"I
must not be guilty of the sin of pride, but I think
perhaps they might, if they were not quite expert in
these things."

"Then you mean that if somebody were to play a
little joke, and, when the things are exhibited, change
the cards round, some people might be taken in?"

Mother Simon-Zelotes chuckled, a nice, fat, pleasant
sound, but refused to answer.   Entirely satisfied, Mrs.
Bradley went over to the guest-house to have lunch.
Ferdinand, to her astonishment, was one of the guests.
Mother Jude herself hovered round him in the parlour
before the meal was served, and informed his mother
that he had had a long and tiring journey, and that she
was going to make special arrangements for him to have
a good afternoon sleep in one of the bedrooms after
lunch.

"But what are you doing here, child?" Mrs. Bradley
enquired, when the rotund little nun had gone to
superintend the serving of the meal.

"Came to see my protégée whom I did not succeed
in protecting," he replied.   "I'm awfully sorry about
that, mother, but I'm afraid it never occurred to me that
the girl would try to get back.   For one thing I'd no idea
that she'd got any money."

"What was that about an attack on the car as you were
going to Wandles that night?"

"Oh, that?   Some form of hysteria, I imagine.
Perhaps she thought we'd have to return to the convent
if she was ill."

"You're quite sure she wasn't attacked?"

"Oh, perfectly certain."

"But you were asleep, George said."

"Oh, well, yes, I may just have dozed off.   I believe
I did, now you mention it.   But, mother, we were doing

about fifty when it happened. She must have done it
herself."

"You are right, probably; but I'm keeping a watchful
eye on her—or, rather, my deputies, two lynx-eyed sisters are. Come along; there's the gong, and we mustn't
be late for grace."

"Grace! Oh, yes, of course."

This time it was the Jesuit, Father Clare, who sat at
the head of the table. The short Latin grace he pronounced—two words—suited his soldierly figure and
stern, hard, handsome face. He was a ruthless-looking
young man, with an unsavoury grubbiness about him. She
sat next to him. He talked well, chiefly about cattle-
rearing in the Argentine. He had lived out there as a boy,
he told Mrs. Bradley; had an Irish father and a Spanish-
Indian mother.

"A good mixture," he observed, without pride, but as
one who stated a fact which none could controvert. Mrs.
Bradley worked the conversation through Mexico to Col-
orado, and from Aztec civilisation and the Grand Canyon
to New York and Timothy Doyle. She learned nothing
new however, and got up from table disliking the priest
but with no other positive feelings.

Ferdinand offered to go for a walk with her after
lunch, but Mrs. Bradley, poking him in the ribs with a
bony forefinger, told him to go and rest, as he had been
invited to do.

"Mother Saint Jude's word is law in this house, dear
child. She is Hospitaller here, and if arrangements are
made for your comfort, comfortable you must be," she
said lightly but firmly. She pushed him towards the little
nun, who, with a grinning Bessie and a blushing Annie at
her heels, was about to show him to his room.

It was the first hour of convent recreation. The time

was just after one. Mrs. Bradley walked over to the
school to watch the games, and then went along through
the pleasant garden to the cloister, and tapped at the
door of the frater. But no one was there except Sister
Lucia, piling up wooden platters on which a few crumbs
of bread and the bones of salt fish bore witness to a
Lenten repast.

"The Community are all in the Common Room, except for those that are superintending the school-
children's meal," she said, with a wide, calm smile and a
little gesture towards the refectory door, "and those will
be out in ten minutes."

Mrs. Bradley smiled in response, and thanked the lay-
sister. She had found out what she wanted to know, that,
at the time the school-children finished their lunch, the
frater was always empty. Sister Lucia would have done
clearing by then.

"Are the children ever allowed in here?" she asked
suddenly.

"There is nothing to prevent them from coming in, if
they wish to do so. In wet weather, when the room is
empty, some of them do."

"Would it occasion any remark if in fine weather any
came in?"

"Not from me, and most likely I would be the only
person to see them, apart from old Sister Catherine, who
helps me most days. But she has a liking for children, and
never would drive them away."

Mrs. Bradley nodded, and in a moment in came old
Sister Catherine, picked up a glass in each hand, carried
the glasses to the kitchen, came back for more, and so on
until she had cleared the glasses from the great bare
wooden board. Every time she passed in front of the
Crucifix on the wall she genuflected profoundly; so,

with less ostentation but perhaps, Mrs. Bradley thought,
more piety, did the calm-eyed Sister Lucia.

"How is the consumptive girl?" she asked her.

"She has returned to the home of her English
husband's parents. They cannot go back to Spain.
His business is ruined. She is not well. She cannot
grow well in England."

In a very few minutes the school-children came from
their refectory, and walked along the cloister to their
games. Mrs. Bradley followed, and caught up Ulrica
Doyle, who was closely attended by her nuns. They
smiled and bowed when they saw Mrs. Bradley. She
returned both courtesies, and said:

"I should like to speak to Ulrica." Obviously
against the girl's will she led her into the frater.

"When you helped Ursula with her Latin and her
Science and other lessons, was it in here you used to
come?" she asked gently.

"Yes—sometimes."

"Did you bring her in here on the day of her death?"
The girl looked terrified.

"I don't remember! Don't look at me like that!
Truly I don't remember! How can you ask me to
remember anything that happened on that day! As
though I know now what I did, or where we went, or
anything!"

"I see. But you came in here sometimes?"

"What does it matter? I've told you we came in
sometimes! We're allowed to. There's nothing
against it in the rules!"

"I know that, Ulrica. You told me, you remember,
that your cousin did not kill herself. You want to know
what killed her, don't you? And that's what I'm
trying to find out."

"It couldn't be anything to do with this place.

There's no gas fire here, or anything! You don't think —it couldn't be here!''

''No, it couldn't be here, gas fire or not,'' said Mrs. Bradley. ''But you did come here sometimes, you say. That's all I wanted to know, just that it was possible for girls to come here, with permission, of course, in their recreation time.''

''Lots of the girls come,'' said Ulrica. She remained staring after Mrs. Bradley when the little old woman went out. One of the guardian nuns came up and touched her on the arm.

CHAPTER 22

RECONNAISSANCE

"Heaven and erthe and also helle,
And all that ever in hem dwelle."
ANON. : Good Day, Sire Cristemas.

"MOTHER SAINT JUDE," SAID MRS. BRADLEY, GOING
back to the guest-house and waylaying the little nun
as she was leaving the guest-house for the cloister,
"don't let me delay you, but I wonder whether you can
remember a trifling point in connection with a child—
one of the orphans—whom Miss Bonnet knocked over
in a netball practice on the day that Ursula Doyle was
found dead."

"I remember that the child was injured."

"How did you come to be brought into the thing?
It isn't part of your work to attend to injured
orphans."

"Miss Bonnet herself came and fetched me from the
guest-house. I stayed with the child and with Sister
Saint Ambrose until it was time for us to go to Vespers,
and then Miss Bonnet kindly offered to stay with the
child until it was time for us to begin the afternoon
lessons."

"But she didn't stay with her, did she?"

"She was with her when we came back. She explained that she had been away for a time to give some
extra coaching in gymnastics."

"Yes, that seems to be true."

"Do you believe, then——?" The nun looked surprised. Mrs. Bradley laughed.

"Mother Saint Francis told me, long ago, that Miss Bonnet was a liar," she observed. "One more question: have you any reason to suspect that one of the gas fires in the guest-house consumed more gas than usual the week the child was found dead!"

"No, certainly not. There is only one gas fire in the guest-house, and that is the one you saw in the northern wall of the parlour, the small portable heater. You did see it, you remember?"

"Yes, of course. What other gas appliances are there, besides the geyser?"

"None at all. There are geysers in all three bathrooms."

"Yes, I know. I have looked at them all. I will be frank with you, Mother Saint Jude. I have to find out whether it is possible that Ursula Doyle was murdered in some place other than the bathroom in which she was found."

"And her body carried to the bathroom?"

"Yes. There is very little possibility of it, I am afraid, but, if it should turn out so, my problem, a pressing one, would be to discover the room where the murder took place."

"There are two gas fires in the Orphanage."

"In the Orphanage?"

Mother Jude smiled and shook her head.

"I agree with you," she said. "It could not have been done at the Orphanage. The risk of discovery would have been too great. It would have been so much easier in the guest-house, too. Undoubtedly it was the parlour. Strange, though, that no one smelt gas."

"We can't be sure that nobody smelt gas," said Mrs. Bradley. "Several people may not be telling the truth

about that.   Besides, the very strong smell of that
creasote, you know!"

"It is dreadful," said the nun.   "Who would have
thought of such a thing?"

"There are several people," Mrs. Bradley replied.
"There is Ulrica Doyle, for example.   We can prove
that she went into the church, but we cannot prove
that she spent the whole of the afternoon school-
time there; it covers the time for the murder, that
couple of hours.   Then there is Miss Bonnet: it is odd,
you must admit, that her half-holiday from Kelsorrow
School coincided with the death of the child, and that
all the untoward incidents, such as the attacks on
me and on Sister Bridget, occurred on the evenings
or nights when Miss Bonnet had been on the
premises."

"Ulrica—I should be certain she did not do it.   It
is too wicked a thing for any young girl to have con-
templated," Mother Jude stoutly affirmed.

"The motive," said Mrs. Bradley.

"You mean the money?   I cannot believe she could
be so dreadfully mercenary."

"For herself, no.   For the church ——?"

"The end and the means," said Mother Jude.   She
shook her head again, gently.   "I do not believe it.
You think she would commit a terrible sin in order to
get money to give to the Church?   No, no!   It is
wrong.   You do not understand.   I am sure you do not.
With all your goodness, my friend, you are not a
Catholic!"

"What about Miss Bonnet, then?"

"I do not know her.   But what would be her reason?
Why should she kill a child—and such a gentle, in-
offensive child?"

"I don't know," said Mrs. Bradley, nodding solemnly,

"unless the child was a menace, in some way, to her. What do you say to Mrs. Maslin?"

"Well, that one!" said Mother Jude. Then, to Mrs. Bradley's concealed amusement, she shut her lips tightly, flushed a little, and concluded: "I will not imagine it. No. It is not possible. Yet—she knows something! She is always hinting."

"Well, somebody did it. I thought perhaps you might give me your opinion. What do you say to Mrs. Waterhouse?"

"But, again, why?"

"Well, she killed her husband."

Mother Jude smiled incredulously.

"Oh, but she did," said Mrs. Bradley. "I agree, however, that it is not a very good reason for suspecting her of killing Ursula Doyle. Still, the fact remains that she is, perhaps, a little—hasty."

"Do you know what I really believe?" said Mother Jude. Mrs. Bradley turned to find the blue eyes fully upon her. "I believe it was poor Sister Bridget. I have thought so from the first. Before the inquest I thought so, and now I am almost certain. There! I have told you at last!"

"Sister Bridget deliberately killed that child? I may tell you that it is extremely unlikely you are right."

"Consider the facts," said Mother Jude. "We know that the child was killed by breathing unlighted gas. We know, too, that the child was not seen to enter the guest-house. We know that she was under supervision until——?"

"Yes. Until when? Until the end of morning school. We hear no more of her until she is found in the bathroom with her head completely submerged."

"Quite. But all that water—do you see my point?"

"No," said Mrs. Bradley, who had seen another of

such significance that she could think of nothing else for the moment.

"But yes! The water! When did all that water run into the bath? Did nobody hear it? Why did nobody hear it?" pursued Mother Jude triumphantly. Mrs. Bradley gave her her whole attention.

"You mean—I see. All the guests except Sister Bridget had gone out. She alone would have heard the water running. Yes, but it doesn't prove that she turned it on, you know."

"But who else *could* have turned it on?"

"The murderer."

"But Sister Bridget would have made some remark to one of us about it. She knows that people don't usually take a bath in the middle of the afternoon. You do not believe me. Let us make an experiment."

She rang a bell and Kitty came to the door.

"My dear child," she said, "I want you to go to Sister Bridget's bedroom and remain there for the next half-hour. I have to go, but Mrs. Bradley will be here, and will have other instructions for you."

"Do I have to be doing nothing but stay in her room, ma'am?" Kitty enquired, when Mrs. Bradley and she were left by themselves, and little Mother Jude, with a swirl of heavy skirts, had hurried out.

"You can take another girl with you," said Mrs. Bradley, "and take all the coverings off the bed and tighten the spring mattress, if you will be so kind. You know how to do it, I suppose?"

"Indeed and I do, ma'am. Bessie is on duty with me to-day. Will I be going to find her?"

"You will. When Sister Bridget spends her after-noons in there, does she have the door open or shut?"

"She shuts it against her mouse. And how does the poor weak creature be getting on, ma'am?"

Judging that the question referred to Sister Bridget and not to the mouse, Mrs. Bradley replied that she was almost well. "And now," she said, "you get along and find Bessie. Oh, and one more thing. Ask Annie and Ethel to come along, too, and sit in the kitchen with the door as they usually have it. What about the front door? Always left unlocked?"

"Until after tea, ma'am, always. The guests do be wanting to get in and out without trouble."

"Yes, naturally. I had anticipated that. That makes no difficulty, then."

While Kitty was gone for Bessie and the others, Mrs. Bradley walked over to the Orphanage, where, since the nuns had all gone to Church, the children were left by themselves. There was a fair amount of noise going on, but immediately she went in such a deathly silence ensued that she was considerably disconcerted by it.

"I want a girl of thirteen," she said. She cast a quick glance over all the assembled children.

"You'll do," she added, picking out a stolid-looking girl. She beckoned the child to go with her.

"Now," she said, when they got outside, "what's your name?"

"Molly Kelly, but I wasn't doing nothing."

"You're doing something now," said Mrs. Bradley. "You are helping me in a very important bit of work, and I want you to do exactly as I tell you. You and I are going to reconstruct a crime. Are you a brave girl, Molly?"

"I screeches at the dentist."

"Well done you. But you mustn't screech now. You mustn't make a sound. You understand?"

"Yes."

"Very well. It is just a game. Have you ever been into the guest-house?"

"No."

"Do you know the way in?"

"Yes. I knows where the door is."

"All right, then. We must wait until the coast is clear."

They waited until Mrs. Bradley had seen Kitty go over with Annie and Ethel. Bessie, she assumed, was already in the guest-house, as she was on duty there, and needed only to be taken up into the seventh bedroom. She gave the girls another three minutes, and then said to Molly Kelly:

"You mustn't mind. I'm going to send you in alone. I want you to go up to the front door, walk in, enter the first door on the left—which is your left hand?— that's it—and stay in the room until I come. I shan't be long. Will you do that?"

"Yes." The heavy-looking child walked off. Mrs. Bradley watched her go. The gates were open; the portress was in church. Round the corner towards the guest-house went the child, and after an interval of less than a minute Mrs. Bradley followed after her. There was no sign whatever that the child had entered the guest-house. She herself pushed open the guest-house door, walked in and entered the parlour. There was the child.

They remained in the room for five minutes by Mrs. Bradley's watch. Then Mrs. Bradley opened the big window which looked out beyond the low wooden fence to the downhill stretches of the moor. The next moment she had gone to the door of the room, opened it, and returned to the child whom she lifted up in her arms.

"Keep still," she whispered. The child, looking frightened, wriggled. "Still!" whispered Mrs. Bradley. She carried her up the stairs and along to the bathroom.

There she set her down, grinned at her reassuringly, shut the door and turned on both taps in a steady, fairly fast trickle, letting the water fall on to a towel to deaden any sound that there might be. She looked at her watch, then took a folding ruler from her pocket and measured the bath. At the end of five minutes she measured the depth of the water. Then she whispered to the child:

"That's all. Go back. You'll still be in time for school. Did you ever read a detective story, by the way?"

"Seen Charlie Chan on the pictures," said the child.

"Well, you and I together have been engaged in the solution of a mystery."

The child made no verbal reply; her face, however, expressed her thoughts, which could be summed up thus: "Garn, you old barmy skinny lizzie!"

Mrs. Bradley cackled, and gave the child a shilling. Then she walked along to the seventh bedroom and tapped on the door. Bessie and Kitty had almost finished their task, and when she went in they were making the bed again. Mrs. Bradley shut the door behind her, and then, with her ear to the inside keyhole, she listened. This time there came a sound of running water. She went back to the bathroom, watched, this time, by the girls, and tied the towel, a big bath-towel—over the tap. Slowly, surely, but now without a sound, the water was gradually rising. The quietness of it fascinated Bessie, who leaned, open-mouthed, on the bath. Mrs. Bradley measured the depth again. She compared the result with some scribbled calculations she had made in the margin of her notebook, and slightly adjusted her figures. She was about to tell the girls to go back to their ordinary duties, when Bessie suddenly said:

"'Ell of a row you made on them there stairs."

Mrs. Bradley started, and then laughed.

"I expect that was Molly Kelly getting back to school in a hurry. I came up about five minutes before you saw me come into the bedroom."

"Thought she was going to be murdered, going by the row," said Bessie. "Just a few minutes ago."

"You heard nothing else, though, did you?"

"Nothing else in the world, ma'am," said Kitty.

"Right. Now, listen, you two. I want you to come up here again at precisely half-past two, and undo everything you've done."

"Not 'arf!" said Bessie, austerely. "Who do you think we are? Carter Paterson or something? Or Alice in Wonderland?"

"I should certainly hate to confuse you with the heroine of a certain music-hall turn I saw some time ago," Mrs. Bradley replied. Suspecting a subtle witticism at her expense, Bessie regarded her tormentor with a wary but belligerent eye.

"What was that?" she demanded abruptly.

"A famous conjuring trick. I watched Horace Goldin saw a girl in half. She was almost the image of you, Bessie. It was most realistic, most. An enormous circular saw."

"'Ere!" said Bessie, backing away in mock trepidation, but casting a sincerely anxious glance over her left shoulder as she did so. "Want to make me dream?"

"At two-thirty, then," said Mrs. Bradley, addressing Kitty as well. "Don't fail me, or you'll spoil a very good show."

"This way for the loony-bin," said Bessie, loudly and rudely. "Or, as the old gal at school used to say, 'Across the stream, girls! You'll soon be across the stream!' The asylum being the other side of the brook."

Mrs. Bradley heard Kitty's giggles coming faintly up the stairs, as the girls made their way to the kitchen to warn Annie and Ethel to stand by. It was almost a sound-proof house, she began to think. She resolved to congratulate the builder.

She went back to the bathroom, opened the window, and looked out. Then she glanced again at the bath. The water was coming in nicely. The bath was nearly half full. She looked at her watch, again revised her calculations a little, then went across to the private school to ask Mother Mary-Joseph to spare her a minute or two.

"I want you to know," she said, "what I am trying to do, and why I can't try the experiment with the assistance of one of the children. I am going to reconstruct what may have happened on the afternoon that Ursula Doyle was murdered, and I have asked particularly for your help because you are the lightest of the grown-up people here. You are not easily frightened, I hope?"

"No. I don't think I am," the young nun answered, smiling.

"Good. Go over to the guest-house and enter the first room on the left. Sit down on a chair beside the portable gas-fire, will you? I'll be over in a minute or two."

The nun left her, and Mrs. Bradley walked into the Orphanage, stood there a minute, then went to the guest-house. She found Mother Mary-Joseph seated in a low fire-side chair.

"Don't be alarmed, dear child," she said, very quietly. "You can struggle as much as you like; in fact, the harder the better." So saying, she knelt on the floor beside the low chair, picked up the rubber nozzle of the gas tube and suddenly put her free arm round the nun in the bundly habit, and gripped her nose with some firmness. The young girl gasped and struggled. Mrs. Bradley held her tight, and, the moment that her mouth came open, she inserted the rubber nozzle, and said quickly:

"Don't bite on the rubber, dear child!"

In spite of every effort that the victim could make, she could not escape nor dislodge the nozzle from her mouth.

"Keep your head still. I don't want to injure your nose. So much for that!" said Mrs. Bradley, letting her go at last. "Feel bad? No? That's good. Well, what do you think of the demonstration? Is it convincing, I wonder? Would it convince the police?"

"Was she—is that how she was killed?" The nun had gone pale. "How horrible! Could it have been like that? So quick and clever and cruel?"

Mrs. Bradley cackled—a sound which, since she took it for an expression of mirth, startled Mother Mary-Joseph—and replied:

"You see, even if the attacker had been only a little stronger than the victim, it seems as though, having taken her so suddenly and at such a disadvantage, she would find the rest quite easy. Long before I let you go you would have been unconscious if the gas tap had been turned on. Thank you so much for your help. I do hope you will forgive me for using you quite so unceremoniously."

"We are all under obedience to help the enquiry," the nun responded, with a little bow to acknowledge Mrs. Bradley's apology. "May I go now? I have a class."

When she had gone Mrs. Bradley turned on the gas tap for a second. The gas rushed out with a sharp hissing sound. She turned it off, walked quietly upstairs, opened the bathroom window and climbed out on to the leads. She was wearing a pair of rubber-soled gymnasium shoes which she had borrowed from one of the girls. The climb, she found, was easy enough. She turned first and pushed the window shut, just as she imagined the murderer must have done. Then she groped her way along the flat piece of roof below the window, climbed carefully over the gable, and found herself facing the flat roof of the short passage which, since the three houses had been incorporated into one, joined the end house to the one next door. Along this she crawled, keeping low, and then found herself in view of what had originally been the roof of a garage. Over this she also climbed. She descended to the ground at the end of the converted houses by means of a water pipe. It was clamped into place very firmly with massive, ornamental iron grips, and would not, she thought, pull away from the wall with her weight. On the roof she had thought she could see why the murderer had not needed to make the complete journey over the three converted houses to avoid being seen by the old gardener slapping creosote on the wooden fence with his back to the guest-house windows. The original fences had not been removed when the three houses had been made into one, and those which separated garden from garden still remained, and were six feet high at least. Once past the first of these, the murderer could lie hidden, or could crawl along to the next garden gate and come out on to the road.

The murderer had had bad luck, Mrs. Bradley concluded. The flaw in a well-constructed scheme had been the death of the child from the gas instead of death by drowning. The gas was meant to make her unconscious only, not to kill her. It is never possible to determine the exact amount of carbon monoxide which will cause death; and it is not possible to tell, in the case of any particular supply of coal gas, how much carbon monoxide is present in its constitution, she reflected. The murderer had killed the child instead of stupefying her, and could have had no plan to cover the dire emergency.

She climbed the pipe again and worked her way back towards the bathroom window. Just as her hand was reaching over the sill to grasp the edge of the window to pull it open, she saw—it was less than a shadow— another hand, from inside, grope towards the sill. She flung herself flat on the leads, as a heavy jar of bath salts, the crystals scattering in every direction, flew clean across her and crashed against the trunk of a small, old tree in the garden down below.

Out from the front door came the four eldest orphans, mouths open, Ethel clutching her chest, Bessie with a shower of oaths, Annie breathless and alarmed, Kitty dancing with excitement. Mrs. Bradley, recognising that they would be her saviours, crawled to the edge and waved to them.

"Stay where you are," she said. "I'm coming down."

"Thought you was killed," said Bessie.

"Who was in the bathroom?" Mrs. Bradley demanded when she joined them in front of the guest-house.

"Why, nobody, madam," they said.

"Let's go and look," said Kitty.

"There won't be anyone there by this time," said Mrs. Bradley. "There's been every chance to get away, with none of you on the look-out."

"Oh, yes, out the back door, but they couldn't climb over the wall, I bet," said Bessie. "What say we run? We might ketch 'em, eh? What say?"

But nobody was in sight, although they all ran round

through the gateway and tore as hard as they could towards the school.

"Dear me," said Mother Francis, when she heard of it. "Surely it was very unsafe, in any case, for you to climb about on the guest-house roof, Mrs. Bradley?"

"Yes, I expect so," Mrs. Bradley meekly replied.

CHAPTER 23

PREPARATION

"Strong the tall ostrich on the ground;
Strong through the turbulent profound
Shoots Xiphias to his aim."

CHRISTOPHER SMART: A Song to David.

THE BISHOP HAD BEEN PUT OFF. MRS. BRADLEY HAD seen to it. Driven by George to Bermondsey, she had interviewed Father Thomas, caught him up in the car and borne him off to conduct the negotiations which should result in the Bishop's visit being put off until Thursday, or, at the earliest, Wednesday afternoon. By Wednesday afternoon Ulrica Doyle would be on her way to Southampton.

This being settled, Father Thomas was restored to his presbytery and George drove Mrs. Bradley to Hiversand Bay, where she had booked a room at the hotel. It was the only hotel in the place, modern and fairly comfortable, and at that time of year almost empty. Ulrica Doyle, who had been sent to it under escort earlier in the evening, discovered, to her horror and annoyance, that she and Mrs. Bradley were to share a room, and, what was worse, not a good room, but one on the third floor, one with a window not only not overlooking the sea, but with a sheer long wall underneath it up which no cat or monkey could have climbed.

"Here we shall be undisturbed," said Mrs. Bradley urbanely, when she arrived. No one but George, the Mother Superior, and the two nuns who had escorted

Ulrica, and who were seated, like two black birds, bolt upright on hard bedroom chairs, knew where Mrs. Bradley was staying. George drove the sisters back to the convent, and took the car on to Blacklock Tor and garaged it there as usual.

Ulrica also had been up when Mrs. Bradley came in, and while she was undressing Mrs. Bradley noticed a sharp-toothed band of metal, like an uncomfortable bracelet, clasping her upper left arm.

"What's that?" she asked, regarding it with the detached scientific interest which she would have displayed for totem worship or a ring worn through the lip or nostril. Ulrica flushed, and answered:

"It's voluntary penance, that's all."

"It will probably fester. And I notice that you are wearing it above the injury which you sustained on your journey to my house at Wandles Parva."

"I don't see why I had to be sent to Wandles, and I don't see why you have brought me here. It can't be necessary," said the girl.

"Tell me what happened, Ulrica," said Mrs. Bradley. She took off her hat and coat, and sat on her own bed, looking towards the girl.

"Nothing happened. At the end of afternoon school Mother Saint Francis sent for me and told me to get my packing done because I should be staying here until Wednesday. It's quite absurd, and, of course, I'm not going to stay."

"It's tiresome for you, I know," said Mrs. Bradley. This mild reply apparently surprised the girl, and she said no more. As it was past eleven o'clock, Mrs. Bradley switched off the light as an encouragement to Ulrica to sleep. She herself did not propose to sleep. She listened to every sound, and strained her eyes for shadows, the approach of death.

Morning came, however, after a night of peace, and
Mrs. Bradley was out of the bedroom and seated in the
lounge of the hotel, by the time that Ulrica awoke. The
girl dressed, and came quietly into the lounge. Nobody
else was there. She crossed to Mrs. Bradley's side, and
said a little nervously, "I suppose I may go for a walk
before breakfast?"

"Yes, if I come with you. You can't go out alone."

"But it's silly, and I won't have it." She stared at
Mrs. Bradley as though she were trying to fathom what
was going on in her mind. Then, after a hasty glance
over her shoulder to make sure that nobody else was
there, she said: "I believe you think I did it."

"Do you?"

"I suppose it isn't the slightest use to tell you that I
loved Ursula, and that I would sooner have died than
have any harm befall her?"

"Not the least use. I shouldn't believe you on either
count," said Mrs. Bradley cheerfully.

"But I was giving up my spare time to helping her
with her Latin! You remember you asked me about it.
And I was——"

"Be quiet," said Mrs. Bradley. "If you want to go
for a walk I am ready to go."

So they walked together along the rough, new
promenade, and the wind blew strongly in their faces
from the west. Ulrica had no idea that a car containing
George and Ferdinand cruised past them several times
along the new marine drive which ended—for they
walked as far—on the moor in a smuggler's mule-track.

Breakfast was eaten in silence. Mrs. Bradley had a
newspaper, and hid behind it without doing very much
reading. Her son was breakfasting at a table in an
alcove near by, but no sign passed between them.
Ulrica ate dry toast and drank sugarless coffee.

"I do wish, please," she said, quite timidly, at last, "that you'd let me go back to school. If you can't, will you drive me into Kelsorrow? There is a church there where I can pray."

"School, then," said Mrs. Bradley, "but you'll have to come back here for the night, and you will go from here to Southampton on Wednesday morning."

It suited her own plans that they should return to the school. Her son sat beside George, but got off before they reached the convent gates, and thanked Mrs. Bradley for the lift as though they had been chance acquaintances. If Ulrica recognised him she made no sign. He walked downhill towards the village. As soon as George had set down his other passengers he drove off at good speed over the bumpy road in the direction from which they had come. He did not stay in Hiversand Bay, however, but drove through it, turned south-east, and arrived in Kelsorrow just after half-past ten. He pulled up outside the High School and rang the bell.

"Message for the headmistress from St. Peter's Convent," he said; and, when he was taken in to see the headmistress, he added, "An S.O.S., madam, from the Reverend Mother Superior. Could you spare one of your physical training ladies to give the St. Peter's young ladies a polishing-up for the Bishop?"

So Miss Bonnet—to her disgust, for it was her day for two free periods at Kelsorrow and she had been going to spend them in overhauling all the apparatus that was not being used by her superior, the full-time mistress—was hustled by George into his car—her own being in the garage, for she did not bother to get it out to go to Kelsorrow School, which was distant about a hundred yards from her lodgings—and driven swiftly and expertly to the convent.

"So very good of Miss Heath. So nice of you, my dear," said Mother Francis, who did not, as a matter of fact, Miss Bonnet thought, give the slightest impression that either opinion was her true one. She sent Miss Bonnet into the gymnasium, where the sixth form awaited instruction. Miss Bonnet began bad-temperedly, but soon the excellent response she got, as usual, from the girls, and the fun of feeling the secret gratification that power over the actions of others always gave her, brought her out bright, like the sun appearing from clouds.

The girls liked her better like this; and always argued that "Dulcie" was jollier after she'd been in the sulks than when she had started cheerful. Besides, they had had it impressed upon them that they must be at their very best for the Bishop. All things were opened for his inspection: the pigsties no less than the gymnasium; the private school no less than the Orphanage; Mother Saint Cyprian's needlework, Mother Saint Benedict's illuminations, Mother Saint Simon-Zelotes' metal-work—had not the Bishop's candlesticks been wrought by her, and his altar cloths and missal adorned by the others?

Miss Bonnet worked with good will, and no one but Mrs. Bradley came and watched. This, in itself, was a departure from custom of more than ordinary significance, for it meant that none of the nuns was on supervising duty. All were extremely busy, as Mrs. Bradley knew, and there was, in any case, no provision for the supervision of physical training that day. Little Mother Jude was superintending the scouring and polishing of all the kitchen utensils, and proposed to go fishing in the moorland streams to give the Bishop a palatable

Lenten dish. That it was just a little early for trout had caused her a sleepless night, but none of the fishing was preserved, and she had her own methods—having poached salmon in her unregenerate days, when she was a barefoot child—for obtaining what she required. Indeed, as she declared, with a smile, to Mrs. Bradley, she would poach fish for the Bishop any day, and on Sundays, too, should he desire it. Mrs. Bradley could scarcely poke a nun in the ribs, but she cackled with great appreciation.

Mother Ambrose was burnishing the Orphanage, and all the orphans were let off school to help her. They polished and scrubbed and fetched and carried, and tripped over pails of water, cleaned paint, slid on the soap and had narrow escapes from death in many forms. They were, most of them, very happy, because they liked anything better than school and their lessons. The Bishop, in fact, was very generally popular, Mrs. Bradley gathered, and soon would arrive, fat and laughing, to have his ring kissed, himself idolised, his every word received with breathless ecstasy. A rather indelicate comparison of a cock among hens, which came unbidden to her mind, Mrs. Bradley quickly smothered out of existence.

Mother Simon-Zelotes, her copies of the chalice and paten now carefully locked away, the originals in the strong-room of the bank, was getting her special class to finish their own designs so that there could be a good show of work for the Bishop to see. Mother Cyprian, her embroidered bookbindings done, was energetically exhorting her pupils to get on with their needlework, decorative stitchery, pattern drafting, knitting and drawn-thread work. Even Mother Francis herself, still calm, but sharp-tongued and critical, was getting drawings and paintings mounted ready for show, and urging her flock to fresh efforts, clear colours, rare images and ideas, so that the Bishop should make favourable comment on her work.

Only the Mother Superior, in the impregnable calm of age, awaited the Bishop without trepidation or excitement; awaited the Bishop merely as one friend will wait for another, knowing well that partings and meetings, even the parting of death and the meeting of souls cannot weaken or strengthen the bonds forged of confidence, sympathy, mutual goodwill and affection.

She sent for Mrs. Bradley to go and see her. She was in the nuns' parlour, a pleasant room except for the inevitable religious picture with its emphasis on suffering and death. It was odd, Mrs. Bradley thought, thus to insist upon death rather than upon life and resurrection.

"My dear," said the Mother Superior, "I asked you to come because I want to know whether you're sure."

"Quite sure."

"It is a case, then, for the police?"

"We shall have to decide about that."

"You have proof?"

"Enough for any prosecuting counsel." The old woman in the heavy black robes sighed profoundly.

"From the very first I feared it," she said.

"Yes," said Mrs. Bradley. "I know. I knew, when first my son came along with the tale, that you feared it. We shall get the girl off to New York by to-morrow's boat. What about the paten and the chalice?"

"If your chauffeur will call for them, and give a receipt to-morrow morning, they should be here about twelve."

"It's the best we can do, I suppose. I would like to leave it as late as we possibly can."

"At what time does Ulrica leave?"

"She is catching a train at ten-thirty."

"Your son is going to meet her?"

"At the docks, and see her on to the boat. There mustn't be any hitch."

"She will be well looked after on the journey. Two of us will take her to her destination."

"Mother Saint Timothy and Mother Saint Dominic isn't it? And that, I hope, will mean the end of this dreadful business. Already rumour has died down, and I think no more children have been taken away from the school. As for me, I am going along to the guest-house to get some sleep. I expect to have another wakeful night."

"You guard the child well. We are indebted to you. Oh, and for more than that."

"I keep awake for my own sake," Mrs. Bradley replied, with a humorous grimace and a shrug. "It is easy enough, for I live the life of a hunted animal." She concluded the statement with a chuckle.

"You are good to us—very good. God will reward you," the other old woman said gently. With very faint faith in this vicarious promise, Mrs. Bradley took her leave. When she had gone the Mother Superior knelt at the prie-dieu and prayed for Mrs. Bradley—for her bodily safety, for the success of her enterprise, and, last but not least, for her to be saved from the sin of unseemly levity.

Mrs. Bradley, who was conscious not of levity, unseemly or otherwise, but of the equally sinful feeling of acute depression, a sensation which she had been trying to fight off for days, walked over to the guest-house with less than her customary briskness. It was a quarter to twelve, for she had remained in the gymnasium some time before going to the Mother Superior. She found Bessie and Maggie in the kitchen peeling potatoes. They had nearly finished this task and apparently were not on speaking terms, for a deathly silence reigned, a silence as foreign to both their natures as to a stream bounding downhill over boulders.

"Oh, Bessie," said Mrs. Bradley, "I am going to my room for a bit. Will you come and wake me, without fail, at twenty past twelve?"

"Yes, certainly, madam," Bessie tonelessly replied. Mrs. Bradley's jaw did not drop, but her mental reaction was the same as if it had done so. She made no comment, however, thanked Bessie, smiled at Maggie, and went up the stairs.

"Won't be the same without her," said Bessie, gazing at the door which had closed behind Mrs. Bradley's small figure. "Not 'arf a corf-drop, she ain't."

This tribute was received with an emotional sniff by Maggie, who always cried very easily, and was forgiven her faults as easily in consequence, since tears were regarded as a sign of penitence, leading to grace, by Mother Ambrose.

"But you don't really *know* she's leaving," she affirmed for the fourteenth time since Bessie had first announced the imminence of Mrs. Bradley's departure. Bessie, who had already made thirteen replies to this gambit, disdained another, flung the last potato into the bowl so that the water leapt up and splashed Maggie from head to foot, rinsed her hands under the tap, and dried them, in austere silence, upon the roller towel.

"Perhaps she'll come back and see us," volunteered Maggie, unresentful of the spattering, and wiping off the water with apparent unconsciousness. She went to the cupboard, took out a cake-tin which was burnished to spotless brilliance, held it up in a good light and re-set her curls. "She might give us all an outing after Easter."

"*Outing!*" said Bessie, spewing out the word as though it were something loathsome. "All you think about, and having a goggle at boys when Mother Saint Ambrose takes her optics off you!"

As this was the exact truth, with no exaggeration whatever as a basis for argument, and as Bessie herself despised boys except in the capacity of gun-men and other law-breakers, there was nothing for Maggie to say. She giggled amiably, put the potatoes on to boil, then went and peeped at the clock in the parlour and set the kitchen clock right. The kitchen clock was supposed to be sacred to the ministrations of Mother Jude, but in her absence the orphans kept it going, for she, unlike Mother Ambrose, was happy-go-lucky as regarded her special privileges, and farmed them out to the deserving and (in Mother Ambrose's tight-lipped, militant opinion) to the undeserving also, in an irresponsible manner for which, later on, she would certainly be called to account.

At twenty minutes past twelve, to the tick, therefore, Bessie was able to go up and wake Mrs. Bradley.

"*You* wasn't very deep off," she announced with disapproval. "Woke up at a touch, you did. Guilty conscience, or something, I should call it."

Mrs. Bradley got up and tidied her hair, and grinned kindly at Bessie, whose crude manifestations of affection touched and pleased her.

"I've a job for you, Bessie," she said.

"Oh, 'elp," said Bessie tartly. "I'm up to me eyes for Mother Saint Jude and Mother Saint Ambrose and Sister Genevieve and Sister Lucia already. The Bishop don't come very often, but when he do—visitation, they calls it. More like the Last Day, I reckon!"

"I hope," said Mrs. Bradley, "that you do not betray

those racy opinions to Mother Saint Ambrose and
Mother Saint Jude."

"Oh, Mother Saint Jude wouldn't mind, although
she's as flighty as any of 'em when it comes to the
Bishop," said Bessie. "And Mother Saint Ambrose
don't really like nothing that upsets what she calls the
routine. Well, what you want me to do?"

"Retire from the guest-house when I do, and take
up a job I've found for you with a friend of mine,"
Mrs. Bradley answered concisely. She described to
Bessie the work which she had in mind. Bessie's face
became transfigured.

"Blimy, if I couldn't give you a smacker," she
pronounced, in accents of awe. Mrs. Bradley, who had
not kissed anyone for more than twenty years, recoiled
in alarm, and Bessie, both diverted and restored by this
sight, grinned devilishly and opened the door for Mrs.
Bradley to go to the bathroom to wash.

She turned at the door and said:

"Who uses bath-salts here, Bessie?"

"Why, that there Mrs. Maslin," Bessie promptly
replied.

"Ah, yes. I might have deduced that," Mrs. Bradley
observed. She dried her hands, went downstairs to
the dining-room and took the chair that was empty.
All the other guests were assembled. The chair
happened to be between Miss Bonnet and Mrs. Maslin.

"So you haven't seen fit to take away Mary?" Mrs.
Bradley observed to Mrs. Maslin. "May I say that I
think you are unwise?"

"We shall go as soon as Ulrica is settled," Mrs.
Maslin responded, with her vacant, insincere smile.
"I shall go to the docks, of course, to see her off, and
shall probably take Mary along. Perhaps you didn't
know, but she and I and her father are going out by the

next boat. We can't afford to let Ulrica have it all her own way now that poor little Ursula is dead. After all, what's a will, if not subject to alteration?"

"You won't need to get this one altered," said Mrs. Bradley. "I fancy it is altered already."

CHAPTER 24

CONFLAGRATION

"But these all night,
Like candles, shed
Their beams, and light
Us into bed.

They are indeed our pillar-fires,
Seen as we go;
They are that City's shining spires
We travel to."

HENRY VAUGHAN: Cheerfulness.

AS SOON AS TEA WAS OVER, GEORGE DROVE MRS.
Bradley and Ulrica Doyle towards Hiversand Bay to
spend the night again at the hotel, but before they had
gone very far it was fairly obvious that they were being
followed. Acting on instructions, therefore, murmured
by his employer down the speaking-tube, George
accelerated, and drove on to the main road to Kelsorrow.
He swung left just before they reached a bridge over the
river, skirted the town, found a by-pass road, and then
drove along it at fifty miles an hour. Mrs. Bradley
looked back. About a hundred yards behind them on
the straight, wide road, a red sports car was bursting
along at a speed great enough to overtake them, at their
present rate, before the wide road ended at the entrance
to the next town.

"Better pull up, George. I don't recognise the car,"
said Mrs. Bradley. "They may not be following us,

324

but if they are I think we'd better see what they want."

George pulled in to the grassy edge of the road. The sports car drew up ten yards in front of them, and out of it got a man whom Mrs. Bradley had never seen before. Ulrica, however, recognised him, and leaving Mrs. Bradley and George, who were standing by the roadside, she walked to meet him.

"Why, Uncle Percival! Is anything wrong?" she said. Mr. Maslin took hold of her hand as though she had been a small child. He did not answer, but walked up to Mrs. Bradley and addressed her by name.

"Mrs. Bradley, my little girl! Will you please return at once to the convent? Mary has gone! I know it's unreasonable to ask you to do any more. My wife has confessed that you urged her to take the child home, but—will you come back with me, please?"

"I am concerned with Ulrica's safety. That is my first responsibility," Mrs. Bradley told him. "But, of course, I will do what I can. George, take Miss Doyle as before, and I'll telephone you, later on. Remain there until you hear from me."

"Very good, madam." He walked to the car, and returned with a small revolver. "I have a licence for this, madam. Please take it. I have another."

"Good heavens, George!" said Mrs. Bradley.

"There's such things as put-up jobs," said George, glowering solemnly at Mr. Maslin, "and the party of the second part might just as well know exactly where they get off."

With these admirable sentiments he went back to the car and opened the door for Ulrica. Then he took his place at the wheel, turned the car in the wide road in one magnificent arc, and drove back towards Hiversand Bay.

"Now, Mr. Maslin," said Mrs. Bradley, when her

own car was out of sight, "don't worry too much. How much is known about the disappearance?"

"Nothing. Nothing at all. Look here, jump in, do you mind?—I'd like to get back to the convent. I've rung up the police, so that's something. I don't know the district, unfortunately, but I'll comb out every inch——" The car shot away.

It was obvious, from the moment of their arrival, that something was seriously wrong. Mrs. Bradley clearly remembered the last occasion on which she had searched for Mary Maslin. This time (she was informed by the white-faced sister portress at the gate) Miss Bonnet, who had actually got into her car to drive back to Kelsorrow, had got out of the car again, put on her trousers, borrowed a hoe from the gardening shed, and had gone off, followed by the ironic applause of Bessie and the hysterical giggles of Kitty, to conduct a search on her own.

"Which way did she go?" asked Mrs. Bradley.

"Quick, I'll show you," said Bessie. "Lor', she didn't half look a cutie!"

"You run off and find Sister Genevieve and ask her to get hot blankets ready," said Mrs. Bradley, turning away from Bessie towards Mrs. Maslin. "I suppose the buildings here and the grounds and the garden have been searched?" she said. "When was the girl first missed?"

"She was to have had tea with her father and me in the guest-house," said Mrs. Maslin, more foxy-looking than ever with fright and anxiety. "It was all arranged, and when she didn't turn up I thought she must have been kept after school or something. How was I to know that they don't keep the children in? *We* were always kept in!" she added, peevish with fear.

"And at what time did you become anxious?"

"At half-past five, just after you had gone off with Ulrica, and now I find that she hasn't been seen since the end of afternoon school."

"Let's see—she would have been having a games lesson with Mother Saint Benedict," said Mrs. Bradley rapidly, "Go and find Mother Saint Benedict, Mrs. Maslin, and ask whether Mary had a fall or sustained any injury during the game. That might help a little, do you see?"

"Oh, dear, oh, dear! This violence! And all this dreadful secrecy about Ulrica! Whatever shall we do? It's too terrible," said Mrs. Maslin, going off to find Mother Saint Benedict.

It was too terrible for Mr. Maslin, as Mrs. Bradley could see. He had been pale when she had first met him; he was now a dreadful grey colour; his nostrils were pinched and his cheeks seemed to have fallen in.

"For God's sake," he kept muttering. "For God's sake! For God's sake!"

"Mr. Maslin," said Mrs. Bradley, "I want you, please, to drive me to the village, and not to worry. Everything is going to be all right."

At the village post office there was a telephone. The post office itself was closed, but the shop was still open, and there was no difficulty about calling up the hotel at Hiversand Bay.

"Here, madam, right in the entrance lobby," George's voice responded. "Nobody can come either in or out without I see them. The young lady went straight to her room on arrival, and says she doesn't want any food. The other young lady has had a dinner sent up, madam, so the head-waiter tells me. It's a homely little hotel, madam, and I am already in fairly close touch with most of the staff. I don't think we need have much fear, madam, but what the young ladies will be safe."

"Excellent, George. As soon as the inspector arrives,

you can come on here and have your own supper.
I'm telephoning him now."

She telephoned the inspector, and went back, grimly
smiling, to the almost frantic Mr. Maslin.

"The inspector thinks his men are well on the trail.
Probably a bare-faced bit of kidnapping, he says," she
observed. "Somebody who's heard that she's Timothy
Doyle's granddaughter, I suppose."

"They may kill her!"

"They won't kill her. The police know where she is."

"Know where she is? Why the devil don't they get
hold of her, then?"

"All in good time," said Mrs. Bradley. "Back to
the convent, please."

The convent had been searched from the attics in the
Orphanage to the cellars beneath the frater. The nuns
were in groups in the Common Room, the frater, the
children's refectory and the cloister. The guests had
congregated miserably in the guest-house parlour; the
orphans, under the jaundiced eye of Mother Saint
Ambrose, were sitting in close rows in the Orphanage
playroom, doing needlework with hands that were sticky
with the sweat of excitement; the boarders, let off
preparation, had been given freedom to help in the
search of the school and the grounds. Mother Saint
Francis was shut away in her room, because she and the
Mother Superior (calm among her daughters, as behoved
the head of the house) were the only members of the
Community who knew that Mary Maslin was safe at
Hiversand Bay, and while Mrs. Bradley knew that
nobody would suspect that the benignity of the Reverend
Mother Superior hid anything but an anxiety that was
natural and general to everybody, she had not the same
faith in the dramatic abilities of the volatile Mother
Francis.

Meanwhile, the object of all the care and suffering was sitting at a small bedside table eating a four-course meal with every appearance of appetite, breaking off occasionally to observe in rapturous tones:

"I say, isn't this a rag! I *say*, won't the girls be sick!"

"I should think you'll be the one to be sick," her cousin coldly observed. "And I refuse to go to sleep with a *policeman* in the room."

It turned out to be a policeman's wife, however, a young and cheery creature, whose husband, a large, young sergeant, was posted on the landing outside the bedroom door, with a chair, a bottle of beer, some tobacco, a tumbler, a large ash-tray, a book and a plate of cold beef, cold ham, mustard pickles and bread. He was there unofficially, having been, however, officially released from duty so that he could be "lent" to Mrs. Bradley as a watchdog.

George, whose task was done, took his leave, and at a leisurely twenty-eight miles, drove over to Blacklock Tor, and garaged the car at the inn. He had a half-pint, went out for a walk on the moor, had another half-pint before they closed, then went up to his room. He was on the second floor, and his window looked over the sloping hill-side of moor towards the convent. He went to the window and looked out, but except for the steady light of Saint Peter's Finger which shone from the church tower lantern, there was nothing else on the landscape visible except the dark stretch of the moor.

He went to bed at a quarter to eleven, gave a last glance at his watch before he put out the light, turned his face towards the window and closed his eyes. At five minutes to eleven he went to sleep.

He did not know what woke him. No light was shining on to his face, and no sudden noise had startled him, but through the uncurtained window he could see

that the sky was alight with a deep, red glow. He got
out of bed very quickly, and went to look out. A
minute later he was putting on his flannel trousers, a
lounge jacket and his boots, and a minute later still he
was running downstairs to get the car.

The garage was a lock-up, and he had a key of his own.
He switched on his lights, drove carefully on to the road,
and then put the car at the moorland track at such a
breakneck pace that it bounded over the ruts, the heather
and the boulders like a car in a comic film.

(2)

Of all the searchers for Mary Maslin, the most
feverish, apart from the Maslins themselves, who had
been into Kelsorrow to interview the police and then
had scoured the country-side in the fast red sports car
for clues, were Mother Benedict and Miss Bonnet.
Fortunately, the useful rule of obedience could be
brought into play to prevent the nun from continuing
the useless search, but not even the news that the
police were on the track of the missing child (brought
back from Kelsorrow police-station by a greatly-relieved
Mr. Maslin as additional information to that supplied
by Mrs. Bradley) could abate Miss Bonnet's ardour or
allay her obvious anxiety. In the end, even she gave up,
and a bed was found for her in the Orphanage on the
top floor where Sister Bridget, now practically recovered,
lay attended, as usual, by the Infirmarian, in the large
infirmary ward.

On the floor below slept the orphans, some thirty-six
of them, their ages ranging from three to seventeen or
eighteen. They were in five dormitories, and in each
dormitory slept a nun. Mother Ambrose and Mother
Jude were always on duty, and the rest of the Com-

munity slept week by week in the Orphanage dormitories by rota, with the exception of Mother Francis, who remained in charge of the private school children in their cubicled dorters on the west side of the cloister.

Before the attack with the hammer Sister Bridget had been a heavy sleeper, but her sleep had been fitful during her sojourn in the Infirmary. Since she had recovered consciousness she had thought a good deal, in her rambling non-consequential way, about her mouse, and had mentioned it once or twice to Mrs. Bradley. Mrs. Bradley had soothed her with accounts of its well-being, and had suggested to Mother Ambrose that it should be imported into the Orphanage. Mother Ambrose, however, with courtesy and finality, had declined to have the mouse brought anywhere near the house of which she was in charge.

"It will breed," was her last and unarguable dictum. So the mouse remained in Mrs. Bradley's room, and she fed it and grew accustomed to its company and to finding it on her pillow, in her shoe, climbing the curtains, and almost drowned in the ewer. On the Tuesday night, when Mary Maslin was missed, the general excitement even penetrated to the Infirmary, for its guardian had joined in the search with everyone else, and had come back, tired and flushed, to sleep a good deal more soundly than usual.

Sister Bridget was wakeful and excited. She was aware of vague cravings, and these crystallised themselves, at about half-past eleven, into a violent desire for the companionship of her mouse. She knew that it was of no use to call her mouse, as she had been wont to do when she slept in her bedroom at the guest-house, for, although she was extremely vague as to where she was, she did know that she had called it, and called it in vain, a good many times just lately, so she made up her mind to go and look for it.

She had managed to steal and secrete two boxes of matches since the accident. She crept from her bed, leering happily, since, childishly, her happiness was rooted in action, not contemplation, and, opening the window, put her hand out between the bars—for all the second- and third-floor windows in the Orphanage were barred—and brought in a box of matches.

Then she waddled, bare-footed, to the door, and went to look for her mouse. She began on the bottom floor —not for any reason, but because she forgot, half-way, what it was she was going to do, and the endless stairs, from the third floor down to the ground, became a kind of pilgrimage which could be undertaken without thought. There were exactly the same number of stairs in each flight, and there were two flights, with a turn, between each floor. She sat down, as a baby will, and shifted her seat from stair to stair, clutching hold of the banisters in the darkness to reassure herself, and so that she did not fall.

When she got to the bottom and found there were no more stairs, she began to whimper. Then she remembered what she had come for, and, striking matches and dropping them, began to look for her mouse.

(3)

Mrs. Bradley had given up her room in the guest-house to Mr. Maslin, for the guest-house had no double rooms. She herself had received accommodation, as before, in the Orphanage, and had gone to bed at eleven, happy in the belief that her responsibilities for the night were over, and that Mary Maslin and Ulrica Doyle were safe at Hiversand Bay.

It was with a feeling of unaccountable anxiety, therefore, that she woke at about midnight, and sat up in bed. She listened, but there was nothing to be heard. She got out of bed and walked to the window, but there was nothing to be seen. She went back to bed again, lay down and tried to go to sleep. It was useless.

She went to the door, which she had locked, and turned the key. Then she knew what had awakened her. Somewhere, lower down in the house, was a muffled crackling and roaring. Mrs. Bradley took George's revolver from under her pillow, put on her peacock dressing-gown and a pair of stout shoes which she used when she walked on the moors, and descended the stairs to find out the cause of the noises.

Fire! The gust of hot air struck against her as she reached the first-floor landing. Fire! The whole of the ground floor appeared to be in flames. As she arrived at the top of it, the whole of the last flight of stairs collapsed almost under her feet.

She raced for the children's dormitories, found Mother Ambrose awake, and told her, quickly but quietly, what had happened. Mother Ambrose got up at once, and—interesting reaction, Mrs. Bradley thought —clothed herself fully and then prayed before she began to make the rounds of the various dormitories and wake the children. Mrs. Bradley left her, and made a systematic tour of the two top floors of the house.

She first roused Miss Bonnet, who immediately pulled over her pyjamas the inevitable pair of trousers, shoved her arms into a blazer, and her feet into brogues. She was as calm as Mother Ambrose had been, Mrs. Bradley noted with relief.

Little Mother Jude knelt and prayed, then put on her habit—perhaps this was part of the rule, Mrs. Bradley thought—and also began to go the round of the beds. Mother Benedict and old Mother Bartholomew, the two nuns who happened to be on duty at the Orphanage that night, placed themselves under the direction of Mother Ambrose.

All this was accomplished with the greatest rapidity and quietness, but, by the time all the children had been roused, the fire had gained ground, and the bottom floor of the house was an inferno. The children were kept in the rooms whilst Mrs. Bradley and Mother Jude went to survey the chances of escape by the staircase. The position, as Mrs. Bradley had known it must be, was hopeless.

"Never mind," said Mother Ambrose, who had lined up the orphans and put each section in charge of one of the eldest, "there's a fire escape from the top storey. Let us all go up there."

So up the stairs they mounted to the Infirmary, and found Sister Bridget, the cause of all the mischief, asleep in her bed. She had run away from the fire, and, by the time she was back in the Infirmary, had forgotten both the danger and her mouse.

They left her asleep for the moment, whilst Miss Bonnet took it upon herself to investigate the chances of escape down the outside ladder.

She opened the Infirmary window, which ended in a broad, perforated iron platform, the top of the fire escape, and lowered herself into the darkness. Suddenly a great tongue of flame leapt out of a window, and in a minute Miss Bonnet came back into view at the top of the ladder.

"No go," she muttered in Mrs. Bradley's ear.

"Smoke?"

"Flames, too. The blinking thing's red hot on the floor below the upper dormitory. I blistered my hands on the metal. *We* might risk it, but these kids will never face it. What are we going to do?"

"Tell the others," said Mrs. Bradley. "The decision, I suppose, must rest with Mother Saint Ambrose."

"Right. You tell 'em. I'll stay here with the kids and quell any riot," Miss Bonnet officiously observed.

Mrs. Bradley drew back from the window to let Miss Bonnet climb in. The girl was trembling, but her voice was steady and her eyes were clear and brave. Mrs. Bradley walked towards the door and gave the nuns a glance to get them to follow. There, away from the children, she told them Miss Bonnet's opinion.

"I'll go down myself, just to confirm what she says, but I'm certain she's right," she added. So, with a jest as she passed the children, who were all assembled in straight, mute lines behind their leaders, she opened the window and crawled out. The dressing-gown was a nuisance, so she shed it, and pushed it back over the sill. Then she began to climb backwards down the ladder.

The air got hotter and hotter. She could hear the roaring of the fire. Soon she was coughing, her lungs full of acrid smoke. Then the metal became hot to the touch, and she imagined that she could feel the heat through her shoes. She tried to get farther down the ladder, but felt herself being suffocated by the smoke which now was billowing in great thick clouds about her. The heat against the palms of her hands was unbearable, and another tongue of flame shot out of a window, this time above her head, and singed her hair.

As quickly as she could she mounted again, pulled herself over the sill, walked, smoke-grimed, to the door, and went outside on the landing to clear her lungs. She leaned against the stair-head, eyes streaming and throat like a rasp, coughing from effects of the smoke.

The children, by this time, could hear the roaring of the fire, and see the smoke drifting past the window, and had become terrified. Some were crying, others were whimpering pathetically for the mothers who had either died or deserted them. One began to scream, and Mother Ambrose, to prevent a general panic, seized the child quickly, muffled her head in her habit, and almost suffocated her into silence.

"Now all of you children sit down on the beds," she said calmly, "and Mother Saint Bartholomew will tell you a nice, quiet story whilst we are waiting. Not a long story, please, Mother. We shall not have to stay here very long."

Old Mother Bartholomew, owing, Mrs. Bradley supposed, to her former profession, was a gifted raconteuse.

She began to tell the children, not stories of saints and angels, but racy tales of a pantomime that she had taken part in as a child. Mrs. Bradley looked at the group ; at Mother Ambrose, justifying gloriously her military habit and address; at little Mother Jude, cherubically smiling in death's face, as though she saw God's face behind it, as a man may show his own expression through a mask; at Mother Benedict, who had never looked more beautiful than she did at that moment, serene, calm and courageous; at old wrinkled Mother Bartholomew, suddenly returned for inspiration to her first love, her eyes sparkling with amusement, her gestures free and occasionally vulgar, as with a flow of anecdote, reported repartee, descriptions of scenes and "business," stories of quarrels, generosity, poverty, travel, she turned once more to take Rosa Cardosa from limbo, and exhibit, in God's name, the former idol of five capitals and two continents.

Last Mrs. Bradley looked sideways at Miss Bonnet's hard young face.

"Take it pretty well, don't they? I suppose they do *know* there's not an earthly?" said Miss Bonnet, meeting her glance.

"And that being so," said Mrs. Bradley, "I suppose that you and I can take it that our short but interesting game of cat and mouse is now at an end?"

"What I can't make out," said Miss Bonnet, drawing away to the farthest corner of the room, so as not to interrupt the pantomime story, "is how you tumbled to it all."

"Well, there was nobody else. I couldn't see for a time how you stood to gain, until, of course, the business of the paten and the chalice came up. Then I remembered that the children's grandfather had made an offer for them to the convent some time previously. It also transpired that he was an unscrupulous old man who had not the slightest objection to purchasing stolen goods as long as they were what he desired, and I heard about you and the pictures——"

"Oh, *damn!*" said Miss Bonnet, dismayed. "How did that come out?"

"You appear to have overlooked the fact that your reputation followed you to Kelsorrow, and from Kelsorrow to the convent."

"But I didn't think the nuns *could* know, when they let me come here and teach in the private school."

"Well, they did know. And the next thing which occurred to me was that you had killed the child because she was the heiress, and would be certain to go to New York at some time when she would immediately identify the stolen property."

"It's quite true that the confounded kid had caught me measuring the beastly things once, before the copies were made. I was really sneaking them then, but she interrupted the good work. However, the rest of your suspicions——''

"I supposed," said Mrs. Bradley, "that you had inserted a cigarette holder in the end of the gas-flex, so that the teeth marks would not show on the rubber nozzle."

"How did you get on to that? It doesn't act, of course, because I don't use a holder. But I can see that it must very soon have dawned on you that all the times fitted in rather well with the days that I came to the convent, and I admit, of course, that I lobbed the hammer at your head that night you sat in the Common Room after the nuns had gone. In fact, it struck me pretty soon that you were altogether too hot. I began to feel beastly unsafe. I tried to get you, too, by firing that room in the guest-house, but only knocked out the poor old lay-sister, and I meant to lay for you on the following Thursday, and then at the pub."

She walked over to the window and looked out. There was nothing to see except smoke. She returned to Mrs. Bradley's side.

"It's all right to discuss the thing, I suppose. Our chances appear to be nil. How did you think you could prove the murder on me? Or mustn't I ask?"

"Well, you could have been the girl on the guest-house roof. She was wearing a tunic. Then, you did not know that the children here are always bathed under a wrap. You knew where to find a guest-house towel— a thing I was pretty sure that scarcely any of my suspects would have known—for *you* had been offered a bath in the guest-house before! Then, you were almost the only person who insisted that the suicide verdict was the right one, so, naturally, I wondered whether you had anything to gain from it!"

"I believe," said Mother Jude, breaking in as Mother

Bartholomew came to the end of her tale, "that it might be better to move a floor higher, Mrs. Bradley."

So the children, very difficult now to control, were marched up the next flight of stairs, those behind pushing hard against those in front, and one poor creature murmuring, "Mummy!   Mummy!" in heart-breaking accents of fear.

"Not too good a move," said Miss Bonnet quietly. "I see her point, but these rooms are so beastly cheerless, and there's nowhere on earth to sit in these beastly attics except on the floor."

She sat on it, and, taking no further notice of Mrs. Bradley, made the children into two concentric circles, feet to the middle, and started some sitting-down physical exercises to occupy the attention of the party.

"She is a good girl.   She has a good heart," said Mother Jude.   "Is there any chance, do you think?"

Mrs. Bradley beckoned her, and the two of them, followed by Bessie's anxious eyes, went out on to the landing.   They crossed it, and entered the room on the opposite side of the house.   The attic windows, being set in the slope of the roof, did not give a very good view, so they went down the next flight of stairs to the Infirmary landing, and stood at the window again, but at the one in a small room on the opposite side of the house where the smoke was not blowing.   A great crowd of people, lighted by the flames that now belched luridly forth from the lower part of the Orphanage, waved to them and shouted.   Mrs. Bradley waved, and scanned the crowd anxiously for George.   He was not to be seen.   There was a sudden movement, and then a struggle, and two of the nuns could be seen holding back another nun who was trying to rush into the building.   It was too uncertain a light in which to distinguish one habited figure from another.   Suddenly there was another commotion, however, and, hatless, there stood George. He cupped his hands and bellowed —for he could see his employer silhouetted against the light which she had turned on in the little room:

"O.K., madam! Hang on! I've been and dug out the brigade!"

"Good heavens, George!" Mrs. Bradley returned, with a sudden screech of laughter. She withdrew her head, and addressed her companion, Mother Jude.

"But the job will be to get these children out in time, even so. It won't be much good to carry them one by one down a ladder, I imagine, even if a ladder can be set up. The fire is gaining rapidly, and the firemen aren't here yet, because George is only just back."

They mounted to the attics again. Miss Bonnet had concluded her table of exercises and the children seemed a little more controlled. It was only a matter of time, though, Mrs. Bradley decided, before there was scream- ing panic. Suddenly Bessie, grim-eyed, set up the languishing theme song of a film. She kept one eye on Mother Ambrose, but the nun made no objection, and after a bit the other orphans joined in.

Taking advantage of this timely assistance from Bessie, Mrs. Bradley explained the position to the nuns.

"Have to chuck 'em out into a sheet, I'd say," said Miss Bonnet. "They won't like it, poor little brutes, but it can't be helped. Even if there were *time* to get 'em down one by one, I doubt whether the men could climb past that red-hot stuff."

The position was now truly terrifying, and the children were kept from the windows. A sentry—Mother Benedict—was posted outside on the landing to keep watch on the progress which the fire was making up the stairs, and Mrs. Bradley herself went back to the floor below—which was burning hot to her feet and might, she knew, at any moment fall through in a rush of flame—to shout down orders to George.

The brigade, she saw, had arrived. She went back to the attics to report.

"These blasted bars!" said Miss Bonnett, tugging with maniac strength at the bars which covered the window. All the upstair Orphanage windows were barred, except for the one which opened on to the useless fire escape.

Mrs. Bradley and Mother Ambrose helped Miss Bonnet to pull. Mrs. Bradley had brought Sister Bridget upstairs with her this time, for the half-witted creature had continued to sleep through the danger. She now sat in a corner whimpering, until Mother Ambrose told her to be quiet. So she squatted down obediently, to Mrs. Bradley's relief, and did not give any more trouble.

"I think," said Mother Ambrose, "that we should all pray."

"Pray, nothing!" said Miss Bonnet, from the window. "They want us to climb on the roof! I'll go up first, if you like, and help haul the kids up. Lord, what a leap in the dark!"

"It's an impossible jump," said Mrs. Bradley, under her breath; but, before she could make any other suggestion, Miss Bonnet was out on the landing and had made a cat-like leap to catch at the edge of the open trap-door. She pulled herself up by her arms—a gymnast's movement—swung her legs, and then was up and through. She lay on her stomach and stretched an arm through the opening.

"Come on, next!" she said. "Make a straight line, you girls, and nobody is to shove! Big ones first, Mother Saint Ambrose. There'll be no one to mind the babies, else, up here. QUIET!'' she added, in a bellow which silenced even the terror-stricken orphans.

"They'll never be able to jump from such a height. It's four stories,'' said Mrs. Bradley, who, assisted by Mother Ambrose, had swung herself up beside her.

"Ladder in a slant from the gatehouse roof,'' said Miss Bonnet. "It's your man. He's a sensible feller. Push us up some of those kids, and hats off to Casabianca!'' she added, with good-humoured roughness, for she was really, it was obvious, horribly frightened.

The little children were carried down first by the firemen. Miss Bonnet and Mrs. Bradley descended again through the trap-door to assist the nuns through the opening on to the roof. It was easy enough to lift Mother Benedict up, and Annie and Bessie, strong girls both, soon hauled her to safety; Mother Jude, too, was not much trouble. But lay-sister Bridget, heavy Mother Ambrose and old Mother Bartholomew taxed the strength and ingenuity of the party, who were now augmented, however, by George and one of the firemen.

In the end, the last of the orphans, children of twelve or thirteen, had to be made to jump. Most of them hung back, and it was pretty to see Miss Bonnet, obviously in her element, lobbing them into the sheet held out by the firemen on the roof of the gatehouse.

CHAPTER 25

CONCLUSION

"He was a shepparde and no mercenarie;
And though he holy were, and vertuous,
He was to sinful man ful piteous."

CHAUCER: The Canterbury Tales.

"WE SHOULD NEVER HAVE MANAGED IT WITHOUT
her," said Mrs. Bradley. It was some weeks later, and
the time was Easter Saturday. Ferdinand, true to his
promise, had come down to see his mother. The school
children had all gone home for the holiday, and the
religious and the orphans were in church for Compline,
Matins and Lauds.

From where she stood, with her son and George on
either side of her, Mrs. Bradley could hear the beginning
of the Alleluias.

"Don't apologise to *me* for having let her go," said
Ferdinand. "I suppose, as long as those two children
and the precious vessels are safe, you don't care whether
the murderer is laid by the heels or not? Queer the
old chap altering his will like that, and leaving all his
money to the convent. Saved the Maslins a journey
to New York! How angry that rather spiteful little
woman was, wasn't she? What's happening to our
young friend Ulrica—the girl I saw on to the boat?"

"She is going to stay over there in the care of a
Catholic community."

"What, as an orphan, do you mean?"

"No. The grandfather has set aside a sum of money

343

for her education, and enough to give her a small dowry if she decides, later on, to take the veil. If she does not become a nun, the sum will secure to her a small income, but she will have to earn a little money as well.''

''It's all a bit odd to me, mother.'' Ferdinand knit his black brows and stared away over the top of his mother's dark head to where, beyond the orchard, the tall church rose to the sky. Mrs. Bradley cackled, and George observed:

''Madam didn't exactly let Miss Bonnet go. It was more that the young lady managed to disappear in the general mêlée of the rescue.''

''Very fairly put, George,'' said Mrs. Bradley. ''And the fact does remain, of course, that I could not have handed her over to the police, for I could not prove much against her, although she confessed that she had attacked Sister Bridget. In any case, I do not think that the attack was meant to kill the victim, although the actual force of the blow was rather dangerously misjudged. But that's Miss Bonnet all over.''

''But the murder of the child! You remember you described to me how you reconstructed the murder with that piece of gas-tubing in the guest-house dining-room?''

''Oh, that? But that was not a reconstruction of the murder! It was to assure myself that that was not a way in which the thing could very well have been done. If the murderer had held that tube of escaping gas so that the victim could breathe from it, she would have run considerable risk of being gassed herself. Have you turned the gas on in there? And the child, you remember, was not injured. Her nose might well have been broken, if the method that I demonstrated was right.'' Ferdinand looked at his mother in some perplexity.

"But the cigarette holder shoved in the nozzle of the gas-tube to form a mouthpiece!" he exclaimed. "That seemed to me so ingenious!"

"Yes, so it was," Mrs. Bradley regretfully conceded. "But it happened to be my ingenuity, not Miss Bonnet's at all. You see, she never used a cigarette holder. On the other hand, Ulrica Doyle, quite suddenly, began helping her cousin Ursula with her Latin *and her Science*. That seemed to me significant."

"Ulrica?"

"Yes. Carbon monoxide is easy enough to make, and Ulrica used to take those mysterious walks, which the Community, believing them harmless, did not supervise."

"You mean children ought to be under constant supervision? I thought you were such an apostle of liberty!"

"I am, dear child, I hope. And it is now part of an inevitable reaction, that Ulrica knows she betrayed the kindness of Mother Francis and the Reverend Mother Superior."

"But I thought you had fixed on Miss Bonnet!"

"Miss Bonnet," said Mrs. Bradley, "is almost a half-wit in some respects, but even she could hardly have missed the conclusion that, if a child was going to be murdered, the time to do it was while the nuns were all in church between two o'clock and half-past. Even if nothing else had indicated that Miss Bonnet was not the culprit, I should have given up thinking her guilty when I heard about that half-hour's special coaching she gave to the private-school girls."

"But she knocked out that orphan child deliberately during the netball practice, you thought."

"Yes, I know she did. She needed an excuse to get into the Orphanage, I think. When she had stolen the chalice and paten she wanted a hiding place very near at hand, from which she could take them when the search had ceased to be local and had widened."

"But why pick the Orphanage?"

"Because nobody would suspect the poor orphans of stealing the chalice and paten, and suspicion would hardly be attached to Mother Ambrose and Mother Jude."

"She just snooped round for a hiding-place?"

"Whilst Mother Ambrose and Mother Jude were busy. Yes, I think so."

"But where was the child killed, mother?"

"In the bathroom where she was found. The carbon monoxide could have been made in several ways by a girl with some knowledge of chemistry—by burning some charcoal, for instance. The problem of how the child got into the guest-house bothered me for a time, but I'm quite sure now that Ulrica told her Miss Bonnet was there and wanted to see her about that extra coaching in physical training. You remember that that was one of the reasons brought forward in favour of the suicide verdict?—that the child was in trouble at school? Well, she was in trouble—if you can call it that!— with Miss Bonnet, and had been told she must have some extra practice."

"But the bathroom?"

"Oh, we can imagine, I think, what happened. First they looked in at the parlour. 'She isn't here. She said she might be upstairs, and we were to find her.' You know what children are, and Ursula would have believed every word from her cousin, the cousin who was helping her with her work, helping her to gain merit badges from her teachers, helping to make her so happy. You remember that many of the nuns decided that so happy a child would not have killed herself? Then, when they got to the bathroom door, the whiff of the carbon monoxide—'look what I'm going to show Mother Saint Simon to-morrow.' The fatal sniff, the climb out of the window to release the rest of the gas where it might harm no one, the horrifying discovery that the child was not merely unconscious, but was dead, the panic-stricken tearing off of the clothes, the water rising higher and higher in the bath, the closed window—to conceal, if possible, even from herself, that she had been out on the roof to get rid of the dangerous evidence—and then, the flight to the church, quite the most characteristic touch. Mind you, I think this: that if all had gone exactly according to plan, and the child had been found, not gassed in the bath, but drowned, and a verdict of Accidental Death had been returned, even Ulrica herself would have forgotten, very soon, that the death was due to her agency. Unfortunately for her, suicide is a dreadful sin from the point of view of the Church. That point of view she accepted, and immediately it worried and confused her. To have her innocent cousin—for she never thought of her except as a cypher and a pawn— accused of mortal sin, and wrongly accused, worked on her mind, and roused in her a dormant suicide complex.''

"But what are you going to do about it now?''

"Nothing, dear child. Why should I? Reverend Mother Superior, Mother Saint Francis, and old Mother Gregory, the Sacristan, were all convinced of her guilt.''

"But she can't get off scot free!''

"Scot free?'' said Mrs. Bradley. She laughed—not her usual cackle, but a harsh sound, sardonic and pitiful. "Why do you think I have had her so carefully watched? The nuns knew, if you do not. That abortive attempt at suicide in the car was her first, although the nuns tell me that after the death she frequently walked in her sleep and always towards an open window or towards the head of the stairs. The tendency to suicide was innate, and it was that which made the murder possible. To a Christian, Catholic or Protestant, murder and suicide should be, alike, impossible. Logically, a belief in the resurrection of the dead must always neutralise any belief in death as a solution of human problems. Murder, including self-murder, is evidence of an innate non-Christian belief that death ends all, and this child's father, remember, an atheist, was a renegade Catholic churchman. The child, brought up without positive religious beliefs, was always in a state of mental conflict, for she could never reconcile her early training with her later religious ecstasies. All adolescents are at war within themselves, but in this child the fight was terrible enough to overwhelm her. Somehow, she had to rehabilitate herself in the eyes of God. Somehow, the family fortune had got to go to the Church. That was how she saw it. She had to expiate, somehow, the terrible sin of her father's atheism. It had become a burden too terrible to be borne, and true reason broke beneath the strain of it.''

"But, mother, she must have been mad.''

"On the contrary, perfectly sane. Her tragedy was that she had a single-track mind, as the vulgar have it. If that mind held two very powerful basic ideas, it followed that those ideas must be in conflict.''

"But you can't just leave it like this!''

"She will never commit another crime.''

"But, mother, you'll have to expose her! The murder was such a wanton, wicked thing. It was something planned for weeks, carefully, painstakingly, devilishly; every circumstance taken into account and used to the best advantage. It was only through the merest accident that it failed to hoodwink everybody! After all, you needn't worry! They wouldn't hang the girl!"

"No, they wouldn't, would they?" said Mrs. Bradley. Walking without her customary briskness, she led the way to the guest-house.

"You had a good deal of evidence against Miss Bonnet, though, hadn't you?" her son observed tentatively, as they passed the wicket gate. "The towel, the absence of the bath-sheet, the fact that she lied about her visit to Kelsorrow School—or, rather, about the time she went there—the fact that she made two or three attempts to 'out' you when she found you were getting rather warm—that jar of bath salts, for instance! Nobody here but Miss Bonnet could have shinned over that high brick wall, and so got back undetected to the school."

"The evidence was nearly all circumstantial, dear child. And Miss Bonnet would never have murdered the girl in the guest-house. For her it would have been risky in the extreme. She would have wrung the child's neck and thrown the body into one of the fissures of the cliff or into a pool on the moor. Miss Bonnet's reactions are lively, violent, and bear all the colourful stigmata of a shallow and rather weak nature. Besides, I don't think at first it occurred to Miss Bonnet that the children could be a menace. Even if they had gone to New York and recognised the chalice and paten in Timothy Doyle's collection, she thought he would tell them that the convent had sold him the copies. Nobody but an expert could tell them from the originals, you see."

"Then you—Oh! So Mrs. Maslin knew that Ulrica was the criminal, and wanted to go to New York to drop the old man a hint!"

"She must have known, yes. She saw her on the roof getting rid of the rest of the evidence. You remember that she came out early from the pictures? She thought of giving Ulrica away, and then saw that to do so might involve considerable risk to herself, since no one could give her an alibi for the probable time of the murder, and she knew that she had lied to me about the time. She said she walked back that day, but she came by taxi."

"Exasperating sort of position to be in, with all that money at stake."

"Yes." They had reached the guest-house, and Ferdinand went inside. George remained at the entrance with his employer.

"Odd the young lady should have found the right towel and that, and not used the bath-sheet, madam," he observed.

"Clever brain, George. The towel came out of her aunt's room. She knew the guest-house pretty well, you see. Had been to tea there before the murder, and knew her way about. I found that out from the cousin, Mary Maslin. All three of those children knew the guest-house. Her school tunic, dirty after climbing on the roof, she discarded, I expect, and wore Ursula's tunic instead. All the school garments are named, but the two of them had the same initial, and if the cousin's tunic seemed a little shorter than her own, Miss Bonnet, she knew, would not notice, and for other lessons she wore that long black overall."

"You don't think the young lady would do herself in in New York, madam? Has she got over that by now?"

"I don't know, George. She may have gone past the stage at which the tendency to suicide is still active. There is very little doubt, I'm afraid, that unless she joins a religious community and establishes an unbreakable inhibition, she will end by killing herself in some fit of despair.''

"Well, there's one thing come right in it, madam. The poor old girl who set the place on fire getting her mind back through you.''

"Yes.   Her   recovery   is   well   advanced,   George. I think the fire actually helped.   It was a shock, and this time the shock was followed by the right reaction.''

"And the young person in the Orphanage you were interested in?''

"Bessie?   Doing very well.   I'm very pleased about Bessie.   Annie, too, has a good place to go to when she leaves.''

"So all's well that ends well, madam.''

"A Jesuitical statement, George, that I did not look for from you.''